Peck's Uncle Ike

AND THE

Red Headed Boy

By George W. Peck

Author of "Peck's Bad Boy and His Pa," "Peck's Fun,'
"Peck's Sunshine," Etc.

Illustrated

———

NEW YORK
HURST & COMPANY
PUBLISHERS.

Illustrations

To the Typical American Boy,

The boy who is not so awfully good, along at first, but just good enough; the boy who does not cry when he gets hurt, and goes into all the dangerous games there are going, and goes in to win; the boy who loves his girl with the same earnestness that he plays football, and who takes the hard knocks of work and play until he becomes hardened to anything that may come to him in after life; the boy who will investigate everything in the way of machinery, even if he gets his fingers pinched, and learns how to make the machine that pinched him; the boy who, by study, experience, and mixing up with the world, knows a little about everything that he will have to deal with when he grows up—the all-around boy, that makes the all-around man, ready for anything, from praying for his country's prosperity to fighting for its honor; the boy who grows up qualified to lead anything, from the german at a dance to an army in battle; the boy who can take up a collection in church, or take up an artery on a man injured in a railroad accident, without losing his nerve; the boy who can ask a blessing if called upon to do so, or ask a girl's ugly father for the hand of his daughter in marriage, without choking up; the boy who grows up to be a man whom all men respect, all women love, and whom everybody wants to see President of the United States, this book is respectfully dedicated by

THE AUTHOR.

PECK'S UNCLE IKE

RED-HEADED BOY

CHAPTER I.

"Here, Uncle Ike, let me give you a nice piece or paper, twisted up beautifully, to light your pipe," said the red-headed boy, as Uncle Ike, with his long clay pipe, filled with ill-smelling tobacco, was feeling in his vest pocket for a match. "I should think nice white paper would be sweeter to light a pipe with than a greasy old match scratched on your pants," and the boy lighted a taper and handed it to the old man.

"No, don't try any new tricks on me," said Uncle Ike, as he brought out a match from his vest pocket, picked off the shoddy that had collected on it in the bottom of his pocket, and hitched his leg around so he could scratch it on his trousers leg. "I have tried lighting my pipe with paper, and the odor of the paper kills the flavor of this 10-cent tobacco. Now, the brimstone on a match, added to the friction of the trousers leg, helps the flavor of the tobacco," and he drew the match across his trousers, and lighted

his pipe, and as the smoke began to fill the room his
good old face lighted up as though he had partaken
of a rich wine. " I like to get a little accustomed to
brimstone here on this earth, so, if I get on the
wrong road when I die, and go where brimstone is
the only fuel, I won't appear to the neighbors down
there as though I was a tenderfoot.   Wherever I go,
I always want to appear as though it wasn't my first
trip away from home.   Ah, children," said the old
man, as he blew smoke enough out of his mouth to
call out a fire department, and laughed till the windows rattled, "there is lots of fun in this old world,
if your pipe don't go out.   Don't miss any fun, because when you die you don't know whether there is
any fun going on or not."

    " I believe, Uncle Ike, that you would have fun
anywhere," said the boy, as he thought of the funny
stories the old man had told him for many years, and
listened to the laugh that acted as punctuation marks
to all of Uncle Ike's remarks.   " I would hate to
trust you at a funeral.   Did you ever laugh at a
funeral, Uncle ? "

    " I came mighty near it once," said the old man,
as he put his little finger in the pipe and pressed
down the ashes, and let the smoke out again like the
chimney of a factory.

    " O, my ! why don't they make you use a smoke
consumer on that pipe, or cause you to use smokeless
tobacco ? " said the boy, as he coughed till the tears
came to his eyes.   " It looks in this room like burn-

ing a tar barrel when Dewey sunk the Spanish fleet.
But tell us about your funny funeral."

"O, it wasn't so funny," said the old man, as he
stroked the stubble on his chin, and a twinkle came
all around his eyes. "It was only my thoughts that
come near breaking up the funeral. There was an
old friend of mine years ago, a newspaper man, who
was the most genial and loving soul I ever knew, but
he stuttered so you couldn't help laughing to hear
him. He could write the most beautiful things without stuttering, but when he began to talk, and the
talk would not come, and he stammered, and puckered up his dear face, and finally got the words out,
chewed up into little pieces, with hyphens between
the syllables, you had to laugh or die. We were
great friends, and used to smoke and tell stories together, and pass evenings that I can now recall as
the sweetest of my life. There were many things in
which we were alike. We smoked the same kind of
tobacco, in clay pipes, and lived on the same street,
and, after an evening of pleasure, whichever of us
was the least wearied with the day's work and night
of enjoyment walked home with the other. We used
to talk about the hereafter, and promised each other
to see that the one that died first should not have a
funeral sermon that would give us taffy. It was my
friend's idea that, if the minister spread it on too
thick, he would raise up in the coffin and protest.
He was not what you would call a good Christian, as
the world goes, but I would trust him to argue with

St. Peter about getting inside the gate, because, if
his stutter ever got St. Peter to laughing, my friend
would surely get in. Well, he died, and I was one of
the bearers at the funeral, with seven others of his
old friends ; and when the minister was picturing the
virtues of the deceased which he never possessed,
one of the bouquets on the coffin rolled off on the
floor, and I thought of what my friend had said about
calling the minister down, and in my imagination I
could see the old fellow raising up in the coffin and
stuttering, and puckering up his face there on that
solemn occasion, and for about ten seconds it seemed
as though I would split with laughter ; but I held it
in, and we got the good old genius buried all right,
but it was a terrible strain on my vest buttons," and
the old smoker lighted another match on his trousers
and started the pipe, which had grown cold as he
talked of the stuttering remains.

"O, say, Uncle Ike," said the boy, as he shuddered
a little at the idea of a stuttering corpse talking back
at a minister, "speaking of heaven, do you think the
men that furnished embalmed beef to the soldiers
and made them sick in Cuba will get to heaven when
they die?"

"That depends a good deal on whether a political
pull is any good over there," said Uncle Ike, as he
reached for the yellow paper of tobacco and filled up
the clay pipe again. *"I think a soldier is the noblest
work of God.* A young man who has got everything
. just as he wants it at home, parents who love him,

"**Why,** a dog biscuit would have been **mince** pie to the soldiers **in** comparison."

and perhaps a girl who believes he is the dearest man
that ever wore a choker collar; who hears that his
country needs help, and gives up his spring mattress,
his happy home, his evenings with the dearest girl in
the world, gives up baking powder biscuits and straw-
berry shortcake, and enlists to go to Cuba, and sleeps
on the ground in the mud, gets malaria, and fights
on his knees when he is too weak to stand up, deserves something better than decayed meat, and I
believe the people who furnished that stuff for the
boys are going right straight to hell when they die,"
and a look of revenge and horror and indignation
came over the old man's face that the boy had not
seen before in all the years he had known his uncle.
" No, sir," said he; "the smell of that canned beef
will stick to the garments of those who prepared it
and those who furnished it to those boys; and if one
of them got into heaven by crawling under the canvas, every angel there would hold her nose and make
up a face, and they would send for the devil with his
pitchfork to throw him out. The verdict of no
board of investigation is going to be received as a
passport to heaven. Why, a dog biscuit would have
been mince pie to the soldiers in comparison to the
stuff the rich beef packers furnished to those young
noblemen with the kyack uniforms on. To make a
little more money, men who have millions of dollars
to burn, bilked a weak and overworked set of officials
with incipient paresis and locomotor ataxia in their
walk and conversation, and sawed on to them stuff

that self-respecting pigs could not have digested without taking pepsin tablets; and with that embalmed
and canned outrage on humanity in their stomachs
those brave men charged in the face of an enemy,
and were hungry heroes, loaded with decayed beef
from a country that produces the finest food in the
world.   Tramps, begging at the back gates of American homes, were living on the fat of the land; dogs
could gnaw fresh and sweet meat off of bones thrown
away, and laugh at our soldiers carrying Old Glory to
victory up hills shelled and bulleted and barbed-wire
fenced.   A bullet from a Spanish gun, entering the
stomach of an American soldier, turned black when
it came in contact with the embalmed beef there, and
poisoned the brave soldier, and made him die, with
thoughts of home, and mother, and sweetheart, and
his lips closed for the last time, silent as to his
wrongs, uncomplaining as to the murder committed
by the millionaires at home.   The business of pack-
ing meat ought to be combined with the undertaking
business, so you could order your meat and your
coffin from the same man.   By cracky! Boy, I am so
mad when I think of it, that I don't want to go to
heaven if those people go there.   Go out, dears, for
a minute, for I want to use language that you can't
find in the school books!" and Uncle Ike got up out
of his chair, pale with anger, and smashed his pipe on
the stone hearth, and a tear rolled down his cheek.

" Why, Uncle Ike, I didn't mean to make you cry,"

said the red-headed boy, as he backed out of the room, frightened at the old man.

" Well, never mind, boy ; don't worry about your Uncle Ike, because at my age, when a man gets mad clear through, he has to have vent, or bust," and the old fellow laughed as hearty as though he had never been mad in his life. " But I have a tender spot for soldiers who go to fight for their country, and when they are abused I feel that somebody is guilty of treason. I was a soldier in the war between the North and South, and have seen soldiers hungry, so hungry that they would take raw corn out of the nosebags of mules that were eating it, until a mule would begin to kick seven ways for Sunday when he saw a soldier coming ; but it couldn't be helped, be-cause the government couldn't keep up with the sol-diers with rations, when they were on the jump night and day. But, do you know we had fun all the time we were hungry ? There were Irish soldiers in my regiment who would keep you good natured when you were ready to die. The Irish soldier is so funny and so cheerful that he should have good pay. If I was going to raise a regiment, I would have one Irish soldier, at least, to every seven other soldiers, and my Irish boy would keep them all laughing by his wit, so they would stand any hardship. I have seen an Irish boy parch his corn that he had stolen from a mule, spread it out on a saddle blanket in four piles, go and ask three officers to dine with him, and, when they sat down on the ground to eat the parched corn, he

wouldn't let them begin the meal until he made a
welcoming speech, and had the chaplain ask a blessing over the corn ; and then he would go without his
share, and tell funny stories until the guests would
laugh until they almost choked. The Irish soldier is
worth his weight in gold in any army, boy, and he is
in all armies, on one side or the other, and generally
on both sides. The only objection I have to an Irishman is that he smokes one of these short pipes," and
the old man lit up his long clay pipe, and let the boy
go out to think over the lesson of the morning.

CHAPTER II.

Uncle Ike sat and smoked his pipe in silence for a few minutes, blew the smoke out in clouds, and looked at it as though searching for something, and there was a serious look on his face, as though he was trying to fathom some mystery, while the red-headed boy was looking at himself in a hand mirror to see if the freckles on his nose were any smaller since he had been using some of his mother's toilet powder to remove them. Finally Uncle Ike put the bowl of the pipe to his nose and smelled of the burning tobacco, turned up his nose and snuffed, and said:

"There is something the matter with this 'ere terbacker. I suppose the terbacker makers have got into a trust, and they don't care how the stuff smells. Condemned if I ain't half a mind to quit smoking and break up the trust."

"Oh, I forgot to tell you," said the red-headed boy, "that I fixed your tobacco for you so it would not smell so bad. I put some cinnamon bark and wiener skins in it."

"Well, of all things!" said Uncle Ike, as he emptied the tobacco out of the pipe by rapping it on the heel of his boot, and looked sick. "What in the name of heaven is wiener skins?"

"Why, it is the envelope that goes around a 'ener sausage. Us boys were smoking cigarettes

"There is something the matter with this 'ere terbacker."

one day made of paper and dried dandelion leaves, and the boy at the butcher shop said if we would dry some wiener skin and cut it up and put it in the cigarette and smoke it, it would make the finest flavor, and make us strong. I tried it, and the cigarette smelled just like camping out and cooking over a camp-fire, and the next day I was so strong ma noticed it. I thought you were getting old, and I would make you strong and young again. Don't you notice how different the smoke smells since I fixed the tobacco? I was going to put in some red pepper pods, but———"

"Here, hold on!" said Uncle Ike. "The butcher has got you mixed up. He was giving you a recipe for a Mexican pudding. But don't you ever try any experiments on your Uncle Ike any more. I don't want to be made strong any more on sausage skins. A gymnasium is good enough for me, and it don't smell like burning a negro at the stake. I know anything would help the flavor of this terbacker, but I have got used to it, after about sixty years burning it under my nose, and, if the trust will not water the stock with baled hay or cut cabbage, I will try and pull through as it is. So you experiment on yourself, condemn you! I knew it was you that had disturbed my terbacker. I can tell by the freckles on your face when you have done anything wrong. A boy that is freckled has got to be square, or I am right on to him. When you are guilty, the freckles on your nose are changeable; one will be yellow, like saffron, and

another freckle seems pale, and little drops of perspiration appear between the freckles ; and then several small freckles will combine into one, like a trust,
and you are given completely away. So remember,
as long as you wear freckles, if you do anything
crooked, there is a sign right on your face that tells
the tale."

"Say, Uncle Ike, what is a trust?" asked the red-
headed boy, anxious to turn the subject away from
wiener skins and freckles. "What good does a trust
do?"

"Well, a trust is one of these things," said Uncle
Ike, as he opened a new paper of tobacco, and threw
the old paper, that had been treated with foreign sub-
stances, into the fire, "one of these things that are
for the benefit of the dear people. You have heard
of selling a gold brick, haven't you? The man who
sells a gold brick has a brass brick made with a hole
in it, in which he puts some gold, and he lets the jay
who wants to invest in raw gold test it by putting
acid on the place where the gold is filled in, and the
jay finds that the brick is solid gold, and he buys it,
after mortgaging his farm to raise the money. The
man sells the gold brick cheap, because the jay is his
friend, and when he has got out of the country the
jay tries to sell his gold brick for eight hundred dollars, and he gets two dollars and eighty cents for it.
That is one kind of a trust. The trust you mean is a
combination of several factories, for instance. The
promoter gets all the factories in one line of business

to combine. They pay each factory proprietor more
than his business is worth, and he is tickled, but they
only pay him part money, and give him stock in the
combine for the balance, and let him run his old business, now owned by others, at a good salary, and he
gets the big head and buys a rubber-tired carriage,
and sends his family to Europe. Then the trust
closes down his factory and throws his men out of
employment, lowers the price of goods to run out others who have not entered the trust, and the people
who get goods cheap say a trust is the noblest work
of God. After the outsiders have been ruined, and
the man who entered the trust in good faith has spent
the money they gave him, and tries to sell the stock
he received, it has gone down to seven cents on a dollar, and the trust buys it in, and he cables his family
to come home in the steerage of a cattle ship. His
old employees have gone to the poorhouse or to selling bananas with a cart, and the former manufacturer
who was happy and prosperous has become poor and
shabby, and he looks at his closed factory, with its
broken windows, and he tries to get a position pushing a scraper on the asphalt pavement, and if he fails
he either jumps off the pier into the lake, or takes a
gun and goes gunning for the trust promoter who
ruined him. And after the factory man is drowned,
or sent to the penitentiary for murder, the stock in
the trust takes a bound and is away above par, and
he hasn't got any of it, and the poor competitors of
the trust having been ruined and closed up, prices of

the goods go up kiting, and the dear people who said
a trust was the noblest work of God say it is the
dumbdest work of man, and they pass resolutions to
down the trust, while the owners of the good stock in
the trust stick out their fat stomachs, full of champagne and canvasback and terrapin, and laugh at the
people till they nearly die of apoplexy, and drive bob-
tailed horses that live better than the people, and carry blanketed dogs on velvet-cushioned carriages, that
would turn up their noses at good wiener skins worse
than I did when you loaded my tobacco, you little
red-headed rascal," and Uncle Ike drew a long breath,
and brought his fist down on the table in anger, as he
got worked up over the wrongs of the people at the
hands of the gold brick trusts.

"Gosh," said the red-headed boy, as his eyes kept
opening wider and wider when he took in all Uncle
Ike had said, "I should think the people would have
the trusts arrested for breach of promise."

"What do you know about breach of promise?"
said Uncle Ike, coloring up and looking foolish.
"Who has been telling you about my being arrested
once for breach of promise? If your mother has told
you about that old trouble I had, I'll leave this house
and go board at a tavern."

"I never heard anything about it, Uncle Ike, so
help me. I never heard that you was ever in love."

"I never was in love," said the old man, as he
loaded up the pipe again, "except with my pipe. That
affair was a clear case of a dog getting stuck on a

man, and the owner of the dog thinking she was being loved. You see I went to a summer resort years
ago, and got acquainted with a widow. She was a
sweet creature, but I never said a word to her about
marriage. She had a pug dog, and I petted the dog,
and called it to me, and, do you know, that dog got
so he would follow me, and set on my lap, and come
to my room, and whine, until I got scared. I talked
with the widow some, and once I took her and the
dog out boat riding, but I never gave her any cause to
think that I was in love with her. But you ought to
have seen that dog. He just doted on me. I encouraged it till all the guests at the hotel began to
notice that I was very dear to the dog, and the widow
looked on smilingly and encouraged the intimacy.
Then I tried to drive the dog away from me, but he
would curl up at my feet and look up at me in such a
loving manner that I weakened. Then the widow
began to hint at her desire to have someone that the
dog could look up to and love, and it was getting too
warm, and I left the summer resort, and was sued for
breach of promise. Of course I didn't know what the
woman or the dog would swear to, so I settled for a
thousand dollars. The next year I called at the summer resort, and found the dog stuck on another man,
and I know just as well as can be that the widow paid
her expenses each summer by that dog getting in love
with men, and I have never looked at a woman twice
since."

"Served them right," said the boy, who had an

idea that Uncle Ike was right about everything. "I don't take much stock in girls myself. I am mighty glad I haven't got any sister. The boys that have got sisters are in hot water all the time, and have to go home with them from parties, and carry their rubbers to school when it rains, and fight for them if the other boys call them tomboys. Sisters are no good," and the red-headed boy looked smart, as though he had said something Uncle Ike would applaud.

"There, that will do," said Uncle Ike, as he put his hand in the boy's hair to warm it. "Don't let me ever hear you say a word against sisters again. You don't know anything about sisters. They are great. Let me tell you a story. I know a man who is away up in public affairs, at the head of his profession in his county, and one the world will hear more about some of these days. He was just such a little shrimp as you are, when he was a boy. He got out of the high school, and was going to clerk in a feed store, when his sister took him one side, one Sunday, and told him she wanted him to go to college. He almost fainted away at the idea. There wasn't much money in the family to burn on a boy's education, and he knew it, and he asked where the money was to come from. This little sister of the poor boy said she would furnish the money. She knew that he would be one of the great men of the country, if he had a college education, and it was arranged for him to go to college, this little sister being his backer financially. She had a musical education, and began to look for chances to make money. She took scholars in music, and was so anxious to make money for this brother to blow in on an education that she fairly forced music into all her pupils, working night and day, often with her head ready to split open with pain, but every week she rounded up money enough to send to that brother at college, and for four years there never was a Monday morning that he did not get a postoffice order from that sweet girl, and every day a letter of encouragement, and advice, and when he graduated a pale girl stood below the platform with bright eyes and a feverish cheek, and when he came down off the platform with his diploma he grasped her in his arms and said, ' Sister, darling,' and kissed her in the presence of five thousand people, and she fainted. She had worked as no man works, for four years, and the result was a brother, a lawyer, a grand man, who loves that sister as though she was an angel from heaven. So, confound you, if I ever hear you say a word against sisters again, I will take you across my knee and you will think the millennium has come and struck you right on the pants," and Uncle Ike patted the boy on the cheek, and said they had better go out and catch a mess of fish.

CHAPTER III.

"Uncle Ike, did you ever take many degrees in secret societies?" asked the red-headed boy, as he saw the old gentleman reading an account of a man who was killed during initiation into a lodge, by being spanked with a clapboard on which cartridges had been placed.

"About a hundred degrees, I should think, without counting up," said Uncle Ike, as he thought over the different lodges he had belonged to in the past fifty years. "What set you to thinking about secret societies?"

"Oh, I thought I would join a few, and have some fun. I read every little while about some one being killed while being initiated, and it seems to me the death rate is about as great as it is in Cuba or the Philippines. Is there much fun in killing a man, Uncle Ike?"

"Well, not much for the man who is killed," said the old man, as he gave the grand hailing sign of distress for the boy to bring him his pipe and tobacco. "Accidents will happen, you know. It isn't one man in ten thousand that gets killed being initiated."

"What do people join lodges for, anyway, when they are liable to croak?" said the boy, as he passed the ingredients for a fumigation to the uncle. "Don't you think there ought to be laws against initiating, the same as clipping horses and cutting their tails off, or cutting off dogs' tails and ears ?   What do the lodges have those funny ceremonies for ?"

"Well, a fool boy can ask more questions than the oldest man can answer," said Uncle Ike, as he hitched around in his chair, and looked mysterious, as he thought of the grips and passwords he once knew. "No, there is no occasion for laws against men going up against any game.   Most men join lodges because they think it is a good thing, and after they have taken a few degrees they want all there are, and after awhile the degrees keep getting harder, and they think of more to come, and by and by they get enough.   In most lodges all men are on an equal footing, the prince and the pauper are all alike.   Occasionally there is a man who thinks because he is rich or prominent in some way, that he is smarter than the ordinary man in a lodge. Then is the time that the rest try to teach him humility, and show him that he is only a poor mortal.   It does some men good to have their diamonds removed, their good clothes replaced by the tattered garments of the tramp, and then let them look at themselves and see how little they amount to.   In some lodges a man is taught a useful lesson by stripping him to the buff and taking a clapboard and letting a common laborer maul him until he finds out that he is not the whole business. If that were done occasionally by society you wouldn't find so many men looking over the common people. It would take the starch out of some people to feel

"It does not take opera music to get people to heaven."

that if they put on too many airs they would be liable
to have a boot hit them any time. Lodges sometimes
make good men out of the worst material. In some
lodges the Prince of Wales would have to walk turkey right beside a well-digger, and it would do the
prince good and not hurt the well-digger. But if I
was in your place I would not join a lodge yet. Try
the Salvation Army first," and Uncle Ike got up and
went to the window, and listened to the bugle and
bass drum and tambourine of the army as it passed on
its nightly round.

"That Salvation army makes me tired," said the
red-headed boy, as he reached for his putty blower.
" Going around the streets palming that noise off on
the public for music, and scaring horses, and taking up
a collection, and singing out of tune. Say, I'll bet I
can blow a chunk of putty into that girl's bonnet and
make her jump like a box car in a collision," and the
boy opened the window and was taking aim at the
tambourine girl's bonnet when Uncle Ike reached out
and took the putty blower away from him and said:

" Don't ever worry those poor people, or let any
other boy bother them when you are around. They
are entitled to the respect of all good people. It does
not take opera music to get people to heaven. Even
that wretched music they give so freely, may turn
some poor wretch from the wrong to the right way,
and a poor devil who becomes a follower of Christ
from practicing following the Salvation army is just as
welcome in heaven as though he went to church with

a four-in-hand and listened to a heavenly choir that is paid a hundred dollars per. It does not seem possible to some rich people that St. Peter is going to extend the glad hand to a dockwolloper, and let the rich man stand out in the cold until he tells how he used his money on earth, whether to oppress the poor or to make them glad. Lots of men are going to be fooled thinking they are going to get inside the pearly gates on the strength of their money, but some of them may have to be vouched for by a Salvation army lassie. So, boy, if you love your old uncle, always respect the religion of every soul on earth, and don't fire putty at any girl's bonnet. You hear me?" and the old man patted the boy on the back, and his old face looked angelic, through the tobacco smoke cloud.

"Well, Uncle Ike, you are the queerest man I ever saw," said the red-headed boy, as he wiped a tear out of his eye with his shirt sleeve. "There is nothing I can do to agree with you, until you have talked to me a little. When I feel funny, and want to laugh, you make me cry; and when I get serious about something, and get you to talking, you get me to laughing. I never agree with you until you have had your say. But I agree with you on one thing; you said the other day, when we were talking about breach of promise, that you were never in love. That's where you and I are alike. It makes me weary to see some boys in love with girls, and run around after them, and make themselves laughing stock of everybody. If a girl should get in love with

me, I would tell her to go to thunder, and I would
laugh at her, and tell all the boys she was silly.
There is no good in love. I thought I liked a girl
once, and gave her a German silver ring that I got
off an old china pipe stem ; and she loved me just a
week, and then she shook me because the German
silver ring corroded on her finger and gave her blood
poison. It wasn't true love, or she would have stuck
to me if she had been obliged to have her finger am-
putated. Bah! I was so discouraged that I will
never have anything to say to a girl again, and I will
grow up to be an old bach like you, who never did
love anybody but a dog. Isn't that so, Uncle Ike?"

"Did I say I never loved any woman?" said Uncle
Ike, as he looked away off, apparently his eyes pene-
trating the dim past, and a wet spot on his cheek that
kept getting wetter, and spreading around his face,
until he wiped it off with one end of his necktie.
"Why, boy, don't you ever tell your ma, but I have
been in love enough to send a man to the insane asylum. You think you will never love any girl again,
on account of that blood poisoning. Why, blood
poison is nowhere beside love. Some day you will
have a girl pass to windward of you, and when cool
air of heaven blows a breath of her presence toward
you, the love microbe will enter your system with the
odor of violets that comes from her, and there is no
medicine on earth that will cure you. The first thing
you know you will follow that girl like a poodle, and
if she wants you to walk on your hands and knees,

and carry her parasol in your mouth, you will do it.
When she looks at you the perspiration will start out
all over you, and you will think there is only one pair
of eyes in the world, that all beautiful eyes have been
consolidated into one pair of blue ones, and that they
are as big as moons.   If you touch her hand you will
feel a thrill go up your arm and down your spine, as
you do when a four-pound bass strikes your frog when
you are fishing.   She will see that your necktie is on
sideways, and she will take hold of it to fix it, and you
will not breathe for fear she will go away, and when
she gets you fixed so you will pass in a crowd, you
will be paralyzed all over, and unable to move, until
she beckons you to come along, and when you start
to walk you will feel all over like your foot is asleep.
Walking a block or two beside this girl will be to you
better than a trip to Europe, and a look at her face
will seem to you a glimpse of heaven, and angels, and
you will leave her after the too short interview, and
you will be glad you are alive, and then you may see
her riding in a street car with another, and you will
want to commit murder.   When these things occur,
boy, you are in love, and you have got it bad.   You
think you don't love anybody, but you will.   I have
been there, boy, and there is no escape without taking
to the woods, and love will make a trail through the
forest, and over glaciers, and catch you if you don't
watch out.   So when love gets into your system, that
way, just hold up your hands as though a hold-up
man had the drop on you with a revolver, and let the

girl go through you. The only way I escaped was
that the girl married. Now go away and let me
alone, boy, or I shall have to take you across my
knee," and the red-headed boy backed out of the room
and left Uncle Ike, his trembling fingers rattling the
yellow paper of tobacco, trying to fill his pipe, and as
the boy got outdoors and blew a charge of putty from
his blower at the washwoman bending over the wash-
tub, he said :

"Well, Uncle Ike hasn't had a picnic all his life."

CHAPTER IV.

"What is the matter with your Aunt Almira this morning?" asked Uncle Ike of the red-headed boy, as he came out into the garden with a sling-shot, and began to shoot birdshot at the little cucumbers that were beginning to grow away from the pickle vine, as the boy called the cucumber tree.

"She's turned nigger," said the boy, turning his sling-shot at an Italian yelling strawberries. "Wait till I hit that dago on the side of the nose, and you will hear a noise that will remind you of Garibaldi crossing the Rubicon."

"Garibaldi never crossed the Rubicon, and you couldn't hit that Italian count on the nose in a week, and if you did he would chase you with a knife, and tree you in the cellar under the kindling wood, and if I interfered he would gash me in the stomach and claim protection from his government, and a war would only be averted between this country and Italy by an apology from the President, saluting the Italian flag by our navy, and an indemnity paid to your dago friend, enough to support him in luxury the balance of his life. So be careful with your birdshot. But, about your Aunt Almira; she was yelling for help this morning, and didn't come down to breakfast."

"Well, sir," said the boy, respectfully, as he

sheathed his trusty sling-shot in his pistol pocket,
after the dago had felt a shot strike his hat, and he
looked around at the boy with the whites of his eyes
glassy and his earrings shaking with wrath, " It was
all on account of the innocentest mistake that aunty
is ill this morning. You see, every night she puts
cold cream all over her face, and on her hands clear
up above her wrists, to make herself soft. Last
night she forgot it until she had got in bed and the
light was put out, and then she yelled to me to bring
the little tin box out of the bathroom, and I was
busy studying my algebra and I made a mistake and
got the shoe dressing, that paste that they put on
patent leather shoes. Well, Aunt Almira put it on
generous, and rubbed it in nice. I didn't know I had
made a mistake until this morning, but I couldn't
sleep a wink all night thinking how funny aunty
would look in the morning."

"Hold on," said Uncle Ike, " don't prevaricate.
You did it on purpose, and knew it all right, and let
that poor lady sleep the sleep of innocence, blacker
than the ace of spades. Say, if you was mine I
would have a continuous performance right here now,"
and Uncle Ike run his tongue a couple of times around
a dry cigar a friend had given him, and licked the
wrapper so it would hold in the shoddy filling. "Don't
interrupt the speaker," said the boy, as he handed
Uncle Ike a match to touch off the Roman candle.
" If you had seen Aunt Almira, just after she had ·
yelled murder the third time this morning, you would

"Then she yelled again and wanted me to send for the doctor."

not scold me. She woke up, and the first thing that
attracted her attention was her hands, and she thought
she had gone to bed with her long black kid party
gloves on, and she tried to pull them off. When she
couldn't get them off, she raised up in bed and looked
at herself in a mirror, and that was the time she
yelled, and I went in the room to help her. Well,
sir, she hadn't missed a place on her face, neck and
arms, and the paste shone just like patent leather. I
said, aunty, you can go into the nigger show business,
and she said, what is it, and I said, I give it up for I
am no end man. Then she yelled again. Oh, dear, I
was never so sorry for a high-born lady in my life, but
to encourage her I told her I read of a white woman
in Alabama that turned black in a single night, and
the niggers would never have anything to say to her,
because she was a hoodoo, and wasn't in their class,
and then she yelled again and wanted me to send for
a doctor, and I told her there wasn't any negro doctor
in town, and what she wanted was to send for a scrub-
woman, and then I showed her the box of shoe paste
and told her she had got in the wrong box, and she
laid it to me and shooed me out of the room like I was
a hen, and she has been all the forenoon trying to
wash that shoe paste off, but it will have to wear off,
'cause it is fast colors, and aunty has got to go to a
heathen meeting at the church to-night, and she will
have to send regrets. Don't you think women are
awful careless about their toilets?" and the boy
rubbed his red hair with a piece of sand-paper, be-

cause some one had told him sand-paper would take
the red out of his hair.

"Do you know," said Uncle Ike, as the cigar
swelled up in the center and began to curl on the
end, and he threw it to the hens, and watched a
rooster pick at it and make up a face, "if I was your
aunt I would skin you alive? If you were a little
older, we would ship you on a naval vessel, where you
couldn't get ashore once a year, and you could get
punished every day."

"I wouldn't go in the navy, unless I could be
Dewey. Dewey has a snap. Every day I read how
he has ordered some man thrown overboard. The
other day a Filipino shoemaker brought him a pair of
shoes and charged him two dollars more for them
than he agreed to, and Dewey turned to a coxswain,
or a belaying pin, or something, and told them to
throw the man overboard. Uncle Ike, do you think
Dewey throws everybody overboard that the papers
say he does?"

"Well, I wouldn't like to contradict a newspaper,"
said Uncle Ike, as he thought the matter over. "It
has seemed to me for some time that Dewey had a
habit of throwing people overboard that would be lia
ble to get him into trouble when he gets home, if the
habit sticks to him. For that reason I would suggest
that the house that is to be presented to him at
Washington be a one-story house, so he could throw
people that did not please him out of a window and
not kill them too dead. When he gets home and

settled down, it is likely he will be called upon by
Mark Hanna, General Alger and others, and they
will be very apt to give Dewey advice as to how he
ought to conduct himself, and what he ought to say;
and if he had an office in the top of a ten-story building, the janitor or the policeman in the street would
be finding the remains of some of those visitors flat-
tened out on the sidewalk so they would have to be
scraped up with a caseknife. Throwing people overboard in Manila bay, and in a ten-story flagship in
Washington, is going to be different."

"Well, boy," said Uncle Ike, as the two wandered
around the garden, looking at the things grow, "there
is a sign that tomato cans are ripe, and you go and get
one and I will hold this big, fat angleworm," and he
put his cane in front of a four-inch worm, which short-
ened up and swelled out as big as a lead pencil. "I
want just a quart of those worms in cold storage, and
tomorrow we will go fishing. Don't you like to go
out in the woods, by a stream, and hook an angleworm
on to a hook, in scallops, so he will look just as though
he was defying the fish, and throw it in, and wait till
you get a nibble, and feel the electric current run up
your arm, and then the fish yanks a little, and you
can't refrain, hardly, from jerking, but you know he
hasn't got hold enough yet, and you make a supreme
effort to control your nerves, and by and by he takes
it way down his neck, and you know he is your meat,
and you pull, and the electricity just gives you a shock,
and——"

"Yes, sir," said the boy, interrupting the old man, "it feels just like going home with a girl from a party, and she accidentally touches you, and it goes all up and down you, and he swallows the bait, and you pull him out and have to take a jackknife and cut the hook out of his gills, and the angleworm is all chewed up, and when she looks at you as you bid her goodnight and says it was kind of you to see her home, and puts out her hand to shake you, you feel as though there was only one girl in the whole world, and when you start to go home you have to blow your fingers to keep them warm, and pry your fingers apart, but I don't like to scale 'em and clean 'em, but when they are fried in butter with bread crumbs, and you have baked potatoes, gosh, say, but you can't sleep all night from thinking maybe the next party you go to some other boy will ask her if he can't see her home, but I like bullheads better than sunfish, don't you, Uncle Ike?" and the boy went on filling his tomato can with worms.

"I have just one favor to ask," said Uncle Ike, as he puckered up his mouth in a smile, then laughed so loud that it sounded like raking a stick along a picket fence, "and that is that you don't mix your fish up that way. When the subject is girls, stick to girls, and when it is fish, stay by the fish. I know there is a great deal of similarity in the way they bite, but when you get them well hooked the result is all the same, and they have to come into the basket, whether it is a fish or a girl. The way a girl acts reminds me a good deal of a black bass. You throw your hook,

nicely baited with a fat angleworm, into the water
near the bass, and you think he will make a hop,
skip, and jump for it, but he looks the other way,
swims around the worm, and pays no attention to it,
but if he sees another bass pointing toward the
worm he sticks up the top fin on his back, and turns
sideways, and looks mad, and seems to say, ' I'll tend
to this worm myself, and you go away,' and the bass
finally goes up and snuffs at the worm, and turns up
his nose, and goes away, as though it was no particular interest to him, but he turns around and keeps
his eye on it, though, and after awhile you think you
will pull the worm out, because the bass isn't very
hungry, anyway, and just as you go to pull it up
there is a disturbance in the water, and the bass that
had seemed to close its eyes for a nice quiet nap,
makes a six-foot jump, swallows the hook, worm, and
eight inches of the line, kicks up his heels, and starts
for the bottom of the river, and you think you have
caught onto a yearling calf, and the reel sings and
burns your fingers, and the bass jumps out of the
water and tries to shake the hook out of his mouth,
and you work hard, and act carefully, for fear you will
lose him, and you try to figure how much he weighs,
and whether you will have him fried or baked, and
whether you will invite a neighbor to dinner, who is
always joking you about never catching any fish, and
then you get him up near you, and he is tired out, and
you think you never saw such a nice bass, and that it
weighs at least six pounds, and just as you are reach-

ing out with the landing net, to take him in, he gives
one kick, chews off the line, you fall over backwards,
and the bass disappears with a parting flop of the tail,
and a man who is fishing a little ways off asks you
what you had on your hook, and you say that it was
nothing but a confounded dogfish, anyway, and you
wind up your reel and go home, and you are so mad
and hot that the leaves on the trees curl up and turn
yellow like late in the fall.   Many a girl has acted
just that way, and finally chewed off the line, and let
the man fall with a dull thud, and after he has got
over it he says to those who have watched the ang-
ling that she was not much account, anyway, but all
the time he knows by the feeling of goneness inside
of him that he lies like a Spaniard," and Uncle Ike
tied a handkerchief over the tomato can to keep the
worms in, and said to the boy, " Now, if you can get
up at four o'clock in the morning we will go and get
a fine mess."

" Mess of bass or girls?" said the boy, as he looked
up at the old man with a twinkle in his eye.

" Bass, by gosh!" said Uncle Ike.

CHAPTER V.

"Here, what you up to, you young heathen?" said
Uncle Ike, as a pair of small boxing gloves, about as
big as goslings, struck him in the solar plexus and all
the way down his stomach, and he noticed a red
streak rushing about the room, side-stepping and
ducking. "You are a nice looking Sunday-school
scholar, you are, dancing around as though you were
in the prize ring. Who taught you that foolishness,
and what are you trying to do?" and the old man
cornered the red-headed boy between the bookcase
and the center-table, and took him across his knee,
and fanned his trousers with a hand as big as a canvas ham, until he said he threw up the sponge.

"Well, I'll tell you," said the red-headed boy, as the
old man let him up and he felt of his trousers to see
if they were warm, "I am going into the prize-fighting business, and Aunt Almira, who is studying for
the stage, is teaching me to box. Gee, but she can
give you a blow with her left across the ear that will
make you think Jeffries has put on a shirt-waist, and
a turquoise ring, and she and I are going to form a
combination and make a barrel of money. Say, Aunt
Almira has got so she can kick clear up to the gas
jet, and she wants to play Juliet. I am going to play
Jeffries to her Juliet."

"Oh, you and your aunt have got things all mixed

up.   She does not have to kick to play Juliet.   And
you can't box well enough to get into the kindergar- ·
ten class of prize fighters.   What you want to fight
for anyway ?   Better go and study your Sunday-school
lesson."

"I don't know," said the boy, as he tied on a boxing
glove by taking the string in his teeth, "there is more
money in prize fighting than anything, and Jeffries
was a nice Sunday-school boy, and his father is a
preacher, and he said the Lord was on the side of Jim
in the fight that knocked out Fitzsimmons.   Do you
believe, Uncle Ike, that the Lord was in the ring there
at Coney Island, seconding Jeffries, and that the
prayers of Jeffries' preacher father had anything to do
with Fitzsimmons getting it right and left in the slats
and on the jaw ?"

"No! No! No!" said Uncle Ike, as he shuddered
with disgust at the thought that the good Lord should
be mixed up in such things just to make newspaper
sensations.   "There is not much going on that the
Lord is not an eye-witness of, but when it comes to
being on one side or the other of a prize fight He has
got other business of more importance.   He watches
even a sparrow's fall, but it is mighty doubtful in my
mind whether he paid any attention as to which of the
two prize-fighting brutes failed to get up in ten seconds.   Boxing is all right, and I believe in it, and want
all boys to learn how to do it, in order that they may
protect themselves, or protect a weak person from
assault, but it ought to stop there.   Men who fight

each other for money ought to be classed with bull-
dogs, wear muzzles and a dog license, and be shunned
by all decent people," and the old man lit his pipe
with deliberation and smoked a long time in silence.

"But they make money, don't they?" said the boy,
who thought that making money was the chief end of
man. "Think of making thirty thousand dollars in
one night!"

"Yes, and think of the train robbers who make a
hundred thousand dollars a night," said the old man;
"and what good did any money made by train robbing or prize fighting ever do anybody? The men
who make money that way, blow it in for something
that does them no good, and when they come to die
you have to take up a collection to bury them. Don't
be a prize fighter or a train robber if you can help it,
boy, and don't ever get the idea that the Lord is
sitting up nights holding pool tickets on a prize fight."

"Uncle Ike, why didn't you go to the circus the
other night? We had more fun, and lemonade, and
peanuts, and the clown was so funny," said the boy;
"and they had a fight, and a circus man threw a man
out of the tent; and a woman rode on a horse with
those great, wide skirts, and rosin on her feet and
everywhere, so she would stick on, and——"

"Oh, don't tell me," said Uncle Ike, as he ran a
broom straw into his pipe stem to open up the pores;
"I was brought up among circuses, and used to sit up
all night and go out on the road to meet the old wagon
show coming to town. Did you ever go away out five

or six miles, in the night, to meet a circus, and get tired, and lay down by the road and go to sleep, and have the dew on the grass wet your bare feet and trousers clear up to your waistband, and suddenly have the other boys wake you up, and there was a fog so you couldn't see far, and suddenly about daylight you hear a noise like a hog that gets frightened and says "Woof!" and there coming out of the fog right on to you is the elephant, looking larger than a house, and you keep still for fear of scaring him, and he passes on and then the camels come, and the cages, and the sleepy drivers letting the six horses go as they please, and the wagons with the tents, and the performers sleeping on the bundles, and the band wagon with all the musicians asleep, and the lions and tigers don't say anything; and you never do anything except keep your eyes bulging out till they get by, and then you realize you are six miles from home, and you follow the procession into town, and when you get home your parents take you across a chair and pet you with a press board for being out all night, until you are so blistered that you cannot sit down on a seat at the circus in the afternoon.   Oh, I have been there, boy, barefooted and bareheaded, with a hickory shirt on open clear down, and torn trousers opened clear up. Lemonade never tastes like it does at a circus, sawdust never smells the same anywhere else, and nothing in the whole world smells like a circus," and the old man's face lighted up as though the recollection had made him young again.

"Did you ever see a fight at a circus, Uncle Ike?" asked the red-headed boy, who seemed to have been more impressed with the fight he had seen than with the performance.

"See a circus fight?" said Uncle Ike. "Gosh, I was right in the midst of a circus fight, where several people were killed, and the whole town was a hospital for a month. See that scar on top of my head," and the old man pointed with pride to a place on his head that looked as though a mule had kicked him. "I was a deputy constable the day Levi J. North's old circus, menagerie and troupe of Indians showed in the old town where I lived. Some country boys got in a muss with a side-show barker and they got to fighting, and some Irish railroad graders heard the row, and they rushed in with spades and picks and clubs, and some gentleman said, 'Hey, Rheube,' and the circus men came rushing out, and I came up with a tin star, and said, 'In the name of the state I command the peace,' and I grabbed a circus man by the arm, and an Irishman named Gibbons said, 'to hell wid 'em,' and then a box car or something struck me on the head, and I laid down, and three hundred circus men and about the same number of countrymen and railroad hands walked on me, and they fought for an hour, and when the people got me home and I woke up the circus had been gone a week, and they had buried those who died, and a whole lot were in jail, and my head didn't get down so I could get my hat on before late in the fall."

"I grabbed a circus man by the arm."

"Did you resign as constable?" asked the red-headed boy, and he looked at Uncle Ike with awe, as he would at a hero of a hundred battles.

"Did I? That's the first thing I did when I came to, and I have never looked at a tin star on a deputy since without a shudder, and I have never let an admiring public force any office on to me to this day. One day in a public office was enough for your Uncle Ike, but I would like to go to a circus once more and listen to those old jokes of the clown, which were so old that we boys knew them by heart sixty years ago," and Uncle Ike lighted his pipe again, and tried to laugh at one of the old jokes.

"Uncle Ike, I've got a scheme to get rich, and I will take you into partnership with me," said the red-headed boy, as Uncle Ike began to cool off from his circus story. "You go in with me and furnish the money, and I will buy a lot of hens, and fix up the back yard with lath, and just let the hens lay eggs and raise chickens, and we will sell them. I have figured it all up, and by starting with ten hens and two roosters, and let them go ahead and attend to business, in twenty years we would have seventeen million nine hundred and sixty-one fowls, which at 10 cents a pound about Thanksgiving time would amount to——"

"There, there, come off," said Uncle Ike, as he lit up the old pipe again, and got his thinker a'thinking. "I know what you want. You want to get me in on the ground floor. I have been in more things on the

ground floor than anybody, but there was always another fellow in the cellar. You are figuring hens the
way you do compound interest, but you are away off.
Life is too short to wait for ccmpound interest on a
dollar to make a fellow rich, and cutting coupons off
a hen is just the same. I started a hen ranch fifty
years ago, on the same theory, and went broke. There
is no way to make money on hens except to turn them
loose on a farm, and have a woman with an apron
over her head hunt eggs, and sell them as quick as
they are laid, before a hen has a chance to get the
fever to set. You open a hen ranch in the back yard,
and your hens will lay like thunder, when eggs are four
cents a dozen, but when eggs are two shillings a dozen
you might take a hen by the neck and shake her and
you couldn't get an egg. When eggs are high, hens
just wander around as though they did not care
whether school kept or not, and they kick up a dust
and lallygag, and get some disease, and eat all the
stuff you can buy for them, and they will make such
a noise the neighbors will set dogs on them, and the
roosters will get on strike and send walking delegates
around to keep hens from laying, and then when eggs
get so cheap they are not good enough to throw at jay
actors, the whole poultry yard will begin to work over-
time, and you have eggs to spare. If the hens in-
creased as you predict in your prospectus to me, it
would take all the money in town to buy food for
them, and if you attempted to realize on your hens to
keep from bankruptcy, everybody would quit eating

chicken and go to eating mutton, and there you are. I decline to invest in a hen ranch right here now, and if you try to inveigle me into it I shall have you arrested as a gold-brick swindler," and Uncle Ike patted the red-headed boy on the shoulder and ran a great hard thumb into his ribs.

CHAPTER VI.

"Say, Uncle Ike, did you see this in the paper about fifty ambulances being lost, on the way to Tampa, Florida, last year?" said the red-headed boy, as Uncle Ike sat in an armchair, with his feet on the center-table, his head down on his bosom, his pipe gone out, yet hanging sideways out of the corner of his mouth, and the ashes spilled all over his shirt bosom. "Seventeen carloads of ambulances that started all right for Tampa, never showed up, and the government is writing everywhere to have them looked up. Wouldn't that skin you?" and the boy stood up beside Uncle Ike, took his pipe out of his mouth, filled it again, brushed the ashes off his shirt, and handed him a lighted wax match that he had found somewhere. Uncle Ike put the match to his pipe, took a few whiffs, stuck up his nose, threw the match into the fireplace, and said:

"Where did you get that tallow match? Gosh, I had just as soon light my pipe with kerosene oil. Always give me a plain, old-fashioned brimstone match, if you love me, and keep out of my sight these cigarette matches, that smell like a candle that has been blown out when it needed snuffing." And the old man began to wake up, as the tobacco smoke went searching through his hair and up to the ceiling. "And so the government lost fifty ambulances in transit, eh? Well, they will be searching the returned soldiers next, to see if the boys got away with them, and never think of looking up the contractors, who probably never shipped them at all. It must be that the boys got tired of embalmed beef, and ate the ambulances. When a man is hungry you take a slice of nice, fresh ambulance, and broil it over the coals, with plenty of seasoning, and a soldier could sustain life on it. The government must be crippled for ambulances, and I think we better get up a subscription to buy some more. An ambulance famine is a terrible thing, and I have my opinion of a soldier who will steal an ambulance. When I was in the army, I remember that at the battle of Stone River we——"

"Oh, Uncle Ike, please don't tell me any of your terrible army experiences," said the boy, as he remembered that he had heard his uncle tell of being in at least a hundred battles, when the history of the family showed that the old man was only south during the war for about six months, and he brought home a blacksnake whip as a souvenir, and it was believed that he had worked in the quartermaster's department, driving mules. "Let us talk about something enjoyable this beautiful day. How would you like to be out on a lake, or river, today, in a boat, drifting around, and forgetting everything, and having fun?"

"I don't want any drifting around in mine," said Uncle Ike, as he got up from his chair, limped a little on his rheumatic leg, and went to the window and looked out, and wished he were young again. "Don't you ever drift when you are out in a boat. You just take the oars and pull, somewhere, it don't make any difference where, as long as you pull. Row against the current, and against the wind, and bend your back, and make the boat jump, but don't drift. If you get in the habit of drifting when you are a boy, you will drift when you are a man, and not pull against the stream. The drifting boy becomes a drifting business man, who sits still and lets those who row get away from him. The drifting lawyer sits and drifts, and waits, and sighs because people do not find out that he is great. He wears out pants instead of shoe leather. When you see a man the seat of whose pants are shiny and almost worn through, while his shoes are not worn, except on the heels, where he puts them on the table, and waits and dreams, you can make up your mind that he drifted instead of rowed, when he was a boy, out in a boat. The merchant who goes to his store late in the morning, and sits around awhile, and leaves early in the afternoon, and only shows enterprise in being cross to the clerk who lets a customer escape with car fare to get home, is a drifter, who stands still in his mercantile boat while his neighbors who row, and push, and paddle, are running away from him. The boy who drifts never catches the right girl. He drifts in to call on her, and drifts through the evening, and nothing has been done, and when she begins to yawn, he drifts away. She stands this drifting sort of love-making as long as she can, and by and

by there comes along a boy who rows, and he keeps
her awake, and they go off on a spin on their wheels,
and they can't drift on wheels if they try, because
they have got to keep pushing, and before he knows
it the drifting boy finds that the boy who rows is
miles ahead with the girl, and all the drifting boy can
do is to yawn and say, " Just my dumbed luck." Dogs
that just drift and lay in the shade, and loll, never
amount to anything. The dog that digs out the
woodchuck does not drift; he digs and barks, and
saws wood, and by and by he has the woodchuck by
the pants, and shakes the daylights out of him. He
might lay by the woodchuck hole and drift all day,
and the woodchuck would just stay in the hole and
laugh at the dog. The pointer dog that stays under
the wagon never comes to a point on chickens, and
the duck dog that stays on the shore and waits for
the dead duck to drift in, is not worth the dog biscuit
he eats.

" No, boy, whatever you do in this world, don't
drift around, but row as though you were going after
the doctor," and the old man turned from the window
and put his arm around the red-headed boy, and
nugged him until he heard something rattle in the
boy's side pocket, and the boy pulled out a box with
the cover off, and a white powder scattered over his
clothes. " What is that powder?" asked the old
uncle.

" That is some of this foot-ease that I saw adver-
tised in the paper. Aunt Almira likes pigs' feet, and

she says they lay hard on her stomach; so I got
some foot-ease and sprinkled a little on her pigs' feet
for lunch, and she ate it all right.   Say, don't you
think it is nice to be trying to do kind acts for your
auntie?"

"Yes; but if she ever finds out about that pigs'
foot ease, she will make you think your trousers are
warmer than your hair.   You strike me as being a
boy that resembles a tornado.   No one knows when
you are going to become dangerous, or where you are
going to strike.   You and a tornado are a good deal
like a cross-eyed man; you don't strike where you
look as though you were aiming, and suddenly you
strike where you are not looking, and where nobody
is looking for you to strike.   Nature must have been
in a curious mood when she produced cross-eyed men,
red-headed boys and tornadoes.   What do you think
ought to be done to Nature for giving me a red-
headed boy to bring up, eh, you rascal?" and the old
man chucked the boy under the chin, as though he
wasn't half as mad at Nature as he pretended to be.

"Uncle Ike, do you think a tornado could be broken up, when it got all ready to tear a town to pieces,
by shooting into it with a cannon, as the scientific
people say?" said the boy, climbing up into the old
man's lap, and slyly putting a handful of peanut
shucks down under the waistband of his uncle's
trousers.

"Well, I don't know," said Uncle Ike, as he wiggled around a little when the first peanut shuck got

down near the small of his back. "These scientific
people make me weary, talking about preventing tornadoes by firing cannon into the funnel-shaped clouds.
Why don't they do it? If a tornado came up, you
would find these cannon sharps in a cellar somewhere.
They are a passel of condemned theorists, and they
want someone else to take sight over a cannon at an
approaching tornado, while the sharps look through a
peep-hole and see how it is going to work. You
might have a million cannon loaded ready for tornadoes, and when one came up it would come so
quick nobody would think of the cannon, and everybody would dig out for a place of safety. Not one
artilleryman in a million could hit a tornado in a vital
part. Do these people think tornadoes are going
around with a target tied on them, for experts to shoot
cannon balls at? A tornado is like one of these
Fourth of July nigger-chasers, that you touch off and
it starts somewhere and changes its mind and turns
around and goes sideways, and when it finds a girl
looking the other way it everlastingly makes for her
and runs into her pantalets when she would swear it
was pointed the other way. No, I am something of a
sportsman myself, and can shoot a gun some, but if I
had a cannon in each hand loaded for elephants, and
I should see a tornado going the other way, I would
drop both guns and crawl into a hole, and the tornado
would probably turn around and pick up the guns and
fire them into the hole I was in. That's the kind of
an insect a tornado is, and don't you ever fool with

"My boy, you are going to lose your Uncle Ike."

59

one. A tornado is worse than a battle. I remember when we were at the battle of Gettysburg——"

"Oh, for Heaven's sake, Uncle Ike, what have I done that you should fight that war all over again every time I try to have a quiet talk with you?" and the boy stuffed his fingers in his ears, and got up off the old man's lap, and the uncle got up and walked around, and when the peanut shells began to work down his legs, and scratch his skin, and he found his foot asleep from holding the big boy in his lap, the old man thought he was stricken with paralysis, and he sat down again, and called the boy to him and said, in a trembling voice:

"My boy, you are going to lose your Uncle Ike. I feel that the end is coming, and before I go to the beautiful beyond I want to say a few serious words to you. It is coming as I had hoped. The disease begins at my feet, and will work up gradually, paralyzing my limbs, then my body, and lastly my brain will be seized by the destroyer, and then it will all be over with your Uncle Ike. Remove my shoes, my boy, and I will tell you a story. When we scaled the perpendicular wall at Lookout Mountain, in the face of the Confederate guns, and——"

"Can this be death?" said the boy, as he took off one of the old man's shoes and emptied out a handful of peanut shucks, and laughed loud and long.

"Well, by gum!" said Uncle Ike, "peanuts instead of paralysis," and he jumped up and kicked high with the lately paralyzed legs; "now, I haven't eaten peanuts in a week, and I suppose those shucks have been in my clothes all this time. I am not going to die. Go dig some worms and I will show you the liveliest corpse that ever caught a mess of bullheads," and the boy dropped the shoe and went out winking and laughing as though he was having plenty of fun, and Uncle Ike went to a mirror and looked at himself to see if he was really alive.

CHAPTER VII.

"You are a nice-looking duck," said Uncle Ike, as the red-headed boy came into the sitting-room with a black eye and a scratch across his nose, and one thumb tied up in a rag, but looking as well, otherwise, as could be expected. "What you been doing? Run over by a trolley car or anything?"

"Nope," said the boy, as he looked in the mirror to see how his eye was coloring, with all the pride of a man who is coloring a meerschaum; "I just had a fight. Licked a boy, that's all," and he put his hand to his head, where a lock of his red hair had been pulled out.

"You look as though you had licked a boy," said the old man taking a good look at the blue spot around the boy's eye. "I suppose he is telling his folks how he licked you, too. My experience has been that in these boys' fights you can't tell which licks until you hear both stories. What was it about, anyway?"

"He lied about you, Uncle Ike, and I choked him until he said 'peunk,' and then I let him up, but he wouldn't apologize, and said he would leave it to you, if what he said was true or not, and here he comes now," and the red-headed boy opened the door and ushered in a boy about his own size, with two black eyes and a piece peeled off his cheek, and one arm in a sling.

"Which is Jeffries?" asked Uncle Ike, as he filled his pipe, and looked over the two companions who had been scrapping.

"He is Jeffries," said the visitor, "and I am Fitz simmons, but I want to have another go at him unless we leave it to arbitration," and the boy looked at the red-headed boy with blood in his eye, and at Uncle Ike with a look of no particular admiration.

"Well, what was the cause of the row?" said Uncle Ike, as he took a chair between the two boys, lit his pipe, and smiled as he saw the marks of combat on their persons.

"He said you used to be a drunkard, Uncle Ike, and had been to the Keeley cure, and I called him a liar, and then we mixed up."

"That's about the size of it," said the other boy; "now, which was right?"

Uncle Ike smoked up and filled the room so it looked like camping out and cocking over a fire made of wet wood, and thought a long time, and looked very serious, and the red-headed boy could see they were in for a talk. Finally the old man said:

"Boys, you are both right and both wrong, and I'll tell you all about it. I never was a drunkard, and never drank much, but I have been to the cure all the same. It was this way: I had a friend who was one of the best men that ever lived, only he got a habit of drinking too much, and no one seemed able to reason with him. He wouldn't take advice from his own mother, his wife, or me, or anybody. He

was just going to the devil on a gallop, and it was
only a question of a year or two when he would die.
I loved that man like a brother, but he would get
mad the minute I spoke of his drinking, and I quit
talking to him, though I wanted to save him. I have
smoked dog-leg tobacco many a night till after midnight, trying to study a way to save the only man in
the world that I ever actually loved, and I finally got
it down fine. I began to act as though I was half
drunk whenever I saw my friend, spilled whisky on
my coat sleeves, and acted disreputable, and got a few
good fellows to talk with him about what a confounded wreck I was getting to be ; and he actually
got to pitying me, and finally got disgusted with me ;
and one day he said to me that I was a disgrace, and
was making more different kinds of a fool of myself
than any drunkard he ever met. I got mad at him,
and told him to attend to his own business and left
him. Then the boys got to telling him that the only
way to save me was to get me to go to a cure ; and,
do you know, that good fellow that I would have
given the world to save, came to me and urged me to
take the cure ; and at first I was indignant that he
should interfere in my affairs, and finally he said he
would go if I would. Then we struck a bargain, and
went to Dwight, and took the medicine. The boys
had told the doctors the story, and they only gave
me one shot in the arm ; but that came near killing
me, because it almost broke me of using tobacco.
Well, I remained there ten days, and, while they were

"Which is Jeffries?" asked Uncle Ike.

pretending to cure me, they were curing my friend
sure enough, putting the gold cure into his system
with injections and drinks, while I didn't get anything
but ginger ale ; and when we were discharged cured,
I was the happiest man in the world, except my
friend, who was happier.   He was not only cured
himself, and an honor to his family, but he thought
he had saved me from a drunkard's grave.   That's
the story, boys, and now you get up and shake hands,
and don't fight any more over your Uncle Ike," and
the old man patted them both on the head, and they
shook hands and laughed at each other's black eyes.
As the red-headed boy showed his late antagonist to
the door, he turned to his uncle and said :

"Uncle Ike, if you have ever held up a railroad train,
or robbed a bank, or stolen horses, or done anything
that would cause you to be arrested, I beg of you to
tell me of it now, so if anybody abuses you in my
presence I won't get into a fight every time," and the
boy put his arm around his Uncle Ike and hugged
him, and added, " You were a thoroughbred when
you bilked that friend of yours to take the cure.'

" Oh, I don't know," said Uncle Ike, "that reminds
me of the battle of Chickamauga.   When Bragg's
forces were——"

" Fire ! Fire !" yelled the red-headed boy, and he
rushed out of doors and left the old man talking to
his pipe.

" Has that battle of Chickamauga been fought out
to a finish yet ?" said the red-headed boy, as he stuck

his head in the door after the imaginary fire alarm
that he had created to escape Uncle Ike's war history,
"for if it is ended I want to come in, but I can't
stand gore, and your war stories are so full of blood
that you must have had to swim in it."

'Oh, you don't know a hero when you see one,"
said the old man, as he straightened up and saluted
the boy in a military manner, only that he used his
left hand instead of his right hand.

"Well, I'll tell you," said the boy as he got inside
the room and stood with his hand on the door knob,
ready to escape if Uncle Ike got excited. "You old
veterans make me sick. I have heard nothing for
fifteen years except war talk, old war talk, back number war talk, about how you old fellows put down the
rebellion, and suffered, and fought, and all that rot.
Why, I heard a bugler who enlisted for the Spanish
war, and who only got as far as Jacksonville, say that
you fellows that put down the rebellion in 1864 were
just a mob, and that you didn't have any fighting, and
that the Southern people were only fooling you, and
that you didn't suffer like the Spanish war heroes did,
and that you just had a picnic from start to finish.
The bugler said he wouldn't ask any better fun than
to fight the way you fellows did, when you had all you
wanted to eat, good beds to sleep on, and servants to
carry your guns, and cook for you. The bugler said
you fellows all get pensions just for making an excursion through the Southern resorts, while the heroes of
the Spanish war, who fought a foreign country to a

standstill, and went without food, and got malaria, are
without pensions, and just existing on the record they
made fighting for their country——" and the boy
stopped nagging the old man when he noticed that
Uncle Ike was turning blue in the face, and choking
to keep down his wrath.

" Where is this heroic bugler of the Spanish war?"
said Uncle Ike, trying to be calm, but actually froth-
ing at the mouth. " Bring him here, ʿ .d let me hear
him say these things, condemn him, and I will take
him across my knee and I will knock the wind out of
him, so that he can never gather enough in his car-
cass to blow another bugle. Why, confound him, he
is a liar. The war of the rebellion was a war, not a
country schuetzenfest, with a chance to go home
every night and sleep in a feather bed, and get a
Turkish bath. The whole Spanish war, except what
the navy did, was not equal to an outpost skirmish in
'63. Of course, the rough riders and the weary
walkers did a nice job going up San Juan hill, but we
had a thousand such fights in the rebellion. After
that skirmish there was nothing done by the army at
Santiago, but to sit down in the mud and wait for
the Spaniards to eat their last cracker, and kill their
last dog and eat it, and then surrender. Ask that
bugler to tell you where he found, in his glorious
career as a wind instrument in the Spanish war, any
Grants, Shermans, Sheridans, Logans, Pap Thomases,
McClellans, Kilpatricks, Custers, McPhersons, Braggs,
and hundreds of such heroes. What has the bugler

got to show for his war? Shafter! And Alger!
And all of them quarreling over the little bone of
victory that was not big enough for a meal for our
old generals of the war of the rebellion. And he
talks about our pensions, the young kid. He probably wears corsets. Why, we didn't get pensions until
we got so old we couldn't get up alone. His gang of
Jacksonville heroes will probably get pensions when
they are old enough. Bring that bugler in here some
day, and don't let him know what he is going to run
up against, and I will give you a dollar, and I will let
you see me dust the carpet with him," and the old
man sat down and fanned himself, while the boy
looked scared for fear Uncle Ike was going to have a
fit. "Why, at the battle of Pea Ridge, when a min-
ie ball struck me, when I was on the firing line——"

"Keno," said the red-headed boy, as he went
through the window head first, and over the picket
fence on his stomach, and disappeared down the
street.

CHAPTER VIII.

"Say, Uncle Ike, don't you think the Fourth of July is sort of played out?" asked the red-headed boy, as he came to Uncle Ike's room on the morning of the 5th, by appointment, to demonstrate to the old man that he had not been quite killed by the celebration of the great day. "It seems to me we don't have half as many accidents and fires as we used to," and the boy counted off to the uncle the dozen injuries he had received by burns, and dug into his eye with a soiled handkerchief in search of some gravel from a torpedo.

"Oh, I don't know," said Uncle Ike, as he lighted the old pipe and began to look over the boy's injuries. "The Fourth is carrying on business at the old stand, apparently. Your injuries are in the right places, on the left hand, principally, and the gravel is in the left eye. That is right. Always keep the right hand and the right eye in good shape, so you can sight a gun and pull a trigger, either in shooting ducks or Filipinos. You see, our country is growing, and we are celebrating the Fourth from Alaska to Porto Rico, and from London to Luzon, so we can't celebrate so very much in any one place. I expect by another Fourth Queen Victoria will be yelling for the glorious Fourth, Emperor William will be touching off dynamite firecrackers, Russia will be eating Roman candles, and Aguinaldo will be touching off nigger-chasers and drinking red lemonade. This is a great country, boy, and don't you forget it."

"Well, you may be right," said the boy, as he poured some witch-hazel on a rag around his thumb, "but it looks to me as though the troops in the Philippines will be climbing aboard transports protected by the fleet, with Aguinaldo slaughtering the boys in the hospitals and looting Manila, if the President does not get a move onto himself and send another army out there to be victorious some more. The way it is now, we shall not have troops enough there to bury the dead. The boys have been debating at school the Philippine question, and it was decided unanimously that the President is up against a tough proposition, and if he does not stop looking at the political side of that war and send troops enough to eat up those shirtless soldiers, who can live on six grains of rice and two grains of quinine a day, we are going to be whipped out of our boots. That's what us boys think."

"Well, you boys don't want to think too much, or you are liable to have brain fever," said the old man, as he realized that there was mutiny brewing among the school children. "What you fellows want the President to do? Haven't we whipped the negroes everywhere, and taken village after village, and burned them, and—and—chased them—and——"

"Sure!" said the boy, as he saw that his uncle was at a loss to defend the policy of his government. "We have had regular foot races with them, and burned the huts of the helpless, and taken villages, and then didn't have troops to hold them, and when we went out of a village on one street, the niggers came in on another, and shot into our pants. We swim rivers and take towns with as brave work as ever was done, and become so exhausted we have to lay down in the mud and have a fit, and the niggers climb trees like monkeys, eat cocoanuts and chatter at us. Say, Uncle Ike, do you know us boys are getting tired of this business, and we are getting up a petition to the President to get a trained nurse to put Alger to sleep and run the war department herself. We are going to have the petition signed by seven million American boys. Why, if those niggers could go off in the woods and shoot at a mark for a week, and get so they could hit anything, our boys would all be dead in a month. The trouble is the niggers just pull up a gun and touch it off like a girl does a fire-cracker. She lights the tip end of the tail of a fire-cracker, and throws it, and you forget all about it, and when her firecracker has ceased to interest you, and you don't know where it is, it goes off in your coat collar, or down the waistband of your pants. A Filipino shoots the way a trained monkey touches off a syphon of seltzer water. He knows it will squirt if he touches the thumbpiece, but it is as liable to hit him in the face, or wet his feet as anything. Some day those niggers will learn how to shoot, and when Funston attempts to swim a river he will get a bullet through the head, and Lawton and MacArthur, who

"We are going to have the petition signed by seven million American boys."

stand up in plain sight and let them practice will wish they hadn't. We boys have decided to support the President until he conquers those people, if that is what he is trying to do, but, by gosh, if he does not wake up and quit looking pleasant, and seeming to hope that Filipino shower is going to blow over, we feel that he will wake up some morning and find that a nigger tornado has struck his brave boys at Manila, and they will be in the cyclone cellars waiting for somebody to come and dig them out. Don't you think so, Uncle Ike?"

"I say, boy," said Uncle Ike, as he lighted up the pipe, after letting it go out while listening to the war talk of the excited boy, "do you think you could arrange your affairs so as to leave here by tomorrow evening and take the limited for Washington? Would you accept the vacancy in the office of secretary of war? I know this offer comes sudden to you, and that you will have no time to consult your debating society as to whether you ought to accept the position, but when you reflect that the country is in a critical situation, and needs a man of blood and iron to steer the craft through among the rocks, I feel that you cannot refuse. The ideas you express are so near like those that General Jackson would express if he were alive, that I feel the country would be blessed if you were in a position to brace up the President. Now go wash your face, and I will wire the President that you will be there day after tomorrow morning. But if you go there thinking, as many people seem to think, that the

President's backbone is made of banana pulp, and that
he is not alive to the situation, you will make a mistake.   There are chumps like you all over this country
that wonder why they have not been selected to run
this country, who think the commander-in-chief is running ward politics instead of the affairs of the country.
Of course, a President gets under obligations to different elements in a campaign, and finds it necessary to
surround himself with a cabinet, a few members of
which are not worth powder to blow them up, but if
they were all weak and vicious on the make, and
political ciphers, and the President himself is all right,
the country will not go very far wrong.   What you
boys want to do is to debate less on questions you do
not understand, and saw more wood.   Let the grown
people run things a while longer, and you boys prepare
to take the burden a quarter of a century hence," and
the old man got up and put his arm around the boy
and felt of his head to see if he could find any soft
spot.

"Well, I was only joshin' any way, Uncle Ike," said
the boy, as he put both arms around the old man,
and felt in his uncle's pistol pocket to discover something that was eatable.   "But, Uncle Ike, I am serious now.   I have got in love with a girl, and she is
mashed on another boy, and I am having more trouble than McKinley.   You know that quarter you
gave me yesterday?   I saved 20 cents of it to treat
her to ice-cream soda ; and when I went to find her,
she was coming out of the drug store with the other

boy, and I found out they had been sitting on stools
at the soda fountain all the forenoon, drinking all the
different kinds of soda, until he had to hold her
down for fear she would go up like a balloon, from
the soda bubbles that she had concealed about her
person. I have not decided whether to kill my rival,
or go and enlist and go to the Philippines and break
her heart. What did you do under such circumstances, Uncle, when you used to get in love?"

"I used to take castor oil," said Uncle Ike, as he
looked at the forlorn-looking boy, "but you don't
need to. Just you take off those tan shoes and put
on black shoes, and change your luck. I never knew
it to fail, when a boy first put on tan shoes and a
high collar. He is bound to get in love before night.
Take off those shoes, and you can go out in the world
and look everybody in the face and never get in love.
It is the same as being vaccinated," and the old man
looked sober and serious, and the boy went to work
to change his shoes, with a bright hope for the future
lighting up his face.

CHAPTER IX.

"Go away from me! Don't you come any nearer or I will smite you!" said Uncle Ike, as the red-headed boy came into the room with his red hair cut short with the clippers, a green neglige shirt, with a red necktie, a white collar, a tan belt with a nickel buckle, and short trousers with golf socks of a plaid pattern that were so loud they would turn out a fire department. "I am afraid of you. Who in the world got you to have your red hair shingled so it looks like red sand-paper? And who is your tailor? Have I got to go down to my grave with the thought that a nephew of mine would appear in daylight looking like that? Get me a piece of smoked glass, or I shall have cataracts on both eyes," and the old man knocked the ashes and deceased tobacco out of his pipe on his boot heel, and dug the stuff out of the bottom of the pipe with a jack-knife.

"Well, I had to have my hair cut, because the boys at the picnic filled my hair with burdock burrs, and it couldn't be combed out," said the boy, as he took a match and scratched it on top of his head, and lit it, while the uncle sniffed at the burned hair. "Aunt Almira cut my hair first with a pair of dull shears, to get the burrs out, and then a barber cut off all there was left, with these horse-clippers, and I feel like a dog that has had his hindquarters clipped to make a

lion of him. Aunt Almira says I have got a great
head. Say, Uncle Ike, did you ever examine the
bumps on my head? I was at a phrenology lecture
once, and the feeler could tell all that was going on
in a man's head just by the bumps. Feel of mine,
Uncle, and tell my fortune," and the red-headed boy
came up to the old man for examination.

"I am no phrenologist," said Uncle Ike, as he
smoked up and got the boy to coughing, "but there
are some bumps I know the names of," and he felt all
around the boy's head, and looked wise. "This place
where there is a dent in your head is where the bump
of veneration will grow, later, if you get in the habit
of letting old people have a show, and get up and offer
them your chair, and run errands for them without expecting them to pay you. This place on the back of
your head, where there is a bump as big as a hickory
nut, is what we call the hat rack bump, because you
can hang your hat on it. The barber ought to have
cut a couple of slices off that bump with his lawn
mower. Here is a bump that shows that you are color
blind. Be careful, or you will marry a negro girl by
mistake. As a precaution, when you begin to get in
love serious, bring the girl to me that I may see if she
is white. Here is a soft bump that indicates that you
will steal——"

"Oh, come off," said the boy, laughing, and remov-
ing his head from the investigation. "That is where
I was struck by a golf ball. You are no phrenologist.
I know what you are, Uncle Ike; you are a fakir.

" Here is a sort bump that indicates that you will steal——"

But, say, I was sick last night, after we had that green watermelon for dinner, and Aunt Almira said I was troubled with sewer gas, and she gave me the peppermint test.   Do you think peppermint will detect sewer gas, Uncle Ike?"

"I know what you want, boy, you want to get me mad," said Uncle Ike, as he threw his pipe into the grate because it wouldn't draw, and took a new one and filled it.   "There is no greater fraud on the earth than this peppermint test for sewer gas.   I had a house to rent, years ago, and was ruined by peppermint. When a tenant had anything the matter, from grip to corns, the doctor would look wise, snuff around, and say he detected sewer gas, and they would call in a health officer and he would put a little peppermint oil in somewhere, and go into another room, and when he smelled the peppermint he would say it was sewer gas, and send for a plumber, and they would begin to plumb, and I had to pay.   I had nine tenants in two years, and every disease they had was laid to sewer gas, and I had to ease up on the rent or stand a lawsuit.   When one family had triplets, and tried to stand me off on the rent on account of sewer gas, I became a walking delegate, and struck, and turned the house into a livery stable, and now, do you know, every time I go to collect rent I am afraid a horse has got sick, and the livery man will lay it to sewer gas.   Why, boy, peppermint oil will go through an asphalt pavement.   You might put peppermint oil on top of the Egyptian pyramids and you could smell

it in fifteen minutes in Cairo. If anybody ever talks
to you about sewer gas and peppermint test, call them
a liar and charge it to me," and the old man was so
mad the boy's hair began to curl.

"Here, Uncle Ike, what you staring out of the
window so for, with your eyes sot, like a dying horse,
and your body as rigid as a statue?" and the boy
rushed up to the window and looked out to see what
had come over the old man.

"Hush, keep still, and don't scare her away," said
Uncle Ike, as he held up his hand and motioned the
boy to keep still.

"By gosh, if it isn't a woman, Uncle Ike, that has
paralyzed you, and you always said you didn't care
for them any more," said the red-headed boy, as he
looked out the window and saw a blonde-haired young
woman standing on the corner waiting for a street
car, and glancing up at Uncle Ike through the frowsy
hair that was loosely flying about her forehead. "And
she is a blonde, too, and blondes have gone out of
style. Didn't you read in the papers that the shows
won't hire blondes any more, and that nothing but
brunettes are in it? It must be pretty tough on a
blonde to get her hair all fixed fluffy, after years of
patient coloring, and then find she has gone out of
style, and no op'ry will hire her to shed blonde hair on
the coats of the chorus fellows. Oh, Uncle Ike,
come away from the window or you will be stolen,"
and the boy dragged the old man away from the win-

dow, handed him his pipe, and said, "Smoke up and
try to forget it."

"Forget nothing," said the old man, as he lit the
torch and a smile came over his good-natured face.
"Don't you worry about blonde girls going out of
style. These bleached ones, who never were the real
thing, may go back to their natural, beautiful brunetti-
cism, and when they realize how foolish they have
been, trying to bunko nature, they will be happier than
ever, but the natural blonde will never go out of style.
She is a joy forever. Do you know, when a man gets
in love with a girl he couldn't tell what the color of
her hair was, to save him? He knows all about her
eyes, and her hands, and her face, but unless he finds
a hair on his coat he can't tell what is the color of the
hair of his beloved. Love is like smoking. You may
smoke in the dark, and if your pipe goes out you
smoke right along and don't know the difference.
You sit up with a girl in the dark and you can't see
her, and she may go to sleep, but love keeps smoking
right along and never seems to go out. When I was
wounded at the battle of Pea Ridge, and was taken to
a young ladies' seminary to be doctored and nursed
back to life——"

"Oh, do quit, Uncle Ike! If you had been taken
wounded to a young ladies' seminary, say in 1863,
thirty-six years ago, you would have been there yet,
and your wound would still be paining you, and the
girls who saved your life would be grown up to be
gray-haired old women," and the boy jollied the old

man until he blushed. "You must have known a
man named Ananias in the army. Say, Uncle Ike,
you know you wanted me to learn a trade, and I have
decided that I would like to learn the trade of a
bishop. I read of the death of a bishop the other
day who was worth half a million dollars, and now
you must tell me how to become a bishop, like Newman," and the boy laughed as though he had got the
old man in a tight place.

"Well," said Uncle Ike, after stopping to think a
moment, "you might do worse. Do you know, boy,
that Bishop Newman, who died recently, did learn a
trade? Well, he did. When he was a boy, he seemed
to be a no-account sort of a duck, some like you. His
parents were poor, and lived in the slums of New
York. His hair was some the color of yours, and he
loafed around, and made fun of his old uncle, no
doubt, the same as you do. He had to do something
to help earn the bread and beer for the family, and
so he went to work stripping tobacco in a factory
near his home. Somehow he got vaccinated with a
desire to learn something, and after he had stripped
tobacco, and snuffed it, and got some sense in his
head, he began to learn to read. A girl stripper
taught him first to read the labels on packages of tobacco, and taught him to spell. Then he got a taste
for education, and became the smarty of the factory,
and the boys who could not read called him 'snuff,'
because his hair and freckles were the color of Scotch
snuff. Some white man connected with the factory

saw that the little rat had stuff in him, and he helped him to get an education, and he stripped tobacco daytimes and studied nights, and became a preacher, and finally a bishop. So, you smarty, if you want to learn the trade of a bishop, strip the wrapper off that package of tobacco and fill my pipe. Who knows but Bishop Newman stripped the very tobacco I am smoking now?" and the old man puffed and laughed at the boy.

"Gosh! it smells old enough to have been stripped when the bishop was a boy," said the red-headed boy, and then he dodged behind a table, while Uncle Ike tried to catch him and teach him how to be a bishop.

CHAPTER X.

Uncle Ike stood with his pipe in his left hand, his thumb pressing the tobacco down tight, and with a match in his right hand, just ready to scratch it on his leg, when he froze stiff in that position, and never moved for five minutes, as he watched the red-headed boy, who had walked into the room listlessly, his eyes staring at a picture he held in his hand, his face so pale that the freckles looked large and dark, his lips white as chalk, his cheeks sunken, his fingers gripping the picture, a faded and forlorn pansy in his button-hole, and his short clipped hair standing up straight in rows like red beet tops in a vegetable garden.

"Anybody very dead?" said Uncle Ike, as he drew the match across the cloth, put it to his pipe, and began to swell out his cheeks and puff, keeping his eye on the boy, through the smoke, who had taken his eyes from the picture, drawn a deep sigh, and sat down on the lounge, as though he never expected to get up again.

"No, nobody dead," said the boy, as he laid his head on a sofa pillow, closed his eyes, and placed the picture inside his vest. "But I wish there was. I wish I was dead."

"How many times have I told you to put oil on cucumbers, and they wouldn't gripe you that way?" said Uncle Ike, as he drew a chair up beside the

lounge and felt of the boy's pulse, and took his handkerchief and wiped the perspiration off his forehead,
and finally took the picture out of his bosom and
looked at it. "She is a nice, warm-looking girl, but
you might have the picture on your stomach a week,
and it wouldn't draw that colic out of you," and Uncle
Ike gazed with some admiration on the picture of the
beautiful girl, whose high forehead, bright eyes, and
beautiful chin, showed that she had the making of a
rare and radiant woman.

"'Tain't colic, and I haven't et no cucumbers,"
said the boy, as he rolled his eyes up toward the
roof of his head. "It's love, that's what it is, and I
am miserable, and Aunt Almira said you had been in
love over six hundred times, and could tell me what
to do."

"Well, I like your Aunt Almira's nerve," said
Uncle Ike, as he looked half pleased at the accusation.
"Of course, I have had some encounters with the
fair sex, but I have never entirely collapsed, the way
you have. What's the symptoms? Don't the girl
love you?"

"Yes! Gosh, she idolizes me," said the boy, sitting up, and getting a little color in his face.

"Oh, then you don't love her," said Uncle Ike,
probing into the wound.

"It's false," said the boy, getting on his feet and
standing before the old man in indignation. "I
love the very ground she walks on. Say, when I
walk a few blocks with her, and can't see her again

"She is a nice warm-looking girl."

for a week, I go around the other six days and look
at the boards she walked on, and it makes me mad to
see anybody else walking where she did.   I want to
get rich enough to buy all the houses we have walked
by, and the street cars we have rode in.   Love her ?
Say, you don't know anything about love, Uncle Ike.
The love you used to have was old style, and didn't
strike in."

"Oh, I don't know," said Uncle Ike, "its all about
the same.   Was the same in Bible times, and will be
the same hundreds of years hence, when we conquer
the Philippines.   Same old thing.   Nobody invents
any new symptoms in the love industry.   There may
be new languages to express it in, but it is just plain,
every-day love.   But if you both love each other, what
is the use of all this colic ? "

"Why, you see, she has to dissemble.   That's what
she says.   She can't go with me all the time, and
when I see her with anybody else it seems as though
it would kill me.   I know she does not smile at anybody else the way she does at me, but the condum
fools might think she did, and love her.   I know if
one of those ducks should squeeze her hand, she
would be mad, and cuff him, but I could squeeze her
hand till her fingers cracked, and she would enjoy it."

"I see," said Uncle Ike, smoking right along.
"You are like a man who owns the most beautiful
diamond in the world, and is not allowed for some
reason to be known as its owner, but is allowed to
wear it only two hours a week, and then other people

are allowed to wear it.   You know it is yours, and yet
when it is in the possession of others, you don't dare
go and claim it, and they wear it as though they own
it, and people see it in their possession and admire it,
as it sparkles and throws rays of sunshine, and think
how lucky is the man who wears it.   Isn't that about
your idea?   She is yours, body and soul, but has not
been delivered to you, eh?"

"Sure!   That's it, exactly.   What shall I do,
Uncle Ike?"

"Shut up!" said the old man; "that is what you
want to do.   Brace up; you have no cause to worry.
I can tell by that face of hers.   When she is going
with other boys, as she must, she is thinking of you
all the time, and wishing your red head was in place
of that of the kid who is buying ice-cream soda for
her.   When she walks about the streets she is thinking of when you were with her at the same place.
And when you are permitted to pass an hour with her
she will convince you in a minute that you are all the
world to her, and that the other ducks are not in it.
I can tell by her eyes, boy, and her mouth, and her
whole face, that she is a thoroughbred."

"Well, I swan, Uncle Ike, you are better than a
doctor," and the red-headed boy began to hug the old
man, and dance around, and kick high, and he took
the picture and looked at it, and said: "Nobody but a
chump would doubt that girl," and the boy suddenly
became himself again, reassured as to the position he
held in the mind of his girl, by a few words of kindly

advice at the right time, when the boy was on the
verge of suicide.   He laughed and pinched himself
to be sure he was awake, and then took on a serious
look and said : " Uncle Ike, do you think it will take
two hundred years, honestly, to subjugate the Filipinos, and tame them, so that they will eat out of
our hands ?"

"Well, we ought to do it in half the time the
Spaniards have been trying and failed," said the old
man, as he slapped a mosquito that was eating him.
" There, you see that mosquito is dead.   No doubt
about that, is there ?   But what effect does the death
of that mosquito have on the nine or ten million of
his race that are out here in the woods ?   This one
simply got through the screen, and bucked up against
a sure thing, and his bravery, or gall, got him killed,
and I may think I am a hero because I killed him.
But let me take my gun and go out in the woods, or
on the marsh, where there are a million mosquitos to
one of me, and what kind of a life will they let me
lead ?   I should have to be slapping and kicking all
the time, and couldn't attend to my shooting.   It is
just so with those Filipinos.   They will stay in the jun-
gles and breed, and enjoy the malaria and the rainy
season, and a few will go around the camps and sing
their songs, and keep the soldiers awake, and bite and
poison them, and shoot and stab, and when the soldiers chase them they will go farther into the jungle,
harass the flanks of the boys that are discouraged,
and when another year is gone there will be more

Filipinos than there are now, better armed, and hat-
ing the Americans worse than ever. We may take
towns, hold them if we have troops enough, and start
a new graveyard at every place we try to hold, and
when we give it up and go away, the human mosquitos will return buzzing and biting, and they will dig
up the remains of some mother's boy, just to get the
gold filling out of his teeth. If the war keeps on a
few hundred years, instead of one large cemetery at
Manila, that can be watched and kept a sacred spot,
we shall have hundreds of small graveyards all over
the archipelago, where the boys in blue that are
buried will find it mighty lonesome when we take the
living soldiers away. No, boy, it will not take two
hundred years to subdue the Filipinos. That is, we
will not be working at the job that long, because we
are not built that way. If we find we have got into
a hornet's nest, and that the hornets don't have any
honey, anyway, and that we don't need hornets in our
regular business, somebody in authority will be apt to
know when we have got enough, and we will probably
shake the dice with some nation that is so addicted to
gambling that it had as soon shake dice for hornets as
anything, and we will let them play loaded dice on us,
and shake sixes, and we will turn up deuces and trays,
and let them win the condemned mess of hornets that
didn't give honey, and that have nothing but stings,
and wish whoever wins the hornets much joy. Understand me, boy, I am not saying anything against the policy of our administration, if it has got one, and I will
hold up my hands and root for the army as long as it

is in the game, and will encourage the President all I
can to do what he thinks is right, but I shall always
feel that Spain sold him a gold brick for 20,000,000
plunks, and that he has not yet found out that it is
made of brass. I know the tobacco trust, and the
cordage trust, and lots of other trusts that are interested, are trying to make him believe that the gold
brick he bought is good stuff, and that he must protect it, or some other nation will get it away from
him, but you wait until that Scotch-Irish blood of the
President begins to boil, when he finds out that he
has been bunkoed, and he will get those trust magnates together some day, and he will get pale around
the gills, and mad as a wet hen, and he will say that
he has heard about all the funeral dirges on the long-
distance telephone from Manila that he wants to hear,
and that the wails of the mourning mothers of the
dying boys are keeping him awake nights, and that he
has got about enough, trying to put bells on the Filipino wildcats, and that they can take the whole Philippine archipelago and go plum to hades with it, for
he is going to stop the death rate, and get those boys
home and set them to plowing corn."

   "Oh, Uncle Ike, don't get excited. I only wanted
to change the subject from my own troubles to the
troubles of our country," and he went out singing,
"There's Only One Girl in All This World for Me,"
while Uncle Ike took off his collar and wiped the perspiration off his neck, and fanned himself awhile, and
then lit his pipe, smoked a spell, and finally said: "Well,
it is none of my condum business, anyway, I s'pose."

CHAPTER XI.

Uncle Ike was sitting in his room with a bath robe on, and his great, big, bare feet in a tub of hot water, in which some dry mustard had been sifted, and on a table beside him was a pitcher of hot lemonade, which he was trying to drink, as it got cool enough to go down his neck without scorching his throat. His head was hot, and he had evidently taken a severe cold, and occasionally he would groan, when he moved his body, and place his hand to the small of his back. His pipe and tobacco were far away on the mantel, though he could smell them, and the odor so satisfying to him when he was well, almost made him sick, and when the red-headed boy came in the room the first thing the old man said was :

" Take that dum pipe and terbacker out of the room, and put it in the woodshed. Your Uncle Ike ain't enjoyin' his terbacker very well," and the old fellow made up a face, and looked as though he was on a steamboat excursion in rough weather. The boy took the pipe by the tail, and the tobacco paper in his other hand, and went out, and soon returned with a heavy blanket coat on, a pair of felt boots, and a toboggan knit-cap, and a pair of yarn mittens on, though it was late in July, and the weather was quite hot. Uncle Ike looked at him in wonder, as though he was not sure but it was winter, and he was so ill as not to

know that summer and fall had passed without his
knowing it.

"What you got them sliding-down-hill clothes on for,
in July?" said the old man, as he put one puckered-up
bare foot on the other, in the water, and sozzled them
around in the mustard in the bottom of the tub. "You
will have me sunstruck yet, if you wear those clothes
around here. What is up, anyway?"

"A lot of us boys are going to the Klondike," said
the red-headed boy, as he took a big hunting knife out
of a sheath, "and I came in to see if you would grubstake me. We have been reading about the millions
of dollars in gold nuggets and dust, that is being
brought out, and we are going to have some of the
gold. Want your corns cut?" said the boy, as he
sharpened the knife on Uncle Ike's boot that lay on
the floor.

"You ducks have been reading about the gold that
has been brought out, but you forgot to read about
the corpses that stayed in the Klondike, didn't you?"
said the old man as he took a drink of the hot lemonade, and pulled the bathrobe around his hind legs.
"You tell the boys you are not going, and that Uncle
Ike will not grubstake you. Tell them you have
found out that for every dollar in gold that comes out
of the mines, a hundred dollars is spent to find it.
Tell them that not one man in a hundred that goes
there ever sees anything yellow, except the janders.
Tell them that seven out of ten men either freeze to
death, or die of disease, or starve to death, and that

"A lot of us boys are going to the Klondike."

every trail in Alaska is marked with graves of just such fools as you boys. Tell them that they can make more money selling picture books at a blind asylum, or tin trumpets at a deaf and dumb school, than they could by digging gold in the Klondike, and that you are going to stay home. Now take off that uniform and get down on your knees and rub my feet dry," and the old man drew one foot out of the tub and rested it on the edge, while the boy took a Turkish towel that looked like a piece of tripe, and began polishing the foot, like a bootblack.

"Gosh, but one of your feet would make about six the size of my girl's feet," said the boy, as he fixed the old man up, and helped him onto a lounge, where he stretched out and went to sleep. For an hour the boy watched the old man, and listened to his snore, and finally he got a gutta-percha bug out of his fishing tackle, and when Uncle Ike woke up and began to stretch the boy said: "Uncle Ike, I have saved your life. This kissing bug was just ready to pounce on you, and poison you, when I grabbed it and killed it. See!" and he held up the bug.

"Yes, I see," said Uncle Ike, as he rubbed his eyes, and looked at the kissing bug. You examine it close, right by the tail, and you will find a trout hook. I used to catch a great many trout with that bug," and Uncle Ike got up and stretched his limbs, and found that his cold was gone, and he was well enough, and he dressed himself and began to act natural, and after the boy had looked him over, and marveled at the sudden cure, he said:

"Uncle Ike, you have deceived me. I thought you was on your last legs, and I was going to have a serious talk with you. Heretofore, when I have tried to talk serious with you, you have turned everything into fun, but now I want a serious opinion from you. What would you think of my going out on a farm and learning to be a farmer? I ride by farms and see farmers and boys at work, or lying in the shade, or drinking out of a jug, or sitting on loads of hay, or riding a horse plowing corn, and it seems to me they have an easy life, and they must make money; and if I can't enlist to fight Filipinos, nor go to the Klondike, I want to be a farmer. What do you think, Uncle Ike?" and the boy looked up into the old man's face appealingly.

"Well, bring back that pipe and terbacker, and I will tell you all about farming, for I was brung up on a farm till I was busted." The boy brought in the smoke consumer, and after the old man had puffed a few times, and found it did not make him sick, he continued: "In the first place, you are getting too old to learn farming. When city people have a call to farm it, they buy a farm, put up a windmill, get plumbers out from town, put in a bathtub with hot and cold water, and buy some carriages with high backs, and go in for enjoyment, regardless of the price of country produce. They put in hammocks and lawn tennis, and the young people wear knicker

bockers and white canvas dresses, and roll their pants
up, and all that.   There is no money in farming that
way.   Now, you have got your city habits formed ;
you don't get up in the morning till after 7, and you
have to take a bath, and have fresh underclothes frequently.   You would want to lay in the shade too
much and ride on the hay.   Did it ever occur to you
that before you could ride on the hay it has to be
cut, and cured, and cocked up, and raked around ?
It takes a whole lot of backaches to get a load of hay
ready for you to ride on.   Now, you are going on 20
years old.   If you had been born on a farm, you
would be just about ready to quit it and come to
town to learn something else.   You would have a
stomach full of farming, for you would have worked
about twelve years, day and night ; your hands would
be muscular, and you would have callouses inside of
them.   You go out on a farm now, at your age, and
when you get the first blister on your hands you want
to send for a doctor, and you throw up the job and
come back on my hands.   Suppose you started out
next Monday morning to learn to be a farmer.   Let
me make out a programme for you.   You would go
to bed Sunday night at 9 o'clock, and lay awake
thinking of the glory of a farmer's life, and at 3 a. m.
you would go to sleep, and at 4 you would hear the
door to the attic open, and a voice that would sound
like an auctioneer would yell to you to come down and
get to work.   You couldn't argue the case with the
farmer, as you do with me when I try to get you up

early to go fishing; and you would get up and put on
a pair of cowhide shoes, brown overalls, a hickory
shirt with bed-ticking suspenders, and you would go
out into a barnyard that smelled like fury, and milk
nine or fifteen cows on an empty stomach; and while
another hired man was taking the milk to a creamery,
you would see that it was not daylight yet, but you
would go in the kitchen and eat a slice of pork, and
hurry about it, and then you would curry off the
horses, and help hitch the team to a reaper; and just
as it was getting light enough to see things, you would
go out to a wheat field, and, after the old man had
cut two or three swaths around the field, several of
you would turn in to bind up the bundles. They
would show you how, and then they would see that
you did your share of work.

"You would hustle for about four hours, and you
would be so hungry it wouldn't be safe for a dog to
come around you, and you would drink warm water
out of a jug till your stomach ached, and you would
wonder if it was not almost supper time, and if you
looked at your watch you would find it was only about
9 o'clock in the morning, with three more solid hours
of work before dinner time. When the horn blew for
dinner you would just be able to climb on one of the
horses to ride to the house, and the harness would
take the skin off your elbows. When you got to the
house you would want to lay down and die, but you
would have to pull water up in buckets to water the
horses, and go up in the hay mow and throw down

hay and carry oats to them, and when you went in to
dinner you would feel as though you could eat a ten
course banquet, but you would find that it was washing day, and they didn't do any cooking, and you
would eat a bowl of bread and milk, and chew about a
bushel of young onions, and when you were filled up
and wanted to lie down and go to sleep, and die, the
old man would tell you to hustle out and hitch up
that team, and you would be so lame you couldn't
ride on top of a hard farm harness, and you would
walk to the field, your heavy shoes wearing the
skin off your ankles, and the old machine would
begin to stutter and rattle, and you would go to
work binding bundles at 1 o'clock and work till
dark, because it looked as though it was going to rain,
and when you got the chores done, milked the cows,
bedded down the horses, carried in wood to the
kitchen and a few things like that, and they told you
supper was ready, you would say you would rather go
to bed than eat, and you would go up in the attic and
fall on the bed, and go to sleep and dream of your
Uncle Ike.   Do you know where I would find you
next ? You would come into town on an early freight
train Tuesday morning, and show up about breakfast
time, and you would hunt the bathtub, and if any man
ever talked farming to you again, you would be sassy
to him.   No, boy, the city man or boy is not intended
for a farmer, but the farmer boy is intended for the
city, when he gets enough of the farm.   About so
much farming has got to be done, but it will be done

by those who are brought up to it, and who know that
every minute has got to be used to produce something, that the appetite must be satisfied easily and
cheaply, and that everything on the farm must be of
marketable value, and nothing must be bought that
can be dispensed with, and that everybody must work
or give a good reason for not working. The pleasure
of farming is largely in anticipation. The big crops
and big prices are always coming next year. You
would be about as good at farming as I would at
preaching," and Uncle Ike gradually ceased speaking,
like an old clock that is running down, and ticking
slower and slower, and then he fell asleep in his chair,
and the red-headed boy sat and thought of what had
been said, and looked at his hands as though he
expected to find a blister, and smelled of them to see
if he had actually been milking cows, and then he
rolled over on the lounge and went to sleep, and the
two snored a match.

CHAPTER XII.

"Uncle Ike, I heard a rumor about you yesterday that tickled me almost to death," said the red-headed boy, as he came into the old gentleman's room while he was shaving, and the boy took the lather brush and worked it up and down in the cup until the lather run over the side, and he had lather enough on hand to shave half the men in town.

"What was it?" said the old man, as he puckered his mouth on one side, and opened it so he could shave around the corner of his mouth. " Nothing disreputable, is it; nothing to bring disgrace on the family?" and he wiped the razor on a piece of newspaper, and stropped it on his hand, as he looked in the mirror to see if there were any new wrinkles in his face.

"Well, I don't know as it would disgrace us so very much, if you looked out for yourself, and didn't steal," said the boy, as he began to sharpen his knife on Uncle Ike's razor strop. " There is a rumor among the boys that you may be nominated for President, and a lot of us boys got together and took a vote, when we were in swimming, and you were elected unanimously. I am to be the boss who deals out the offices, and all the boys are going to have a soft snap. Before the thing goes any further the boys wanted me to see you, and have you promise that anything I promised should be good, see?"

"Uncle Ike, I heard a rumor about you yesterday that tickled me almost to death."

" Well, you are a dum nice lot of politicians, to work up this boom for me, without my consent," and the old man put up his razor, and began to wash the lather off his face, and while he was rubbing his red and laughing face with a towel, he said : " If I am elected President, and I want you to understand that I have not yet consented to take the nomination, I would, the first thing I did, have all my relatives either sent to jail, or confined in various asylums of one kind or another. I think I would send you to a home for the feeble-minded."

" What's the matter with relatives ? " said the boy, as he took the razor, and searched around on his lip for some hairs, and finally got hold of one, and the razor pulled it so hard the tears came in his eyes ; " seems to me a President with all his relatives in jail would be looked upon as a disgrace to society."

" Well, I wouldn't care," said the old man, as he struggled to make a fourteen-inch collar button on to a sixteen-inch shirt, and nearly choked himself before he found out he had got the boy's collar by mistake. " I have watched this President business a good many years, and have concluded that the most of the trouble a President has is through fool relatives. Look at Grant. You couldn't throw a stone in Washington without hitting a relative, and they got into more scrapes, and dragged Grant into more disgrace, and fool schemes, than anything. There wasn't offices enough for all of them, and some had to live in other ways, which didn't help Ulysses very much. Harri-

son never had any pleasure until he had an operation
performed on his son to remove his talking utensils.
That boy would be interviewed and jollied, and he
would tell more things that were not so, about pa's
policy, than the President could stand. But a brother
is the worst relative a President can have, if he is a
half-way lawyer. A President cannot kill a brother
that is older than he is, and can't prevent his being
retained, and can't keep his brother's fingers out of
all the contracts, and his being attorney for contractors, and can't tell him to keep away from the White
House, and don't dare to tell his brother not to go
around looking wise, as though he was running the
whole administration. No, sir ; there ought to be a
law that when a man is elected President, all male
relatives that are old enough to talk, should have
their mouths sewed up, and be compelled to put
on gloves that are fastened with a time lock, so
they couldn't get their hands into anything that would
bring disgrace on the chief magistrate. Now, if you
boys want me for President, with this understanding,
that you shall all keep away from me after the 4th of
March, and never let anybody know that you ever
heard of me, and that you will never write me even a
postal card, why, you can go ahead with your boom,"
and the old man tied his necktie so it looked like a
scrambled egg, and he and the boy went in to breakfast, the boy opening the outside door and whistling
a weird whistle, which brought three boys up on the
porch, when he said to them :

" By the way, that presidential boom for Uncle Ike
is off.   Don't let the gang do another thing.   He is
a lobster," and the boys went out into the world looking for another candidate, followed by a dog that
jumped up and down in front of them as though he
could lead them to a presidential candidate or a woodchuck hole mighty quick.

" Speaking of dogs," said Uncle Ike, as he and the
boy sat down to breakfast, and the other boys went
out on the street to wait for the red-headed boy to
finish eating, " where you boys going ? "

" Just going to follow the dog," said the warm-
haired proposition, as he kicked because the melon
was not ripe.   " Did you ever drown out a gopher,
Uncle Ike ? "

" Bet your life," said Uncle Ike, as he dished out
enough food for the boy to have fed an orphan asylum.   " Oh, I had a dog once that knew more than
an alderman.   Do you know, boy, that a dog is the
best thing a boy can associate with ?   A boy never
does anything very mean, if he has a dog that loves
him.   Many a time I have been just about ready to
do a mean trick, when the dog would sit down in
front of me, and look up into my eyes in an appeal-
ing way, and raise up one ear at a time and drop it,
and raise the other, and he would jump up on me and
lick my hand, and seem to say, ' Don't,' and, by
gosh ! I didn't.   Say, if a mean boy has a dog that
loves him, the dog is better than he is, and the boy is
careful about doing mean things, for fear he will

shame the dog. I don't suppose a dog will get to
heaven, but, if his master goes to heaven, the dog is
mighty likely to lay down on the outside of the pearly
gates, and just starve to death, waiting to hear the
familiar whistle of his master, who is enjoying himself
inside. Now, let's go out on the porch while I
smoke ;" and the old man led the way, and lighted up
the old churn, and puffed away a while, and the boy
was in a hurry to get away with the other boys ; and
finally the boys came up on the porch, and the dog
went up to Uncle Ike and licked his hand, as though
he knew the old man was a friend of dogs and boys.

"What's this scar on his nose? Woodchuck bite
him ? "

" Yes, sir," said one of the boys.

"And this one on the under lip?" said the old
man. "Looks like a gopher had took a bite out of
that lip."

" That's what it was," said another boy, and they
all laughed to think that a dignified old man like Uncle Ike could tell all about the scars on a cheap dog.

" Well, boys, I won't detain you if you are going
out to exercise the dog on woodchucks or gophers.
But let me tell you this," and he puffed quite a little
while on the pipe, and seemed to be harking away
back to the bark of the dog friend of his boyhood, and
the boys could almost see the dirt flying out of an old-
time woodchuck hole as the dog of Uncle Ike's memory was digging and biting at roots, and snarling at a
woodchuck that was safe enough away down below the

ground. " Let me tell you something. You want to
play fair with the dog. A dog has got more sense
than some men. He can tell a loafer, after one woodchuck hunt. The boy who gets interested when the
dog is digging out a woodchuck, gets down on his
knees and pushes the dirt away, and pats the dog, and
encourages him, and when he comes to a root, takes
his knife and cuts it away, is the thoroughbred that
the dog will tie to ; but the boy who sits in the shade
and sicks the dog on, and don't help, but bets they
don't get the woodchuck, and when the dog and his
working partner pulls the woodchuck out, gets up out
of the shade and begins to talk about how we got the
woodchuck, is the loafer. He is the kind of fellow
who will encourage others to enlist and go to war, in
later life, while he stays home and kicks about the
way the war is conducted, and shaves mortgages
on the homes of soldiers, and forecloses them. That
kind of a boy will be the one who will lie in the shade
when he grows up, and not work in the sun. Didn't
you ever see a dog half-way down a woodchuck hole,
kicking dirt into the bosom of the boy's pants who is
backing him, suddenly back out of the hole, wag his
tail and wink his eyes, full of dirt, at the boy who is
working the hole with him, and then run out his
tongue and loll, and look at the fellows who are sitting
around waiting for the last act, in the shade, and say
to them, as plain as a dog can talk, ' You fellows make
me tired. Why don't you get some style about you,
and come in on this game on the ground floor ? ' and

then he gets rested a little, and you say, 'dig him out,'
and he swallows a big sigh at their laziness, and goes
down in the hole and digs and growls so the lazy boys
think he has forgotten that they are deadheads in the
enterprise, but the dog does not forget."

"Well, I swow, if your Uncle Ike ain't away up in
G on woodchuck hunting," said one of the neighbor
boys as they all sat around the old man, with their
eyes wide open. "How about drowning out a gopher?"

" Same thing, exactly," said Uncle Ike, as he filled
up the pipe again, and lit it, and run a broom straw
through the stem, to give it air. " The dog watches
the hole, and keeps tab on the boys who carry water.
You have got to keep the water going down the
gopher hole, and you got to work like sixty. Gophers
know better than to have holes too near the water,
and the dog knows what boy flunks after he carries
one pail of water, and says, ' Oh, darn a gopher anyway ; I hain't lost no gopher,' and goes and sits down
and lets the other boys carry water. The dog knows
that the boy who keeps carrying water and pouring it
in the hole is the thoroughbred, and that the quitter
has got a streak of yellow in him. When the hole is
filled up with water, and the gopher comes to the sur-
face, and the dog grabs for it, and the boy who took
off his clothes and carried water also grabs, and either
the dog or the boy gets bit, usually the boy, the dog
knows that the boy who worked with him on that
gopher hole has got the making of a good business
man in him. A business or professional career, boys,

is just like digging out a woodchuck, or drowning out a gopher, and the fellows who help the dog when they are boys, are the ones who are mighty apt to get the business woodchuck when they grow up. I will bet you ten dollars that if you pick out the most success-ful business man in town, and go look at his left thumb nail, you will find a scar on it where a half-drowned gopher bit him, because he was at the hole at the right time. Now, go and have fun, and be sure and play fair with the dog," and Uncle Ike took down a broom and shook it at them as they scattered down the street, the dog barking joyously.

"I speak for carrying the water to drown out the gopher!" yelled the red-headed boy.

"Me, too!" shouted the other boys in chorus, as they disappeared from sight, and Uncle Ike listened until they were out of hearing, and then he limped down to the gate and looked up the road toward the country, but all he could see was a cloud of dust with a dog in it, and he walked back to the house sadly, and as he lifted the lame leg upon the porch, and took his hat, he said :

"Blamed if I don't hitch up the mare and drive out there where those boys have gone. I'll bet I know woodchuck holes and gopher holes them kids never would find if they had a whole passel of dogs," and he went out to the barn and pretty soon Aunt Almira heard him yell, "Whoa, gosh darn ye, take in that bit!" and she put on her sunbonnet and went out to the barn to see if he had actually gone crazy.

CHAPTER XIII.

"What you scratching yourself on the chest for?" said Uncle Ike, as the red-headed boy stood with one hand inside his vest, digging as though his life depended on his doing a good job. "Is there anything the matter with you that soap and water will not cure?" and the old man punched the boy in the ribs with a great big, hard thumb, as big as a banana.

"Uncle Ike, how long will a porous plaster stay on, and isn't there any way to stop its itching? I have had one on for seventeen days and nights, and it seems to be getting worse all the time," said the boy, as he dug away at his chest.

"Good heavens, take it off quick!" said Uncle Ike, as he laid his lighted pipe down on the table, on a nice, clean cloth, and the ashes and fire spilled out, and burned a hole in it. "You will die of mortification. Those plasters are only intended to be used as posters for a day or two. What in the name of common sense have you worn it seventeen days for? Let's rip it off."

"No, I have got to wear it eighteen days more," said the boy, with a look of resignation. "Now, don't laugh, Uncle Ike, will you? You see my girl has gone to the seashore to be gone five weeks, and she gave me a tintype and told me to wear it next my heart till she got back, and I thought I could get it nearer my heart by putting it right against the skin, and putting a porous plaster over it, and by gum, I can feel her on my heart every minute. Now don't laugh, Uncle."

"Well, I guess not," said Uncle Ike, as he put out the fire on the table-cloth, and smoked a little while to settle his thoughts "Here, this plaster has got to be removed before the fatal day of her return, or you will be holding down a job as a red-headed angel. Now, open your shirt," and the old man reached in and got a corner of the plaster, and gave a jerk that caused every hair on the boy's head to raise up and crack like a whiplash, while the tintype of the girl, covered with crude India rubber and medicated glue, dropped on the floor, and the boy turned pale and yelled bloody murder. "Now, don't ever do that again. A picture in your inside pocket is near enough to the heart for all practical purposes. Next, you will be swallowing her picture in the hope that it will lodge near your heart. Now I got something serious to talk with you about. One of the park policemen was here this morning looking for you. He said some of you boys just raised merry hades at the park concert last night. What did you do?"

"Just flushed quails," said the boy, as he buttoned his shirt, and gave the sore spot a parting dig. "We played we were hunting quail, and we had more fun than you ever saw."

"There are no quail in the park," said Uncle Ike. as he looked curiously at the boy through the smoke,

"Here, this plaster has got to be removed before the fatal day
of her return."

and puffed until his cheeks sank in, and the tears
came to his eyes. " What is this quail fable, anyway ?"

" You see," said the boy, as he took a piece of ice
out of the water pitcher and held it in his bosom,
where the plaster came off, "when there is an evening concert at the park, the boys and girls go off in
couples and sit under the trees in the dark, or on the
grass, where no one can see them very well, and they
take hold of hands and put their arms around each
other, and all the time they are scared for fear they
will be caught, and ordered to quit. Well, us boys go
around in the dark, and when we see a couple in that
way, one boy comes to a point, like a dog, another
boy walks up to the couple and flushes them, and as
they get up quick to go somewhere else, I blow up a
paper bag and bust it, and they start off on a run.
Say, Uncle Ike, it is fun. We chased one couple
clear to the lake."

" You did, did you, you little imp ?" said the old
man, as his sympathies were aroused for the young
people who were disturbed at a critical time. " Don't
let me ever hear of your flushing any more couples,
or I'll flush you the first time I catch you with your
girl. How would you like to be flushed ? The parks
are the only places many young people have to talk
love to each other, and it is cruel to disturb them by
bursting paper bags in their vicinity. If I was mayor
I would build a thousand little summer houses in the
parks, just big enough for a poor young couple to sit
in, and talk over the future, and I would set police-

men to watch out that nobody disturbed them, and if one of you ducks come along, I would have you thrown in the lake. The idea of a boy who is in love the way you pretend to be, having no charity for others, makes me sick. I'll bet none of those you flushed last night had it so bad they had tintypes of the girls glued on their hearts with a porous plaster. Bah! you meddler!" and the old man stamped his foot on the floor, and the boy looked ashamed.

"Well, that's the last time I will mix in another fellow's love affair," said the boy, as he climbed up on Uncle Ike's knee.

"Now, I want to talk to you seriously," said the boy, as he looked up into Uncle Ike's round, smooth, red and smiling face. "Us boys have been reading about the serious condition of our country, when its wealthy citizens are leaving it and going abroad to live. Do you think, uncle, that William Waldorf Astor's deserting this country, and joining England, is going to cause this country to fail up in business? In case of war with England, do you think he would fight this country?"

"Well, you kids can borrow more trouble about this poor old country of ours than the men who own it can borrow. Astor! Why, boy, his deserting his country will have about as much effect as it would for that man working in the street to pack up his household goods and move to Indiana. Do you suppose this state would tip up sideways if he should quit running that scraper and move out of the state?

Not much. The Astors have been rich so long that
they are un-American. It is not the natural condition of an American to be rich. When a man gets
too rich, he is worried as to what to do with his
money. There is no great enjoyment that the very
rich can have in this country that the poor cannot
have a little of. The first thing a very rich man ac-
quires is a bad stomach. He becomes too lazy to
take exercise, and lets a hired man take exercise for
him. He looks at his money, and thinks of his stomach. In Astor's case there was nothing in this country that he could enjoy, not even sleep. Nobody
respected him any more than they did every other
honest man. Only a few toadies would act toward
him as though he was a world's wonder, on account
of his wealth. People with souls, and health, and
good nature, in the West, got rich as he, and went to
New York, and knew how to spend money and have
fun, and do good with it ; and Astor couldn't understand it. He wanted to be considered the only, but
he never had learned how to blow in money to make
others happy. If he gave to the poor, an agent did
it for him, and squeezed it, and made a memorandum
and showed it to him once a year, and he frowned,
and his stomach ached, and he took a pill, and sighed.
I suppose two girls from California, daughters of an
old Roman of the mines and the railroads, who died
too soon, a senator with a soul, taught Astor how to
do good with money, and maybe scared him out of
the country. Those girls seemed to know where

there was a chance for suffering among the poor, and
they kept people in their employ on the run to get to
places before the bread was all gone, until half a million of the people that only knew there was an Astor
by the signs on buildings for rent, knew these Fair
girls by sight, and worshiped them as they passed.
The girls are married now, but they give just the
same, and wherever they are in the world there is
the crowd, and there is the love of those who believe
them angels.   Astor could not find any one to love
him for any good he ever did that did not have rent
or interest as the object, and he went away where a
man is respected in a half-way manner, in proportion
to the money he spends on royalty, in imitating royalty, and he will run a race there, and get tired of it ;
and some day, if he lives, he will come back to this
country in the steerage, as his ancestors did, and take
out his first papers and vote, and maybe he will be
happy.   The only way for a rich man to be very
happy is to find avenues for getting his congested
wealth off his mind, where it will cause some one who
is 'poor and suffering to look up to him, and say that
riches have not spoiled him.   But to inherit money
and go through life letting it accumulate, and not
finding any avenue where it can leak out and be
caught in the apron of a needy soul, is tough.   No,
you boys need not worry about the desertion of Astor.
If we have a war with Great Britain, you would find
Astor taking a night trip across the channel, and
France would draw him in the lottery.   One for-

eigner who landed in this country the day Astor
sailed away, will be of more value in peace or war
than Astor could be if he had remained."

"Gosh!" said the boy, as he got up out of Uncle
Ike's lap, "if you are not a comfort! Between that
porous plaster, and Astor's going to England, and my
girl at the seashore, I was about down with nervous
prostration, but I am all right now," and the red-
headed boy went out to round up the gang and tell
them the country was all safe enough, as long as they
had Uncle Ike to run it.

CHAPTER XIV.

"Well, you are a sight!" said Uncle Ike, as the red-headed boy came in the room, all out of breath, his shirt unbuttoned and his hair wet and dripping, and his face so clean that it was noticeable. "Why don't you make your toilet before you come into a gentleman's room? Where you been, anyway?"

"Been in swimming at the old swimming hole," said the boy, as he finished buttoning his shirt, and sat down to put on his shoes and stockings, which he had carried in his hat. "Had more fun than a barrel of monkeys. Stole the clothes of a boy, and left him a paper flour sack to go home in. Wait a minute and you will see him go by," and the boy rushed to the window and yelled to Uncle Ike to come and see the fun. Presently a boy came down the street from toward the river with nothing on but a flour sack. He had cut holes in the bottom to put his feet through, and pulled it up to his body, and the upper part covered his chest to the arms, which were bare and sunburned, and the boy was marching along the street as unconcerned as possible, while all who saw him were laughing.

"What did you do that for?" said Uncle Ike, as he called to the boy to come in.

"Just for a joke," said the red-headed boy, laughing, and jollying the boy dressed in the flour sack, as he came in at Uncle Ike's invitation.

"Well, that is a good enough joke for two," said Uncle Ike. "Now take off your clothes and change with this boy, and put on the flour sack yourself," and he superintended the change, until the other boy had on a full suit of clothes, and the red-headed boy had on the flour sack. "Now I want you to go to the grocery and get me a paper of tobacco."

"O, gosh, I don't want to go out in the street with this flour sack on. Some dog will chase me, and the people will make fun of me," said the boy, with an entirely new view of a practical joke.

"But you go all the same," said Uncle Ike, taking down a leather strap that he sharpened his razor on, and driving the boy outdoors. "Bring back this boy's clothes, also," and he sat down and waited for the boy to return. He came back after awhile with the tobacco and the clothes, followed by a lot of other boys, and after the two had changed clothes, and all had enjoyed a good laugh, Uncle Ike said:

"Boys, playing practical jokes is a good deal like jumping on a man when he is down. You will notice that the weaker boy always has the joke played on him. Boys always combine against the weak boy. The boy that can whip any of you never has to wear a flour sack home from the swimming hole, does he? Any joke that you can take turns at having played on you is fair, but when you combine against the weak, you become a monopoly, or a trust. When I was a

"Presently a boy came down the street from toward the **river** with nothing on but a flour sack."

boy we used to tie the clothes of the biggest and
meanest boy in knots, and if he couldn't take a joke
we all turned in and mauled him.   After this, if there
is to be any jokes, let the biggest boy take his turn
first, and then I don't care how soon the others take
their dose, but this trust business has got to be broke
up," and Uncle Ike patted the boys on the head
and said they could go and have all the fun they
wanted to.

"Speaking of trusts, Uncle Ike, I thought you
said, a spell ago, that the trusts would be brought up
with a round turn," said the red-headed boy, reading,
as he glanced at a heading in a morning paper, "but
here is an article says that a thousand million billion
dollars have been invested in trusts in New Jersey,
and the manager of one of the biggest trusts says
nobody can do anything to stop them.   He says :
' What are you going to do about it ? ' "

"Well," said Uncle Ike, as he filled the air with
strong tobacco smoke, and his eyes snapped like they
did when he was mad, "you wait.   I am older than
you are.   I remember when old Bill Tweed, the great
robber of New York, who had stolen millions of dollars from the city, and was in his greatest power, became arrogant, and asked the people what they were
going to do about it.   When people think they are
invincible they always ask what anybody is going to
do about it.   When a bully steps on the foot of a quiet
and inoffensive man, purposely to get into a row,
he looks at his victim in an impudent manner and

says, 'What are you going to do about it?' and the
victim gets up deliberately and thrashes the ground
with the bully.   The people got mad at Tweed when
he said that, and they chased him over the world, and
landed him in the penitentiary, where he died.   That
will be the fate of some of these trust magnates.   The
foundation of the trust is corruption.   Its trade mark
was uttered years ago by a great railroad man who
said, 'The public be d——d.'   That expression is in
the mind of every man connected with a trust.   He
turns the thumbscrews on the public, raises prices,
and if they complain, he says, 'What are you going to
do about it?' and if anybody says the public cannot
stand it, they say 'the public be blessed,' or the other
thing.   Now, wait.   The public will be making laws,
and the first law that is made will be one that sends
a man to the penitentiary who robs through a trust.
If three men combine to rob it is a conspiracy.   If a
hundred or a thousand combine to rob seventy million people, it is treason.   You wait, boys, and you
will hear a noise one of these days when the people
speak, and you will hear trust magnates who fail to
get across the ocean before the tornado of public indignation strikes, begging for mercy.   Now, gosh blast
you, run away.   You have got me to talking again,"
and Uncle Ike lighted his pipe and shut up like a
clam, while the boys went out looking for trouble.

Uncle Ike had been dozing and smoking, and fixing
his fishing tackle, and oiling his gun, and whistling,
and trying to sing, all alone, for an hour, after the

boys had gone out to have fun, and when he saw them
coming in the gate, two of them carrying a big striped
watermelon, and the others watching that it did not
fall on the ground, he was rather glad the boys had
come back, and he opened the door and went out on
the porch and met them.

"S-h-h !" said the red-headed boy, as Uncle Ike
thumped the melon with his hard old middle finger,
to see if it was ripe. "Don't say a word. Let's get
it inside the house, quick, and you carve it, Uncle,"
and they brought it in and laid it on the table, and
the boys looked down the street as though they were
expecting some one.

"We never used to ask any questions when I was
a boy, when a melon suddenly showed up, and nobody
knew from whence it came," said Uncle Ike, as he
put both hands on the melon and pressed down upon
it, and listened to it crack. "Do you know, if a person takes potatoes, or baled hay, that does not belong
to him, it is stealing, but if a melon elopes with a boy,
or several boys, the melon is always considered guilty
of contributory negligence," and the old man laughed
and winked at the boys. "But a house is no place to
eat a melon in, and a knife is not good enough to cut
a melon. Now, you fetch that melon out in the garden,
by the cucumber vines, and I will show you the conditions that should surround a melon barbecue," and the
old man led the way to the garden, followed by the
boys, and he got them seated around in the dirt, with
the growing corn on one side, a patch of sunflowers

on another, a crabapple tree on one side, giving a little shade where they sat, and the alley fence on the
other.   The boys were anxious to begin, and each
produced a toad-stabber, but Uncle Ike told them to
put away the knives, and said :

"The only way to eat a melon is to break it by putting your knee on it, and taking the chunks and running your face right down into it.   A nigger is the
only natural melon eater.   There," said he, as he
crushed the brittle melon rind into a dozen pieces,
and spread it open, red, and juicy, and glorious.
"Now 'fall in,' as we used to say in the army," and the
boys each grabbed a piece and began to eat and drink
out of the rind, the juice smearing their faces and
running down on their shirt bosoms, and Uncle Ike
taking a piece of the core in his hands and trying to
eat as fast as the boys did, the red and sticky juice
trickling through his fingers, and the pulp painting
pictures around his dear old mouth, and up his cheeks
to his ears, while he tried to tell them of a day during
the war when he was on the skirmish line going
through a melon patch, and how the order came to
lie down, and every last soldier dropped beside a
melon, broke it with his bayonet, and filled himself,
while the bullet whistled, and how they were all sick
afterwards, and had to go to the rear because the
people who owned the melons had put croton oil in
them.

"Gosh, but this is great!" said the red-headed boy,
as he stopped eating long enough to loosen his belt.

"You bet!" said one of the other boys; "Uncle Ike is a James dandy," and he looked up and bowed to a boy with an apron on, who came into the garden with a piece of paper in his hand, which he handed to Uncle Ike.

"What is this, a telegram?" says Uncle Ike, as he takes it with his sticky fingers and feels for his glasses.

"No, it is the bill for the melon—50 cents," said the grocer's boy.

"Bunkoed, by gosh!" says Uncle Ike, as he looks around at the laughing boys who have played it on him.

"Don't ever ask where a melon comes from," said the red-headed boy.

"Sawed a gold brick on me, you young bunko-steerers," says Uncle Ike, as he wipes his hands on some mustard and feels in his pocket for the change; "but it was worth it, by ginger," and he pays for the melon, they all go in the house and wash the melon off their hands and faces, the old man lights his pipe and says: "Boys, come around here to-morrow and play this trick on Aunt Almira, and I'll set up the root beer."

CHAPTER XV.

" Say, where you been all day ? " asked Uncle Ike of the red-headed boy, as he showed up late in the afternoon, chewing a gob of gum so big that it made his ear ache. " Here, I've been waiting all day for you, with so many things on my mind to tell you about that I have had to make memorandums," and the old man took out his knife and shaved some tobacco off a plug, rolled it in his hands and scraped it into the pipe, and lit up for a long talk.

" I been working," said the boy, as he took some pieces of chocolate out of his pocket and offered them to his uncle. " I am working for a syndicate, and have got a soft snap, with all the money I can spend," and the boy shook the pennies in his pocket so they sounded like emptying a collection plate.

" Working for a syndicate, a-hem !" said the old man. " A syndicate is a great thing, if you are the syndicate, but if you work for it you get left, that's all. Now tell me about it. What you doing for a syndicate, and who furnishes you the money to spend? Tell me, so I can see whether it is honest. Somehow I can't feel that a syndicate means any good to a boy."

"It is this way, Uncle Ike," said the boy, as he threw away his gum and took another stick out of his pocket, and chewed it until he fairly drooled, " you know these slot machines in the depots and hotels,

where people put in a penny and pull out a knob and
get a stick of gum or a chocolate, or some peppermint
drops.   Well, the syndicate wants a boy to go around
and put in pennies, and get the prizes, when people
are looking on, so as to get them interested, so they
will put in pennies, see?"

"Sure! You are a sort of capper for a gum bunko
game, eh?   Rope in the people and get them next to
a good thing," said Uncle Ike, looking at the boy
over his glasses.   "What particular talent does this
new business bring to the front?   Do you make
speeches to the people, encouraging them to invest
their hard-earned pennies in your great scheme for the
amelioration of the condition of the down-trodden, or
what do you do?   Tell me how the thing works."

"Why, my work is all pantomime.   The man who
hired me said I had a face that was worth a fortune.
I go up to a slot machine, and act as though I never
saw such a thing before.   Then I monkey around,
and seem to be puzzled, and my face looks serious,
and the people in the depot waiting for trains gather
around and watch me, and when the jays are all ripe,
ready to pick, I put a penny in the slot, draw out a
stick of gum, put it in my mouth, and then I smile
one of those broad smiles, like this, and the people
begin to put in pennies, and they surround the machine, and money just flows in, until their train goes,
when another crowd comes in and I work them on the
chocolate slot, and just blow in pennies belonging to
the syndicate that owns the machines.   Oh, it's a **great**

snap, Uncle Ike.   You ought to go into it," and the boy threw away his gum and went to eating chocolate.

"Is that so?   My face would be my fortune, too, would it?" said Uncle Ike, who was beginning to show that he was mad.   "And what salary does the syndicate pay you for your valuable services as a piece of human fly paper?"

"O, they don't pay me any salary," said the boy, as he took out a handful of syndicate pennies and poured them from one hand into another, to show the old man that he had wealth.   "I don't ask anything for my services.   I just get pay in fun, and have all the gum, and chocolate, and lemon drops that I can eat.   The man told me it would be an experience that would be valuable to me in after life, being in the eye of the public, leading the people.   He said this would be the making of me, and open up a career that would astonish my friends.   Don't you think so, Uncle?   Can't you see a change in me since I went to work for the syndicate?"

"Well, I don't know but I do," said Uncle Ike, as he pondered over the remarks of the boy.   "You begin to look more bilious, probably on account of the chocolate you have eaten, to deceive the people at the depot into the idea that it is good stuff.   And perhaps this experience will be the opening of a career.   If you can, by your actions, cause strangers to run up against a slot machine, I don't see why you couldn't, in time, be a pretty good capper for a three-card monte game, where you could pick out the right card, and the jay

loses his money.   If this is the kind of business you
have selected for a career, it will not be long before
you will be in demand as a bunko-steerer.   You would
be invaluable, with that innocent face of yours, in
roping in strangers to a robbers' roost, where they
would be fleeced and thrown down stairs on their necks.
With about two days more experience on a slot machine, some gold-brick swindler will come along and
raise the syndicate out on your salary, and put you on
the road selling gold bricks.   Starting in business as
a fakir, you will rise to become a barker for a side-
show, graduate into bunko and gold bricks, and if you
are not sent to the penitentiary, there is a great opening for you as a promoter of a trust in the air we
breathe.   We shall have to part company.   My reputation is dear to me.   I have never turned a jack from
the bottom when I had one to go in seven-up, and to
associate with a boy who will rope people to buy
mouldy gum, and be an advance agent of prosperity as
recorded on a slot machine, is too much, and I bid you
good-bye.   I have loved you, but it was because you
were innocent and tried to do the fair thing, but—
good-bye," and the old man laid down his pipe, picked
up his hat and started for the door.

    " Hold on, Uncle Ike," said the boy, taking the
handful of pennies out of his pocket and laying them
on the table, " I didn't know it was so bad.   I won't
do it any more.   Come back, please."

    " Well, I got to go downtown," said the old man,
" and I will be back in an hour.   In the meantime

"Been trying to smoke the old man's pipe, eh?"

you write out a letter of resignation to the syndicate.
Say that you find a diet of decayed chocolate and
glucose candy is sapping the foundation of your man-
hood, and that your Uncle Ike has offered you a position on the staff of a gold-brick syndicate," and the
old man went out, leaving the boy to write his
resignation.

"Well, how is my decoy duck, and has he sent in
his resignation?" said the old man, as he came in a
little later and found writing material and pennies on
the table, and the boy lying on the lounge looking pale
and sick. "What is this? Sick the first time you have
to resign an office?   That won't do.   You never will
make a politician if you can't write out a resignation
without having it go to your head," and the old man
sat down by the boy and found that he was as sick as
a horse, his face white, and cold perspiration on his
upper lip among the red hairs, and on his brow among
the freckles.   The boy's bosom was heaving, and his
stomach was clearly the seat of the disease, and suddenly the boy rushed out of the room, into the bathroom, and there was a noise such as is frequently
heard on steamboat excursions. The old man thought
it was the chocolate and gum that had made the boy
sick, until he looked at his pipe on the table, which
was smoking, although he had been away an hour or
more.

"Been trying to smoke the old man's pipe, eh?"
said he, as the boy staggered out of the bathroom so
weak he could hardly stand. " Well, that plug tobacco

in the pipe is a little strong for a bunko-steerer, but I suppose you thought if you were going to be a business man, and leave me, you ought to take with you some of my bad habits. Let me fill the pipe with some of this mild switchman's delight, and you try that," and he brought the pipe near to the boy.

"Take it away, take it away," said a weak voice, coming from under a pillow on the lounge. "Oh, Uncle Ike, I will never touch a pipe again. You look so happy when you are smoking that I thought I would like to learn, so I lit the pipe, and drew on it, and the smoke wouldn't come, and I drew in my breath whole length, as I do when I dive off a spring board, and the whole inside of the pipe came into my mouth, and I swallowed the whole business, and pretty soon it felt as though a pin-wheel had been touched off inside of me, and the sparks flew out of my nose, and the smoke came out of my ears, and they turned on the water in my eyes, and my mouth puckered up and acted salivated, like I had eaten choke-cherries, and pretty soon the pin-wheel in my stomach began to run down, and I thought I was going to stop celebrating, when the pin-wheel seemed to touch off a nigger-chaser, and it went to fizzing all around inside of me, up into my lungs, and down around my liver, and it called at all my vital parts and registered its name, and when the nigger-chaser seemed to be dying it touched off an internal sky-rocket, and s-i-z-boom—that was when I went in the bathroom, 'cause I was afraid of the stick. Say,

Uncle Ike, does anyone ever die from smoking plug tobacco?"

"Oh, yes, about half of them die, when they smoke it the first time. When their eyes roll up, like yours, and they cease to be hungry, and feel as though they had rather lie down than stand up, they don't last very long," and the old man looked serious, and reached for his pipe and a match, and said: "Any last message you want to send to anybody; any touching good-bye? If you do, whisper it to me, and I will write your dying statement."

"Don't light that dum pipe!" said the boy, rolling over and looking like a seasick ghost, as Uncle Ike was about to scratch a match on his trousers. "Here is the address of my girl. Write to her that I am dead. That I died thinking of her, and smelling of plug tobacco. Put it in that I died of appendicitis, or something fashionable, and say that eight doctors performed eight operations on me, but peritonitis had set in, and there was no use, but that they cut a swath in me big enough to drive an automobile through. I had rather she would think of me as dying a heroic death, than dying smoking plug tobacco. And, say, Uncle Ike, after you have written her, don't make a mistake and send my resignation to the syndicate to her. O, God! but it is hard to die so young," and the boy went to sleep on the lounge, and Uncle Ike went to taking the kinks out of a fish line, knowing that when the boy woke up he wouldn't be dead worth a cent. About half an hour later the boy rolled over, opened his big eyes, sat up, and stared around, and Uncle Ike said :

"Now, you go in the bath-room and wash your face in cold water, and you will be all right," and the boy did so, and came back with almost a smile on his face, and he looked at the papers on the table, and said :

"Uncle Ike, you didn't send that appendicitis story to my girl, did you ? Gosh, but I am all right now, and I am not going to die."

"No, I didn't send it ; but next time I will, by ginger," and the old man laughed. "Here, have a smoke on me," but the boy went out in the open air and kicked himself.

CHAPTER XVI.

It was a beautiful, hot, sunny morning, and after breakfast Uncle Ike came out on the porch in his shirt sleeves, and with a pair of old hunting shoes on, and his shirt sleeves rolled up, showing the sleeves of a red flannel undershirt, a kind he always wore, winter and summer. He leaned against the post of the porch, lit his pipe, and looked away toward the hazy, hot horizon, and thought of old days that had been brought to his mind the day before, when he saw the parade of a Wild West show. The old man was a '49er, who went across the plains for gold when the country was young, and the yells of the Indians had made him nervous, as they did half a century ago. He had staked the red-headed boy and several of his chums to go to the show, and was waiting for them to show up and report. He stepped down on the lawn and took up the nozzle of a sprinkler and turned it on a lilac bush, when suddenly there was a yell that was unmistakably that of a Comanche Indian ; and he stopped and looked at the bush, and could plainly see a moccasin and a leg with buckskin fringe on it, and he knew the boys were laying for him, to scalp him and have fun with him ; so he held the nozzle as his only protection against the bloodthirsty band of savages, headed by Chief Red Head, his nephew, but a bad Indian when off the reservation. From behind an evergreen tree down by the gate there came a blood-curdling yell, which was evidently from the throat of "Watermelon Jim," a neighbor's boy, while from the wild cucumber vine on the south porch came a noise like that of a pack of wolves breakfasting on a fawn.

"Surrender!" shouted a damp voice from behind the lilac bush, where the hose was turned. "Surrender, or we burn down your ranch over your head!" and a painted Indian, with red, short hair showing under the feather, crawled toward a rosebush, where it was dry.

"Never!" said Uncle Ike, as he bit the stem of his pipe, and smiled at the boys who were peeking out from behind the different hiding places. "Your Uncle Ike often dies, but he never surrenders," and he cocked the nozzle of the lawn sprinkler, and stood ready for the attack.

The red-headed Indian lit a parlor match and held it aloft, which was apparently a smoke signal, for an Indian behind the porch appeared and suddenly a swish was heard in the air, and a piece of clothesline with a noose in it came near going over Uncle Ike's head; so near that it broke his clay pipe, leaving the stem between his lips.

"Ah, ha! You will, will you? Vamoose!" said Uncle Ike, as he turned the hose on the Indian with the lasso, and drove him behind the porch with water dripping down his calico shirt, taking the color out. **Then an Indian near the gate began to fire blank**

cartridges with a toy pistol and Uncle Ike put his
elbow up in front of his face, as he said afterward, to
save his beauty, and Uncle Ike started toward that
Indian, dragging the hose, and shouting, " Take to
the chaparral, condemn you, or I will drown you out
like a gopher!"

For a moment there was an ominous silence. The
Indians had withdrawn behind the currant bushes,
but Uncle Ike knew enough of Indian warfare to
know that the silence was only temporary. Suddenly
there was a blazing and crackling, and a big smoke
from the back of the house, and it seemed the red-
skins had set fire to the house, the hired girl yelled
fire and murder, and came out with a pail of water,
while the chief yelled "Charge!" and in a minute Uncle
Ike was surrounded by the tribe, his legs tied with
the clothesline, though he fought with the garden
hose until there was not a dry rag on one of the boys
or himself.

" Burn him at the stake!" shouted a little shrimp
who carries papers every afternoon, after school, as
he wiped the red paint off his cheek on to his bare
arm, and shook water out of his trousers leg.

" No, let's hold him for a ransom," said the red-
headed boy.   " Aunt Almira will give us enough to
buy a melon, and make us a pail of lemonade, if we
let this gray-haired old settler off without scalp-
ing him."

" Chief, spare me, please," said Uncle Ike, as he
sat up in a puddle of water on the battle ground, with

"Take to the chaparral, condemn you, or I will drown you out
like a gopher!"

his legs tied. "I am the mother of eleven orphan children. O, spare me! and don't walk on that pipe of mine on the grass there, with your moccasins. I will compromise this thing myself, and pay the ransom. Here is a dollar. Go and buy melons, and we will have a big feed right here. But what was the fire behind the house, and is it put out?"

"The ransom is agreed to," said the red-headed boy, as he took off his string of feathers, and gave a yell, hitting his lips with the back of his hand so it would "gargle," "and the fire is out. We put some kerosene on an empty beer case, that was all." So Uncle Ike handed over the dollar, and was released, while a boy who had washed his paint off was sent to a grocery after a melon. Then they wiped the mud off Uncle Ike, and all went upon the porch, a new pipe of peace was provided, and they talked about the Wild West show of the night before, while Uncle Ike did the most of the smoking of the pipe of peace, though he wiped the stem once and handed it to the red-headed chief to take a whiff, but the chief, after his experience with plug tobacco cholera a few days before, declined with thanks.

"What interested you most at the show?" said Uncle Ike, puffing away, as he sat on the floor of the porch, and leaned his back against one of the posts. "When you go to a show you always want to get your mind on something that makes an impression on you."

"Well, sir," said the boy who had worked the lasso

on Uncle Ike, "the way these Mexicans handled the
lariat struck me the hardest, only they look so darned
lazy.   They just wait for a horse to get in the right
place, and then pull up.   I would like to see them
chase something, and catch it by the leg, that was
trying to get away.   But the Cossacks!   O, my!
couldn't they ride, standing up, or dragging on the
ground with one foot in the stirrup.   Gosh! if Russia
turned about a million of those Cossacks loose on
China, they wouldn't do a thing to John Chinaman."

"The Indians got me," said another boy, as he
took off a moccasin and hung it up in the sun to dry,
after his fight to the death with Uncle Ike's water-
works.   "I would like to be an Indian, or a squaw,
and never have anything to do but travel with a show,
and yell.   They just have a soft snap, dressing up in
feathers, and paint, and buckskin, and living on the
fat of the land, and yelling ki-yi! in a falsetto voice."

"Oh, I don't know," said the red-headed boy,
"what struck me as the most exciting was the battle
of San Juan hill.   Say, did you see our boys just
walk right up to the Spaniards, in the face of a perfect hailstorm of blank cartridges, with a gatling gun
stuttering smokeless powder, and the boys in blue firing volleys, and the rough riders walking on foot, and
the Spaniards just falling back, and pretty soon we
went right over them, and down came the Spanish
flag, and then the Stars and Stripes went up, and
there was where I yelled so the roof ripped.   But
what made me cry was to see Old Glory and the

British flag get together, every little while, and float
side by side, and seem to be grown together as one
flag, and everybody seemed glad.   What you think
about things, Uncle Ike ?   Don't sit there and smoke
up, all the time, but tell us what you think about the
American and British flags waving together so much
lately.   Are you in favor of an alliance?   Do you
want to be an assistant Englishman, Uncle Ike?"

"Well, I don't want to be quoted much on this
business," said Uncle Ike, as he looked around at the
boys, who were listening intently.   " I have watched
the course of England and all the countries, for over
fifty years, in their relations with this country, and
the only friendship England ever showed to us was in
the last war. They did us good, no doubt, and I trust
I am grateful, as becomes a good citizen.   It was like
a big boy and little boy fighting.   The big boy can
whip if he is not interfered with, but a lot of boys are
standing around, ready to mix in to help the little fellow.   They are ready to trip up the big fellow, so the
little one can jump on him, and they are getting
ready to throw stones at him, and kick him on the
shins.   Then a big bully that they are all afraid to
tackle, comes along and says : ' This little fellow
picked on the big fellow, and kept nagging him till he
had to fight or run.   Now the little fool has got to
take his medicine, and you fellows mustn't mix in, or
you got me to fight.   Just keep hands off, that's all.'
That's all there was to it, but it came in mighty
handy, and we appreciate it, but there is too much

grand stand play about an alliance.   In other wars
with England, Germans and French and Poles have
fought with us, and for us, and yet we have never felt
like having an alliance with them.   Do you ever take
much stock in Russia, boys?   Don't ever forget
Russia.   During our war between the North and
South, we were once in a tight place.   England and
other countries were about to recognize the Southern
Confederacy, and England was doing everything possible to break us up, furnishing privateers, and har-
boring confederate gunboats, and making it warm for
us.   Boys, your Uncle Abraham Lincoln was perspir-
ing a good deal those days.   They say he couldn't wear
a collar, he sweat so.   It was believed that England
and several other countries were going to simultane-
ously recognize the Confederacy, and maybe turn in and
fight us.   Warships from other countries were hovering around our southern coast, and our soldiers were
feeling pretty blue, the cabinet never smiled, and nobody laughed out loud except Uncle Abe, and even
his laugh seemed to have a hollow, croupy sound.
One day, when the strain was the greatest, and everybody felt as though there was a funeral in the family,
and there were funerals in most families, a flock of
warships flying the flag of Russia, steamed by Sandy
Hook, and up to New York, saluted the forts and the
Stars and Stripes all along up to the Battery.   It
seemed as though those battleships never would stop
coming.   They lined up all around New York, and
their guns pointed toward the sea, and every Russian

on board acted as though he was loaded for bear. The
news went to Washington that night, and they say
Uncle Abe had night sweats. The next morning a
Russian admiral, who had gone over to Washington
on a night train, called to pay his respects to the
President, and presented him with a document in the
Russian language, which had to be interpreted by the
Russian minister. When it was interpreted they say
old Abe danced a highland fling, and hugged the Rus-
sians and danced all hands around. That document
has never been published, but it was to the effect that
the Russian fleet was at the disposal of the President
of the United States, to fight any country on the face
of God's green earth that attempted to mix in. See?
It was not long before other nations discovered that
Russia had sent her fleet to stay, and every Russian
on every vessel acted as though he was spoiling for a
fight, and seemed to say to the world, 'Come on,
condemn you!' And nobody ever came along to
fight. And Uncle Abe began to be in a laughing
mood, and you know the rest, if you have read up
about the war. Nobody has ever suggested an alliance with Russia, and yet we are under more obligations to that old Czar than to anybody. In fact, we
don't want an alliance with anybody. We want the
friendship of all. If I have any more love for one
country than another, I do not know which it is, only
when I see a Russian, even one of those Cossacks
that rode so well, I feel like taking him by the hand
and telling him, when he goes home, to go up to the

Winter palace and give my love to the Czar, because
I always have before me the picture of that Russian
fleet in New York harbor, when things were hot.
England has done a similar favor during this last war,
and if we had another war, and the newspapers would
quit nagging him, you would find the young emperor
of Germany doing something for us equally as good.
So, boys, don't get stuck on one country, but give
them all a chance to be good to us."

"Gosh, Uncle Ike, I never heard anything about
that Russian fleet," said the red-headed boy. "England can go plum to thunder. I thought England
was the only country that was ever even polite to us."

"Come on, boys, let's go and play Cossack," said
one of the Indians, and they went rolling over the
picket fence on their stomachs, leaving Uncle Ike
to go and put on some dry clothes.

CHAPTER XVII.

Uncle Ike had been having twinges of rheumatism in one of his legs ever since he had the scrap with the Indians, and turned the hose on them and got wet himself, and he sat out on the porch one morning with a blanket over his leg trying to warm it up, smoking his pipe in silence, and wondering why the good Lord arranged things so a good man should grow old, and have pains. The red-headed boy and quite a flock of kids of about his age were sitting on the sidewalk, outside the fence, arguing something in loud voices, and finally he heard them agree to leave it to Uncle Ike, and then they piled over the fence and came up to the porch, and the red-headed boy was the spokesman. He said :

" Say, Uncle Ike, us boys have got a bet and you are to decide it. Isn't it true that the people of Cuba, Porto Rico and the Philippines are gamblers, and hasn't our government fought them to a standstill to send people there to induce them to stop gambling and to attend to business? Isn't gambling a sin, and is it not our duty as a nation, to teach these ignorant people the wickedness of gambling, bull fighting, cock fighting, and all that?" and the boys sat all around Uncle Ike, waiting for a decision to be handed down, as they say in court.

The old man rapped the bowl of his pipe on the arm

of the rocking chair, blew through the stem, made up
a face when he got some of the nicotine on his tongue,
took a piece off the broom and run through it, blew
again, reached for the tobacco bag, filled it up, lighted
it, smoked a minute or two in silence, while five pairs
of big boys' eyes watched him as though he was a chief
justice. He wiggled around a little, to ease his leg,
knitted his brow as the pain shot through his leg, almost said darnn; then the pain let up, his face cleared
off, a smile came over it, he looked at the little statesmen around him, and finally said:

"Well, boys, you must not grow up with the idea
that our own beloved country has no faults. Just
love it, with all its faults; fight for it, if necessary,
but don't get daffy over it. In the countries you
speak of, everybody gambles more or less. In this
country only a small proportion gamble, and yet the
element of chance is something that is very attractive
to most people here at home. The other evening
your Aunt Almira brought home a beautiful goblet
she won at a progressive euchre party of neighbors.
How much more of a sin is it for the Cuban woman
to win five dollars at monte, and buy a goblet? It is
scarcely three years since tickets in Havana lotteries
were publicly sold in this country. There is more
money lost and won on draw poker in one day in New
York than is lost and won in Havana on monte and
roulette. You can find almost any gambling game in
Chicago or Milwaukee that you can find in the Philippines; and while we do not have bull fighting, we

have prize fighting every night in the week, far more brutal. It is the gambling instinct in men and women that keeps the stock exchanges going, and industrial stocks, manipulated by those who control the prices, is tinhorn gambling, as much as pulling faro cards from a silver box in a brace game, where the dealer gets a rake-off, the same as the commission man, who deals the cards in stock or wheat. I don't know whether it is the object of our government to attempt to show the people of these new possessions the wickedness of gambling, and cock fighting, and all that ; but if it is, thousands of men who have become bankrupt from gambling here at home could be sent there as object lessons ; but the chances are they would put up a job to skin the natives out of their last dollar on some game they did not understand. If gambling is a sin, let he who is without sin throw the first stone into a Porto Rican cock fight. Let the senator who never played draw poker be the first to introduce a resolution to stop gambling in Manila. Let the army general that never sat up all night at a faro bank issue the first order against monte and roulette in Havana. Let the men who furnished embalmed beef for widows' sons, issue edicts against making fresh meat out of live bulls. I can't decide your bet. You better call it a draw," and the old man looked at the boys as though he wanted to change the subject.

"Say, boys, Uncle Ike knows more than any man in the world," said the red-headed boy, " but he argues

"I can't decide your bet. You better call it a draw."

too much. Let's go and play shinny and call it golf,"
and they went off on a gallop, leaving Uncle Ike with
his lame leg and his pipe.

Uncle Ike sat and thought for an hour or more, or
the porch, occasionally moving his rheumatic leg so it
hurt him worse than it did before he moved it, and then
he wondered what in the deuce he had moved it for.
He thought of his experience as a gambler, since the
boys had talked about gambling. He thought of the
time he went to a State fair, when he was a boy, right
fresh off the farm, with his white shirt his mother had
sat up the night before to iron for him, his ready-
made black frock-coat that the sun had faded out on
the shoulders, the old brown slouch hat he had traded
another one for with a lightning rod peddler, his shoes
blacked with stove blacking, instead of being greased,
as usual. He thought how a gambler at the State
fair picked him out for a greeny before he had fairly
got through the gate, and wondered how the gambler
could have known he was so green without being told,
and yet he carried a sign of greenness, from the faded
and sunburned hair of his head to the sole of his
stove-blacking shoes. He thought how the gambler
got him to bet that he could find the pea in the shell,
and how he had been so confident that he could find
it that he had bet his whole month's wages, and when
the gambler had taken it, and wound it around a wad
he had, and put it in his vest pocket, he remembered,
here sitting on the porch with his rheumatic leg, how
mad he was when the gambler who had ruined him,

shouted, "Next gentleman, now! Roll up, tumble up, any way to get up!" As he sat there waiting for the boys to come back and be company for him, he thought how destitute he was when the gambler had taken his money, how he was twenty miles from home, with only 20 cents in his pocket, and he sat down on a chicken coop, and ate 10 cents' worth of the hardest-hearted pie that ever was, and the tears came to his eyes, and the great crowd at the fair all mixed up with the horses and cattle, and he wandered about like a crazy person, all the afternoon, and at night started to walk home, with the balance of his wealth invested in gingerbread that stuck in his throat as he walked along the road in the dust, and he drank at all the wells he passed, until before he got home the peaches he had eaten before he gambled, combined with the corrugated iron pie, and the gingerbread and the various waters, gave him a case of cholera morbus big enough for a grown person, and when he got home along toward morning he wanted to die, and rather thought he would. Then he began to wonder if that gambler ever prospered, and whether he wound up his career in the penitentiary, or in politics, when he saw a big dust down the road, where the boys had gone, and presently the whole crowd came on a run, barefooted, and the first to arrive hit Uncle Ike on the arm and said, "Tag; you're it," and they all laid down on the grass and panted, and accused each other of shoving, and not running fair. After they had got so they could breathe easy, and each had taken a lot of green apples out of his shirt, and were biting into them and looking sorry they did so, the red-headed boy said:

"Uncle Ike, we have been talking it over, and have decided that some day you are to take us down to Pullman, the town founded by George Pullman. We have read a book about the town, and all about the philanthropist who laid it out, and made a little Utopia—I think that's the word—for the laboring men in his employ, where they have little brick houses made to fit a family, with gas and water. The book says he was a regular father to them, and we want to see a place where everybody is happy and contented. Will you take us there some time, Uncle Ike? Isn't Pullman the greatest and happiest man in the world?"

"Look a here," said Uncle Ike, as he got up and tried his lame leg, and found the pain was gone, and walked down on the lawn where the boys were rolling in the grass, and sat down on a lawn chair; "when you read a book of fairy stories, you want to look at the date. That book was written a dozen years ago to advertise Pullman cars. It is out of date."

"Well, isn't the town there, and are not the laboring people happy, and singing praises to the great and good Mr. Pullman, and showering blessings on his family, and helping to make a heaven upon earth of the town he built for them?"

"I thought you boys were up to the times," said the old man, as he lighted up his pipe, and crossed his legs so the lame one was on top, "but you are

back numbers.   You read too much algebra, English
history and fables.   Why, Pullman has been dead for
years, both the man and the town.   I guess I'll have
to educate you a little in American history, that you
don't get in the ward school.   Pullman was a carpenter who worked with a jack plane, and a saw, and
things.   It is said he took advantage of some ideas
another man forgot to patent, got the ideas patented,
and the result was the sleeping car.   He made money
by the barrel, and when the callouses and blood blisters were off his hands, and they became soft, he began to blow in money, and made people acquainted
with the fact that he was too rich for words.   He
still looked like a carpenter, but smelled like a rose
garden, for he learned to take a bath every few minutes and perfume himself, so the old-fashioned perspiration that had been so healthy for him would not
be noticed.   He hunted dollars as a pointer dog
hunts chickens, and finally he got so much money he
could not count it, and he hired men who were good
at figures to count it for him.   Then his brain took a
day off and studied out Pullman, and he built it on the
prairie.   His idea was all right, only that he couldn't
get over the idea that he must have a big percentage
on his outlay, in rents.   He wanted his men to be
happy, but he wanted them to pay big prices.   Another thing he wanted was for them not to think, but
to let him do all the thinking.   For a few years they
were happy, but they kept getting in debt; he cut
down on wages, but kept rents up, and the price of

gas and water never went down. If they did not like
it they could go somewhere else, and leave some of
the furniture to square up, if they were behind in
rent, but usually the bookkeeper took it out of the
wages. Then they traded at his stores, attended his
theater, and he got most all the velvet. They stood
it as long as possible, and asked for more wages, and
more work, and his agents—Pullman was never there
himself, he had an island in the St. Lawrence, and
residences everywhere except at his Utopia—told
them to hush up and go to work, and be mighty quick
about it, or he would fire them bodily out of the town.
Then they struck, and wanted to arbitrate, but Pullman telegraphed that there was nothing to arbitrate,
and then the Utopia became a Tophet, which it had
resembled for some time. Everything was closed up,
men saw their children hungry, and they were moved
away by charity to new places, where they might get
some work. The cold-blooded proposition that is not
popular with American citizens was that if men would
get on their knees, apologize, and beg, the authorities
would see what could be done for them. Men became
desperate, troops were sent to guard the premises and
to jab with bayonets these happy workmen that did
not move along fast enough. Pullman himself stayed
at his island, or at the seashore, and the men who had
dared to think without a dog license were growing
thinner, and by and by nearly all were gone; others
took their places, but the old town was not what it
used to be. Workmen preferred to live miles away,

in attics, or anywhere, in preference to the Pullman cottages. Then, one morning Pullman died, quick action, at his house, and millionaire neighbors buried him. Few flowers were sent by the old laborers. His boys, twins, had developed a partiality for jags, and having been cut off with little money in his will, they have wandered around, from one drunk cure to another, marrying occasionally, and otherwise enjoying themselves, until their poor mother was almost crazy, and the Pullman works are run by men who happened to be in on the ground floor, but who don't care much about the laboring man. No, sir," said the old man, warming up to the subject, " I will not take you kids to Pullman. I had rather take you to a cemetery, or visit the homes of the cliff dwellers of Mexico. Now, go wash up for dinner. You get me to talking, and I forget all about my rheumatism, and my dinner, and everything," and the old man started for the house, and the boys looked at each other as though they had learned something not in the school books.

CHAPTER XVIII.

It was the first cool and bracing morning since the
extreme heat of the summer, and Uncle Ike had begun to feel like going duck shooting.   He could
almost smell duck feathers in the air, and he had put
on an old dead-grass colored sweater, with a high collar that rubbed against his unshaven neck, and he
had got out his gun to wipe it for the hundredth time
since he laid it away at the close of the last season.
He looked it over and petted it, and finally sat down
in a rocking chair, with the gun between his knees
and a few cartridges in his hand that he had found in
the pocket of his sweater ; and he got to thinking of
the days that he had passed, in the last half century,
shooting ducks, and hoping that the clock of time
could be turned back, in his case, and that he might
be permitted to enjoy many years more of the sport
that had given him so much enjoyment, and con-
tributed so greatly to his health and hardness of
muscle.   He was cocking the old gun and letting
down the hammers in a contemplative mood, and occasionally aiming at a fly on the opposite wall, as
though it was a duck, when the door opened and the
red-headed boy, accompanied by eight other boys,
armed to the teeth with such weapons as they could
find, marched in and formed a line on the opposite
side of the room, and at the command, " Present

arms!" given by the red-headed captain, they saluted Uncle Ike. He arose from the rocking chair, placed his shotgun at a "carry," and acknowledged the salute, and said:

"If that horse pistol that No. 2 soldier has got pointed at my stomach is loaded, I want to declare that this war is over, and you can go to the cook and get your discharges, and fill out your blanks for pensions. But now, what does this all mean? Why this martial array? Why do you break in on a peaceful man this way, a man who does not believe in shedding human gore, so early in the morning?"

"Uncle Ike," said the red-headed boy, stepping one pace to the front, and saluting with a piece of lath, "we came to offer you the position of colonel of our regiment. We have thought over all the men who have been suggested as leaders, and have concluded that you are the jim dandy, and we want you to accept."

"Well, this takes me entirely by surprise;" said Uncle Ike, as he laid the shotgun on the table; "I certainly have not sought this office. But I cannot accept the trust until I know what is the object of the organization. Who do you propose to fight?"

"We are organized to fight the French, both with weapons and by the boycott," said the leader, swelling out his chest, and each red hair sticking up straight. "We have watched the trial of Dreyfus, and the outrage of his conviction without a particle of testimony against him, has just made us sick, and we are form-

ing a regiment to fight Frenchmen wherever we find
them.   We had the first battle at daylight this morning, when a French milkman drove along, and we
threw eggs at him, and his horse run away and spilled
four cans of milk.   We are for blood, or milk, or any
old thing that Frenchmen deal in.   We will not drink
any French champagne, and have decided not to visit
the Paris Exposition."

"Well, I swow! you have got it up your noses
pretty bad, haven't you?" said the old man as he
ordered the platoon to sit down on the floor and go
into camp.   "It is pretty tough, the way the French
treated Dreyfus, but how are you going to make your
boycott work?"

"We are going to petition the President to cut off
supplies for the Paris Exposition, withdraw from par-
ticipation in it, and we are going to ask all the people
that were intending to go to Paris to stay away."

"I see, I see," said Uncle Ike, feeling in the pocket
of his old sweater, and finding a handful of leaves,
twigs and plug tobacco that had accumulated there
for years.   "How many Jew boys have you got
enlisted in your army?   You know this Dreyfus
trouble is a fight on the Jews, not only in France, but
of the whole world.   You ought to have a whole regiment of Jew boys.   How many have you got?"

"Well, we haven't got any yet, but a whole lot of
them are going to think about it, and ask their parents
if they can join," said the captain.

"Yes, they will think about it, but they won't join,"

"Uncle Ike, we came to offer you the position of Colonel of our regiment."

said the old man, reaching for his pipe, and lighting up for a talk. "The Jews are the most patient, peaceful people in the world. They come the nearest to acting on the theory of the Golden Rule, of any class of people, and they are about the only people that will turn the other cheek, when hit on the jaw. They have been assailed for thousands of years, until they look upon being ostracised and trodden upon as one of the things they must expect, and they don't kick half as much as they ought to. If they had the enthusiasm and the fighting qualities of the Irish, they would take blackthorn clubs and mow a swath through France wide enough for an army to march over. Why don't you fellows wait until the Jews map out a plan of campaign, and then follow them? It is no dead sure thing that if the people of other countries boycotted France, that they would not ruin more Jews than Frenchmen, as the Jews are in business that the Exposition will make or break, while the French just sit around and drink absinthe and shout "viva la armee!" Don't you see you may ruin the very people you want to help? Then, stop and think of another thing. It is not many months ago that a Jew cadet at West Point was hazed and abused and ostracised by the other cadets, and had his life made such a burden that he had to resign and go home, heart-broken to a heart-broken mother. That was almost as bad as the Dreyfus case, as far as it went. How can the President boycott France for abusing Jews when our own army officers, that are to be, have shown a meanness that will size up pretty fairly with the French army devils. I'll tell you, boys, what you do. Let your sympathy go out to Dreyfus, and all his people, but don't go off half-cocked. Wait until the representative Jews of this country decide what it is their duty to do in this case, and then join them, and help them, whether it is to fight or to pray. If they conclude to sit down, and look sorry, and turn the other cheek, and be swatted some more, you be sorry also. If they decide to get on their ears, and fight, with money, or guns, or boycott, you do as you like about helping them out. But if you read, in a day or two, that France has borrowed a few more millions of Rothschild, to pay off these officers who have persecuted Dreyfus, you can make up your minds that it is a good deal like our politics here at home, mighty badly mixed. Now you go and get me a wash basin of hot soft water, and some rags, and I will clean this gun, and you disband your army, and appoint a good Jew for colonel, and when he says the affair is ripe for a fight you can spiel," and the old man took the gun apart and prepared to clean it.

"Atten-shun!" shouted the red-headed boy to his army, and each soldier jumped up off the carpet and stood erect as possible. "I will now disband you, and deliver my farewell address." Then he whispered to Uncle Ike, and the old man handed him a half dollar, when the captain gave the money to a boy who seemed to be second in command, and added, "Go and buy you some ice-cream soda, and be prepared to respond to the call to arms at a minute's notice. If France does not pardon Dreyfus, and I can get a lot of Jew boys to join us, we won't do a ting to France. Break ranks! Git!" and the boys went outdoors and made a rush for a soda fountain.

"Now, Uncle Ike," said the boy, as he watched his army going down the street, "I have got a favor to ask of you. I want you to give me music lessons."

"Well, I'll be bunkoed," said Uncle Ike, as he began to pull the sweater off over his head. "I can't sing anything but 'Marching Through Georgia.' What you want music lessons for?"

"Well, sir, I'll tell you, if you won't laugh at me," said the boy, blushing. "You see, my girl has got back from the seashore, where she has been taking salt-water baths. She was too fresh, but she is salty enough now, and her face and arms are tanned just like these Russia leather moccasins. You couldn't tell her from an Indian, only she doesn't smell like buckskin. She has been taking lessons all summer at a conservatory of music, and she can sing away up so high that when she strikes a high note and gargles on it, it makes your hair raise right up, and bristle, it is so full of electricity. She has got a tenor voice that——"

"Hold on, hold on, you have got all mixed up," said the old man. "She does not gargle. That is called warbling, or trilling, or trolling, or something. And no girl has a tenor voice. She must be a soprano."

"Well, that's what I want to take music lessons for, so I can talk with her intelligently about her music. Why, last night we were at a party, and I turned the music while she played and sang, and I got the wrong page, and got her all tangled up, and when she got through, and the people were telling her how beautiful she sang, I told her she had the most beautiful bass voice I ever saw, and she was so mad she wouldn't speak to me, so I want you to teach me which is tenor, and which is baritone, and which is that other thing, you know, Uncle Ike."

"Yes, I think I do," said the old man as he turned his head away to keep from laughing. "You want to learn to be a he Patti, in four easy lessons. Why, you couldn't learn enough about music to be in her class in fourteen years. What you want to do is to look wise, and applaud when anybody gets through singing, and say bravo, and beautiful, and all that, but not give yourself away by commenting on the technique, see?"

"Stopper! Backerup! What is technique on a girl, Uncle Ike?" asked the red-headed boy, as his eyes stuck out like peeled onions. "I have been around girls ever since I was big enough to go home alone after seeing them home, without being afraid of spooks, but I hope to die if I ever saw a technique."

"The technique," said Uncle Ike, looking wise, "is what we musicians call the—the—get there, Eli. You know when a girl is singing, and gets away up on a high note, and keeps getting it down finer all the

time, until it is not much bigger than a cambric
needle, and she draws in a whole lot of air, and just
fools with that wee bit of a note, and draws it out
fine like a silk thread, and keeps letting go of it a little at a time until it seems as though it was a mile
long, and the audience stops talking and eating candy,
and just holds its breath, and listens for her to bite it
off, and she wiggles with it, and catches another
breath when it is keeping right on, and it seems so
sweet and smooth that you can almost see angels
hovering around up in the roof, and she stands there
with her beautiful eyes shining like stars, and her
face wreathed in smiles, and that little note keeps
paying out like a silk fish line with a four-pound bass
running away with the bait, and the audience gets
red in the face for not breathing, and when everybody
thinks she is going to keep on all night, or bust and
fill the house with little notes that smell of violets,
she wakes up, raises her voice two or three degrees
higher, and finds a note that is more beautiful still,
but which is as rare as the bloom of a century plant,
so rare and radiant that she can't keep it long without
spoiling, and just as you feel like dying in your tracks
and going to heaven where they sing that way all the
time, she shakes that note into little showers of crys-
tal musical snowflakes, and then raises her voice one
note higher just for a second, and backs away with a
low bow and a sweet smile, and the audience is dumb
for a minute, and when it comes to, and she has
almost gone behind the scenes, everybody cheers,

and waves handkerchiefs, and stands up and yells
until she comes back and does it over again, that is
technique."

"Well, sir, my girl has got a technique just like
that. She can sing the socks right off of——"

"Oh, hold on; don't work any of your slang into
this musical discussion. When you want to know
anything about music, or falling in love, or farming,
come to your Uncle Ike. Office hours from 9 a. m.
to 4 p. m. No cure no pay. If you are not satisfied
your money will be cheerfully refunded," and the old
man got an oil can and begun to oil the old shotgun,
while the boy started to sing "Killarney" in a bass
voice, and Uncle Ike drew the gun on him and said:
"If you are looking for trouble, sing in that buzz-saw
voice in my presence. I could murder a person that
sang like that."

CHAPTER XIX.

Uncle Ike was leaning over the gate late in the afternoon, waiting for the red-headed boy and some of his chums to come back from the State fair. He had gone to the fair with them, and gone around to look at the stock with them, and had staked them for admission to all the side shows, and when they had come out of the last side show, and were hungry, he had bought a mess of hot wiener sausages for them, and while they were eating them somebody yelled that the balloon was going to go up, and the boys grabbed their wieners and run across the fair grounds, losing Uncle Ike; and being tired, and not caring to see a young girl go up a mile in the air, and come down with a parachute, with a good prospect of flattening herself on the hard ground, he had concluded to go home before the crowd rushed for the cars, and here he was at the gate waiting for the boys, saddened because a pickpocket had taken his watch and a big seal fob that had been in the family almost a hundred years. As he waited for the boys to come back he smoked hard, and wondered what a pickpocket wanted to fool an old man for, a man who would divide his money with any one out of luck, and he wondered what they could get on that poor old silver watch, that never kept time that could be relied on, and a tear came to his eye as he thought of some jeweler melting up that old fob that his father and grandfather used to wear before him, and he wondered if the boys would guy him for having his pocket picked, he, who had mixed up with the world for half a century and never been touched. It was almost dark when the red-headed boy and his partners in crime, came down the sidewalk, so tired their shoes interfered, and they stubbed their toes on the holes in the walk, even.

"Well, I s'pose you ducks spent every cent you had and had to walk five miles from the fair ground," said Uncle Ike, as he opened the gate and let them fall inside and drop on the grass, their shoes covered with dust, and their clothes the same. He invited them in to supper, but the peanuts, the popcorn, the waffles, the lemonade, the cider and the wieners had been plenty for them, and it did not seem as though they ever wanted to eat a mouthful again.

"Where is your fob and watch?" said the red-headed boy, as he noticed that the big stomach of the old man carried no ornament.

"Well, I decided this afternoon that it did not become a man of my age to be wearing gaudy jewelry," said Uncle Ike, "and hereafter you have got to take your uncle just as he is, without any ornaments. The watch never did keep time much, and I have had enough of guessing whether it was 1 o'clock or 3."

"Never going to wear it any more?" asked the red-headed boy, with a twinkle in his eye.

"No, I guess not," said Uncle Ike, as he heaved a sigh.

"Then I guess we can draw cuts for the old rattle-box," said the boy, as he pulled the watch and fob out of his pants pocket.

"Here! where did you get that watch?" said Uncle Ike, in excitement. "I thought a pickpocket on the trolley car got it, and I was hot. Say, that is one of the best watches in this town. Where did you find it? Did the police get the man?"

"Oh, police nothin'," said the boy. "Say, Uncle Ike, you were the easiest mark on the fair ground. There you stood, looking up at the kites, with your hands behind your back, like a jay from way back, and I knew somebody would get your watch; so I just reached up and took it, and left you standing there. I wanted to teach you a lesson. Don't ever wear your jewelry at a fair. Here's your old ticker. Sounds as though it had palpitation of the heart," and the boy handed it to the old man.

"Well, by gum! To think I should live all these years, and go through what I have, and then have an amateur pickpocket take me for a Reuben, and go through me! But how did you like the great agricultural display?"

"Oh, I don't know," said the boy, taking off his shoes and emptying the sand out. "It seems to me the farmers ought to be encouraged. I wonder how many hundred dollars it cost to hire that girl to go up in a balloon; and what good could that exhibition do the farmers? If that girl's parachute hadn't parachuted at the proper time, and she had come down

"Here! where did you get that watch?"

and been killed, wouldn't the people have been so
horrified they would never go to another fair, and
couldn't the state have been sued for damages for
hiring her to kill herself?"

"Oh, maybe," said the old man, winding up his
watch a lot ahead, and holding it to his ears to see if
it had heart disease, as the boy had intimated. "But,
you see, people have got to be amused. It has got
so there is not the inspiration in looking at vegetables
that there used to be, and the patchwork quilt does
not draw like a house afire. The farmers are not
going to blow in money to exhibit things for a blue
ribbon, and the wealthy people who have fancy stock
take the premiums and advertise their business.
Money is paid for exhibits that more properly belong
to the circus and the vaudeville, that ought to be paid
in premiums to farmers who raise things. We hire a
balloonist, believing that she will fall and kill herself
before the season is over. We take the chance that
she will kill herself at our fair, but if she does not,
and is killed at some cheap fair, somewhere else, we
feel that we are abused, and have been trifled with.
What interested you the most at the fair?" asked the
old man.

"The wieners," said the boys, all at once. And
the red-headed boy added: "When a feller is so hungry his eyes look straight ahead, and he can't turn
them in the sockets, there is nothing like a hot
wiener to start things moving, and the man who invented wieners ought to have a chromo. By gosh, I

am going to bed," and the boys all started for their resting places, while Uncle Ike felt of his stomach where the fob rested, and looked as happy as though he had never been robbed.

"Come on, Mr. Train-robber," said Uncle Ike the next morning, as the boy showed up in the breakfast room, and the old man held up his hands as he supposed passengers did when train-robbers attacked a train. "Go through me, condemn you, and take every last dollar I have got. I have brought you up to be an honest boy, and you turn out to be a pickpocket, and rob me of my watch. Oh, I tell you, no old bachelor ever had so much trouble bringing up a boy as I have. Now, I expect you will graduate in burglary, bunko, and politics, won't you?" and the old man looked at the laughing boy with such pride that the boy knew he was only fooling.

"No, if I went into burglary and kindred industries, I could never find such easy marks to practice on as dear old Uncle Ike," and the boy put his arms around the old man and asked him what time it was, and the Uncle grabbed his fob as though he was not sure whether it was there or not. "Now, let's eat breakfast," and they sat down together, and Aunt Almira poured the coffee, while Uncle Ike looked over the morning paper.

"You can disband your army, and let them go back to the paths of peace, for Dreyfus has been pardoned," said the old man. "I knew that they would pardon that man."

"Now, wouldn't that kill you," said the boy, as he sampled two or three pieces of canteloupe to find one to his taste. "That breaks up my scheme to fight the French. Uncle Ike, I have about made up my mind to lead a different life and become a minister, and preach, and go to sociables, and just have a dandy time. Say, it's a snap to be a minister, and only have to preach an hour Sunday, and have all the week to go fishing and hunting. What denomination would you advise me to become a minister of?"

"Well," said Uncle Ike, as he dropped a few lumps of sugar into his coffee, and looked at the boy across the table, "from the color of your hair, and your constant talk about falling in love every time you see a pretty girl, and the manner in which you take up a collection every time you see me anywhere, I should say you would make a pretty fair Mormon. Yes, if I was in your place I would preach Mormonism, as your experience in taking things out of people's pockets, in the way of watches, would come handy, and you are so confounded freckled you would have to have wives sealed to you or they would not stay. A minister has got to be pretty condemned good-looking, nowadays, to hold a job in a fashionable church."

"But the minister business is easy, ain't it? They don't have to work, anyway," and the boy looked at Uncle Ike as though he expected an opinion that was sound.

"If you took a job preaching," said the old man, whirling around from the table, and sitting down in his old armchair, and lighting his pipe, "you wouldn't have any soft snap. Do you know anything about what a minister has to do? Let's take one week out of the life of a regular minister. He starts in on Monday morning by having a woman call at the parsonage, a woman dressed poorly, and whose pained face makes his heart ache, and she tells him a tale of woe, and he goes to his wife and gets a basket of stuff out of the kitchen to give her, a kitchen not stocked any too well, and sends her home with immediate relief, and then goes out to hunt up the relief committee of his church to give the woman permanent relief. He comes back after a while and finds other callers, some to have him make a diagnosis of their souls, over which they are worrying, another to have him help get a son out of the police station, who used to belong to the Sunday-school, and one man wants him to preach a funeral sermon in the afternoon. He gets out of the police station in time for the funeral, and they make him go clear to the cemetery, and stop at the house with the mourners on the way back, and he gets a cold dinner that night, and has to call on several sick friends that evening, and one of them is so nearly gone that he remains with him to the last, and gets home at midnight. The other days of the week are the same, only more so, and in addition he has to run a prayer meeting, several society meetings, a sociable, settle a quarrel in the choir, and bring two members of the church together who have not spoken to each other for months,

attend a ministers' meeting and map out a plan of
campaign against the old boy, run out into the country
to preach a little for a neighboring preacher who is
sick, or off on a vacation, attend a missionary meeting, marry a few couples, and prepare two sermons for
Sunday forenoon and evening, sermons that are new,
and on texts that have not been preached on before.
One night in the week he can get on his slippers and
sit in the library, and the other nights he is running
from one place to another to make a lot of other people
happier, and he has more sickness at home than any
man in his congregation, and he works harder than the
man who digs in the sewer, and half the time the
people kick on his salary and wonder why he doesn't
do more, and say he looks so dressed up it can't be
possible he has much to do, and when he gets worn
down to the bone, and his cheeks are sunken, and his
voice fails, and his step is not so active, they saw him
off on to some country church that never did pay a
minister enough to live on, and he never kicks, but
just keeps on praying for them until he kicks the
bucket, when he ought to give them a piece of his
mind.   How do you like it?"

"Say, Uncle Ike, I surrender.   I don't want to
preach.   Where can a man enlist as a pirate?   The
pirate business appeals to me," and the boy got up
and took his golf club to go out.

"Yes, you have many qualifications that would
come in handy as a pirate, and I will use my influence
to get you into politics, you young heathen," and the

old man gave the red-headed boy a poke in the ribs with his big hard thumb, and they separated for the day, the old man to smoke and dream, and the boy to have fun and get tired and hungry.

CHAPTER XX.

Uncle Ike did not get up very early, on account of a little pain in one of his hind legs, as he expressed it, a rheumatic pain that he had almost come to believe, as the pension agent had often suggested, was caused by his service in the army thirty-five years ago. The pension agent, who desired to have the honor of securing a pension for the old man, had asked him to try and remember if he was not exposed to a sudden draft, some time in the army, which might have caused him to take cold, and thus sow the seeds of rheumatism in his system, which had lain dormant all these years and finally appeared in his legs. The old man had thought it over, and remembered hundreds of occasions when he was soaked through with icy water, and had slept on the wet ground, and gone hungry and taken cold, but he realized that he had taken no more colds in the army than he had at home, and he could not see how he could swear that a chill he received thirty-five years ago could have anything to do with his present aches, and though he knew thousands of the old boys were receiving pensions, that were no worse off than he was, he had told the pension agent that he need not apply for a pension for his pain in the knee. He said he felt that he might just as well apply for a pension on account of inheriting rheumatism from an uncle who fought in

the Mexican war, and he would wait until the government did not insist on a veteran having such an
abnormal memory about sneezing during the war, as a
basis for pension claims, and when it got so a pension
would come to a soldier by simply looking up his
record, and examining his physical condition, he
would take a pension. The old man had heard a
peculiar clicking down in the sitting room, all the
morning, while he was dressing, and he wondered
what it was.   As he limped into the sitting room,
with his dressing-gown on, and began to round up his
shaving utensils, preparatory to his morning shave,
he found the red-headed boy in his night shirt, sitting
at a table with an old telegraph instrument that
looked as though it had been picked out of a scrap-
pile, and the boy was ticking away for dear life, his
hair standing on end, his brow corrugated, and his
eyes glaring.

"What dum foolishness you got on hand now?"
asked the old man, as he set a cup of hot water on
the mantel, and began to mix up the lather.   "What
you ticking away on that contrivance for, and looking wise?"

"This is a telegraph office," said the boy, as he
stopped operations long enough to draw his cold bare
feet up under him, and pulled his night shirt down to
cover his knees.   "I am learning to telegraph, and
am going into training for president of a railroad.
Did you see in the papers the other day that Mr.
Earling was elected president of a railroad, and did

you know that he started in as a telegraph operator and a poor boy, with hair the color of tow? They used to call him Tow-Head."

"Yes, I read about that," said Uncle Ike, as he looked in the glass to see if the lather was all right on his face, and began to strop his razor. "I knew that boy when he was telegraphing. But he knew what all those sounds meant. You just keep ticking away, and don't know one tick from another."

"Yes, I do," said the boy, as he smashed away at the key. "That long sound, and the short one, and the one about half as long as the long one—that spells d–a–m, dam."

"Well, what do you commence your education spelling out cuss words for?" asked the old man, as he raked the razor down one side of his face, pulling his mouth around to one side so it looked like the mouth of a red-horse fish. "Anybody would think you were in training for one of these railroad superintendents who swear at the men so their hair will stand, and then swear at them because they don't get their hair cut. The railroad presidents and general managers nowadays don't swear a blue streak, and keep the men guessing whether they will get discharged for talking back. This man Earling never swore a half a string in his life, and in thirty years of railroading he never spoke a cross word to a living soul, and his brow was never corrugated as much as yours has been spelling out that word dam. Got any idea what railroad you will be president of?" and the

"What dum foolishness you got on hand now?"

old man wiped his razor, stropped it on the palm of his hand, put it in a case, and went to a washbowl to wash the soap off his face.

" Well, I thought I would start in on some narrow-gauge railroad, and work up gradually for a year or two, and finally take charge of one of those Eastern roads, where I can have a private car, and travel all over the country for nothing. As quick as I get this telegraph business down fine I shall apply for a position of train dispatcher, and then jump right along up.   Uncle Ike, you will never have to pay a cent on my railroad.   I will have a caboose fixed up for you, with guns and dogs, and you can hunt and fish all your life, with a nigger to cook for you, and a porter to put on your bait, and another nigger chambermaid to make up your bed, and I will wire them from the general office to sidetrack you, and pick you up, and all that."

" Is that so ?" said the old man, as he stood rubbing his face with a crash towel till it shone like a boiled lobster.   "You are hurrying your railroad career mighty fast, and if you are not careful you will re- place Chauncey Depew before you get long pants on. Now, you go get your clothes on and come to break- fast, and after breakfast I will tell you something." The boy dropped the key, after ticking to the imagi- nary general office not to disturb him with any mes- sages for half an hour, as he was going to be busy on an important matter, and he went to his room and soon appeared at the breakfast table, and after the breakfast was over, and the old man had lighted his pipe, the boy said :

"Now, Uncle Ike, tell me all you know about railroading in one easy lesson, for I have to go to a directors' meeting at ten, and then we are going out to look over the right of way," and the boy ticked off a message to have his special car ready at eleven-thirty, stocked for a trip over the line.

"I see you are getting well along in your railroad career, and like nine out of ten boys who want to be railroad men, you are beginning at the private car instead of the gravel train, issuing general orders instead of working in the ranks," and the old man smoked up and thought a long time, and continued : "The successful railroad man begins at the bottom, and learns the first lesson well.   Do you know how long this man Earling has been getting where he is today ? Thirty-five years.   More than the average age of man. The successful railroad man, if he begins telegraphing, gets so he can send or receive anything, with his eyes shut, and never makes a mistake.   After a long time he gets a measly country station, where he does all kinds of work, and he is satisfied.   He goes to work to increase the business of that station, to clean up around the depot, and please all the customers, as though he was going to live there all his life.   He never thinks he is going to be a high official, but just makes the best of the present.   Some day he is awfully surprised to be given a better station, and he hates to leave, and maybe sheds a tear as he parts with the friends he has made there. But he goes to his new place and improves it, and gets in with a new, pushing class of people, and begins to grow. He maybe works there ten years, and his work shows so the officials recognize it, and he never makes a mistake in his telegraphing, and some day they call him into headquarters during a rush, to help the train dispatcher, and then he has to move into the city and watch trains on thousands of miles of road, to see that they don't get together, as train dispatcher. He thinks that position is good enough, and he hopes they will let him alone in it, but some day he assists the superintendent, and he is so well posted they are all surprised. They wonder how that station agent got to knowing all the men on the road, and how much a train of freight cars weigh, and how many cents per mile each loaded car earns for the company, and what cars ought to go to the shops for repairs, and how many new cars will have to be bought to handle the crops on his division. The 'old man,' as the president is always called, gets to leaning on this always good-natured, promoted, station agent, who is so modest he wouldn't offer a suggestion unless asked his opinion, and when asked gives it so intelligently that you could set your watch by it, as the boys say. He is always sober, never sleepy, and whether figuring on the wheat crop of Dakota to a carload, or wearing rubber boots and dining on sausage and bread for a couple of days fixing up a washout, he is always calm and smiling, and every man works as though his own house was afire, till the

washout is repaired and the first train pulls over.
When the rich, fat, gouty directors come around,
once a year, to take an account of stock, and see the
property at work, they see the modest man, and by
and by he is taken off his feet by a promotion that
almost makes him dizzy.   Other railroads see that he
is all wool, and they try to steal him away, but he
says he has got used to his old man, and he knows
every spike in the system, and there are gray hairs
beginning to come around his ears, and he guesses he
will not go away and have to make new acquaintances,
and he remains with the road where he learned to
tick, as you are ticking, and one day he is at the head
of it.   But if you examine into the head of the man
who gets up from station agent to president, you will
find that there is brain there and no cut feed.   Another station agent might get the bighead the first
time he was promoted, and they would have to pro-
mote him backward, on that account, but it would be
because there was excelsior in his head, instead of
brain, and he would be mad and jealous, and say
mean things about those who got promoted, and
stayed promoted.   Now, let me give you a pointer.
Don't train for general manager or president of a road.
Train for the thing you are going to get first, whether
it is operator or brakeman, and when you have mas-
tered the details of that place, learn something about
the next above.   It is like going up a ladder ; you
have got to go up one step at a time, and get your
foot on the step so it will stay, then go up another

step. If you attempt to step from the ground to the top of the ladder, you are going to split your pants from Genesis to Revelations, and come down on your neck, and show your nakedness to those who have watched you try to climb too fast, and they will laugh at you. Now, go on with your condum ticking, but tick out something besides d—a—m, dam," and the old man went out to see if there had been any frost the night before, with an idea that if there was he would shoot a few teal duck, and cure his rheumatism that way, instead of putting on liniment.

CHAPTER XXI.

Uncle Ike was out in the front yard in the early morning, in his shirt sleeves, with no collar on, an old pair of rubber boots to keep the dew from wetting his feet, and he was helping the Indian summer haze all he could, by smoking the clay pipe and blowing the smoke up among the red and yellow leaves of autumn, and as he kicked the beautiful leaves on the lawn into piles he thought what foolish people they were who claimed last week that winter had come, because it was a little chilly, when he could have told them, by half a century's experience, that the most beautiful part of the year was to come, the Indian summer, the lazy days when you want to shoot snipe, and eat grapes, and have appendicitis. The red-headed boy came out yawning, half awake, and raised his arms and stretched until it seemed that he would break his back.

"You remind me of Indian summer," said the old man, as he stepped on the boy's bare foot with his soft rubber boot.

"Oh, I don't know," said the boy. as he let out a secret school society yell at some boys across the street, which brought them all over into the yard, as though there was a dog fight on. "Uncle Ike, you remind me of Father Time, after he has been to a

barber and got shaved, with your smooth old laughing
face. Why do I remind you of Indian summer ?"

" Well, your red hair resembles the frosted leaf of
the maple tree, your brown freckles look like the dead
and dying leaves of the oak, your unwashed chalky
face looks like the leaves of the ash, your sparkling
eyes like the dewy diamonds on the grass, and your
sleepy look as you just come from your bed makes me
think of the hazy atmosphere that the Indians loved
so well. What all you boys around here for so early
in the morning, anyway, disturbing your Uncle Ike
when he wants to think ?" and he grabbed half a dozen
boys and piled them up in a heap on the grass, and
put one of his big rubber boots on the top one, and
held them down, squirming like a lot of angleworms
in a tomato can. The red-headed boy took Uncle Ike
by the suspenders and pulled him off the boys, and
then they all grabbed his legs and threw him down
and sat on him, breaking his pipe, and pulling off his
rubber boots and making him yell, " Enough !" before
they would let him up, but he laughed and spanked
them with a leg of a rubber boot, and finally they all
sat down on the porch, panting, and Uncle Ike was
the youngest boy in the gang, apparently.

" Come to order," said the red-headed boy, and
every boy took off his hat, and braced back against
the side c the house, and Uncle Ike looked on, wondering what was coming next. " We have met, gentlemen," said the red-headed boy, "to make arrange-
ments to nominate Dewey for President. We have

"Squirming like a lot of angle worms in a tomato can."

watched the manner in which the people have received him at New York and Washington; have
noticed his modesty and level-headedness, and us boys,
Uncle Ike, have decided that Dewey shall be the next
President. If any person has got anything to say
why he should not be President, let him speak now, or
forever after hold his peace. It is up to you, Uncle Ike,
and this assemblage would like to hear a few casual
remarks from you, before breakfast, on this subject.
Now, boys, hurrah for Uncle Ike, the jolliest old
scrapper in the business. Now, give the yell, 'Who
are we! who are we! we are the kids for old
Dewe-e—siz! boom! yah!'" and the boys yelled until
Uncle Ike had to respond.

"Well, you condum heathen can settle more public questions here on this porch than all the political
parties," said the old man. as he fixed a broken suspender with a nail, and came up to the boys with one
rubber boot in his hand, and reached for a new pipe
on the window sill, loaded it, and lit it for a talk.
"You ought to have better sense than to think of
Dewey placing himself in the hands of the politicians,
and going into politics, where he will have to be cat-
hauled by all the disreputable critters in the country.
Look at Grant! When he got out of the war he
was just like Dewey, and would be alive today if
he had not got into the hands of the politicians.
Dewey can sit down in Washington as he is, and have
more power for good than any President, and he will
be proud of himself and his country. If he went

into politics he would be betrayed, and made responsible for all the stealing and mistakes of those under
him, and in a little while he would hate himself, and
would like to get all the politicians into a Spanish ship
and turn the Olympia loose on them."

"Yes, but nobody could say anything against
Dewey," said the red-headed boy, interrupting Uncle
Ike. "All he would have to do would be to appoint
a cabinet of admirals, and give all the other offices to
the midshipmen and jackies, and send army officers
abroad as ministers and things. The people would
lynch a man that said anything against Dewey."

"They couldn't say anything against him, could
they?" said Uncle Ike, pulling on the rubber boot.
"Well, you are an amateur in politics. Do you know
what they would do if Dewey were nominated? They
would prove that he murdered a man in Vermont in
1852, in cold blood, and produce the corpse. They
would swear that he was the inventor of the wooden
nutmeg, and that he had six wives living, and that he
was in cahoots with Aguinaldo, and that he didn't
sink the Spanish fleet, but that it got waterlogged
and went down without a shot being fired. They
would claim that he was the originator of the process
of boiling maple roots and putting the juice into glucose, and selling it for pure Vermont maple syrup.
They would claim that the reception he received at
the hands of the American people was a put-up job;
that he paid all the expenses himself, out of money
he stole from the government, and that all the cheer-

ing was done by hired claquers, who were all promised an office when he was elected. And then if he
was elected, every man that knew him before he went
to Manila would claim to have been the making of
him, and want to be in the cabinet, and every man
that has shook hands with him since, would expect
the best office at his disposal, and if they didn't get
the offices they would prove that he was responsible
for the embalmed beef scandal, and that he was in
partnership with Capt. Carter in robbing the government, and ought to be in jail. Oh, you can't tell me
anything about politics, and if I could see Dewey I
would tell him to say nothing but 'nixy' to every
proposition to mix him up. Now, all you boys come
in to breakfast," and the old man tossed the boys
toward the dining room door as though they were
footballs.

"Well, Uncle Ike, you have punctured our tire
again. Every time we get a scheme to save the
country, you come in with your condumed talky-talk,
and throw us in the air. Guess you will have to take
the nomination yourself, and run on a platform of
seven words, 'Here's to the boys, God bless 'em,'" and
the red-headed boy got under Uncle Ike's arm, and
the gang went in to breakfast, Uncle Ike trying to
argue against being nominated, and having to go to
the White House with a lot of tough boys making
life a burden to him, when he would have to get married, for no President is a success as a bachelor, as
Cleveland found out. As Uncle Ike got the boys all

around the table, he bent his head and reverently
asked a blessing—something he had never done before
in the presence of the red-headed boy, and when the
meal was over and the boys had all gone away, except
the warm-haired one, and Uncle Ike had begun to
smoke again, the boy said to him :

"Uncle Ike, I did not know that you belonged to
any church."

"Well, I don't," said Uncle Ike, as he got up and
looked out of the window, and blew smoke at a fly
that was buzzing on the glass.

"Then how could you ask a blessing, and expect
that it will be heard? I supposed a person had to be
initiated in a church, and be sworn in, and given the
password, and take the degrees, before he was ordained to ask a blessing," said the boy.

"No, that is not necessary," the old man said.
"Now, you haven't got much religion, and never jined,
but you give thanks to the Lord quite often. When
you are happy, and enjoying yourself, and smile and
laugh, you are unconsciously thanking the Ruler for
making things so comfortable. All pleasure is made
possible by a higher power, and all you got to do is to
feel grateful, same as you would to me if I gave you
a dollar, and there you are. You just be square, and
do business on the golden rule plan, and you have got
a heap more religion than some people who are blat-
ting about all the time. I just thought I would par-
alyze you kids by showing you that I was all wool,
and wanted the Lord to keep tab on us, and know

that we appreciated good health, and all that.   Now,
you go to school, and don't say anything to that blue-
eyed teacher of yours that you have nominated me
for President.   I don't want to get girls after me,
thinking they will be mistress of the White House,"
and the old man took his gun and went down into the
marsh looking for snipe.

CHAPTER XXII.

Uncle Ike had been reading the morning paper, as he sat before the grate fire, in the sitting room, while the red-headed boy was using a slate and pencil trying to figure out something to make it match the answer as given in the arithmetic, and having guessed the answer right he was drawing a picture of Uncle Ike and his pipe, and occasionally wetting his finger in his mouth and rubbing out some feature of the old man that didn't suit. He had the old man pictured in a football costume of padded trousers, nose guard, ear guard, knee pads, and all the different things used in football, and when he showed the picture to Uncle Ike, that old citizen sighed, though he looked a bit pleased that he should be the study of so eminent an artist. Uncle Ike had been reading that there was to be a football game that afternoon, between the State university and Beloit college, and he wanted to go like a dog, but he had abused football so much that he was ashamed to speak of going.

"I hope you are not interested in that disreputable game," said Uncle Ike, knocking the ashes out of his pipe on the andirons of the fireplace. "I hope you don't want to go and see respectable boys maimed and killed, and knocked down and dragged out, and sand-bagged, and brained. I have seen a bull fight in Mexico, but I never want to see anything as bloody

as a football game," and the old man winked to himself, and filled the pipe.

"Oh, what you giving me?" said the boy, jumping
up in indignation. "Football is no worse than the
old-fashioned pullaway you used to play. I am going
to see this game through a knothole in the fence I
rented from a boy who has the knothole concession at
the baseball park."

"No, you don't," said Uncle Ike, "you will go in
the gate like a gentleman. No nephew of mine is going to grow up and be a knothole audience. You get
two or three of your chums and come around here
about 2 o'clock, and I will go with you, and stand between you and the sluggers, and see this game out. I
don't want to go, and detest the game, but I will go
to please you," and the old man looked wise and
fatherly.

"Oh, you don't want to go, like the way the woman
kept tavern in Michigan," said the boy, as he edged
toward the door.

"How was it that the woman kept the hotel in
Michigan?" he asked, looking mad.

"Like hades," said the boy, "only the man who
told me about it said she kept tavern like h—l, but I
wouldn't say that in the presence of my dear old
uncle," and the boy slipped out ahead of a slipper that
was kicked at him by the laughing old man.

So in the afternoon Uncle Ike, the red-headed boy
and two chums appeared at the gate, the old man
plunked down two dollars with a chuckle, asked if he

could smoke his pipe in there, and was told that he
could smoke a factory chimney if he wanted to, and
they went in and got seats on the bleachers, and as
they sat down the old man said it was almost exactly
like the bull ring in Mexico.   The boys explained to
him that the red ribbons were university colors and
the yellow belonged to Beloit, and he must choose
which side he would root for.   As the red matched
his flannel underwear and his flushed face, he said he
was for the university, and then the boys explained
the game, about carrying the ball, getting touchdowns,
kicking goal, and half-back and quarter-back, and when
the teams came in and the crowd yelled, Uncle Ike felt
hurt, because it made so much noise, and people acted
crazy. Uncle Ike looked the players over, and he said
that big fellow from Beloit was John L. Sullivan in dis-
guise, and wanted him ruled off.   The play began,
the ball shot out behind the crowd, a man grabbed it
and started to run, when someone grabbed him by the
legs and he went down, with the whole crowd on top
of him.   Uncle Ike raised up on his feet and waved
his pipe, and when one of the men did not get up and
they brought water and tried to bring him back to
life, he shouted : " That is murder.   I saw that fellow
with the black socks strike him with a hatchet.   Police !" but someone behind him yelled to him to sit
down, and the red-headed boy pulled his coat tail, he
sat down, and the game went on, but Uncle Ike was
mad, because the dead boy was playing as lively as
anybody.

Then a man got the ball and started on a run down the field, with the whole crowd after him, and finally they got him down and Uncle Ike stood up again and said : "Stop the game.   I saw a fellow trip him up, and pound him with a billy, and stab him.   Say, boys, he's dead, sure.   Where's the police?   Ain't there no ambulance here?   Kill the umpire!" he shouted, remembering that he was an old baseball fan.

"Oh, don't worry, Uncle Ike, they are all right," said the boy, waving a long piece of red ribbon, as the two bands tried to play a "Hot Time" and a waltz at the same time.   "Now watch the kangaroo kick off," and as he kicked the ball the whole length of the field the old man simply sat still and said :

"Gee whiz, but that was a corker.   U-rah-u-rah!" and the only way to stop him was to feed him peanuts.

From an enemy of football the old man was rapidly becoming its friend.   When the men came together at first, and went down in a heap, legs flying in all directions, and noises like heavy blows coming to him, he would swear he saw a man strike another with a mallet, but later in the game he said it served the man right, and he ought to have been hit with an ax, and before the game was over he was so interested that he got down off the bleachers, leaned over the railing and yelled at the combatants to eat 'em up, and when the game was over he rushed into the field, hugging the players, and saying that it was the greatest thing that ever was, and offering to act as one of the bearers to the funeral, if anybody had been killed,

"Police!"

and when the boys got him out of the grounds he took up the whole sidewalk, waving his ribbons, tied on his cane, shouting the university yell till he frothed at the mouth, and on the way home he took the boys into a store and bought them a new football, and insisted that they come into the front yard and play a game every morning, and offered to have the shrubbery cut down to give them room. As they got home, and the other boys had gone away, the red-headed boy said:

"Uncle Ike, you have disgraced the whole family. You went to the football game under protest, a quiet, inoffensive citizen, ostensibly to take care of us boys, and the first jump out of the box you got crazy, and we had a terrible time to get you home. I don't suppose you remember what you did do out there. Do you remember of putting your arm around a strange lady, and hugging her, and telling her to yell? Her husband is looking for you with a gun. Do you remember of grabbing a young woman sitting in front of you, just as they made a touchdown, pulling her head over into your lap, and patting her cheeks with your great big hands, and telling her she ought to marry a football player? Her brother is coming up street now with a baseball club. I suppose you have no recollection of jumping up and sitting down in the lap of a woman in the seat behind you, throwing your arms around her, and telling her she was a darling, and squeezing her till you broke her corset. She says you offered her marriage, and her lawyer will be here in the morning to find out what you are going to do about it. I think you better be examined by doctors to see if you are not getting nutty, and let them send you to a sanitarium," and the boy sighed, and looked at the old man as though his heart was broken.

"Say, did I do any of those things?" asked Uncle Ike, as he got up and looked out of the window, and then locked the door, and acted frightened. "Well, I'll be dumbed! I recollect the woman in front of me, and the one behind, but I pledge you my word that I did not know that I hugged anybody. I am willing to apologize, but I'll be condemned if I marry any of 'em, and I'm not crazy. That confounded game got me all mixed up, and I may have acted different from what I would ordinarily, but it was not my intention to propose to any female."

"But say, Uncle Ike, what did you think of the game as a means of building up muscle, pluck, push, get there, and general usefulness?" asked the boy.

"Greatest thing I ever saw," said Uncle Ike, as he looked out of the window, to see if any females he might have hugged in his excitement were out there waiting for him. "Say, I saw young fellows in that game that I used to know, who would cry if taken across their father's knee, and beg for mercy, and they would rush into the most dangerous position, and if knocked silly they would smile, never groan, and suck a swallow of water out of a sponge, and go in for another knockdown. That game will make men of the weak boys, and cause them to be afraid of nothing that walks. The boy who pushes, and tackles, and runs through a wilderness of other boys who are trying to down him, and get his pigskin away, will become the pushing business man who will go through the line of business progress, and make a touchdown in his enterprise, and he will kick a commercial or professional goal, over the heads of all competitors. Life is only a football game, after all. Every man in business who is worth his salt is a pusher, a shover, a tackler, a punter, or half-back, and the unsuccessful ones are the ones who carry the water to bring the business players to, when they become overheated, and do the yelling and hurrahing when the pushing business man in the football game of life makes a touchdown. It is these rough players that become the rough riders when war comes to the country, and they rush the ball up San Juan hill in the face of the Spanish tacklers, and the interference of barbed wire and other things. War is a football game also, and the recruiting officers are not looking for the weak sisters who can't push and shove, and fight, and fall over each other, and when wounded laugh and say it is nothing serious. A country that has a majority of its boys growing up to fight on the football field for fun, has no cause to fear any war that may come to it, for if they will fight like that in good nature, to uphold the colors of their college, what will they do to uphold 'Old Glory,' which comprises the dearest colors in all the world? Yes, boy, you can go on playing football, and if you are injured your Uncle Ike will pay all the expenses, and sit up nights with you, but you better not take me to any more games, for the first thing you know I will be bringing home here more wives than that Utah congressman has got.   Now, go rest up, and next week I will take you to see President McKinley, at the hotel here, and you will see him throw his arms around me and say, 'Hello, Uncle Ike!' I used to know him when he wasn't President," and Uncle Ike dismissed the boy, and sat by the window till dark, looking out to see if anybody was coming to claim his hand in marriage, and wondering if he did make as big a fool of himself at the football game as the boys said he did.

CHAPTER XXIII.

It was Sunday afternoon, and Uncle Ike had been
to church with the red-headed boy, and they had listened to a sermon on patriotism, and the minister
had expressed himself on the subject of the Philippines, and the duty the President owed to civilization
to keep on killing those negroes until they learned
better than to kick at having a strange race of people
boss them around, and Uncle Ike had walked home
along the bank of the lake, and breathed the free air that
was his because his ancestors had conquered it from
England, and he couldn't help having a little sympathy for those Filipinos who had been bought from
a country that didn't own them, by a country that
had no use for them, and wished it could get rid of
them honorably, without hurting the political party
that was acting as overseer over them.   He didn't
want to seem disloyal to a country that he loved and
had fought to preserve, but when he thought of those
poor, ignorant people, trying to learn what freedom
meant, and what there was in it for them, studying
the constitution of the United States to find out how
to be good and great, and dodging bullets, he felt as
though he wished he knew just what the Savior of
Man would do in the matter if He had been elected
President.   He had left the red-headed boy at Sunday-school, and now they were both back home, wait-

ing for the dinner bell to ring. The boy was studying some pamphlet he had brought home, and looking
mighty serious.

"Any great problem been presented to you at
Sunday-school that you are unable to solve?" said
Uncle Ike, as he walked by the boy and tried to
stroke the corrugated lines out of his forehead, and
patted him on the head. "For if there is anything
you are in doubt about, all you got to do is to let your
Uncle Ike be umpire, and he will straighten it out
for you."

"Thank you, awfully," said the boy, as he dropped
his book, walked up to the old man, and looked him
squarely in the face. "You are the man I have been
looking for. Uncle Ike, suppose a man should haul
off, without provocation, and smash you on the side of
the face, a regular stinger, that would jar your head
until you could see stars, what would you do?"

"Oh, say, that is an easy one," said the old man,
as he filled the pipe and lighted it, and threw the
match in the grate. "Do you know what I would do?
I would give him one on the nose with my left hand,
and when he was off his guard I would paste him one
under the ear, or on the point of the jaw, and then I
would stand over him and count ten, and if he came
to, I would give him some more, and when he had got
enough, I would say to him: 'Now, when you feel
that way again, and want to enjoy yourself, you come
right to me, for I don't have any too much exercise,
anyway.' But why do you ask? You knew all the

time what I would do if a man hit me," and the old
man walked around the room as though he would like
to see someone hit him.

"That's what I feared," said the boy, as the twink-
les played around his eyes. "You see, among the
verses in the Sunday-school lesson was this one, ' If
they smite you on one cheek, turn the other cheek,
also,' and I thought I would like to get the opinion of
an expert as to how to go about it, to turn the other
cheek the right way."

"Say, here, you don't take advantage of an old man
that way," said Uncle Ike, as the boy began laughing.
"When you ask questions like that you want to read
the verse first, and give a man a chance. 'Course, if
they smite you on one cheek, you want to do just
what the Bible says. Some of you kids make me
tired," and the old man wished dinner was ready, so
they could change the subject.

"I told my teacher I didn't see how a fellow could
turn the other cheek, also, and maintain his standing
in society, but she said it was the way to do, and then
the Sunday-school superintendent came along, and she
asked him about it. He belongs to the athletic club
of the Y. M. C. A., and I have seen him box with
soft gloves, and he said it was right to turn the other
cheek, but I noticed he smiled, and then the minister
visited our class, and the teacher asked him to im-
press on us boys the idea of turning the other cheek.
He looked pious, and said you must turn the other

"I would give him one on the nose with my left hand."

205

cheek when smote, as it showed a meek and forgiving
disposition, but I know the minister is a boxer, also,
and I heard that he almost jarred the head off a tramp
last summer for sassing him, so I am worried as to
what it is best to do, in a case of smoting. The
teacher, you know her, the pretty girl that let you
hold her hand so long at the picnic, when you was in-
troduced to her, and you told her you used to know
her mother when she was a girl, and used to go with
her, and all that rot, she told me I better talk it over
with you, Uncle Ike, and see what you thought about
it. So you honestly think it is best for a boy to grow
up letting people get in the habit of smiting, so to
see him turn his other cheek, and get another bat on
that cheek, eh? Don't you think a boy that takes
that kind of medicine, without making up a face,
ought to say, 'Thank you, ever so much,' and always
wear pinafores, and stay in the kindergarten, and if
he ever grows up and goes into business he better become a he-milliner, or a manicure, say? It's up to you,
now, Uncle Ike, and I am ready to listen, and to follow your advice, and be a boy or a girl, just as you
say, but I don't know any girl in my set that would
let anybody smite her much, without pulling hair a
little, at least."

Uncle Ike had been thinking pretty hard, as the
boy talked, had let his pipe go out, and his face had
taken on a serious look, a look also of pride as he listened to the boy, but he was trying to think how to

steer him right on that turning the other cheek also
business. He fumbled for the tobacco bag, and as
he emptied some tobacco into the pipe, his hand was
unsteady, and he spilled a good deal on the floor, and
he had to scratch two or three matches on his pants
before he could get one that wouldn't break off, or go
out. Finally he got the pipe lighted, and he puffed a
long time, and looked at himself in the big mirror
over the mantel, to see if he was looking his best, and
finally he said :

"I'll tell you, my boy, I don't think they are turning the other cheek also when smote, as much as they
used to. The theory is all right, and if everybody
would do so, there would not be any trouble, and all
would be peace. I suppose that verse in the Bible
was written when the Jews were trying to get along
without having scraps all the time. There were people there, Jew-baiters, I suppose, who just laid for
them, and knowing them to be opposed to a fight,
they would smash them, and on the advice of leaders
they would turn the other cheek and go home with a
black eye. I don't suppose I could write a Bible half
as good as the old one, but I think if that verse had
been changed a little, so the Jews would have stood
up for their rights, and everlastingly lambasted anybody that came around jarring them on the cheeks,
and been brought up to fight their way through, from
Jerusalem to France, things would have been different. But, as I say, things have changed a good deal

since Bible times. I think, now, if I was a boy, growing up to take my place in the business world, I
might try to forget that verse, or think of it as we do
of the Golden Rule, or the 'love one another' verse.
You may try as hard as you like and you can't love
your neighbor as yourself, unless he, or she, as the
case may be, is a lovable person, and loves back.
There can be no arbitrary rules that will bind you
against what you think is right. Suppose your neighbor is a horsethief, or a liar, who belongs to another
political party, and backbites, and steals your wood,
and kicks your dog, and puts up jobs on you, how you
going to love that neighbor as yourself? Two or
three thousand years ago maybe these things would
have been all right, when they didn't have any newspapers, and trolley cars, and there was no business except selling fish, and no money but coppers. I'll tell
you how I shall bring up my boys, when I have any, and
that is to keep their cheeks away from the smoter who
smotes. Be on your guard, and if a boy tries to smite you
on one cheek, you duck, and side-step, and smile at him,
and keep your hands up so if he makes a feint to
smite you on one cheek, just stand him off, and maybe he will think that you are onto his smiting on the
cheek business yourself, and are no chicken, that is
going to keep cheeks for other people to smite, and he
may quit, and you can laugh over it, and consider the
incident closed. But if he gets gay, and it seems to
be his day to smite cheeks, and he acts as though he

had picked you out for a soft mark, and rushes in to
do you up, if I ever hear of your running, or putting
your hands down, and letting him biff you, one, two,
on both cheeks, and you come home here crying, with
the nosebleed, and your eye blacked, and you haven't
done a thing to that cheek smiter, I will warm your
jacket so you will think there is a hornets' nest in it,
hear me?" and the old man looked cross and sassy.
" No, sir ; you just let him search for your cheeks, and
if he won't quit, you finally give him your left in the
neck, and side-step, and keep out of his way, and if
he wants more, find a place where there is an opening,
and jab him until he quits looking for cheeks to smite,
and other cheeks to turn also.   I don't know as it is
right, but turning the other cheek also has gone out
of style, and nobody is doing it that has got any
gravel in their crop.   Don't let me ever catch you
fighting, that is, bringing on a fight, but don't you
ever let anybody use you to practice that verse on,
because your minister or your Sunday-school superintendent wouldn't allow anybody to smite them without
getting hurt."

" Well, I like that," said the boy, getting up and
starting for the dining room.   " I will do just as
you say, Uncle Ike, and try to avoid trouble.   But
what shall I tell that blue-eyed teacher you advised
me—the one, you know, that you was so sweet on at
the picnic ?"

" Oh, tell her I told you to try and grow up to be

a regular thoroughbred, like your Uncle Ike, and only turn the other cheek to girls, see! And tell her I never squeezed anybody's hand at a picnic, unless they commenced it, by gosh !" and the old man took the red-headed boy in his arms and carried him bodily into the dining room, and there was a smile on his good old face that was good to look upon.

CHAPTER XXIV.

Uncle Ike had met with a misfortune that troubled him, and he was smoking and trying to think of some way to explain the affair. All his life he had been an all-around sport, and duck shooting had been his hobby. He had prided himself that he could ride any boat that an Indian could, and bragged that he had never got his feet wet in his forty years as a duck shooter; but this morning he had gone out in a boat, before anybody was up about the house, and when he was not looking, a wave tipped the boat up on one side, filled it with water, and had gone down with him before he could say Jack Robinson, and he had floundered around in mud and water up to his armpits, singing "A life on the ocean wave," and yelling for somebody to come and tie him loose. A neighbor had come with a boat, and dragged him ashore, and he had taken off his wet clothes, hung them on the fence to dry, put on some dry clothes, and he was smoking his pipe and wringing the water out of his wet pants, when the red-headed boy came out to inquire into the marine disaster.

"Getting your washing out pretty early in the morning, Uncle Ike," said the boy, as he lifted a wet sweater off the fence, and took some wet cartridges out of the pockets. "Is it healthy to go in swimming with so many clothes on? How did this thing happen, anyway?"

"Now, don't get gay," said Uncle Ike, "and I will
tell you.   It was blowing a hurricane, and the wind
took the boat up in the air about ten feet, and it dove
down head first, and what could I do but get out?
A cramp took me in the leg, and I stood on t'other
leg, but I wasn't afraid.   I didn't yell, but just said
to a man who was about half a mile away, says I,
'Kindly assist me to land,' and he took me by the
shirt collar and escorted me to the shore."

"I see," said the boy; "you whispered to him,
when he was half a mile away, but did not yell for
help.   Oh, you're a mark, trying to make believe you
are young enough to enjoy sport.   Say, you ought to
have a shawl strap on you, so your rescuer can have
something to take hold of; and if I were in your
place, I would get the dimensions of Noah's ark,
and have one made to fit me.   You better buy your
ducks, and stay on land.   But now that the Prodigal
Uncle has got back, I am going out to kill a fatted
calf, and we will have a calf banquet.   Say, Uncle
Ike, did you ever read about the Prodigal Son?   We
had it in our Sunday-school lesson last Sunday.   They
didn't do a thing to him, did they?"

"Yes, I have read about the Prodigal Son, and I
give it to you straight--he was the greatest chump
mentioned in the Bible, and sometimes I think you
are a dead ringer for him!" and the old man laughed
at the boy.

"Oh, I don't know," said the boy, as he poured
some water out of Uncle Ike's rubber boots, that

"A life on the ocean wave."

hung on the fence; "you and Noah size up about
right. If you had been running that ark, you would
have spilled the whole outfit, and nobody ever would
have got ashore. But that Prodigal Son makes me
tired. He was a regular jay. He run away from
home, and got in with a terrible crowd, and they
pulled his leg for all the money he had. They
steered him up against barrel houses, and filled him
with liquor that would burn a hole in a copper kettle,
got him mixed up with queer women, and he painted
the towns red; and when his money was all gone,
they kicked him out with a case of indigestion and a
head on him that hurt so he could not wink without
thinking there was an earthquake. Say, Uncle Ike,
do you know that fellow had some sense after all?
When he found that all his new-found friends wanted
was his money, and to help him spend it, and that
they shook him when it was gone, he had a right to
be disgusted with the world; and if he had been like
some of our present day prodigals, he would have
turned tramp, or held up a train, or stolen a horse
and been lynched; but he just tumbled to himself
and took the first job that came along, herding hogs,
but he didn't live high. He worked for his board and
furnished his own husks. Do you know, I can't help
thinking the man that hired Prod. to drive hogs was
in a trust, and made all the money there was in the
deal. But he was repaid for all his suffering. When
he thought of the old folks at home, and drew his
wages and started back, without clothes enough on

him to wad a gun, thinking maybe they would stick
up their noses and say he smelled bad, and quarantine
him, and make him take a bath, but, instead of doing
so, they just fell on his neck and wept, and set up a
calf lunch for him, he must have thought the world
was worth living in.   Uncle Ike, were you ever a
prodigal son?" and the boy turned over the wet
clothes so the sun would dry the other side.

  "Yes, sir, I have been a prodigal son, and every
boy who goes away from home to make his own living is a prodigal son, in a way," and he and the boy
sat down under a tree, the one to talk and the other
to listen.   "When a boy decides to leave the old
roof tree at home to go out into the world, it is most
always against the wishes of his parents; but he argues with them, and finally prevails on them to let
him go.   It is what he amounts to after he gets away
that makes him either a prodigal or a thoroughbred.
If a boy goes into bad company, and thinks the world
is made to spend unearned money in, instead of to
earn money in and save it, it is only a matter of time
when he comes back home a prodigal son, either
alive and needing a doctor and a mother's care, or he
comes in a box to be buried, his father to pay the express charges.   On the other hand, if he gets a job,
doing something, anything, masters the business, and
becomes a valuable citizen, maybe in time at the head
of his profession or business, some day he comes home
to the old folks, and there are smiles instead of tears,
a brass band instead of the singing by the funeral

choir, and he pays the mortgage on the old home-
stead, instead of having his father pay express charges
on the remains. That is the difference. All boys
can be prodigals if they have the prodigal bacillus in
their systems when they go out into the world; but
if they have the get-there-Eli microbe concealed in
their pajamas when they go away, they can laugh at
the traps and nets that are thrown out to catch them,
stand off the alleged friends who try to induce them
to go into the red paint business, use the red liquor
to rub on bruises and strained muscles on the outside,
instead of taking it internally to build fires that never
quench. Which kind of a prodigal nephew you want
to be—one who comes home with a suit of clothes
and a bank account, the glow of health on your
cheek, and a love of life and all that goes with it; or
a prodigal with a blanket, a haversack full of husks
that the hogs won't eat, all the diseases that are going in the set you have moved in, and a desire to die
on the doorstep of the old home before they can cook
the calf? Which you want to be, boy?"

"I'll tell you, Uncle Ike," said the boy, laying his
head in the old man's lap, as they sat under the tree;
"I am going to be the kind of a prodigal who comes
home with the good health, and the money, and the
appetite for calf; and when you are old, Uncle Ike,
you sha'n't get wet any more, for I will buy you a
duck boat that can't be tipped over with jackscrews,
that you can't break with an ax, and that has air
chambers in both ends, so it couldn't be sunk if

loaded with railroad iron ; and I will buy you a pump gun that will shoot ducks without your aiming it, and you shall have a picnic as long as you live. That is the kind of prodigal nephew I am going to be "; and the old man stroked the red hair on the head that lay in his lap, and the tears stole down his cheeks as he thought what a difference there was in prodigals. He thought of his own prodigal days, when he went out from the home roof tree to make his way in the world; how he worked on a farm from long before daylight in the morning, till all the rest had gone to bed, and his back ached so he could not sleep; how he jumped the farm when he found his wages decreased as the work became harder and the weather colder, and he went into the city and worked at many different trades, and finally became a printer, and grew up to be an editor, made money and went back home a grown man, with a moustache that actually had to be combed; and how the girls that would not speak to him when he was a dirty, freckled boy, wanted to give parties in his honor, and how he shook them; and now he regretted, old bachelor that he was, that he had not allowed them to entertain him, so he might have picked out the best one of them for his wife ; and he sighed, and got up and wrung some more water out of his wet clothes hanging on the fence, and wondered how in the world he could have allowed himself to be tipped over in a boat, and if he actually did make a fool of himself when he was there in the water, wishing he hadn't gone hunting at all.

Peck's
Red-Headed Boy

By

Geo. W. Peck
Author of " Peck's Bad Boy and His Pa,"
" Sunbeams," "Peck's Uncle Ike," etc.

Illustrated by
G. C. WIDNEY

NEW YORK
HURST & COMPANY
PUBLISHERS.

PECK'S RED-HEADED BOY.

LOVE AND OTHER THINGS.

"Uncle Ike, how old does a man have to be before he ceases to get in love?" asked the red-headed boy, as he sat reading the morning paper, while Uncle Ike was grunting and trying to get his left foot up onto the right knee, so he could lace his shoe.

"Well, you'll have to ask somebody older than I am," said the old man, as he tied the string in a hard knot, and dropped his foot with a sigh of relief. "There is a man ninety years old living down in the Third Ward, and you better go and ask him. Methuselah was the oldest man I ever heard of, and they say he was getting in love regularly the last few hundred years of his life. But what has started you on this everlasting question of love? Something happened in Chicago?"

"No, not as I know of. But Dewey has announced that he is going to marry a widow some time this month," and the boy turned the paper to the sporting column.

"Well, wouldn't that kill you," said the old man, as he broke up a campaign cigar some politician had given him, and fed the fragments into his pipe, lit it, and turned pale. "Does the widow know it? Has he picked her out yet? Say, do you know that man could have any widow he might select, in this whole country, but I was in hopes he would marry Helen Gould. You don't suppose he has taken the first one that came along, do you? Such a kind-hearted man, he wouldn't want to see any widow suffer, and I thought likely as not he had let some widow just pick him out, and take him into camp. You'd think he would sail his fleet right into Washington society, over the torpedoes of widowhood, and see them explode all around him, and never pay any more attention to them than he would at the torpedoes at the entrance of Manila bay. That man ought to have had a gardeen appointed over him, as soon as he got home, and he should have been protected, poor man," and Uncle Ike sighed as though he felt personally hurt at the capture of Dewey.

"Dewey is a fraud," said the boy, reading further along on the article announcing the matrimonial intentions of the admiral. "He has deceived the American people. Here it says he has been corresponding with that widow all the time he has been away. That he knew her when she was a girl, and loved her as much as he dared, and all the time the people supposed that he was worrying over the conditions at Manila, and having dyspepsia, and telling the German admiral to go chase himself, he

was either reading her love letters or writing letters
to her, and when he came home and the people
thought he belonged to them, and gave him a
house to keep bach. in, he was fooling them, and
was calling on her, and pulling down the curtains,
and shutting out the people that owned him, and

Probably holding her hand.

probably holding her hand, and pulverizing her
diamond rings, unless she took them off and laid
them on the table. O, these widows make me tired,
snatching up a man before he has time to go
around and lay all the corner-stones and shake
hands with the people. Say, after squeezing a
widow's hand for a while, he will never want to
shake hands with a million people, it will be so

different. That settles Dewey. He will just want to stay home, and love that widow, and I'll bet you he never comes west at all."

"Well, I don't know about that," said Uncle Ike, after he had taken the paper from the boy and read the account of Dewey's engagement. "Here it says she is about forty years old, handsome, rich, the most intelligent woman in Washington, charitable, loved by everybody, finest family in Ohio; that settles it. That will be the making of Dewey. She will cure his dyspepsia, and by the first of January they will have to publish new pictures of Dewey, with the lines left out of his face by the corners of the mouth, and no tired look in his eyes, and there will be a smile instead of a look of pain on his face. Do you know, boy, if I was a doctor, and I had a patient, a man sixty years old, who had been a widower twenty years, and had been through what Dewey has, until his stomach was lop-sided, his digestion bad, and malaria from a dozen different climates in his system, I would not give him any pills, nor quinine, nor Turkish baths, nor trips to Carlsbad, nor Kneipp cure. I would make out a prescription with nothing in it to give him a bad taste in the mouth, or to make his ears ring. My prescription would be a widow, forty years old, with good looks, smart as a whip, to be shaken, and taken to the altar, and there you have it," and the old man lit up his mangled cigar again. "No, boy, don't let's worry about Dewey any more.

What he wants is a home with a woman in it, and as long as no woman went with the house they gave him, he has taken advantage of the provision of the Declaration of Independence, that man is entitled to the pursuit of happiness, and he is on the right track. That will be a happier home than the white house, and nobody will come in unless invited, and when they get in they will find two of the happiest people on earth. Gosh, but I have half a mind to get married myself," and the old man went to the window and watched a girl go by, who looked up at him and bowed, and that was all, but he blushed like a girl, as she was the only girl in the world that he cared the snap of his finger for, and he never saw her except as she went by the window, and then he had to keep watch to see that nobody caught him blushing. Uncle Ike stepped out on the porch, and as he saw the front gate hanging up in a tree on the lawn, his eyes opened wide, and he pinched himself. He looked into the street and saw a buggy bottom side up, the wheels kicking the air, and a horse hitched to a post by its tail, and he groaned, and turned his eyes upward, and seen that the door mat was fastened to the ceiling of the porch, over his head, and he thought his time had come. A wheelbarrow was standing in the yard on its handles, the old rocking chair was poised on the ends of its rockers, and everything looked to him bottom side up, or in italics, and he called the boy out and said:

"Go right after a doctor, for my brain is affected. I have felt it coming on for some time."

"O, that is all on account of Halloween," said the boy, as he tipped the chair and wheelbarrow into their natural position. "Some of the neighbor boys have been celebrating last night."

"What do they celebrate Halloween for?" asked Uncle Ike, as he brushed his eyes, and began to think his brain was still on straight, like a woman's hat.

"O, I don't know," said the boy. "Nobody that celebrates knows what they do it for. It's just an excuse to do something different. As long as you have got an excuse to do anything, you don't get pulled. Boys are the same as a government that wants to fight another government, they have got to have an excuse, a chance to fight without being questioned by other governments. Now, England has wanted an excuse to fight the Boers in Africa, ever so long, and so they published pictures of Kruger with those peculiar whiskers, until every Englishman was excited, and swore that Kruger should be made to wear side whiskers, at the point of English bayonets, and they had a Halloween at Ladysmith the other night that they will remember a long time. They tried to unhinge Kruger's gate, and hang it on a tree, and Kruger got their fingers in the gate, and just leaned against it, and had the boys prisoners. Say, Uncle Ike, which side are you

on in that fight between the Boers and the Englishmen? Us boys are all for the Boers."

"Well, there's sides enough for all, in that fight,"
said Uncle Ike, as he looked thoughtful, and sat
down on the lawn, while the hired man rescued the
gate from the tree. "You boys are with the Boers
because they seem to be the under dog in the
fight, but they are not en-
tirely blameless. You see,
no people can go off alone
and run a country these
days. These Boers have got
a government that is so corrupt that it discounts any
other on earth. They tax
strangers out of sight, and
a man who tries to get nat-
uralized, and become a citizen, has to almost serve as
a slave for fourteen years,
and during that time he has
to give up his own country,
and until the fourteen years
expire he has no country.

And just leaned
against it.

A foreigner cannot get protection, and cannot
protect himself. Every sixteen-year-old Boer boy
can carry a gun and a revolver, but if an American
carries a pistol he is thrown in prison. They keep
towns built by foreigners, entirely in Boer control,
and if the foreign tax-payers want to educate their

children they can only learn the language of the Boers. Kruger is a farmer, but he has made $25,000,000 in ten years, out of foreigners. Englishmen ask their home government for protection, and what can a government do but protect its citizens, or go out of business? On the other hand, the Boers claim if the foreigners do not like the way things are run they can go away and leave the gold mines they have developed for the Boers to work. O, it is a condition of things that will make a man crazy to think of, and if I was in your place, boy, I would cease to worry over the affairs of any other country, and turn your attention to your own country, and its fight in the Philippines, where we are trying to benevolently assimilate cannibals and Tagals, monkeys and cliff-dwellers to study the constitution of the United States while they drink milk out of cocoanuts and lie in hammocks and let bread fruit drop into their mouths," and Uncle Ike wandered off into the Indian summer day, thinking of the troubles of trying to run a government easy, while the red-headed boy studies his geography to find what colonies belonged to what countries, and where the next fight was going to be, to teach naked savages to be pious.

UNCLE IKE AS A BOY.

Uncle Ike had been reading in the morning paper about the boys at the State university marching around the campus on Halloween night, in ghostly apparel, and how some of them forgot that they had sisters, and made a rush for Ladies' hall, where the girls were having a ghost dance also, and how the boys had stolen some female garments as souvenirs, and his heart was full when the red-headed boy came galloping down stairs, singing a college song, for the boy was preparing to enter college.

"Here, come right here," said Uncle Ike, as he spread out the paper in front of the boy. "I want you to read that, and swear to me, that when you go to the university you will never do a thing like that," and the old man got his pipe to going while the boy was reading the article. "The boys of the present day are too full of the devil to suit me. I don't endorse any such foolishness, and when you go to college I want you to go on another street when there is any feather-head business going on. You just study, and let the 5 per cent of rioters, which is the percentage of duffers in all schools, attend to the monkey business."

"You think boys are worse nowadays than they were forty years ago," said the boy, as he winked at himself in a mirror, and drew Uncle Ike on like an old boot.

"Worse! There never was anything of that kind going on forty years ago. Boys used to study, and stay in nights, and go to church Sundays, and attend Sabbath school, and try to do as they would be done by," and the old man smoked along quietly and looked as though butter would not melt in his mouth.

"Is that so?" said the boy, as he pulled a memorandum book out of the desk, and turned to a page where the leaf was turned down. "Ah, here it is; Exhibit A. When you went to school, Uncle Ike, there was a case which I have taken down from some former remarks you made, in which you and a lot of other loafers got a highly-seasoned billy goat, one night, and put it in the recitation room of the school, and when the teacher was doing something on the blackboard, with his back turned, you fellows tied the goat loose, and he bucked the teacher in the pants, and the teacher run down stairs, with the goat after him, and you remember there was some doubt as to whether the goat got down stairs first, or the teacher, and school had to be dismissed that day, until the teacher got over being nervous. How about that, Uncle Ike?" and the boy closed the book, with his thumb in another place, and looked at the old man inquiringly.

"Well, I snum, I didn't know as anybody remem·

bered about that," and the old man looked thoughtful, and ashamed, blushed a little, and finally said,
"The fact is, that teacher was mean as pusly. He
had a great big hickory ruler, and he used to maul
us boys, and we revolted, after we had stood it as
long as possible, same as the colonies revolted
against England's oppression, and we carried the
day. That we considered a patriotic duty, but we

There was some doubt about which **got**
down first.

didn't make war on women, like those fellows **at**
Madison, stealing corsets and underwear," and the
old man looked wise, as though he had got out of
a hole that squeezed him some.

"Yes, I see," said the boy, as he opened the book
again. "You wanted to fight the teacher for a
principle, and you got a Hessian goat to fight for

you. A very nice scheme, and I will make a mem·
orandum, 'remember the goat, when you get in
trouble.' But here is another patriotic war in which
you were engaged, Uncle Ike. when you were a
boy. Exhibit B. When there was a revival at the
town in which you studied, and was so good and
pious, some of you boys put some cayenne pepper
on a red-hot stove, in the church, and when the
people got up off their knees and rushed for the
doors, coughing and strangling, and falling over
each other to get to the fresh winter air, you told
that old fellow who spent the evening with you
last summer, that you nearly died a laughing to
see 'em snort and sneeze, and get outdoors. How
about that, Uncle Ike?" and the boy yawned, as
though calling up these reminiscences of the old
man's early life was a mere matter of form.

"Say, you red-headed young villain, were you
awake when that old man and I were talking, that
night? You were lying on the lounge, snoring,
and I thought you were asleep," and the old man
colored up and acted as though he didn't know
what to say. "The fact was, those people in the
church were all friends of ours, and we only did it
for a joke, and after it was all over they laughed
about it. Why, we boys went home with some of
those girls that very night. Why," said the old
man, thinking he was making a pretty fair defense
of his early misdoings, "it was the custom in those
days to have fun with each other. There were no

theaters, and no amusements, and people had to depend on the boys to keep things lively."

"Why, certainly," said the boy, "I understand how it was. If you choked anybody to death with the red pepper, and broke up a revival, you were doing a great work in educating the masses, eh? O, you are a pretty man to be giving boys advice. Say, Uncle Ike, now confess before it is everlastingly too late. Did you ever steal girls' clothes? Answer, quick!"

"No, sir, by gum, I never did," said the old man, getting ready to load his pipe, if the boy ever let up long enough for him to do so. "But we better postpone this interesting subject till after breakfast."

"No, don't hurry about breakfast," said the boy, as he wet his thumb and turned over several leaves. "This is one of the most interesting subjects I have ever got next to. It shows how much worse boys are now than boys were forty years ago. Here is Exhibit C. At the time of the reunion here a year ago, when those old soldiers stayed here in the house a couple of days, and eat us out of house and home, and sat up nights and drank Aunt Almira's home-made rhubarb wine, you got to talking about raiding a town in the South, during the war, and how the town was destroyed, and how a lot of you went through a female seminary, and each one of you got a souvenir. If I remember right you got a long home-knit yarn stocking, such as mother

used to make, and your soldier friends each got
something, a sun-bonnet, or a necktie, or a shoe.
How was that, Uncle Ike? Did you need those
things, or were you young soldiers out for a Halloween lark?"

"Here, give me that condum book," said Uncle
Ike, as he scratched a match and lit his pipe, his
face as red as a beet, and the perspiration running
down his cheeks. "I don't want no boy to keep
tab on me. I say things, sometimes, that I am
sorry for, but I never supposed anybody was taking what I said down in shorthand. Here, I'll give
you a dollar for that book," and the boy handed it
to him, he gave the dollar, and threw the book in
the fireplace, and then he stood with his back to
the fireplace for some time, thinking over the past,
and comparing with the present, and finally he
said:

"I'll tell you. Human nature is about the same,
taking one year with another. It was the same a
hundred years ago, and it will be the same a hundred years hence. Condemn a boy anyway. When
you think he has the most sense, he is liable to slip
a cog, and go whizzing off into space, and he is
not responsible for what he does until he comes to.
I suppose those boys at Madison had no more idea,
when they started out to celebrate, of doing anything they would be ashamed of, than us soldiers
did at Tangipaho, in '64. They just went from one
thing to another, and the first thing they knew

they were in it up to their ears, a few of them, and
a thousand outside yelling and cheering, and nothing was safe. Well, do you know how I would cure
those boys that stole the girls' clothes? The same
way the general in command at Tangipaho did,
that time you read about, when I was a fool soldier
in the South, thirty-five years ago. The boys certainly did overdo the thing, when that town was
burning, and they took tobacco, underclothes out
of stores, which they needed, and which they were
allowed to take in such cases. But I remember
seeing one soldier come out of a burning store with
a hoopskirt, just for a lark. The old General Fonda
saw him, and said, 'Did you get that to wear?' The
soldier thought the general was joking, and to
carry out the joke he said, 'Yes, sir.' 'Put it on,
then,' said the general. The man got into the
hoopskirt, and buckled it around his waist, laughing, and the general told him to get on his horse.
He got on his horse with the hoopskirt on, and the
general put him in charge of a guard, and on the
march through to the coast at Pascagoula, Miss.,
for a week, that man wore that hoopskirt, and he
was the laughing stock of the whole command.
He had to sleep in it in the guardhouse, and the
boys came to look at him. He wore it on the
march, until his horse was ashamed of him, and
he cut off from his coat the number of his regiment
and the letter of his company. When a pontoon
bridge was thrown across a river, the man in the

hoopskirt dismounted and led his horse across,
alone, with ten thousand men watching him and
laughing at him. When there was to be a charge
on the picket posts of the enemy, the hoopskirt
man was in the lead, and he acted as though he
wanted to be killed. Finally the object lesson was
considered sufficient, and he was allowed to take

And make them wear it.

off the hoopskirt, and dig a grave and bury it, and
put a cover of a hard-tack box up at the head of
the grave, inscribed, 'Death to Jayhawking,' and
he joined his company, and from that time nothing
but eatables was ever stolen by that lot of raiding
cavalrymen. Now, if I was at the head of the

university I would find some of the ringleaders and
smart Alecks of that girl raid, put onto them some
of the wearing apparel they stole, and make them
wear it on the campus from sunrise to sunset, and
march the students by in review, and I would not
suspend them, or send them home in disgrace.
Just let them have the disgrace right where they
disgraced themselves, and then have it over with,
and let them go to work bucking to make up for
the time they have lost in worrying over having
made fools of themselves. That would settle it.
Now, condemn you, boy, let us go to breakfast,
and try and forget this terrible ordeal that I have
gone through with your old memorandums, and
if you ever keep tab on me again, when I am telling
stories about old times, I am liable to take a fall
out of you, and I am a bad man when you get me
mad," and Uncle Ike put his arm around the boy
and they went out laughing to the breakfast room.

"Say, Uncle Ike, I didn't do a thing to you, did
I?" said the boy, as he sat down to the table opposite the old man.

"You did a thing to me that I shall always
remember, by gosh," said the old man.

ABOUT CHURCH BAZAARS.

It was after 10 o'clock at night when Uncle Ike and the red-headed boy came into the house from an entertainment the boy had induced the old man to attend, a church fair, and the boy dropped down on the rug in front of the fireplace, shaking his sides with laughter, while Uncle Ike sat down on the lounge in a heart-broken sort of manner, and began to pull things that he had bought at the fair out of his pockets and pile them up on the table in front of him.

"You was the easiest mark I ever saw at a bazaar in all my born days," said the boy, as he rolled over on the floor, and yelled so Aunt Almira pounded on the stovepipe for him to keep still. "You bought everything the girls asked you to, from chances on an undressed doll to a ticket on a church organ. Now, what are you going to do with dolls and church organs, if you draw them?"

"Never you mind what I am going to do with them," said the old man, as he spread a doily over his lap, and got out his bag of tobacco and put it on the beautiful doily, and scattered tobacco all over it, while he filled his pipe. "But this settles it, and I don't go to any more fairs with a fool boy. If I had been alone, and those girls had asked me to buy anything I didn't want, I could have stood

them off, but you just sicked them on to me, and
I couldn't get away as long as I had a cent. Gosh,
we didn't save street car fare, and had to walk
home, but it was worth all it cost. Say, did you
see that girl with the black eyes, selling those
tickets, how she clung to me? Well, I am getting

Did you see how she clung to me?

along in years, but the girls know the difference
between an elderly man, who is well preserved, and
all that, and a young dude that don't know bran.
I may bring home a young and bright aunt for you
some day, and then if I catch you calling her
'auntie,' and sitting in her lap, I will make you
think you have been in a football game. I am not
as old as Dewey, and you can't tell about us old

devils," and the old man smoked, and blinked, and got sleepy.

"O, don't make me laugh when my lips are chapped, Uncle Ike," said the boy, as he sat up in front of the fire and held his sides. "Those girls wouldn't marry you if you was lined with diamonds. They were laughing at you all the time behind your back. When one was pulling your leg for half a dollar the others were laughing at you and waiting for their turn to come to get you to pull your weasel and buy. O, they didn't do a thing to you. And to think that they made you think they were gone on you. O, Uncle Ike, you will kill me dead. But there is one thing I want you to understand. If you bring a young wife into this house your doom is sealed. Every time you are in sight I will just love my auntie, and when you have rheumatics so you can't go out nights, I will go with her to church and to theaters, and I will walk out with her, because she will not want to be tied down to a cross old man, and I will make you think you are not in it. You would make a nice husband, wouldn't you, kicking about the pancakes, swearing you could make better coffee out of burnt corn, grumbling because it was too hot or too cold. A girl that married you would need a nice red-headed boy around to make her feel that she had a companion, and wasn't acting as a nurse in the home for the aged. When you going to marry that girl?"

"Not till I get you entered as a student in the

reform school, condum you," said the old man, thinking seriously of what the boy had said. "When I marry it is not going to be a partnership affair with young kids. Now, what we going to do with all this truck I bought at the bazaar?"

"The Lord only knows. What in the name of common sense did you buy it for? Now, there is a

What in the name of common sense did you
buy it for?

nigger doll. What earthly use is a nigger doll in this bachelor home, anyway?" and the boy got up to look the stuff over.

"Now that you have had your say, and had all the fun you wanted to with the old man, I'll tell what I am going to do with it, and what I bought it for," said the old fellow, as he pulled off his boots and put his feet, covered with warm woolen socks, into the hair of a bearskin rug on the floor, and started the old pipe going again. "You thought you was having fun at the bazaar, but I had more than you did. There is a charm that cannot be found in blowing in money in ordinary ways, that is found in visiting a fair, given for the benefit of a church, to buy something for ten cents, and give a half a dollar, and tell the girl to never mind the change, it does good. The girl who is working for her church opens her eyes wide, the color comes to her face, and she is so glad she almost wants to scream for joy, and you can see the happiness scatter all around. I have seen a man out on a toot, or in a campaign, buy some drinks at a bar, throw down a bill and say never mind the change, and what good did it do? The bartender got the difference, probably, and it didn't do him any good. But at a church fair there is nobody to knock down the extra change, and the church gets it all. The meanest man in the world would not beat a church on the change. Say, boy, do you know that you can't make a better investment in this world, than to let some of your money drift into a church, and it does not make any difference what church it is. All of them are good. You see a great big church, and you think it is rich, and that there is no worry there about finances, but there are people laying awake nights thinking of ways and means to take care of the sick, bury the dead that have no provision made, and to take care of the thousands of expenses that nobody outside knows anything about. Then the pastor decides to hold a fair, and old and young are drawn on to help, and they get us old duffers to come in and help, and we let the girls have fun with us, and we shed money, and you fool boys think we don't know what we are about, but we do it to help the good Lord, who sends the bright-eyed girls as His agents to do a little mercantile business, and swell the treasury. Now I'll tell you what I am going to do with this stuff. To-morrow we will take it back, give it to the girls to sell again, and to-morrow night we will go again, and maybe buy it all over again. That's what I call casting bread upon the waters," and the old man got up and pulled off his coat and vest, and took off his necktie, and felt of the bald spot on his head, and said it beat all how, in a man about the age of him and Dewey, the hair grew so confounded short on top of the head, and so long on the tips of the ears, and he got ready to go to bed.

"Just a minute, Uncle Ike, before you go to bed," said the boy, as he raised his arms above his head, and stretched, and yawned, until he almost had lockjaw. "I want to have you settle this war between the British and the Boers before you go to bed. What I want to know is if the British have a right to use this new explosive, lyddite, which knocks things galley-west, and blows the enemy into fragments? Is this humane? Is it right?

When a man is killed in war, hadn't there ought to be enough left of him for a funeral, so his friends can collect him in a basket and have something for the chaplain to work on? I see the Boer commander has protested against the use of the stuff, and what you going to do about it, Uncle Ike?"

"Well, I am about the neutralest old fellow you ever saw, in these wars that are going on," said the old man, as he took some hot tallow off a candle and greased his nose, so he wouldn't take cold going to bed with his pores all open from the draft at the bazaar. "I don't want to mix in in anybody else's war. The subject of powerful explosives has been discussed by all nations, and each nation is anxious that every other nation shall not use such explosives, but all are experimenting on them just the same, and all are anxious to get a chance to try them on an enemy. Even our own peaceful American nation has a new kind of stuff called thorite, that it is trying to get to the Philippines in time to use on your friend Aguinaldo, but it will have to be good on the run to catch that sprinter. I imagine that if the Boers, who have a monopoly of dynamite in the Transvaal, had any means for dropping a few wagonloads of it down amongst the British, they would not stop to ask whether it was a humane method of warfare or not, but would touch it off too quick. It has got so everything goes in war, from a dum-dum bullet to an earthquake. Don't you remember how we had a vessel constructed on purpose to throw dynamite in Cuba, and how they fired a few shots at Cuba, and thought it would sink the island, and how the Cubans kicked when a mountain began to topple over and they thought it was going to fall on them? The only damage done was to have the vessel that fired the dynamite kicked by the discharge half way to Porto Rico, and the men on the vessel said their 'now I lay me down to sleep,' expecting to die in their tracks. Nations are experimenting on balloons that will take a carload of dynamite over a town or an enemy, and drop it, and if the thing is not stopped there will be someone killed awfully dead. But I don't think any country has got any kick coming, as long as they are all trying to kill the greatest number of people, and kill them the deadest. The only way I can think of for the Boers to save themselves from the British explosives is to move further inland. They are not so careful of how they kill their enemies. You remember the other day they loosened the top of a mountain and rolled it down on the British. Lyddite couldn't kill a man any deader than a mountain rolling over him. Now, let's go to bed and forget about somebody else's war," and the old man began to climb the stairs.

CHURCH FAIRS.

"Well, Uncle Ike, you better brush up your church fair clothes, and get ready for a week's hard work," said the red-headed boy, as he came in the room late at night, from attending a meeting of his Sunday-school class in the church, and found the old man nodding over an evening paper, his pipe gone out, and his eyes trying to keep open. "Our church is going to give a fair Thanksgiving week, and we are going to raise money enough to paint the church, put new cushions in the pews, and what there is left is to be used all winter for charity. You are to be it, and now wake up and give your ideas of how we can make the most money," and the boy slapped his uncle on the shoulder so hard that he woke up with a start.

"I knew it would come," said the old man, fishing for the tobacco bag in the pocket of his old smoking jacket. "We are all imitators, and if one church has a fair, and makes a barrel of money, the rest catch the epidemic, and every leg in the congregation is going to get pulled. All right, boy, if the church wants me for anything you can tell them your Uncle Ike will be there at early candle light, and stay till the last victim has escaped. What they want me to do, anyway?"

"One thing is to get up a voting contest,

between you and a rich old Jew who lives near our church. He does not belong to our church, of course, but he is one of the most charitable men that ever was. Why, when the steeple blew down on our church, and we raised money by subscription to rebuild it, this good-natured old Jew sent a big check, though he don't believe a thing in our religion. We thought we would buy a gold-headed cane, and pick you out for the most popular man in our set to vote for, and run the Jew old man against you, and you and he could just buck against each other with money. You could take a roll and give it out to the boys to vote for you, and when his friends heard that you were ahead on the vote they would come into the fair with wads, and we would keep the polls open as long as anybody had a dollar to blow in, see?"

"Yes, I think I begin to see," said Uncle Ike, as he got his pipe going so hard he couldn't see much. "You think this rich old Jew, who has been accu-mulating money by saving, and denying himself luxuries, who has walked to his place of business instead of riding, and who has worn his last year's clothes, and been economical until he has got a million, and is residing on easy street, will forget the traditions of two thousand years, and let you young ducks get him so excited over a seven-dollar cane that he will spend enough money to get it to support his family for a year. That your idea?"

"Yes, sir, that's it," said the boy, as he began to get excited, "you can jolly him, and say you will have that cane if it takes a million dollars, and you can walk around waving a roll of bills, and that rich old Jew will tell you you are not so warm, and he will just pour out money, and he will get the cane, and you will have the satisfaction of having done a big thing by the church. Say, in a cane voting contest in an Eastern city, a spell ago, the cane brought over three thousand dollars, and didn't cost twelve dollars. We are going to pay fifteen dollars for the cane, and we ought to raise four thousand dollars, if the Jew gets excited, and you put up as you ought to. Now, Uncle Ike, be a good fellow this time, won't you, and help us pull that Jew's leg for the benefit of the church."

"Who is going to have charge of the gold brick industry of your fair?" said Uncle Ike, as he blew rings up to the ceiling, and saw them roll up, things of beauty, but soon dissipated into nothing but bad-smelling smoke. "Are you going to have any-body to run a bunco department in your fair? What is the matter of having a few hold-up men and sandbaggers in the ante-room and in the alleys back of the church? If you could scatter a few pickpockets around they would get what was left. No, you fellows are all wrong. You would have to have something better for a bait than a gold-headed cane, that might not stand acid, to catch that old Jew. If you needed money to help the poor, to

buy fuel for the cold houses where poverty is at
work day and night, or medicine for the sick, you
could go to that old fellow and tell your story, and
a tear would steal out of his eye, and run down on
his hard-looking old face, and he would give you
all the money you needed and never ask whether
the poor people belonged to your church, or his

Have a few hold-up men in the ante-room.

church, or no church at all, but if you try to play
him for a sucker, he will be onto you, and he will
shy like a horse without blinders on. You might
get a rich American, who had made a million dollars in a million minutes, or a rich Irishman who
had so much money that it made his head ache to

try to think of figures big enough to count his wealth, to become so excited at a fair, in the glare of electric lights, and in the presence of handsome women, that he would vote twenty-dollar bills as carelessly as he would vote ballots at a caucus for alderman of his ward, but the Jew is not built that way. I had a friend once who was connected with a charity fair, and he had an idea if he put up a big armchair to be voted to the most popular minister, and included a Jewish rabbi in the lot, the Jews would come in with money by the barrel. He got fooled. The Jews who attended the fair looked the chair over, felt of the plush covering, examined the woodwork, and made a mental calculation of what the chair was worth, and then they kept away from the voting contest, though they gave checks to the treasurer of the fair in large numbers, to be used for charity, but my friend couldn't get them excited over the idea of voting a thousand dollars for a twenty-dollar chair. It is easy enough for you boys to pull my leg in this fair business, but instead of the old Jew you better pick out some fellow as weak-minded as I am, who will get excited and drop his wad. But spare the Jew. Now let's go to bed and dream a million or two dollars to the church."

"Well, Uncle Ike, you have ruined a very promising scheme, by your talk. I thought you would do anything for the church," and the boy sighed at the downfall of one of the greatest financial prop-

ositions of the century. "But before going to bed
I want you to tell me what you think of this latest
Dewey business, his deeding that house the people
gave him, to his wife. Us boys have been discussing it at recess, at school, and we have decided that
Dewey is about the greatest chump the country
has produced. A man that had the world at his
feet, to get so stuck on a woman that he would
give her everything he had on earth, and become
nothing but a lodger, liable to be fired out if he
became cross. What you think about it?"

"O, I don't think you fellows that didn't put up
anything towards that house that was given to
Dewey have any call to criticise his action. When
an old man gets in love, he gives right up, and
wants the woman he loves to think there is no one
on earth but her. Dewey had been for two years
away from the refining influence of woman's society, except Chinese women, whose eyes are put in
sideways, Japanese who are too small to be considered in any other light except as children with
dolls, and Filipino women who are darker than a
stack of black cats and who eat onions three times
a day. Now, what chance has he had to be sociable? He comes home and finds a woman who is
as radiant as a queen, and whom he tried to keep
from loving years ago when he had no right to love
her, and she is ready to be loved, and he has
everything he wants except woman's love. He
didn't realize his greatness among the men of the

world, but was just the lonesome old man, who didn't know whether he would put in the evening playing whist with a lot of other old salts, or go to a nigger show and try to laugh at the old jokes, and go home to his hall bedroom and try to think the world was his. So he reached out his hand to this charming woman, who could make him happier than a king, and said: 'Come, Mildred, don't let us live in so many houses. One is enough. Let us both be happy.' And they combine, form a trust in happiness, close up the houses that are not needed, and when he finds how to get the most happiness out of the few remaining years of life, gives her the house and all there is in it, you cheap ducks kick, and worry him. He is all right, and knows what he

They form a trust in happiness.

is about, and ought to tell them all to go to——"

"But say, Uncle Ike, do you believe there is anything in the story that he has offered to marry other women, and that some one of them was going to sue him for breach of promise, and so he got the property out of his hands?" said the boy.

"It wouldn't be strange," said the old man, un-

buttoning his collar, preparatory to going to bed.
"There are better facilities in Washington for a
breach of promise than any place I know of, and
Dewey was there a good deal before he became so
great. A captain, unassigned, with plenty of time
on his hands, is apt to say things to women that he
would not say if he knew that next year he was
going to be an admiral. Everything Dewey has
ever said or done in the matter of love ought to be
wiped off the slate, and a new set of books ought to
be opened. Now let that cat outdoors, and we will
go to bed."

ALL ABOUT AGUINALDO.

"Uncle Ike, have they caught Aguinaldo yet?"
shouted the red-headed boy down the stovepipe
hole from his room, where he was dressing, to the
old man who was in the sitting room below reading
the morning paper.

"No, I don't see any account of his capture in
the paper," said the old man, turning the paper
inside out and looking at the headlines sharply.
"But they have got his wife's underclothes. All
they got to do is to hold the underclothes and wait
for him to come back and claim them. A Filipino
don't stay away from his wife's wardrobe very
long."

"What do you think is the reason they can't catch him, Uncle Ike?" said the boy, as he came downstairs, pulling his suspenders over his shoulders, and acting excited. "Seems as though these long-legged Yankees could sprint as fast as a little nigger."

"They can't tell whether they have got him till they separate the jungle, and look under the leaves and logs. Did you ever chase a frog into a marsh and then, when you had him in sight, make a jump and fall all over him in the grass and mud?" asked Uncle Ike. "You knew the frog was under you, but you couldn't locate him, and you dug around in the stuff, looking for a green back or a white leg to show up, so you could grab it, but half the time the frog would get away, and you would have a handful of mud and grass."

"What do you think makes him run so?" asked the boy. "Certainly he is a brave man, and is well armed, and has quite a mess of niggers to help him. I should think he would just fight until he died, and have an end to it."

"Oh, it's the confounded yelling of those American soldiers that scares him. If they would keep still they could get him tamed down so he could be caught," and the old man looked disgusted at the lack of strategy on the part of the soldiers. "This thing reminds me of old times in a country town, when the boys and men wanted to get rid of a tramp dog. They would take an oyster can and fill it with stones, and tie it to the dog's tail, and give him a kick and start him off, and when he heard the rattle of the stones in the can, and saw the strange thing following him, and the crowd yelling, the dog would go off yelping, other dogs would chase him, and everybody would yell, and the dog would run as long as he had breath, and then crawl under a barn and go to sleep. Sometimes they would tie firecrackers to the dog's tail, and when he went under the barn he would set the barn on fire. That may be the way Lawton has fixed Aguinaldo. Certainly he has got him running, and the faster he goes the more noise there is, and maybe he thinks there is an oyster can tied to him. Anyway, he has lost confidence in the enemy, and he may set something on fire, and burn up with it. But I think Lawton don't want to catch him at all."

"Well, I wouldn't compare him to a dog, if I was you, Uncle Ike," said the boy, as he looked at a picture of Aguinaldo that he had cut out of an illustrated paper. "He has a good head of hair, and wears a frock coat, and a four-in-hand tie, and creased pants, and patent leather shoes. Ain't you ashamed, Uncle Ike, to call him a dog?"

"Well, hand me my pipe," said the old man, who always got nervous when the boy began to advise him. "There, that will do, it is lit enough, and you needn't shove that match, with its sulphur, away down into the tobacco. I'll tell you what I

think. Your Aguinaldo, with all his imitation of a
gentleman, and posing as a second George Washington, is a coward. He has never been on the
firing line, anywhere, that I can find out, since he
opened up the war. He has always been back with
the women, taking up a collection. He has cared
for nothing but money, and you will find if they
catch him, that his baggage consists of specie that
he has stolen. He is gun shy, that is what ails

He is gun shy.

Aguinaldo," and the old man puffed on the pipe
hard.

"Gun shy, what does that mean?" said the boy,
as he laced up his shoes.

"Never trained a bird dog, did you?" said Uncle
Ike. "When a sportsman decides that he will have
a dog of his own, to hunt chickens, he picks out a

likely pup and begins to train him. He gets him
house broke during the winter, and teaches him to
hunt for bones, and old gloves, and come to a point
on them. All the spring and summer he trains the
pup on robins and larks, and gets him so he will
hunt, and he tells everybody that he has the finest
pointer on earth, and when the season is open he
is going to slaughter chickens. He goes out the
first of September with his dog, and when the first
gun goes off, the dog gives a howl and starts across
the country for the nearest farm house, and crawls
under the corn crib. The dog is gun shy. The
owner hunts him up, and ties a bed cord to him,
and gets him back to the chicken ground, and he
finally comes to a point, and when a bird gets up,
and a shot is fired, he breaks away and drags his
owner by the bed cord, through the stubble, and
finally slips the cord off his neck and starts for the
setting sun, and the owner, with his nose skinned,
and his hair full of soil, picks up his gun and fires
a charge of buckshot into the rear of his pet
pointer, and the animal puts his tail between his
legs, yells nine kinds of murder, and becomes a
speck in the distance, and is never heard of again,
and the owner goes limping home, swearing about
the man who gave him a gun shy dog. Now, I
think that Lawton has found that Aguinaldo is gun
shy, and has put a charge of bird shot into the portion of his pajamas that was nearest, and the great
Filipino is looking for a doctor to pick the shot out.

You know when a person is after a doctor, he is in a hurry."

"Yes, but won't some of the other generals head Aguinaldo off and capture him?" asked the boy.

"Not if they obey instructions, I reckon," said the old man, looking wise. "You see, if he stood up and fought, and was captured, we should have to take him, and take care of him, and he would be an elephant. But if he gets away, and goes to a country that is neutral ground, he can stay there and do nothing all the day long except issue proclamations denouncing our government, and we can go along civilizing the Filipinos, and showing them how to live happy, and die poor, and we can benevolently assimilate them, and let them raise tobacco and sugar for us to take away, and we will pay them by letting them eat the rice they raise. O, we are all right. We are a great people," and Uncle Ike got up and stretched himself, and looked like a diplomat, who knew everything worth knowing.

"Gee! Uncle Ike, I should think it would make your head ache to know so much," and the boy went up to the old man and began feeling of the bumps on the bald head, to see if he could feel the brain throb. "I suppose you keep thinking all the week, and get things thought up all ready, so when I touch the button, and ask you questions, all you have to do is to scratch a match, light your pipe, and reel off a whole lot of statesmanship. Gosh, but I should be afraid my head would get so full it would up and bust. I say, Uncle Ike, don't you think Dewey has got the thing all settled, now, about that house, so he can be happy, and never have any more trouble, if he don't talk too much?"

"Well, I'll tell you, boy, everything looks smooth for Dewey now. The house is deeded to his son, and there is a string to the deed which gives Dewey and his wife the use of it as long as they live, and all the boy has to do is to wait thirty or forty years, and he can get married and move in. But suppose a case. Suppose, in the course of human events, the same thing happens to the Dewey family that happened to President Harrison, and in a year or two Dewey is

Gee! I should think it would make your head ache to know so much.

seen around Washington wheeling a baby wagon! I am no alarmist, and I wouldn't swear such a thing would happen, but you can't tell anything about a great hero. Before it becomes time for him to go on the retired list, as an admiral and a husband, there may be a flock of young Deweys that will fill that house clear to the roof. Now, when they grow up are they going to let their big half-brother walk off with the house, and leave them on the sidewalk, under an umbrella? Not in a town where every other man is a lawyer. I tell you, boy, the future is liable to be full of trouble, and baby wagons, and lawsuits."

"But wouldn't young Dewey deed the house to the children, and save trouble?" said the boy.

"Not on your life. He is no chump. He is a traveling man. Did you ever know a traveling man who didn't know when he had struck a good thing? But come on, let's adjourn this inquest," and the old man took the boy by the red hair, to warm his fingers, and they went along, hand in hair, to breakfast.

A COLD MORNING FOR THE OLD MAN.

It was the first real cold morning of the winter, and Uncle Ike had laid awake for a couple of hours, before getting up, waiting for the furnace heat to warm up his room, but as it seemed to be getting colder all the time he had got out of bed, shivering, put on a few clothes and gone down into the sitting room, started a grate fire, and was standing with his bent back to the blaze, to thaw out his spine, which seemed to have the marrow frozen, so he could not straighten up. When he came down stairs he could plainly hear his toes crack with the cold, and he realized that he was getting old. As he stood there with his back to the blaze, he thought of the days, years ago, when he was a boy, days that he would have been outdoors before this time, dragging a squeaky sled up a hill, and sliding down facing the biting wind that would fairly crack his face, or skating on a pond with feet so stiff they were liable to break off, and he remembered that he was having fun all the time. Then he tried to straighten up his back, and felt something break, and as he held his hand on the particular piece of vertebra that seemed to have uncoupled, he thought of the winter he spent in Florida, wearing thin underclothes, and sitting under the trees with a negligee shirt and a belt, and how he had to be brought home in the spring by a trained nurse and a doctor, and how it took all the next summer of strict attention to a quinine diet to cure him of the malaria he brought home on a special car. As the spine thawed out, and he smelled woolen burning, he found his morning gown was on fire, and presently he had put it out, and the exertion straightened his back, and he was himself again, and he yelled up the stovepipe hole for the boy to come down and go with him to the toboggan slide.

"Gee, but this is a hot one," said the red-headed boy, as he came down stairs, the steam puffing out

of his mouth with his breath, and all his clothes
under his arms. "Guess I'll dress here by the fire,
if you will stand around a little. What's your
notion of burning off the tail of your dressing
gown, just as a hard winter is coming on?"

"O, they are wearing them shorter this year,"
said Uncle Ike, his face having thawed out so he

What was your notion in burning off
the tail of your dressing gown?

could smile and wink. "Say, when I was your age
I would have been out before this, shoveling off
snow, or skating. You are getting to be a regular
pet. You want to be done up in pink cotton. Get
on your clothes, now, and we will go out and run

around a block, and warm up, and get ozone into us."

"Not me," said the red-headed boy, as he sat on the floor lacing up his shoes, "not till the sun gets up and warms and melts the jagged frozen corners off the air. I don't want to breathe any Klondike special brand of air, that cuts gashes in my windpipe, and causes my lungs to peunk. When it gets comfortable I will go out and stroll with you, Uncle Ike, and pick you a nice bouquet of icicles, but your little warm-haired boy has not lost any north pole, and is not going out on any expedition to be rescued. See!" and he got up and put his arms around the old man, and hugged until the spine began to hurt.

When I was your age.

"Well, Congress has got started," said Uncle Ike, as he glanced at the morning paper. "This is going to be the most momentous session of Congress we have had since the Civil war, and congressmen will have many sleepless nights."

"Yes, they will have sleepless nights because

they stay up till morning drinking budge, and eating cheese sandwiches," said the boy, as he lit a piece of paper at the grate, and put it on the bowl of the old man's pipe, and saw the blue smoke puff out of the old fellow's mouth. "Congressmen don't worry much, except about being re-elected. What they got to do, except drive out the Mormon, Roberts, and pass the appropriation bill?"

"O, say, you don't know anything about it," said the old man. "Haven't they got to settle the status of the Philippine question? What they going to do with Aguinaldo, unless Congress settles it? Humph! You boys got to grow before you know much."

"O, I don't know," said the red-headed boy, as he put his feet up to the grate to thaw out his shoes. "Us boys have been settling these things for more than a month, at our debating society. In the first place, that coon hunt in Luzon is about over, anyway. All they got to do is to tree Aguinaldo, and cut down the tree, or run him into a hollow log, and run a forked stick in, and when it strikes his pants, twist it, and pull him out, squealing like a coon or a rabbit. And when they get him, send him over here under guard of a sick soldier armed with a syphon of seltzer water, and play him at the dime museums. Then let the other Filipinos go to work and learn how to mark a ticket so they can vote for McKinley when they think they are voting for Bryan. Then Congress

can decide whether to give the Filipinos chloroform to keep them quiet, so they won't get up any
revolution till after election, so the soldiers can
come home in time to vote next fall. O, you can't
fool us boys much."

"Well, I should think so," said the old man, as
he looked at the boy as he would at a boy who had
used profane language. "You are a sacrilegious
rascal to think that Congress will have any political
motive in dealing with these questions. What you
boys going to decide about Roberts, the Mormon?"

"Well, we are divided on that matter," said the
boy. "Some of us think that a man who will, as a
religious duty, support three families, and glory in
it, is as good as a congressman who prowls around
in eight or nine families and don't support any of
them, and that the one who supports so many
families during a panic, when money is tight, ought
to be encouraged by high official position, and then
some of us think he ought to be arrested for dis-
orderly conduct, and sent to the house of correc-
tion instead of to the lower House of Congress.
But we are willing to let Congress figure that out.
What we are watching the closest, though, is
whether Congress will grant Dewey prize money
for sinking the Spanish fleet and capturing the
Ohio widow without firing a gun. We think he is
entitled to prize money in his love affair, anyway,
and if the Sultan of Sulu is sent as a missionary to

Utah, us boys will endorse the proposition, and **we** are starting a subscription to give Otis a house and lot when he gets the war over, and is proclaimed a hero, by the trust newspapers, and we are discussing Mark Hanna's health, trying to find out whether he can do more for the trusts in the Senate than he can in the next political campaign as a committeeman. Say, us boys are going to be heard from next year. We don't know which side we are going to be on, but when we decide, the other side will go out of business, and don't you forget it."

"Do you know what you kids remind me of?" said the old man, after listening to the red-headed boy settling questions before breakfast that statesmen are working hard to solve. "You make me think of a flock of sparrows in the street, taking lunch. They eat and talk, and kick up the dirt, and look sassy, and each one seems to have a chip on its shoulder, looking for trouble. A dog comes along, and they all fly up in a tree, and have a debating society, and pass resolutions against dogs. The dog goes along about his business, and the sparrows fly down and gather around the banquet board again, and before they finish the second course a wagon comes along, and they fly up in the tree again and pass resolutions denouncing the city authorities for permitting wagons to run on the streets. When the wagon has passed by they fly down again, and each one swears he will never leave the banquet table again, whatever comes

along, and just as they get into the third course, a
woman with a short dress, and long stockings, a
red jacket, a blue tam o'shanter, and a green necktie comes along on a wheel, and gets right
amongst the sparrows before they see her, when
one sparrow yells murder, and they all fly away,
saying that settles it, and they go off on another
street, where they can eat the bread of idleness
undisturbed, and when they have all got filled up
they go and sit in a row on a telephone wire, and
talk and twitter to themselves about how hard it is
to earn an honest living, and how everything has
got in a trust so an honest sparrow is liable to
starve unless he has got stock in a combine, and
they pass resolutions against the existing order of
things and imagine the wires on which they sit are
carrying the report of their deliberations to the
four corners of the globe, and that they are really
and truly a factor in the affairs of the world, when
they are only sparrows, with no influence, no vote,
no friends, no nothing but an appetite, and a desire
to increase the sparrow population.   Now, you
red-headed human sparrow, with freckles on your
bill, and an empty stomach, let's stop running the
affairs of the world, and go out to breakfast, and
see if Aunt Almira has forgotten the combination
on those buckwheat pancakes," and the old man,
whose spine had got thawed out, so he could walk
upright, took the boy by the hand and led him to
the slaughter.

THEY DISCUSS THE PRESIDENT'S
MESSAGE.

"I s'pose McKinley has got a great load off his mind, since he sugared off that message, and will go off duck-shooting, and try to forget it," said the red-headed boy, as he and Uncle Ike sat looking out of the window at the snow, that was flying around with the wind, uncertain as to whether it was best to settle down on the ground here, or go out West to make drifts for railroad men to plow out. "It must have made a man's stomach ache to get so much wind in it at once, and fire it off all in one cyclone." ,

"O, I don't know," said Uncle Ike, as he laid down his paper and got ready for a heated argument with the boy, who was always nagging the old man, so he would get hot under the collar, and talk with his eyes shut. "It's your old Democratic Presidents who go duck-shooting, after office hours. Mr. McKinley will stay right there, and watch public business, and buy ducks."

"What's the matter with Hanna?" said the boy, as he got on the other side of the room, to be out of reach of Uncle Ike's big, horny hand. "The boys say that Hanna is the whole shooting match, and that the President never changes his shirt unless Hanna tells him to. Just read that message about trusts. He just makes me think of an old story about a father who had his son across his knee, spanking him lightly with one hand, and feeding him chocolate caramels with the other. He seems to say to Congress, 'You must try and do something before the next campaign to scare the trusts, so they will not raise prices on barbed wire and things any higher, but not scare them enough so they will forget to whack up to the campaign fund.' Are you on, Uncle Ike?"

"Say, you goshblasted young copperhead, where you been listening to such traitorous talk? You boys must be associating with bad people when you are out nights," and the old man really looked grieved at the disloyalty of the young rebel. "Some of these people who are always against the government are always talking about great men, and claiming that someone else runs them. Why, Mark Hanna has no more control over the President than I do. He can suggest, but when old McKinley makes up his mind what is the right thing to do, he just opens the door and tells the boys to go out and play, and he goes to work and thinks it out. Every President since Washington has had the same kind of abuse. I tell you, every man and boy who abuses a President ought to be branded with a frozen boot."

"Yes, but why didn't the President say something to encourage the Boers in their fight against the British, to protect their homes and firesides?"

said the boy, with a bluff at being indignant. "Why didn't he say anything in his message about the Milwaukee street car franchise? Here is Henry Payne, working night and day for McKinley, and getting in trouble about having his franchise extended, and McKinley goes and writes a message about everything else on earth, and never so much as mentions the street car franchise. If I was Henry Payne I would come out for Bryan, and make McKinley jump like a box car."

"Well, you make me weary," said the old man, as he looked around for his bag of tobacco. "The President may have his personal sympathy aroused for the Boers, but he can't work any advertisements for them into his message, no more than he could advertise a brand of baking powder. He has to talk about being at peace with all nations, and wishing them well. Your idea of his mixing up in a street car fight is on a par with your political ideas generally. You are not broad enough for a politician. If he should mix up in the local affairs of Milwaukee he would have to do the same by Toledo and Detroit. You want to try and look at things beyond your immediate surroundings," and the old man finally got his pipe lit, and was ready to talk at a mark.

"Now, Uncle Ike, I want to ask you a very important question, and I don't want any quibbling," said the boy, as he looked right into the old man's eyes. "Your answer will have great effect on us boys. We are studying the question carefully, and want to be prepared to act intelligently. Which side are you on in this war in South Africa? Are you in favor of the Boers or the British, and why are you in favor of one against the other? Now answer quick, without stopping to smoke up a lot ahead."

"Well, I'll tell you," said the old man puffing

Which side are you on in this war?

away at his pipe and trying to kill time while he thought how to answer the red-headed boy. "When I read of the way the Boers went away off away from everybody, and killed off the wild animals, and hewed out farms in the Transvaal, and made little churches, and minded their own business, I am in favor of the Boers, but when I read how they treated the natives, and made slaves of them, and made them work for nothing, and board them·

selves, and how they killed them off, when they
revolted at the injustice, I am against the Boers.
When I think of their building up a country that
was prosperous and happy, and every citizen went
to church and prayed and sung hymns, I am for
the Boers, but when I read about their getting a
monopoly on everything, and charging five dollars
a bottle for poor gin, to the Outlanders, I am
against the Boers. When I read about their getting into trouble with the natives, and when almost
whipped, they called upon the English for help
and the English came in and saved them from ex-
termination, I am for the English. When I read
of the discovery of gold and diamonds by the English, and how they built up cities, and found
hundreds of millions of dollars' worth of precious
metals and stones, and developed the country, I
favor the English, and when I read that the English
took all the gold and diamonds away, and got so
rich they drank champagne for breakfast and let
the Boers drink black coffee, I favor the Boers,
but when I find that the Boers would not let the
English vote, or have anything to say about anything, except to pay taxes, I favor the English,
but when I read that the English got so rich that
they had natives do all the work, and they just laid
around and played lawn tennis, and rode in rubber-
tired carriages, and got their skins full of high
wines, I favor the Boers, but when I read that the
Boer policemen hit an English head whenever they

got a chance, and made them feel that they were
not wanted there, I favor the English. When I
think that the Boers nor the English had any right
in that country, without the consent of the negroes
who owned the country, and how both the Boers
and the English had it in for the natives, and treated
them worse than they did the wild animals, I am
for the niggers, by gosh! When I think of the
good Englishmen, of aristocratic parentage, who
are being shot through the right eyes by the Boers,
causing mourning all over Great Britain, my sympathies are with the British, but when I read of
the casualties among the old Dutch farmers, and
the mourning at the little farm houses where the
father or the son will never come back, I am for
the Boers. When I read that the Boers fire on
flags of truce, and blow up Red Cross ambulances
and nurses, I am for the English, but when I read
that the Lancers charge on the Boers and do not
spare them when they are on their knees praying
for mercy, but run lances through them, kill them
in their tracks after they surrender, and call it pig-
sticking, I am for the Boers, but when I think all
these things over, and go to bed and dream about
it, I make up my mind that I will leave it to the
good Lord to figure it out, and I will remain neutral, by ginger."

"O, I see," said the boy, drawing a long breath,
after Uncle Ike's speech, "you would advise us
boys to saw the whole responsibility onto the

Lord, and not mix up in the scrap. Is that your idea?"

"That's about the size of it," said the old man, who had got enough of the argument. "The Lord has had more experience in these things than you and I."

"Well, then, why not leave the street car fight, and the fight against the Mormon, Roberts, and the gold standard question, and the tariff, and the

Left uncle wondering.

war in the Philippines, and the embalmed beef, and everything, to the Lord? I tell you, Uncle Ike, you are a coward! You haven't got —nd enough to come out and take sides on anything but the game law. What this country wants is men who will get on one side or the other of all questions, and not straddle. Uncle Ike, you are a straddler, and you have straddled every question before the public until you are bow-legged. I want to announce to you right here that I am in favor of the————''

"Say, look at the dog fight in the street," said Uncle Ike, as he went to the window, and the boy put on his hat and rushed outdoors, and left Uncle Ike wondering which side he really was on.

THEY DISCUSS THE WARS.

Uncle Ike sat by the window, watching the people go along with packages of Christmas presents, and he was plainly worried. It was evening, and he had come home on the crowded street car, standing up and holding on to a strap, and he had not had a chance to read the evening paper on the car, so he had glanced over the headings as he sat down by the window, in the fading twilight, and he saw that General Lawton had been killed in the Philippines, and General Buller had been whipped in South Africa by the Boers, and he was wondering how he could explain these things to the red-

headed boy when he came home from school. For
weeks he had been telling the boy that the war in
the Philippines was practically over, that the troops
had scattered the insurgent army all over the island
of Luzon, and that there would be peace before
Christmas, and our army would be ordered home.
He had told the boy that the British would be
chasing the Boers into Pretoria on the run, jabbing
them in the pants with lances, and would take their
Christmas dinner there, and that Kruger would be
a fugitive like Aguinaldo. And here it was three
days before Christmas, the Filipinos had killed
Lawton within six miles of General Otis' headquarters, and the Boers had knocked Buller out
in one round, and they sat on their entrenchments
eating summer sausage and laughing at the army
of Great Britain, which was kicking up a dust down
in the valley, to get out of range of the Boer guns
such as Krupp used to make.

"Guess you better throw up your job as a military expert," said the red-headed boy, as he came
in from school, and slammed the door so Uncle
Ike woke up with a start. "A feller up at the drug
store was just reading that the Filipinos are so
close to Manila that Otis has been taken with chills,
and they killed General Lawton just outside of
town. Thought you said there were not insurgents
enough left in Luzon to make a corporal's guard.
This man said Manila was just surrounded with

niggers, spoiling for a fight.   Where is Aguinaldo?"

"How do I know?" said **Uncle Ike,** as he filled
his pipe and began to fill the room with fog.   "I
took it for granted, from what they said at Washington, that this business was about over.   The
President, and his cabinet, and all the senators who

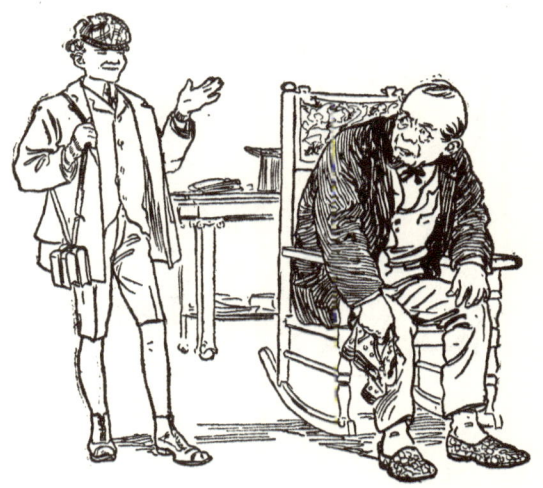

Guess you better throw up your job as a
military expert.

are loyal, have said the war was over, and all that
was necessary was to send a policeman out after
Aguinaldo, and I thought they must know.   Thirty
years ago I was quite an old fighter, but I don't
understand this new method of fighting, taking
an army and going off two hundred miles on a

blind trail, looking for one common boss nigger, and letting twenty thousand other niggers come and settle within gunshot of your base of supplies, and pick off your generals. Next they will cut Otis' cable, and then we won't get any news at all."

"Then we will be in luck. I tell you, Uncle Ike, those Filipinos are playing us for suckers. It is just

Thirty years ago I was an old fighter.

like a game of football. Aguinaldo, the half back, starts off on a run, and we think he has got the ball, and we chase him, and try to tackle him, and finally we look around and a quarter back has got the ball, and has made a touch-down while we have chased the wrong man. I'll bet you it wasn't Aguinaldo at all that they have been chasing up through the mountains, but another nigger made up to look like him, and the first thing we know he will sneak into Manila and steal Otis' typewriter. Gosh, but this kind of way to run a war makes me tired. What they ought to do is to send a committee of senators and congressmen over there, with a range finder, to locate Aguinaldo, then let Billy Mason dress up as Santa Claus, and carry a lot of toys for the niggers to play with, and when Aguinaldo got to playing with a monkey on a stick, let Billy jump on him and hold him down until Otis could get there and tie him with a piece of clothes-line. Us boys have been planning a campaign since school was out, and we could show the President how to wind up that business too quick. If they would take over there a transport loaded with opossums, and turn them loose on the firing line, and scare them over to the enemy, every nigger in the insurgent army would drop his gun and go catching 'possums. There don't seem to be any head work over there at all."

"Well, you got to have patience," said Uncle Ike, as he got up and walked the floor, and looked as though things had not been going to suit him. "You see, a war has got to be run a good deal with a view to its effect on the politics of the country. The idea seems to have been to have the war almost ended just as Congress met, so they would not kick too much, and pass resolutions denouncing the way the war was being conducted. Now there is a recess of two weeks, and it is proper to let the insurgents have their inning, and scare us out of our boots,

while the congressmen are home eating Christmas
dinners and fixing their fences for the next campaign.   When the recess is over we will have vic-
tories until the appropriation bills are passed, and
then we will be licked some along towards spring,
and then the people will say it won't do to go back
on the administration while they are fighting. Then
next fall, during the campaign, every time there is
a political meeting we can have a victory in the
afternoon papers, and the people will cheer for the
old flag, and sing the 'Star Spangled Banner,' and
get daffy.   I am satisfied it is a political necessity
not to take Aguinaldo till about the first of next
September, and then they can bring him here two
weeks before election and show him on the rear
platform of the car, while Otis and the other fellows
make speeches to the cheering multitude, and there
you are.   Victory in the field, politics in the air,
and prosperity on every hand, except when there
is a panic in trust stocks.   Boy, you don't know
as much as your Uncle Ike, if you do go to school,"
and the old man sat down and fanned himself with
a newspaper.

"Yes, Uncle Ike, that sounds well, but nothing
that you predict comes true," said the boy, as he
sat down on Uncle Ike's knee. "You were going
to have the British wipe the Boers off the earth
before Christmas. How do you account for their
getting licked every time they show up in front
of the Boers?"

"Well, I'll tell you. England has not had a war for a hundred years or so, except with savages, and they can kill savages with any old smooth-bore gun. They are behind the times in artillery, except in their navy. They take a lot of guns that will shoot a mile, if they don't bust, and go against Boers that have guns that will shoot five miles, and before they can get near enough to hit the Boers they are blown sky high by the Krupps. See? England has got to get a move on, and get up to date, and then she will stand a chance. A man might as well take a saber and charge on a man half a mile away who is armed with a repeating rifle. Before he got near enough to cut a gash in the man with his saber he would be so full of lead that he would sink in a fog. I am going to write to Queen Victoria, this evening, and tell her to buy more new-style cannon and less chocolate drops for her soldiers," and the old man and the boy declared an armistice and went to supper.

BEFORE AND AFTER TAKING.

Uncle Ike knew better than to eat so much at dinner on Christmas day. For years he had enjoyed a bit of dyspepsia when he was not careful, and he knew just what he ought not to eat as well as anybody, but Aunt Almira had got up an old-fashioned Christmas dinner, and invited in a few chums of the red-headed boy, and as the house became filled with odors of turkey, goose, mince pie and dozens of other things, the old man sent for the carving knife, and as he sharpened it on a scythe stone he thought what a good carver he was, and how he would slice the fowls so they would make the mouth water. He sat down to the table in the dressing gown the boy had given him, and as the red-headed boy sat down, with a new red sweater, pulled up so it would not entirely cover his new red vest, and so he could get at his gold watch every few minutes, to tell somebody what time it was, his feet, encased in new moose-hide moccasins, made things so quiet you could have heard a gum drop. The other boys looked at the steaming turkeys and things, and Aunt Almira sat opposite Uncle Ike so as to be ready to tell him to put more dressing on the plates, and a little more of the white meat, and to be careful and not spill anything on the tablecloth. Uncle Ike felt of the edge of the knife with his thumb, stuck the fork straddle of the breastbone, said something about Christmas coming but once a year, and began hacking away at the birds and loading the plates, which needed sideboards to hold it all.

"There is nothing like Christmas, after all. Will you have light or dark meat?" said he to one of the boys.

"Both light and dark meat, and some of the

goose, and plenty of dressing, but I think Thanksgiving is the best," said the chum of the red-
headed boy.

"Guess I'll give you the platter, turkey and all,"
said the old man, as the hungry-looking red-headed
boy was becoming anxious, and then he passed a
plate well loaded to Aunt Almira, others to the
other boys, and finally
fixed the red-headed
boy with an instalment,
loaded his own plate to
the guards, and soon all
were eating as though it
was the last meal to be
served on earth. Uncle
Ike forgot all about his
stomach, and the rich
gravy, the mashed pota-
toes, the pickled peaches,
the corn, asparagus, the
mince pie, the nuts and
raisins, the fruit and

Began hacking away.

coffee, the candy, the popcorn, everything came
to his net, and no boy ever stopped eating until
Uncle Ike did, and when they got up from the
table Uncle Ike's vest was unbuttoned and the
boy's moccasins were too tight.

They went into the sitting room and Uncle Ike
was asked to tell about his Christmas in the army,
when he was a young man, and he told them how,

in 1864, he was on the march, in the rain, on Christmas, and how all he had was a piece of mule meat and a few hard tack, how he put an iron ram rod through a chunk of mule, held it over the coals of a rosin tree fire, and burned it so it tasted like the calking of a boat, and how he soaked the hard tack in water, and fried them in a piece of tin off a canteen, in rusty pork fat, and that he never had anything taste so good in all his life, and how he went into a fight after dinner and never did know how many people he killed, but he said there was nothing that made a man so brave as to eat mule meat. He lighted his pipe and stood with his back to the fireplace, with his legs spread wide apart, when the red-headed boy said, "If the Spaniards had been fed on mule meat they wouldn't a done a thing to our troops, would they?"

"Well, I'll tell you," said Uncle Ike, as he lifted the tails of his new dressing gown, to see if they were burning, "I don't know as mule meat would have helped the Spaniards. Spaniards are brave enough, if they can get you at a disadvantage, and can have plenty of people looking on. They like to play to the grand stand. If any great battle with the Spaniards could be fought with ladies looking on, the Spaniards would do deeds of valor that would surprise the world, but take a Spaniard and an American, fighting hand to hand, alone, and the Spaniard would run, unless he could get a jab in behind the American. That is what makes

a Spanish bull fighter so brave, is the fact that
thousands of ladies are looking on. He will run
chances of being killed for the applause of women.
If he went out into a pasture, alone, and a bull calf
came at him, he would run like a whitehead, and
if a big bull, with long horns, should go for him,
and no one was looking, he would jump a fence,
or climb a tree, and yell for help."

"Uncle Ike, do you think it is mule meat that
makes the Boers so brave?" asked the red-headed
boy, as the other boys began to rattle their skates,
and get ready to go out on the river.

"Well, it may be," said Uncle Ike, as he hesitated
and placed one hand on his stomach, as though
there was a small pain there, not bigger than a
man's hand. "They eat a good deal of sausage
which they import from other countries, and there
may be mule in it. But I think what makes the
Boers brave is because they are built that way.
They have never known a minute but what they
had to be brave. First they had to kill wild animals, lions, tigers and wolves, to get into the
Transvaal, and then they had to kill Zulus to stay
in. Every farm, for half a century, has had to be
an arsenal, and the women and children have had
to fight to protect themselves. A Boer who was a
coward would be shamed to death by his women
folks. There is no such thing as a Boer coward,
because such a person could not live in that cli-
mate, and in those surroundings. Where a race

for several generations has had to fight, it gets so
accustomed to it that nothing can keep them from
fighting, when they think they are right. If Russia, and Germany, France and America, should go
in to help England in this war, it would make no
difference to the Boer. He would get behind a
rock, or a tree, eat his summer sausage, or his dried
beef, smoke his pipe, think of the family at the little
farmhouse away back on the prairie, or in the
mountains, and when an enemy got in sight, whether it was one man or a thousand, he would say his
prayers, sing a hymn, pull the trigger, and look to
his God for commendation, and if his commander
ordered the Boer to retreat he would take it as an
offense, and have to be pulled away with a rope.
He is a stayer, and England will find that for every
mile of advance into the Boer country, there will
be a graveyard."

"Gosh, if Aguinaldo was only a Boer, wouldn't
he make Otis look for a canoe to get out of Manila?" said the red-headed boy.

"O, Aguinaldo couldn't be a Boer. He is im-
mune," said Uncle Ike, as he laid his pipe on the
mantel, and looked as though something didn't
taste good. "There is the same difference between
the Boers and the Filipinos as there is between
fine old coach horses and zebras. The coach horses
have brains and muscle, and can haul a load and
enjoy it. They will stand without hitching, and
seem to enter into the spirit of the labor and pleas-

ure of their owners.   The zebra looks like a circus,
works only because he thinks he is playing, and is
so nervous that if he hears a firecracker go off he
jumps over a fence, runs away, and you can't catch
him with a lariat.   Aguinaldo is like the zebra of
the equine race.   When the troops catch him, he
will be all out of breath, the traces broken, his head-

Something I have eaten seems to have disagreed
with me.

stall dragging in the mud, and the dashboard
kicked through, and they will have to put blinders
on him to lead him, and he will snort and rear up,
until some soldier kicks him in the ribs, and then
he will be quiet.   He is just a runaway horse, without any brain."

"Well, come on, boys, let's go skating," said the red-headed boy, as he took off his new moccasins and put on some old shoes. "But what's the matter, Uncle Ike, you look sick?"

"O, I am all right, but if you will go up to my room and get that little bottle of dyspepsia tablets, I will be much obliged. Something I have eaten seems to have disagreed with me," and the old man looked as though he knew he should die.

"O, I know what it was; it was that half a mince pie," said the boy, as he handed the old man the medicine. "But you never will learn to take care of yourself. Well, so long," and the boys went out to skate, leaving Uncle Ike with several kinds of trouble on his stomach.

THE BOYS GET SKATES ON HIM.

Uncle Ike was a complete wreck, and he lay upon the lounge in the sitting room, wishing that he was as young as he used to be, or that he knew as much as he thought he knew. He had been buncoed by the boys, and could not stand a "dare." He had told the boys that he was one of the best skaters in the whole country, when he was a boy, how he had won prizes for long-distance skating, taken premiums for fancy skating, when he wrote the names of a whole class in Sunday school on the ice, in a space of ten feet, and how once, in an early day, he had been chased by a pack of wolves on the ice, and had saved his life by dodging wolves, and skating away from them, where if a skate-strap had become unfastened he would have been eaten without salt, and pulled into pieces by the ravenous wolves. The eyes of the boys stuck out when he told of the red tongues of the wolves, the hot breath, and the eyes of the animals like balls of fire, and they thought he was either the greatest hero of modern times, or the biggest single-handed liar that had ever told wolf stories that were out of date. Uncle Ike even brought a pair of old-fashioned skates down from the attic, to clinch his argument, a pair with wooden frames, and a goose neck that turned over in a coil, with a brass acorn on the end, a pair of skates fifty years old, with regular harness to keep them on the feet. The boys looked at them, and compared them with the club skates that they owned, sneered at Uncle Ike's old back numbers, and finally they dared him to go to the rink with them and put them on. They said he probably couldn't skate a lick, and would straddle out and split himself, and fall all over, and the police would have to bring him home in a patrol wagon.

Human nature is about the same, in old or young, and when the boys intimated that he must have forgotten how to skate, if he really ever did know how, and that he would have difficulty in standing erect, let alone skating, the old man thought of his youth, and how he used to skate all night with frozen feet, and build a bonfire on the ice; he thought of the girl with the red mittens, of his youth, and he told the boys he would be condemned if he wouldn't get out with them that New Year's morning, and open up the Twentieth century with a whoop, if it was the last thing he ever did. He would show them that a few years more or less on a healthy man didn't make any difference with his kittenishness, and he greased the straps on the old skates that had not been used since the war, run a whetstone down the sides of the runners, found an old rat-tail file and filed the rust out of the old-fashioned grooves, put on an old red comforter that wound around his neck five times, and hung down his old lumbago back half way to his heels, found an old coon-skin cap in the attic, with one tail hanging down behind and the other tail eaten off by a generation of moths, put on an old pair of yarn-streaked mittens that had been knit when he went South in '62, but which were no good for a campaign in the South, and he told the boys to come on.

The boys looked him over, and thought what a sensation he would create at the rink, skating left-handed, and smoking his old clay pipe, but they took him along, and on the way to the rink he jumped up and cracked his heels together, and laughed so a policeman frowned and shook his club, and Uncle Ike was the youngest boy of the lot.

But oh, what a difference in the morning! Uncle Ike had got his long skates on, struck out for a race with wolves, apparently, took the whole floor space, and just as he was dodging a panting wolf, the runner came out of the wood of one of the skates, and he went down on all fours, the toe of

They slid across the rink.

the other skate caught in a woman's dress, and they slid clear across the rink, the ice and snow going up their trousers, everybody fell over Uncle Ike and the woman fastened to him, and when they picked them up, and the old man was uncoupled from the woman, and her husband had confided to Uncle Ike what he thought of him, and they had put out the fire in his comforter, which had caught from the tobacco in his broken pipe, the manager of the rink said Uncle Ike would have to get off the floor, or be roped and branded, the old man called a carriage and went home and sent for a doctor. And here he was on the lounge, after the doctor had patched him up with court plaster, and reduced the swelling on his head, and he pulled a quilt over his head and tried to sleep away the New Year's afternoon, and forget that he had made a fool of himself. The boys had skated all the forenoon, and had come home to see how Uncle Ike was, and as they tip-toed into the room, looking hot from skating and frightened about the old man, and Aunt Almira appeared in the door and said "Hush," the boys were paralyzed.

"Has any time been set for the funeral?" said the red-headed boy, as he looked at the remains on the lounge.

"Condum you, I ain't dead," said Uncle Ike, throwing the quilt off his head, and displaying strips of court plaster on his head and face. "Think a man is dead just 'cause his skates come off? I am all right; only the doc says I am not to get up."

"The doc is right," said the boy. "You won't get up in a week. But didn't he do a dandy job pasting on Uncle Ike's ear with court plaster? When the boys found that ear on the ice nobody thought it could ever be saved."

"The ear didn't come clear off," said Uncle Ike.

"It struck the ice sort of a glancing blow, and wouldn't have got hurt much only that condum woman hung her skate down the side of my head and it lodged on my ear."

"What was your notion, Uncle Ike, of straddling out there so with your legs? You ought to be hobbled when you skate. You must believe in expansion. McKinley ought to have seen you,"

Condemn you, I ain't dead yet.

and the boy winked at the other boys, who were looking at Uncle Ike as though he was a wonder to be alive.

"Why, you see, since I had the rheumatism in my knees, they don't act like they used to, and when my skates got to going in opposite directions there was not enough unity of purpose in my knee-

to get back to first principles. Ruined a new pair
of pants on that stunt—split from Alpha to Omega,
up one side and down the other, and I guess I
took cold in my throat. Say, boys, did many people there at the rink see me when I fell?" and the
old man tried to roll over, and yelled with the backache.

"Did they see him? Listen to that, will you?"
said the red-headed boy, turning to the other boys.
"Why, Uncle Ike, you were the whole thing. When
you started off whooping, after that woman in the
red dress, your old red comforter trailing out behind, you seemed to imagine you were saving her
from a pack of wolves, and every skater stopped to
see if the police would not run you in and take you
back to the asylum. They all thought a crazy man
with bats in his belfry had got loose, and some are
running yet. That woman you assaulted has been
taken to the Emergency hospital, and a horse doctor says she is foundered from sliding with you on
the ice clear across the rink, and her husband is
going to sue the rink managers for damages, and
have you arrested on a criminal warrant for grabbing her as no gentleman would grab a woman
unless he knew her real well."

"Where did I grab her?" said the old man, trying to sit up and argue the case. "She didn't get
out of the way when I whistled, and when my skate
got loose and I began to fall, sort of in instalments,
I saw that I couldn't go around her, so I slid on

both sides of her, and when I struck her feet, going ninety miles an hour, she sat down on my neck and loosened the vertebra, besides choking me. Say, she was no fairy, either. Seems as though she is on my neck now. I like to go into society as well as any man, but not feet first, with a society lady sitting on my neck. Lucky I had my comforter wound around my neck, to break her fall. Gosh, but my Adam's apple feels as though it had been pounded. Was I going to lay there, after we had slid in that way a whole block, and she cutting off my wind, sitting on my throat, and choke to death? No, sir. I know how I want to die when the time comes, but it is not with a two-hundred pound female that I never met sitting straddle of my neck, yelling 'take him off.' How were they going to take me off, when I was the under dog? I had to do something, so I reached up and took her by the first thing I could get hold of, with one hand, and with the other I reached for her hair, and she got off, and then I breathed for the first time. Say, she is an actress, I'll bet, for she said 'Unhand me, villain,' and then she got up and shook herself. Here, see my shirt bosom. One of that female's skates got in under my vest, and skated down my shirt bosom, and the way she kicked while we were sliding along the ice was a caution. I said to her, 'For heaven's sake, don't kick so, for it will soon be over,' but she kicked the bosom all out of my shirt, and broke my suspenders. I slept once with a man

out West who had Mexican spurs on, but I felt
safer than I did sliding with that woman, with her
weight on my throat, and her skates in my stomach.
Hand me that tumbler with the spoon on, the doctor says I must try to sleep," and the old man took
his medicine, rolled over and went to sleep, while
the boys went back to the rink for the afternoon
performance, the red-headed boy giving Uncle Ike
this parting shot:

"Uncle Ike, you better wear a side-saddle on
your neck the next time you chase a woman on
skates."

HE KICKS ON CAFETERIA.

It was after 4 o'clock in the afternoon and Uncle
Ike was sitting in a stuffed chair, his leg on an adja-
cent lounge, pillows to his back, one arm in a sling,
and looking about as mad and disgusted as a man
can be and live. It was a week since he had gone
out skating with the boys, and while he thought
he was not much hurt, when he was brought home,
every day since some new ache had appeared, in
some new place, until now he had not a bone but
needed a soothing application, and not a muscle
did he own that was not cramped and uncomfort-
able, while the lumbago in his back was worse than
it had ever been, and he had thrown his old skates

in the stove and taken an oath never to try to be a boy again. To add to his discomfort, the red-headed boy had not come home from school at luncheon time, and the old man was lonesome and cross, and as he listened he heard the boy stamping the snow off his boots on the front steps, and he decided that he would be indignant at being left alone, and make the boy feel bad.

"Gosh, but I am hungry," said the boy, as he came in the room, steaming with perspiration from playing shinny all the way home, and left the front door open. "Uncle Ike, do you suppose there is any of that turkey left that we had last Thanksgiving? I could chew a frozen drumstick to the queen's taste," and he rushed for the pantry.

"Shut that door, condum you," shouted Uncle Ike, holding up his smoking pipe so the stem, with a tear on the extreme end, pointed to the open door policy of the crazy boy. "Get a man bundled up, sick as a horse, his pores all open, and then open the barn door, and freeze him to death. Say, where were you at lunch time, staying away and leaving me to carve my own hash, and no one to help me into my chair, and put my foot on a hassock? Golblast a boy, anyway. Don't think of old folks, but just want to run and play, and yell, and eat."

"O, I took lunch at the Cafeteria," said the boy, as he came out of the pantry with a few links of cold fried sausage, which he was swallowing, strings and all, with the hunger of a school boy.

"O, you took lunch at the Cafeteria," said the old man, with no idea on earth what a Cafeteria was, or where it was. "This extravagance will hurt you. You get in the habit of going to Cafeterias, and blowing in your money, and you will get so Delmonico will have to open a place here, and you will not feel that you have dined unless you have a cold bottle and a warm bird. What is a Cafeteria, anyway, and what did you eat for lunch that makes you so confounded hungry?"

"O, I thought you smart people knew all about it," said the boy, as Uncle Ike fixed his leg on the lounge so the boy could sit down beside it. "Well, a young lady, who had noticed that school children are gradually starving to death, from their inability to get enough to eat at home, has opened a restaurant called a Cafeteria, in the school, where we can go and pay five cents and get a dandy lunch, just like at a party. You can get pea soup, and creamed potatoes, and milk, and fruit, and sandwiches, and paper napkins, and the paper napkins make the finest spitballs to throw at the teacher, or up to the ceiling, cause they stick just like putty balls. But you can't get enough Cafeteria for five cents to gorge yourself, and after you have had lunch you are just as hollow as can be, and can run a foot race. If I was in training for a prize fight, and wanted to reduce my weight, I would diet at a

Cafeteria. Say, Uncle Ike, to-morrow I am going
to take a quarter, and go to the Cafeteria, the first
one, and eat the whole blamed business. You
ought to go up there once, and see that girl that
runs the Cafeteria, and turn yourself loose and
create a famine."

"How old is she?" asked Uncle Ike.

"O, about forty-five," said the boy, as he rested
his elbow on Uncle Ike's lame foot.

"I'll not go," said Uncle Ike. "And so they have
opened a swell restaurant in the school house.
Well, my boy, this world is getting too gay for me,
and I guess I better move on to the beautiful beyond. When I think of the old school days of my
youth, when the boys brought their dinner to
school in baskets and tin pails, and sat down in the
snow and filled up, and then think of children of
to-day at school eating split pea soup and sponge
cake, and making a society function of it, with paper napkins and finger bowls, I am ready to die.
Say, if you had lived forty years ago, and gone to
a district school with us boys, and eaten cold boiled
potatoes, pork and mince pies, such as mother used
to make, and had to cut wood and carry it in, and
slide down hill a mile long, you would not be so
pale, and your hair would lie down, instead of each
hair standing up to be counted. It was that kind
of living that made school boys grow up to be men.
You will turn out to be a milliner, or a dressmaker,
if you are brought up this way. Cafeteria! O, fill

my pipe, boy, and get me some rough on rats, and
let me die while I have some respect for the school
system of my country."

"O, Uncle Ike, don't feel that way," said the boy,
as he put his hand on the old man's bald head, and
skirmished around there for a hair that had with-

If you had gone to a district school with us boys.

stood the frosts of sixty winters. "We will soon
put a stop to the Cafeteria business. Us boys have
already formed a conspiracy to break it up. We are
going to eat everything the woman has got, the
first round, to-morrow, and then organize the
scholars who don't get anything into a bread riot,
and we are going to paint banners, 'Down with the
Cafeteria! A bas the Cafeteria! Viva the tin din-

ner pail!' and scare that woman out of business.
Don't you worry, Uncle Ike. Trust us anarchists.
We won't do a thing to the paper napkin outfit.
Now, Uncle Ike, we have settled this Cafeteria
affair, and the incident being closed, I want you to
tell me how it is that General Buller does not go to
the relief of General White at Ladysmith. I want
to write an essay on the subject, to deliver in
school, and I want my information right from the
fountain head.   Are the Boers so much better
fighters than the Confederates were in our war?
Are there any mountains in this country that could
keep American soldiers from going where they
want to go? What is the reason the British do not
walk right through the Boers, or go around them?
Is it because they don't want to be killed?"

"Sh-sh! Now come up close, and I will tell you
something," said Uncle Ike, as he lit up the old
pipe again. "The facilities for sending news home
is too good, and they have too many officers who
belong to the aristocracy. Don't you notice that
when the names of a mess of killed and wounded is
sent to London the country goes into hysterics,
and the papers jump onto the general who loses
men, and wants him removed? Instead of sending
the names home in instalments the way to do is to
cut the telegraph wires and have one Gettysburg
there on the Modder river. Just start, and keep
going, walk over the hills and have a trail, get the
Boers on the run, and beat them to Ladysmith,

and let White come out and maul them. You
can't run a war without having plenty of dead people, and if a general waits till he whips his enemy,
and then tells about how many men he has lost,
the mourning can all be done at once. There is no
soft snap in war. You can't economize in human
life very well. When a soldier enlists he should
make his will the week before he signs the enlist-

There is no soft snap in **war**.

ment paper, then think it over a week, and then
go in, with the belief that he never will come back.
If he comes back he is ahead of the game of war.
When a general feels that the list of killed that
he sends home is the same as a confession of in-
competency, and that he is liable to give his place
to some one who can send in smaller death lists,
he is losing his usefulness. The way for people at

home to do is to take rosters of the regiments at
the front, and look upon them all as dead, until
they show up after the war. Consider that they
have gone to war to die, the same as a man takes
poison. If the soldier is lucky in dodging bullets,
he ranks with the attempted suicide who has a doctor get into his midst with a stomach pump before
it is everlastingly too late. A general should not
feel as though he was obliged to apologize to his
government and his people every time some of his
men are killed. He should go right on and fight,
and win, and when he sends the news, it should be
about as follows:

" 'The enemy is defeated and on the run, and we
are chasing them towards the sea. The following is
the roll of honor,' and then give a list of the dead
and wounded. The telegraph should only be used
after the fight is over."

THEY TALK ENTIRELY OF DOGS.

It was Sunday afternoon, and Uncle Ike and the
red-headed boy were trying to kill time, by reading
the papers and talking over the contents. They
had discussed the different wars until there were
blisters on their tongues, and were looking for
something else to take opposite sides on, when

suddenly the tears came to the boy's eyes, and he
laid down the paper and looked out at the snow-
storm that was rapidly covering the ground.

"What you crying about?" said Uncle Ike, as
he lit the pipe for the hundredth time, and smoked,
and made up a face as though the tobacco did not
smell as good as usual, and blew a blast to cool the
blister on his tongue. "I know what ails you. You
have found some love story, where a girl has kept
a fellow on a string a long time, and then married
somebody else. I know it, because you always
choke up when you read a love story. Tell me,
isn't it a love story you have been reading?"

"Yes, Uncle Ike, it is a love story, but not the
kind you think it is. Here it is, a story about a man
being found dead in a marsh, near the railroad
track, and his little spaniel dog sitting up on the
bank, waiting for the master to come back out of
the marsh, and go home. Say, Uncle Ike, to me
that is about the most touching thing in the papers.
This man was a German saloonkeeper, who had
been drinking hard, and had had delirium tremens.
He gets up in the night and goes out on the railroad track, and the faithful dog gets up and
stretches himself, and says, 'I don't know what
the old man is going out for, this time of night,
but I shall go with him,' and he leaves his warm
bed and follows the staggering footsteps of his master away out on the railroad track, and the man
walks down to the edge of the marsh and is

drowned in the mud and water. The dog does not know the meaning of it all, but thinks it is all right, probably, though he is a little nervous because the master stays so long, and he whines, and runs up and down the track and makes a path on the gravel, keeping guard over the master, a few feet away, dead. The dog waits until daylight, and then he can see the face of his master, and his hat, and he thinks the old man has probably discovered some new way of fishing, and he lies down between the ends of two ties, and shivers, and closes one eye and keeps the other on the master, there in the marsh, whom he loves, notwithstanding his bad habits. And when the sun rises, and the master does not move, the dog is sure something is the matter, so he goes down to the marsh, as near the body as possible, and sniffs, and whines, and wags his tail, and jumps up and down as he has often done when he wanted the master to play with him, and then he picks up a stick and runs up and down the track, hoping the master will come and throw it away off in the water, so he can go after it, but the dead master pays no attention to him, and then he drops the stick and sets up a mournful howl that brings the bridgetender from away up the track, and when the bridgetender comes the dog licks his hand, and wags his tail, and runs toward the place where the master is at rest, as much as to say, 'I do wish you would see what is the reason my master does not come out of that nasty place, for he has been there half the night, and pays no more attention to me than as though I was no relation to him,' and then the bridgetender sees the man is dead and calls the police, and the ambulance, and when the procession moves the dog walks behind the ambulance, knowing something awful has happened, and so sad that when a policeman pats him on the head he only wags his tail the least bit, and

Sets up a mournful howl.

so slow that the long hairs on the tail do not seem to move, and his eyes show that his heart is breaking."

"O, say, let up," said Uncle Ike, as he took off his glasses and wiped the perspiration off them, and then wiped wet water out of his eyes, and his nose looked red. "What's the use of harrowing up a fellow that way, on Sunday, when he wants to be gay? Gosh, but there is something about a dog that appeals to me. A dog is the most faithful animal that ever was made, and he sticks to you when all the world has turned its back on you. He looks upon his master as the chief, and will starve for him, fight for him, die for him."

"Uncle Ike, don't you think a dog has a soul?" said the boy, thinking of all the good things he had ever known.

"Well, I wouldn't hardly want to accuse a dog of that," said Uncle Ike, crushing some cut plug tobacco between the palms of his hands, and filling his pipe again, and standing on one leg to scratch a match on the bottom of his shoe, to save his Sunday trousers. "When I think of some men who have souls, supposedly, and are so mean and treacherous and cruel that a dog wouldn't have anything to do with them, I think it is just as well that a dog has no soul, because a decent dog, with a soul, a dog that never did any harm, and would live by the golden rule, might go to heaven, while some men would not, and that would create trouble for St. Peter, as the people who didn't get inside the golden gates would bring it up against good old St. Peter in the next campaign, and score him in the platform, and get out injunctions restraining him from letting dogs in, while men who had always voted the straight ticket, and spent their money for the party, were turned down. No, I guess it is better for a dog to be just a dog, with no worry about where he is going to when he dies. Did you ever have a strange dog fall in love with you, and you try to drive him away, and have him keep right on loving you, until you had to surrender?"

"I don't know," said the boy, trying to think over his love affairs, "I have had everything in love with me, I guess, that knows how. Did you ever have a dog get mashed on you, Uncle Ike?"

"Got a case now, worst you ever saw," said Uncle Ike, blushing as though it was a woman in love with him. "Along last fall I was walking along the sidewalk, when I saw a red Irish setter dog, looking hungry, with burrs in his tail, and as I got beside him he looked up at me inquiringly, and I said, 'Hello, old man, you look hungry,' and I put out my hand and touched him on the nose, just a little love pat, such as you might give to a girl on her hair, kind of stroking it, till she looked up at you as much as to say, 'Can this be love?' When I touched that dog he wagged his tail, and walked right behind me, clear home. I sat down on the steps and he came up to me and put his head in my lap, and looked up at me with his beautiful hazel eyes, and I pulled the burrs out of his tail, and then I got him something to eat, and then told him to run along home. At the word 'home' the dog looked so sad that I felt he had no home, but I knew your Aunt Almira wouldn't let me have a dog around, so I tried to drive him away. Do you know that dog went off a little way and laid down beside a telephone pole, with his nose towards the house, and wouldn't go any farther. I went in the house, and was busy for a couple of hours, when I looked out of the window, and there he was, watching the door. I went out to take a walk, and the dog got up and followed me, wagging his tail all the time, and occasionally putting his cold nose on my hand. I thought I would take him off somewhere and leave him, but he had a 'you can't lose me, old man' air about him that touched me, and he came home with me. I could see he was mashed on me, but I didn't want the intimacy to go too far, and I told the dog he must break away, and fix his affections on some man who was in position to return them, but he wouldn't have it. I was the only man there was, that was all. It was that time you were off camping, a couple of weeks, and I must admit that the dog took your place as a companion to a certain extent. He had fleas, and when he would scratch himself, and bite a flea place as though he was mad, I enjoyed him. One day when Aunt Almira was at a whist party I took the dog to the bathroom and washed him with toilet soap, and filled him with flea powder, and I think every flea left him right there. I know your aunt has complained of fleas off and on ever since. Well, as long as it was warm he stayed out in the street, but in the morning he would be at the door watching for me, and your aunt has driven him away with a broom a hundred times, and she has asked me whose dog it was, and I have told her I didn't know. She has seen him following me, and has asked me why I allowed that dog to follow me, and I have told her that the constitution provides that a dog may follow anybody, as long as he does not interfere with their happiness. The dog seems to know that he must dissemble, and not let your aunt know that he is in love with me, so when she

is in sight he pretends that he is just out for a stroll,
and it has just happened so, that he and I have met.
He does not come near the house now, for since
the cold weather came on I have hired him boarded
and lodged at a livery stable around the corner.
I have thought that the dog might become at-

He tries to tell me in the dog language.

tached to some one else, but he is as true to me
as though I was the only man, and when he is fed
in the morning he comes as near the house as he
thinks is wise, and waits for me, and he never rec-
ognizes me until he has looked all around, to see

if your aunt is looking, and when he finds the coast
is clear, he winks one eye, wags his tail a little, as
much as to say, 'We understand each other, boss,'
but when we turn a corner, and are out of sight of
the house, he jumps upon me, and barks and plays,
and licks my hand, and tries to tell me in the dog
language that he just loves the ground I walk on.
O boy, there is something about a dog that you
can't explain."

"Well, what are you going to do about this case
of love at first sight?" said the boy. "You going
to keep this mash boarding around? Why don't
you announce to the world that he is your dog, and
stop leading this Doctor Jekyll and Mr. Hyde
double life?"

"I have got it all fixed," said Uncle Ike, laughing. "I am going to pretend to be sick, and I have
got the doctor to prescribe a dog for me, on account of my needing constant companionship, and
when your aunt feels that it is a case of life and
death with me, she will let me keep a dog, see, and I
will round up that old setter, too quick, and we will
have a new lease of life. Ah, there he is now, see,
there on the corner! I must go out and walk with
the old fellow!" and Uncle Ike put on his overcoat
and went out to the trysting place, with a smile
and the air was soon full of dog tail and bark.

DOGS, AGAIN, IN THE FAMILY.

Uncle Ike had made it up with Aunt Almira so she would let the setter dog that had become so attached to the old man come into the house, and become one of the family, on the understanding that Uncle Ike should be responsible that the dog should stay on a mat constantly when it was in the house, and that its feet should be wiped before it came in, that the dog should not scratch the door with its nails, should not scratch itself, nor bite itself, as though seeking fleas, while in the house, should not be fed anything at the table, though it might sit quietly beside Uncle Ike during the meal hours; that it should not jump up onto anybody with its forefeet, and act tickled; that it should not get up on a lounge until a blanket had been spread on the lounge for it to lie on, and that the dog should not shed its hair. Uncle Ike knew it was an awful responsibility for him to take, to vouch for the dog, but he wanted the dog's company so bad that he would agree to anything, so he stood sponsor for the setter, and he and the dog had spent all the afternoon in the sitting room, talking it over, and arriving at an understanding. The dog proved to be too long for the mat that had been provided, and while a portion of its body was on the mat all right enough, when Aunt Almira came into the room and caught it unawares, its hind legs reached over onto the carpet, on one end, and its head and shoulders lapped over on the other end. She complained of this, and Uncle Ike offered to have a part of the dog cut off, but being a member of the Humane society, she would not hear to that, so it was decided to take the dog's measure, and buy a new mat. Uncle Ike tried to avoid the expense of the new mat, by telling her it was one of these telescope dogs that would close up if you touched the combination, but he couldn't find the combination. The dog had broken the compact, at breakfast time, and had frightened Aunt Almira. The dog was sitting on the floor beside Uncle Ike, its head raised far above the table, and Aunt Almira had declared that if she had known that the dog was so much taller when he sat down than when he stood up, she never would have consented to have him in the house, but Uncle Ike had made the dog "charge," and surreptitiously given it a crust of bread to chew on. All would have been well if the red-headed boy had not taken a link of sausage on a fork, held it towards the dog and said "Speak." The dog raised up on its hind legs till its head was near the gas fixtures, and gave vent to a prolonged combination of bark and howl, like a pack of hounds after a rabbit, and grabbed the sausage, a piece of the fork and some of the boy's fingers, and showed its cannibalistic tendencies by swallowing the sausage whole and barking for more, while Aunt Almira held her hands to her ears, the curls that habitually hung down beside her face standing up straight, and the color leaving her face, while she yelled:

"Uncle Ike, take that dog out doors."

"He won't come," said Uncle Ike, as he grabbed the dog's tail, as the dog went under the table, and raised up till the table seemed on a pivot. "He

He won't come, said Uncle Ike.

likes it in the house. You don't know anything about dogs. When you get this dog filled up once, he will lie down as quiet as a lamb, and sleep the sleep of innocence, and then all you got to do is to feed him a little each day, but now he is empty." To have peace, Aunt Almira fed the dog, and Uncle Ike fed him, and the red-headed boy fed him, and when breakfast was over all were hungry, including the dog.

It was now afternoon, near time for the boy to return from school, and Uncle Ike was a bit weary of watching the dog, to keep it from scratching itself, and had finally told Aunt Almira that it was the same way with a dog about scratching itself as it was about eating. Let it scratch itself until it had got all scratched up plenty ahead, and it wouldn't scratch any more, and the old lady had concluded to let it scratch, though she didn't believe that would stop it, and now she was filling a carpet sweeper with dog hair, and the dog, who had had his tail drawn into the sweeper, sat on its haunches, with its tail curled under it, and had its nose on Uncle Ike's knee, and was looking up into the old man's face as though saying, "There is no nuisance around a house any greater than a woman with a carpet sweeper," and Uncle Ike winked at the dog as though saying, "What the good Lord ever made women for, beats me." Uncle Ike looked out of the window, up the street, and saw the red-headed boy coming towards home leisurely, with a bundle under his arm, and some long thing in his hand, the end of which he was chewing, and he was looking into windows on both sides of the street, smiling in a vacant sort of way, not as though he was tickled, but as though his face was made of putty. Uncle Ike felt as though the boy had been studying too hard, and having given his breakfast largely to the dog, had got hungry, bought a loaf of rye bread, and lost his mind while chewing it. He watched the boy in sorrow, as he came up the walk, and thought he would get him in bed at once, and put ice on his head, when the boy bounded into the room, the dog barked and jumped all over him, stole his bread and crawled under the lounge and began to tear the loaf to pieces, while Aunt Almira jabbed him with the carpet sweeper and he growled at her and showed his teeth.

"What is the matter, my poor boy?" said Uncle Ike, as he stood between the old lady and the rapidly filling well bread dog. "Why are you acting like this on the street, eating bread as you go along, and looking at people as though your mind was weak?"

"I was trying to make a Franklin mash," said the boy, as he winked at Uncle Ike. "Didn't you ever read about Ben Franklin?"

"Why, yes, I have read the biography of Franklin, the statesman, the signer of the Declaration of Independence, the scientist who brought lightning from the clouds onto his head, the ambassador, the editor, and all that," said Uncle Ike, looking for something to get behind if the boy should go crazy and get violent.

"Well, we had Franklin exercises at school to-day and everybody read something about Benjamin Franklin, and we were all advised to emulate the example of Franklin. You remember when Franklin entered Philadelphia as an apprentice looking for a job, he was poor, and hungry, and he spent his last money for a loaf of bread, and he walked along Market street, eating the bread, while he carried a soiled shirt under his arm, done up in a newspaper. History relates that while he was chewing the bread, and leaning against a railing, his eye c a u g h t the most beautiful girl that was ever seen. She looked at him, and he looked at her, and fire flashed from both their eyes, and he smiled at her with a broad, open-faced smile, with printer's ink on it, and her face lighted up, and she looked sweet at him, and came down and took hold of

The Benjamin Franklin Mash.

Franklin's hand, and he began to squeeze her hand, and wipe printer's ink on her knuckles, and before he could take a second bite of the bread they were in love, and he offered himself to her, and offered to endow her with all his worldly goods, which consisted of the loaf of bread and the shirt, and he broke off half the bread, and gave it to her, and she kept it for a souvenir, and she sent his shirt to the wash with her own clothes, and thus compromised herself, and finally they were married. Well, I worked the Franklin mash act all the way from school, and winked at girls, and smiled on them, but never caught a single one. One girl sent her brother after me with a baseball bat, another set a dog on me, and at one place a policeman told me to 'move on,' and one girl called her father to the window, and when he saw me he started after his gun, and I run two blocks. Say, Uncle Ike, times must have changed terribly since Franklin was mashing. He seemed to strike a snap the first jump out of the box. How do you account for it?"

"Well, I am glad to know you are not as crazy as you look," said Uncle Ike, lighting his pipe, and looking relieved, as the smoke began to appear. "But you should emulate some of Franklin's statesmanlike qualities, instead of that simple incident of his early career. Mashing is a good deal like speculating in stocks. If you go into it deliberately, you lay down your bundle, and get busted, but if you take a flyer once in a while, you may win. A man might pass a million women, and never feel the effects at all, but if it should happen that he met the right one, the one ordained for him, the first time he saw her he would feel it all over him, and he would think lightning had struck him. That was the way it was with Franklin. His footsteps were directed to that girl by a higher power, and it would have been all the same if he had been riding in a coach and four, as it was when he appeared as a tramp printer looking for a job."

"What's that dog eating?" said the boy, looking under the lounge.

"Condemned if he hasn't ruined my hat, chewing it. He must be cutting teeth," and the old man grabbed the dog by a hind leg and threw him out-doors, and the dog scratched to get in, thinking he was having fun.

———

ON THE FIRING LINE IN SOUTH AFRICA AND KENTUCKY.

It was twenty degrees below zero, and Uncle Ike had got up out of bed before daylight, because it was too cold to sleep. He had put on a hunting sweater, and thick woolen socks, pulled an old pair of moccasins over them, and with a moth-eaten fur cap on, and buckskin mittens that he used to chop wood in thirty years ago, he had gone down to the sitting room, built a fire in the grate, lit up his old clay pipe, and was standing with his back to the grate fire and his face towards the register, slowly freezing to death, he thought. He had yelled to the red-headed boy that he needn't get up to go to school that morning, but he could come down pretty soon and bring up a lot of soft coal from the cellar, to keep warm. The boy could smell the tobacco smoke up in his room, and he could hear the old man sing "From Greenland's Icy Mountains," and he yelled back, in a muffled voice, for

He built a fire in the grate.

Uncle Ike to change his luck by singing "My Old Kentucky Home," or "My Warm Baby," but the old man said he was afraid to sing the "Old Kentucky Home," for fear some one would shoot him.

"Come down here and read about the shooting of your friend Goebel in Kentucky," said Uncle Ike, as he heard the boy jump out of bed, and heard his toes crack with the cold. "The paper is full of news this morning. Goebel has been driven across the Tagula river with great loss, and Buller's army has been headed off in the mountains of Kentucky and can't get to Frankfort to arrest the Legislature."

"O, what you giving us, Uncle Ike?" said the boy, as he came into the sitting room, shivering, with the most of his clothes under his arm, and backed up to the fireplace in his nightshirt and tried to get warm. "Gosh, you must have got a new brand of tobacco," and the boy took a long sniff, and said that was the best tobacco he ever knew Uncle Ike to smoke.

Uncle Ike sniffed for a moment, looked anxious and uncertain, and finally grabbed hold of the tail of the boy's nightshirt, and after rolling in his hands for a moment, he said, "Tain't tobacco you smell at all. Your nightshirt is afire."

"That's so, sure as you live," said the boy, as he took off the nightshirt, looked at the scorched tail, and then put on his clothes. "But, Uncle Ike, if I was in your place I would cut up that nightshirt and smoke it with that dog-leg tobacco, as it gives it a flavor that is regular Havana." It was not long before they got warmed up so they could read the headlines in the morning paper, and the boy began to nag the old man.

"Uncle Ike, us boys had a meeting last night, and we decided to discharge you as our military

expert. We have been listening to you, telling how
the British were going to walk right through the
Boers, and every day you get the red coats licked
to a standstill, and yet you keep saying it is going to
be all right. We are about sick of standing by the
British on your account, and have about concluded
we are for the Boers. How do you account for the
British taking that Spion-kop, and staying there
over night, just long enough to get used to dodging shells from the Boers, and then stampeding,
say?" and the boy looked hurt at being deceived
by the old gentleman, who had claimed to know all
about the object of the movements of the British.

"Well," said Uncle Ike, smoking and smoking,
to give him time to think what to say, and trying
to look wise, but making a failure of it, "I'll tell
you. You see, in war, a portion of the army has to
go out and feel of the enemy, and get its position
located, so the main army can take advantage of it,
and go in and knock 'em, see? Buller was just
fooling the Boers, by making a demonstration, and
getting their attention, and while they are watching Buller, some other general will sly up in the
rear, and drive them to the woods. You just
watch."

"Yes, I been watching—all us boys been watching," said the boy, looking the great military
expert squarely in the eye. "Buller's army was not
a scouting party. He took every man Jack he had
across that river, expecting to scare those Dutch-

men out of their boots, and get them on the run,
eating their summer sausage as they ran, and he
told friends of mine he would relieve Ladysmith.
What did he do? He run his brave men up against
a katzenjammer kop, and they let him take it, after
they had got the range so they could drop shells
right into every spot, and after Buller had telegraphed his congratulations to the Queen, on having a new kop in the family, the Boers began to cut
loose, and drop shells right on top of them, and
pretty soon you couldn't see the British for the
dust they kicked up going down that hill, and Buller thought a million Boers were chasing them, and
he trekked his whole army back across the river,
and the Boers laughed so their sides ached, and
Buller telegraphed his regrets, while Gen. Roberts,
with seventy-five thousand men, was two hundred
miles away, playing seven-up with Kitchener, waiting for Buller to throw up his hands and beg for
help. The whole thing shows a jealousy between
the British officers, and I'll bet Gen. Roberts never
strikes a blow until Buller commits suicide and
White surrenders. What the British ought to have
is Gen. Otis, and an Alger in its war department."

"O, get out," said the old man, as he bit off a
piece of the end of his pipe, "you are just a sample
of the critics of the conduct of a war. In all cases
where smart Alecks kick at generals in any war,
you will find, if you inquire into their condition,
they don't know enough to keep their shirts out of

the fire. You just repeat what you read in the newspapers, written by reporters who wouldn't know a war when they saw one. Did you read Queen Victoria's speech to Parliament? It is as full of good stuff as anything McKinley ever did. Say, when the British get over those mountains, and get the Boers chasing each other back to Pretoria, and the Duke of Marlborough and some of the chappies get to firing off champagne bottles in their rear, and hitting them on the back with their golf clubs and tennis rackets, those Boers will throw up their hands, and say their prayers, and surrender. But you better run some war nearer home. Why don't you take Kentucky? Now what would you do with Kentucky, if I should turn it over to you to settle that scrap?"

"Well, I'll tell you," said the boy, as he tore off a piece of his burned nightshirt, and stuffed it into Uncle Ike's pipe, under the tobacco, and gave the pipe to him, and handed him a match, "I would put the Democrats in a line below Louisville, and the Republicans in a line at Knoxville, and march them towards each other. Every man should have a Winchester and four revolvers, and a bushel of cartridges, and ten bottles each of ten-year-old whisky. I would move the women, children and prohibitionists away from the firing line, over into Tennessee, and let them come together, and just keep shooting and drinking, and burying, until the thing was settled. Then I would take the survivors and put them in charge of state affairs, and make them pass a law that no whisky should ever be made or sold in the state for forty years. Then there would be peace in that state. I tell you, Uncle Ike, there is too much whisky and too little beer in Kentucky. Middle-aged men brag that they have drank whisky all their lives and never were drunk. They mistake drunkenness for a condition of staggering, and think as long as a man can walk he is sober, when the fact is that a man with much whisky in his system is drunk. The brain is in a bad state, the nerves are at a tension, and in the forenoon, until they are nicely filled up, they are dangerous. Most of these fights take place in the forenoon, when the hair pulls from the whisky drank the day before, and they are looking for trouble. Along in the afternoon, when a man has had eight or nine drinks, he don't want to fight, but before that, and after he has had fifteen or twenty drinks, you want to look out. There ought to be a law that a man should wear on his breast a memorandum of the number of drinks he has taken, so that when he has arrived at the danger point, they can all walk on some other street, and give the man a wide berth. If all the whisky in Kentucky could be destroyed, and all the grand fellows in that state should take to drinking beer, it would not be long before you would see the opposite parties in a vendetta laughing with each other, and going about with their arms around their enemies, and they would drink beer together, and say **'Prosit,'** and forget that they ever had a gun or a grudge. The Kentucky men are all right, only they have been brought up on too rich and fiery a drink. Their hair pulls constantly, and they are too nervous. Give them beer, and the wars would soon be over

Their arms around their enemies.

in Kentucky. What you think about it, **Uncle** Ike?"

"Say, you're a dandy," said Uncle Ike, as he took his knife blade and dug the piece of burnt offering out of his pipe. "The breweries ought to send you as a missionary to Kentucky."

ALL ABOUT LIQUID AIR.

"Well, Uncle Ike, what did you think about it?" said the red-headed boy.

"Beats me, bigosh," said the old man.

The cause of this interesting question and answer was a visit to Tripler's exhibit of the wonderful powers of liquid air. Uncle Ike and the boy had been reading about the new discovery and the wonderful things it was going to do in revolutionizing the motive power of the world, that when it was announced that Prof. Tripler, the discoverer, was going to show all about it, the old man got two seats right up in front, and took the boy, with an opera glass, and for two hours they had sat and listened to the rambling remarks of the Professor, and seen the liquid air do things that didn't amount to anything, in a manner to cause people to look at each other and wonder what it was all about. And after the show they had gone home, where Uncle Ike could make up lost time in smoking his pipe, which he had sadly missed at the theater. They were going to talk it over before going to bed.

"I think it is all a fake," said the boy, as he yawned and unlaced his shoes. "How does anybody know it was liquid air that he dipped out of the tank? It looked to me a good deal like a seidlitz powder."

"Oh, don't talk that way about great inventions," said the old man, as he parted his coat-tails and stood with his back to the grate, to warm up his thoughts, as the heat went up his spine to his hair. "There were kickers when the telegraph was first discovered. When the telephone was invented lots of idiots wouldn't believe you could talk over a wire, and steam was considered a work of the devil. Before you are old enough to vote you will see our houses heated by liquid air, which will freeze the microbes and boil ice so it will be red hot. You will see the locomotives squirting liquid air into the fields as they go along, and freezing the cattle so they can be carried to market all refrigerated ready to embalm. The embalmed beef for the soldiers will be frozen so stiff that a soldier will have to file his breakfast off a cold chunk with a rat-tail file. Carriages will be run by liquid air, and it will be used for all purposes that steam is used for. You hear me?"

"Uncle Ike, you are too sanguine," said the boy, as he tried to keep from going to sleep in his chair. "Now, what did Tripler do that demonstrated your theories?"

"Why, where were your eyes? Didn't you see him set a teakettle filled with water on a cake of ice, and see the water boil, while the bottom of the teakettle was covered with ice? What did you think of that, eh? Gosh, that convinced me."

"Convinced you of what?" said the boy, getting

up with his eyes wide open, and standing in front
of the old man.   "How do you know it was water
in the teakettle, or steam coming out of it? Kellar,
the magician, can make a woman disappear from a
cabinet when you are looking right at it, and reap-
pear in another cabinet, ten feet away.   You saw it,
and yet you didn't think Kellar could produce full
grown women out of nothing, did you? You
didn't think he was going to revolutionize the pro-

Why don't Tripler turn it to practical account?

duction of the increase to the human race, by moving a fairy wand, did you, and saying presto,
change? Bah! You can't fool me. Suppose you
can put some chemical in a teakettle, and make it
look as though it was boiling on a cake of ice, what
good is it going to do? Who wants to boil a teakettle on ice anyway, the way ice is selling? That
is all poppy-cock. What I would like to see is

liquid air doing something, besides making a mon-key show of itself. Why don't Tripler turn it to practical account? If he would hitch it up and run a coffee mill by the use of this new wonderful power, the people could see that it would do some-thing. Any chemist can mix doses of things to-gether, and do things that will astonish the beholder. What the people want to see is some-thing done with liquid air besides burning the fin-gers of the operator. You hear me?"

"Yes, I hear you," said the old man, filling his pipe again, and looking mad because the boy would not swallow liquid air without choking up. "Didn't you hear the man say he could freeze three hundred degrees colder than a woman's feet? Think of any-thing being frozen as stiff as that. Didn't you see him soak a piece of felt, that is practically non-combustible, in liquid air, and when he touched a match to it, it exploded like dynamite, and burned him so he had to put liquid air on his hand to cure it? Humph! You are an anarchist, that's what you are."

"What do you know about women's feet being cold, Uncle Ike?" said the boy, as the old man blushed like a schoolboy. "What good is there in freezing anything three hundred degrees below zero? When a thing is frozen down along zero, it is cold enough for all practical purposes. What good is it to soak a piece of felt so it will burn? You can touch off red fire and it will do the same, and

yet nobody claims red fire is going to revolutionize the motive power of the world.   I think the
whole thing is a fake, to draw money at the box
office.   Say, if this liquid air was capable of doing
all that is claimed, wouldn't the inventor stay in
his laboratory and turn it to some account?
Wouldn't he hitch it up onto a wheelbarrow, and
show that it would pull?   Why, so far as was practically demonstrated to-night, a goat hitched to a
soap box is a more valuable power to the world.
A billy goat couldn't boil a teakettle on a piece of
ice, but he can haul a wagon, and his motive power
is cheap, because you don't have to use coal to get
up goat steam.   All you got to do is to feed him
circus posters, and you can have power.   I'll bet an
engine run by ten billy-goat power will discount
any engine that will ever be run by liquid air.
What's the use of showing this stuff to mystify an
audience and not teach them anything?   Suppose
Edison, when he invented anything that was to
revolutionize the world, had left his laboratory and
gone to the theaters and talked at a mark, would
the people have had confidence that he knew what
he was talking about? When Edison got a bee in his
bonnet about telephone, or phonograph, or any of
those things, he locked the door, and had his meals
pushed in through a cat hole, and he worked until
something began to buzz, and when he threw open
the doors something had been done that the world
could understand, see?   The Professor talks about

curing cancer with liquid air, and yet doctors listen
and laugh. A hundred men in this country advertise to cure cancer, and yet if there was one authen-
tic case of a cancer being cured, a regular old he
cancer, the man who cured it would have money to
throw at birds. There are a dozen things that will
act as an antiseptic and cleanse a sore, and heal it,
temporarily, and liquid air may do it as well, but
when there is a cancer in the system nothing will
cure it, unless the patient is born again, and nobody
claims liquid air will born anybody again. How
are you going to harness this liquid air so it will
pull a load? How do you know it will not balk or
buck like a broncho? Even in experiments in a
theater everybody is afraid of it, and it burns or
freezes the inventor so he is scratched like a man
taming a wild cat. Why don't you tell me, Uncle
Ike? You are older than I am."

"Why, boy, I don't know myself. Why didn't
you ask questions of the Professor down at the
theater? He invited everybody to ask him questions."

"Yes, and the first question that was asked, by
a retired officer of the U. S. army, as to whether it
didn't cost more to produce the liquid air than it
was worth as a power, the Professor snubbed the
questioner, with an answer that was mighty near
insulting, and then he backed off and dismissed the
audience, because his hand pained him, when there
were a hundred questions all ready to be fired at

him, by men who wanted to know what all that fizzing and sissing all the evening had amounted to. No, sir, I only ask questions of you, Uncle Ike, because if you know, you will tell me."

"Yes, but didn't you see him freeze that mercury so you could use it for a hammer? That ought to

The old man and boy went upstairs.

convince you of the power of liquid air," said the old man, as he put the heel of one boot against the toe of the other, and began to pull it off.

"Well, what did that amount to?" asked the boy. "I can take a piece of summer sausage as big as a window weight, and leave it outdoors and freeze it, when the thermometer is below zero, and I can drive a nail with it, and not bust the skin on the sausage, but what good is it going to do to the world to make that demonstration? Nobody wants frozen sausage, and there is no horse power in it after the horse out of which the sausage is made is dead. I tell you, Uncle Ike, if you will show me one thing liquid air will do to help the world, I will surrender. If you can run a sewing machine with it, better than you can with electricity, or run a street car, or an engine, or do anything except fool away time on a theater stage without demonstrating anything, I will be on your side, but I can see more good now in a bottle of citrate of magnesia. Let liquid air turn a grindstone, and I cave."

"Well, gol blast the liquid air anyway, let's go to bed and forget it," and the old man and the boy went upstairs, hot under their collars.

THE RED-HEADED BOY GROWS OLDER.

Uncle Ike had begun to realize that the red-headed boy was rapidly growing to be a young man, and he was pleased, in his arguments with the boy, to find that he had opinions of his own and did not hesitate to express them, even though they might conflict with the opinions of his dear old uncle, and he had got so it delighted him beyond measure to stir the boy up on some subject that seemed beyond him, and find that he was pretty well posted. The reports from the high school showed that the boy stood well in everything but "deportment," but he thought he would improve on that. He had noticed a new kind of a badge pinned on the boy's vest, and had discovered that it was the badge of a secret society which had been formed in school, a badge with a Latin name. He did not approve of boy secret societies, but he feared to say much about it, for fear he would not understand the Latin words, and the boy would have a joke on him. He had noticed that the boy was wearing a dress suit, or Tuxedo, that Aunt Almira had caused to be made out of one of Uncle Ike's old coats, and the standing collars the boy wore when he went off to dancing school seemed to the old man little less than suicidal, and he feared the boy's neck would be cut off, but the boy seemed to enjoy it. The boy was upstairs putting on his first pair of long trousers, and Uncle Ike was sitting in the twilight, smoking his pipe. waiting for the boy to come down.

"How do they look, Uncle Ike?" said the boy, as he came into the room, bent over so he could look at the new trousers from top to bottom, proud that for the first time in his life the calves of his legs were covered from the sight of the populace.

"Oh, so-so," said Uncle Ike, as he gave one look

at the boy, and turned his head away in sorrow, because the boy seemed to have grown five years in a minute or two, and he realized suddenly that it would not be long before he would be beyond control.

"Well, so-so don't express it," said the boy, as

I think they are a mighty good fit.

he got up on a chair and looked at his trousers in the mirror on the mantel. "I think they are a mighty good fit, and they make me feel like getting shaved. Feel that rough spot on my upper lip, Uncle Ike? One of the girls at school noticed it to-day, and——"

"You hold on right where you are," said the old man, getting up out of his chair and standing in front of the boy, apparently very much hurt. "Don't you ever let me hear of your getting near enough to a girl so she will notice the prickling sensation of that mustache. Going around scratching girls' faces with your mustache! Say, more boys are driven into society by their first mustache, and lost to their friends, than you have any idea of. That isn't a beard, that you feel. That lip is chapped."

"No, sir," said the boy, as he took Uncle Ike's big thumb and rubbed it on the lip, "that is sure enough hair. Everybody in my class noticed it to-day, and I let some of my most intimate friends pull it, but the boys have all promised to let me pull their mustaches when they first show up."

"Ouch, I guess it is hair, by ginger," said the old man, as he suddenly jerked his thumb away, and put some witch hazel on it. "Say, in a month or six weeks you will have a beard hanging away down on your chest, like a Boer."

"Uncle Ike, I wish you would get some new collars," said the boy, as he run his finger over the edge of the collar that was sawing into his neck. "I have been wearing your collars all winter, to parties, and the edges are just like saw teeth."

"Well, I swan! I thought I was getting short of collars," said the old man, as he examined the collar the boy had on, and took his jack-knife and trimmed off some of the edges. "Next thing you will be wearing my Sunday pants."

"S-h-s-h," said the boy, looking around to see if anybody was listening. "Don't ever say 'pants' again, Uncle Ike. You must say trousers. In the society in which I move a man who says pants is looked upon as a relic of the dark ages. You can't trot in my class if you use such language."

"Is that so," said the old man, as he took the boy by the collar and elbow, and tried to wrestle with him square hold, and found that the boy could wrestle some himself. "What I want to know is, what were you fellows doing with that boy in the back lot at school this afternoon when I passed, standing him on his head in the snow?"

"Oh, that was nothing," said the boy, as he released his hold on the old man's suspenders, and left him puffing like a porpoise, from wrestling. "We were giving him the gimlet degree in our secret society, the Wun Lung, a Latin phrase which signifies great courage. It is a Greek society, with a Latin name, because we do not want to show partiality to any nationality, as we may want to go into politics when we grow up.

"The first degree is exemplified by standing a boy on his head and taking his legs for sweeps, and walking around like they do on a turn table, and boring a hole in the snow with his head, until he suffocates, and then we bring him to by rolling him in the snow. He didn't get the whole degree,

for when we bored him down about a foot in the
snow, and he was just suffocating nicely, one of his
legs got loose, and he kicked a boy's front tooth
out, and we had to postpone the exercises. Uncle
Ike, I would like to propose your name in our
society, and if you will join, I will see that they go

One of his legs got loose.

easy on you in the gimlet degree, on account of
your being bald-headed."

"Well, I guess not," said Uncle Ike, as he looked
at the boy in astonishment. "I don't believe in
any of this secret society foolishness, and you ought
to be ashamed of yourselves. Besides I have taken
more gimlet degrees, and standing on your head
degrees, and scratching gravel with your toe nails

degrees, than you will ever take in all your life. Say, once I fell down three flights of stairs, and landed in a tank of ice water, taking a degree, and if the tank hadn't happened to be right there, your Uncle Ike wouldn't have had a whole bone in his body. They let go of me some way and my foot slipped. Too bad about that boy losing his tooth, but you can take it out of your candidate when you give him the next degree. Well, I see Congress has got down to business at last and has begun to pass the bills," said the old man, picking up the evening paper.

"Let's see, said the boy, looking under Uncle Ike's arm at the paper. "I want to know when one bill passes, so I can renounce my country, take the veil, and move to New Jersey, and go into retirement, and never speak the language of my native land again."

"What bill is it, the one in favor of woman suffrage, or making Filipinos star-spangled American citizens?" said the old man, looking under his glasses at the excited boy.

"Neither of 'em," said the boy, poring over the paper. "I could stand it to go to the polls and vote with women, and I hope I may do so some time, and I could welcome a Tagal to citizenship, if he could guess at his A, B, C's, but that bill to remove all disabilities from deserters and allow them to draw pensions, is the one that makes me want to resign. I could stand for it if the govern-

ment should decide to give scme of the old Confederate soldiers who are destitute a little money to
live on, in their old age, because that would be
rendering good for evil, but when it comes to pen-
sioning the bounty jumpers and the cowards who
enlisted for what there was in it, and then deserted
to the enemy, or run away when the battle opened,
and nobody ever did hear from them until the war
was over, and then they were traveling under an
assumed name, I want to register my protest.
Why, it would be an insult to every soldier who
ever wore the blue, and would be a premium on
white livers, a badge of honor to the coward and
the sneakthief, a laurel crown cf greenbacks on the
brow of the dastard, and an encouragement to be a
cur instead of a hero. If that bill should pass every
schoolboy in this country would join a secret society whose life mission it should be to walk with
hob-nailed shoes on the neck of every man who
voted for it."

"Here, here, don't get excited. Your eyes are
flashing fire, and it is not right to get your back up
the first time you wear long pants. You will break
your suspenders, and then you will be sorry," and
the old man patted the boy on the shoulder. "You
take these things too serious, and get rattled too
easy. The fact is that nobody wants that bill passed
except a few deserters who want to live down their
treason, and a few pension agents who want to bilk
ten dollars out of the deserters, and who do not

care who gets money out of the pension fund, as long as they get a rake-off. They got a poor old senator, who did not know it was loaded, to introduce the bill, but nobody would vote for it. Now, you go out and walk around a block and get used to your long pants, or trousers, rather, but don't look down at them. Just let the people find out that you have arrived at the covered leg period, without telling them about it, and then come here to supper, and I will buy you a mess of collars your own size, that will not chew your ears off, and you can go to dancing school to-night, and take a night-key, and nobody shall sit up for you."

"Gosh, won't it be nice to come in late at night and not hear any sleepy old man say, 'Is that you? It is a wonder you wouldn't stay out all night,'" and the red-headed boy hugged Uncle Ike, and went out to try his new pants on a policeman.

THE OLD KICKER AND STREET CARS.

The Old Kicker stood on the corner waiting for a car, which had been delayed at a crossing, and when it came to the corner where he stood it whizzed by without stopping for him, and he was mad enough to eat nails, but another was right behind, and when it stopped for him he glared at the conductor and said:

"Why didn't that car ahead stop for me? Keep a man standing on the corner all the fall waiting for a car."

"I do not know why it did not stop," said the conductor politely. "Another gentleman is running that car, and he probably had his reasons. The car was probably full, and he was behind time, and he thought it best to have you wait a few seconds rather than to crowd and inconvenience all the passengers. This car is pretty full, but there is a nice new strap you can hang on to. Fare, please."

"Not a cent of fare until I get a seat," said the Old Kicker, as he pushed his way through the crowd like a center rush of a football game, his face pale, and his eyes snapping fire. "I will teach this railroad a lesson."

"The rules are that if a man refuses to pay fare he shall be invited to get off," said the conductor. "Fare, please."

"Talk about getting a franchise extended for a hundred years," said the Old Kicker, as he clutched the strap, and looked around at the passengers to see if they would back him. "The franchise ought to be taken away from the company. Condemdest service I ever saw. Conductors impudent, trolley runs off all the time, and they crowd the cars so a man is in luck if he gets on, and doubly lucky if he gets off alive," and he looked around again at the passengers, but they had all closed their eyes, and appeared to be asleep.

"Take my seat, sir," said a young girl with a bundle of books, who got off at the schoolhouse, and the Old Kicker sat down, and the conductor said, "Fare, please," and he paid with a snarl.

"Pretty tough old road, ain't it?" said the Old Kicker, turning to the man in the seat with him who had opened his eyes when he found he had drawn the Old Kicker for a companion. "I am

You are a lot of lobsters.

going to organize a boycott on this road. Every man that will agree to walk down town every morning, raise his hand." As no one raised a hand the Old Kicker said, "You are a lot of lobsters. You would let a monopoly walk on your necks and never peep," and he looked disgusted.

"I have kept tab on you for twenty years," said the old man in the seat with the Old Kicker, "and you have never done anything but kick. When we had bobtail cars with a single mule and a

trough to feed our nickels into, you kicked. Then
we had two mules, and a conductor, and you
kicked, and when the mules were overloaded you
would never get off and walk uphill, but would
sit still in your seat and kick. Then come the electric power, and you kicked because it was dangerous, and everybody was going to be struck by
lightning, and you kicked because they didn't get
new cars fast enough. You have kicked every time
the company tore up old tracks to put down new
ones, and now that the company has got ten million dollars invested, the best cars to be bought,
and has the most perfect system of any road in
the country, and can handle a crowd of hundreds
of thousands, running cars every minute, day and
night, and never harming a hair of any man's
head, you kick worse than during the old mule
days. I'll tell you what I think. You ought to
be prohibited, by law, from riding on a street car
for six months, and then you would appreciate the
electric railroad."

"Kill him! Kill him!" shouted the passengers,
as the Old Kicker was getting ready to kick some
more, and one big passenger took him by the neck,
and another by the trousers, and they were about
to throw him through a window, when the conductor he had abused came along and said:

"Gentlemen, I beg you not to injure my friend
in any way. While he is on this car he is my guest,
and I am responsible for his safety. He means

well, but his habit of kicking is his greatest fault. Next year we shall run a line of balloons for those who do not like the earth."

"Say, conductor," said the Old Kicker, as he straightened out his coat collar, that the passenger had italicized, "you come down to my office after you get off your run, and I will give you a box of cigars. You are all right, and the road is all right, and I am the champion fool of the whole business. Only I do think they ought to carry us laboring men for four cents," and the Old Kicker got off, looking silly.

THE PASSENGERS SETTLE THE STREET CAR CONTROVERSY.

"Well, I see the fight against the street car extension franchise is getting hot," said the man in the street car with the summer overcoat on, the collar pulled up around his neck, and he trying to look too warm. "Guess the railroad company has got those aldermen all right enough."

"Oh, I don't know," said the man with dandruff on his coat collar, "the street car company is all right enough, and the aldermen know what they are about. I have a brother-in-law in the council, who is in favor of the ordinance, and anybody who says he is not an honest man has got to fight me.

The company is going to let the poor laboring
men ride for four cents, going and coming from
work, and they ought to have the franchise extended a hundred years. You hear me!"

"Yah!" said the man with the egg on his whiskers, as he sat down in a seat near the stove, and
handed the conductor a smooth nickel, "I know

You're a liar.

the alderman you speak of. He used to carry a
can to his work, with a little cup on top to warm
coffee in. Now he lunches at a big hotel, and
drinks champagne out of a bottle, and wears cuffs.
Say, I wouldn't trust——"

"You're a liar, and I can whip you in ten seconds if you will step outside," said the man with

the dandruff on his coat. "Conductor, stop the car!"

"Not much I won't get out and fight you," said the man with the egg on his whiskers. "Get off and maul you, pay five cents extra to get down town, and then you go and complain of me and I have to pay ten dollars and costs for two minutes' pleasure. It comes too high. Let's leave it to arbitration, here, to the Old Kicker."

"What is all this row about?" said the Old Kicker, as he came in puffing and smelling of buckwheat cakes, from having to run half a block to catch the car. "What beats me is how a car always passes your house when you are putting on your overcoat, and when you yell to stop it, the motorman looks the other way. Talk about extending the franchise, for giving a four-cent fare in the morning and evening, I would never get any benefit from it, because I would not get up early enough. I would take away the franchise entirely, and make 'em take passengers for three cents," and the Old Kicker took hold of a strap and grated his teeth.

"You would ruin men who have got twelve millions of dollars invested in the road, because you couldn't catch a car when you thought it ought to stop for you," said the old lawyer, who had been reading a paper, as he looked at the Old Kicker as though he had him on the witness stand. "A man who would advocate the breaking of a contract with a railroad, made in good faith, would break a marriage contract, rob a clothes line, or use a jimmy to get into a neighbor's smoke house."

"Well, condum you, when did they hire you?" said the Old Kicker as he began to look sorry. "Here only t'other day you said if the people would back you, you would make the company carry passengers for three cents, and that the council had a right to take possession of the road, by gosh."

"Well, I have been reading some decisions since, and I find that all you fellows could be arrested for conspiracy for talking the way you do. You are inciting the people to revolution, and are liable for damages for destroying the value of a vested right, and I am keeping tab on you."

There was silence for a minute or two, when the Old Kicker said:

"Looks as though we were going to have some snow."

"I notice the Boers are not doing a thing to the British," said the man with the dandruff on his coat.

"Say, did you see that in the paper about Roberts going back on his second wife, and denying the twins?" said the man with the egg on his whiskers.

"Well, I get off here," said the lawyer, "and I will meet some of you anarchists in court."

The car went on and nobody said a word.

THE FRIGHTENED SALVATION LASSIE.

There was quite a gathering of Oshkosh citizens at one of the hotels a few nights ago, politicians and all kinds of good fellows, with wide hats tipped on one side, and everybody was jolly and taking turns telling stories. A Salvation Army girl came in taking up a collection, and each Oshkosh man plunked a piece of heavy silver down in the tambourine so it sang and rattled the brass fixings, and made the girl smile.

"How is old Gabe Bouck getting along up there?" asked a reporter. "Is he getting old and any more cross than he used to be?"

"Gabe is the same old cuss," said one of the Oshkosh men, "growling and grumbling, and giving away money to anybody who is deserving, and scaring them out of their boots before he gives it to them, and making them cry for joy when he shows them out of the office with courtly grace. He just about supports the Salvation Army. Ever hear about the first Salvation Army girl that ever tackled Gabe?"

"No; what did he do?" said the reporter. "Throw her down stairs?"

"No, never did anything but look at her, and ask her what she wanted. You know Gabe never was a beauty," said the Oshkosh man, looking at himself in a glass, and stroking his chin. "Well, I think this Salvation Army girl was a tenderfoot, and it is my idea that Earl Finch, or Charley Barber, or some of those ducks, put up a job on her, by telling her Mr. Bouck was an easy mark, and shed his wealth easily. Anyway, she went up to his office. Gabe had been jawing George Hilton,

She gave one yell.

and was pacing the floor, mad about something, or studying into a law case, in his shirt sleeves, and one leg of his trousers caught on top of his boot-leg. His face was as pale as Gabe's face can be, without whitewashing it, and his black eyes were flashing fire north and south, and just then the girl opened the door and went in. Gabe was just coming out of the other room, where he was arguing with George, and it is more than probable he let fall some remark that had a dam or two in it, as he was retained in a dam case about that time. He strode towards the girl and said, 'What you want, huh?' in what he took to be a polite inquiry, but the girl, O where was she? She gave one yell and went outdoors, and down the stairs head over appetite, losing her bonnet, and went down Main street towards the river yelling that an Indian had chased her. Before she got to the bridge a policeman, assisted by a lawyer named Weed, grabbed her, thinking she was going to jump into the river. When they got her quiet she told how she had been frightened by an Indian up in an office, who swore, and then come towards her, with his eyes glaring on her, and then she said she fled for her life, and she must have left her bonnet in his office. Mr. Hilton came out of his room when he heard the scream, and the woman and the tambourine going down stairs, and said, 'Colonel, what seems to be the matter?' Gabe said he didn't know. He said a woman with a bonnet like a covered wagon came in, and he politely asked her what it was that she wanted, and he'd be cussed if she didn't set up a war whoop, and go down stairs on all fours, and he thought she must have escaped from the asylum. Say, that Salvation Army woman would be running yet if the boys hadn't caught her."

"Well, how did it turn out?" asked the reporter. "Did Gabe ever find out who she was, and does she shy now when she sees him?"

"Oh, George Hilton, I guess, told Gabe who the girl was, and Gabe sent her a five-dollar note, and sent word to her that when the army got short of rations to come around, and she could have anything there was in his haversack. Anyway, once in a while, you will see a Salvation Army girl, with a smile that has no fear in it, go into Gabe's office, and she does not have to say a word, for he hands her money, and when he says 'huh,' she thinks it is a sweet sound, and if the truth was known she probably thinks the stories about old Gabe being homely are overdrawn, for a man who has done as much for the poor and needy as he has, has lines of beauty around his face. What you fellows going to drink?" and the Oshkosh man got up and moved towards the bar.

THE CHUTES FIRE ESCAPE.

The question of the best means of getting children safely out of school buildings in case of fire, is one in which all persons are interested, whether they have children or not. Cincinnati school officials have devised a cylindrical toboggan slide, which goes around in a circle inside an iron pipe.

The floor is smooth as glass, and a person goes down in two seconds, from the third story, turning around several times, and striking outdoors on the ground perfectly safe, but scared out of their boots. A fireman is at the exit to help them to their feet, after they have come down the chute in a sitting posture. The new device was tried the other day, by superintendent, teachers, and children, as well as parents, and it is said to have been successful. Of course the persons who went down the chutes had plenty of time to fix themselves properly, and not be in a hurry, but how it would be in case of a panic, when children were rushed in in flocks, no one knows. Whether the chutes would get clogged up, and hurt the children, it is impossible to tell. It will not be possible to have the children practice going down the chute frequently, because every trip down wears a pair of pants to the bone. It is not an enjoyable trip, though many took it once, just to demonstrate that it would save life, in case of fire, although after they had got down safely, it seemed to those who had not placed a board inside the basement of their clothes that they had been quite near a fire; in fact, when the school superintendent, who weighs over 200 pounds, was helped to his feet at the bottom of the shaft, he placed his hands on the small of his back and yelled "fire," and tried to sit down on an ice wagon that had stopped near where the experiment was being tried. Some of the lady teachers insisted on going down the chute, saying that they could never advise their pupils to go down until they were able to tell them it was not dangerous, but since they went down two of the young lady teachers have resigned, saying that teaching school was getting to be too much like riding barebacked in a circus.   One of

And yelled "Fire!"

them wouldn't get up off the bottom of the chute until they gave her a cloak to wrap around her, as she was sure she had worn her clothes clear through, and she said she felt as though she would like to visit the north pole, where the chairs were all cut out of solid ice. One young woman thought she would feel better to wear a mackintosh, but when she got to the bottom of the chute there was an odor of burning india-rubber that smelled as though an overshoe had been put in the oven to dry, and when she came to have the mackintosh removed it was found to be welded to her, so it had to be taken off with a caseknife. They got a big German to slide down, and when he reached the bottom and met the firemen, he gave the grand hailing sign of distress of the Order of Elks, saying he felt just as he did the night he was initiated into that order. It made one woman who went down the chutes seasick, and she said they ought to have a doctor, and lemons, to go with it. One woman fainted away, and when they brought her to, she placed her hand on herself, and raised her hand to high heaven, and said she would prosecute the inventor of that fire escape for incendiarism. They got a Chinaman to go down, and when he struck the earth he started on a run and they didn't find him for two days, and when asked how he liked the new fire escape he said, "Melican man heap smart Aleck. Chinaman heap dlama fool. Chinaman walk alle same burn up next time." All who went down the chute declined to take a second trip, but they were anxious to have everybody else go, like people who have joined a lodge, and want to see others take the degrees. There is no doubt the chute will be a good thing in case of panic, but it will not be a favorite slide for those who desire to have fun with themselves.

OLD KICKER HAS HARD LUCK.

The "Old Kicker" stood cn the corner waiting for the street car, and he didn't feel any too pleasant, having attended the McKinley banquet the night before, where he remained till almost daylight. There was a chocolate-cream taste in his mouth, and his hair hurt him as he tried to push it down flat. He noticed, as he entered the car, that every seat had a single passenger, all trying to fill the whole seat, and all looking out of windows, pretending not to notice the Old Kicker, and hoping he would not sit down with them and talk. He walked through the car almost to the front, scowling, and finally saw a friend whom he loved, and with whom he could always have the loveliest quarrel, at a moment's notice, and he punched his friend on the shoulder and said, "Come, hunch along and let a gentleman have a show on this cattle train. You fellows all act like stockholders," and he pushed himself in the narrow seat, beside his friend, and spread out.

"It has come at last," said the friend with a sigh. "I have escaped your sitting with me on the way downtown for over a month, by taking a car a little later than you, but it had to come. I have prayed to be spared such a fate. Now, think, but don't talk, or I will murder you. There ought to be a law against cranks riding with people."

"Well, I like that," said the Old Kicker, punching his friend with his elbow, and squeezing him against the window. "You ought to have been to the banquet. Greatest thing I ever saw. Says McKinley to me, as we were coming out of the banquet hall at 3:30 a. m., says he, as he put his hand on my shoulder——"

"Oh, say, don't give yourself away like that. Well, boys, wouldn't that kill you? This bacillus was so drunk last night that he thinks McKinley spoke to him, and he will go down to his grave boring people about what McKinley said to him. You ought to take something to get that out of your system. What did they have to drink there? You smell like one of those empty kegs on the sidewalk," and the friend laughed until the Old Kicker grated his teeth.

"You know I don't drink," said the Old Kicker. "I just drank Apollinaris water all night, and never swallowed a particle of wine. But I couldn't make my wife believe it, for the boys spilled wine all over my coat."

"Yes, I suppose so," said the friend, "but there is a place where they send people to be cured of the Apollinaris water habit; and I have known several to come out after two weeks' treatment perfectly cured. Nice story, about the boys spilling wine on your clothes. No wonder your wife did not believe it."

"I hope to die if it isn't true," said the Old Kicker, warmly. "Fellows sat on each side of me, young dubs that wanted to get their twelve dollars a plate back, and they would clink glasses over

I'll holler if it wasn't a bunch
of celery.

me, and I just got it all. There ought to be missionaries sent around among wives, to induce them to believe what their husbands say when they get home from a banquet. Now, I went home perfectly sober, but I was tired. Had to walk home,

the cars having stopped running. Say, a railroad
company that will stop running cars before a banquet is over, never ought to have a franchise extended. Well, I didn't have my key, and had to
ring the bell, and my wife came down to the door
just about as mad as she could be at that time
of night. When she opened the door, and got a
whiff of five kinds of wine, she just froze stiff, but
she never said a word. I tried to be cheerful, and
began to tell her that McKinley sent his compli-
ments to her, and a few roses, and when I handed
the roses to her, I hope to holler if it wasn't a
bunch of celery. Then she was madder than ever.
Well, I had on a pair of these last year's long-toed
patent leather shoes, and I stubbed them on every
stair, and stumbled, and when I got upstairs I staggered against both sides of the hall, I was so tired,
and my wife went off in a huff and left me to get
my things off. I got everything off except one
of these patent neckties, with a rubber band, and
I left that on and slept in it. Say, I fooled my
wife, though, this morning. I knew she was loaded
for a lecture, and I got up and dressed, and came
downtown without my breakfast. When I go home
to-night I am going to ride up with the driver of
the Emergency hospital ambulance, who lives up
my way, and when that ambulance stops at the
house she will think I am hurt, and when I come
in, looking pale, she will be so glad I am able to
get in without help that she will throw her arms

around my—why, I have passed my corner. I
ought to have got off two blocks back. Now what
kind of a conductor is that to carry a man by?"
and the Old Kicker walked down the car glaring
at the passengers, and told the conductor he ought
to be discharged.

THE CHURCH ROOF GARDEN.

In discussing, before a meeting of ministers in
New York, the subject of getting people to go to
church in summer, Mr. Moody made the suggestion that they provide roof gardens on top of the
churches, to draw the people away from the ordinary roof gardens and summer gardens, and one
Boston minister has decided to build a roof garden on top of his church, for an experiment. Before expressing an opinion on the success of the
enterprise, the writer would like to know what
they are going to provide in the way of refresh-
ments at these church roof gardens. The people
who visit the worldly roof gardens do not go there
particularly because they are on the roof. They
would go to a basement if there was no garden
on the roof. They go to hear the music, see the
play, and sit around tables and drink something
soft. A church roof garden with nothing but a
prayer meeting, or a sermon, would not take very

well.   People would go once or twice, from curios-
ity, but soon their legs would ache climbing up
there, and they would get dizzy coming down,
and all that.   But if the church gives a sociable
on the roof, where the people are just jolly, instead
of so serious, as they often are in church, and sell
ice-cream and some sort of innocent drink, like
lemonade with some aniline dye in it, and the visitors are allowed to have a good time, the garden
may succeed.   It is getting so you have to get
religion into people by some new method, dis-
guised.   The taking of medicine has changed entirely, and you now get the bitterest in capsules,
or fixed so you can drink it with soda.   If you
have a leg taken off now, you don't know anything about it till you try to put on a boot.   The
editor does not advocate chloroform or ether to
get religion into the sinner, but the days of driving
it into people with a club, or scaring it into them,
has passed.   Nowadays you have got to tame your
sinner, and get him so he will walk up to you
without shying, and when you get his confidence
you can slip it into him when he is not looking,
and the first thing you know he is halter broke,
and later you can hitch him up with some steady
old deacon, and he will learn to help pull the load
all right.   This roof garden idea for a church may
be the turning point in church affairs, but you
have got to give a first-class show, and compete
with the sinner's roof garden.   In summer, saints

and sinners alike are thirsty, and they don't want water. They get water enough all the time, but when they go out for an evening's enjoyment they want something wet that is not water. The trouble is that when people try to invent a drink to quench thirst, that has got no alcohol in it, they make it so innocent that no one wants it, and if they do drink it under protest, it is liable to tie them up in a knot. Cider used to be considered a most

In summer, saints and sinners alike are thirsty.

innocent drink, about proper for a church roof garden, but the confounded stuff is unreliable. If you drink it when it is new it gives you the stomachache, and if you wait till it works, and gets hard, there is alcohol in it, and if you served it in that condition at a church roof garden, the people would feel its effects, all the old church quarrels that have lain dormant for years would be sud-

denly remembered, and before they all got downstairs somebody would get to fighting, the choir
would claw the congregation, the deacons would
fall over each other and resign with their fists full
of hair, so cider will not do. If the church roof
garden is coming in, somebody has got to invent a
beverage that is as smooth as champagne, yet as
innocent as water, that the truly good can drink
and keep perfectly sober, and at the same time
imagine they feel creeping over them slight evi-
dences of a jag, but are mistaken. Whoever will
get up such a drink can take the collection, plate
and all.

THE WOMAN TOUCHER AND TWO SWORDS.

Perhaps the most surprised man that ever lived
is a photographer at Eau Claire. He is a soldier
of the regular army, of the National Guard, and
served his country in the Cuban war, and on being
honorably discharged he opened a peaceful photograph gallery at Eau Claire, and ceased to dream
of blood. He ceased to smell gore, and only
smelled the collodion and the other drug store
things in the dark room. Business came to him,
and in time he wanted a toucher. A toucher is
not one of those people who touch you for the

price of a drink, but a young lady with delicate fingers and a clear liquid eye, who takes a crude photograph of a person of 50 and which looks like a person of 80, and by gently marking out the lines of grief and dissipation, makes it look like a young person of 25. She is the most important person in a photograph gallery. The artist asked for sealed proposals for a toucher, and a young woman answered the summons, who was beautiful in the extreme, and whose touch was as fine as velvet. She could make the picture of a decrepit old man look like a freshman in college, and the artist was well pleased. He did not know her from Mrs. Adam, and didn't care where she came from as long as her touch was right, and her presence like a rare painting. The artist had no more idea that she was a married woman than he would that a schoolgirl with books under her arm was the mother of a family of children. He is not a large man, but as plucky a one as ever wore the blue. The toucher had only touched one day when a 6-foot man, a perfect Hercules, came in the studio and began to abuse the young woman, and finally, it is alleged, took her by the neck, or sleeve, or somewhere, and she screamed for help. The small artist could not see his little toucher touched by a big stranger, so he interfered; the man said the toucher was his wife, and he took an ornamental sword from the wall and went for the soldier, who grabbed another sword, which he had brought

home as a relic from the Cuban trouble, and in a
moment the scene of war was transferred from the
Philippines to Eau Claire.   In passing at each
other's vital parts with the broadswords cameras
were upset, as well as the toucher, showcases were
tipped over, and blood flowed upon the carpet,

Was preparing to saw his head off.

while the head rest rolled around and tripped up
the combatants, and punched each in the neck,
while the toucher yelled all kinds of murder. The
big visitor got the little artist down on the floor
and sat astride his body, and was preparing to saw
his head off with a dull sabre, when neighbors

came in and pulled the big man off, and he started down stairs with a sword, while the artist followed with another, and the affair was transferred to the street. The little soldier had got his fighting blood up, and would have made a record, but the large man got on a street car and told the conductor that the little man coming was a lunatic, and the conductor pulled the fast bell, and the motorman pulled out at a mile a minute for Chippewa Falls, leaving the artist bloody and mad in the middle of the street. When he went back to the studio there was a scene of wreck, the toucher was in a swoon with her feet on a lounge, her head under a midwinter scene painted on canvas, and the big camera across her stomach, while a lawyer was throwing what was supposed to be water on her face, which he got out of a plate in the dark room, but which would color a white graven image the color of a cigarette smoker's fingers. The artist was mad because he had not been informed of her social condition as to husbands, and she cried and said she had not lived with her husband in so long, that she was not sure whether she was married or not. She offered to resign, but when she told the artist of the abuse she had been subjected to, and proved that she was a good wife, he told her she could stay as long as she pleased, and touch all she had a mind to, and if that husband came around again he would fill him so full of lead that he would sink if he fell in the river. As ten thousand people

visited the studio during the two days succeeding
the sword exercise, some are inclined to believe the
whole thing is a scheme to advertise the business.

THE RETIRED SHOOTER.

Those who know what an intense gold Democrat Hon. J. J. Hogan of La Crosse has been since
1896, will be pleased to learn that the genial ex-
speaker has accepted an invitation from Colonel
Wetmore of St. Louis, to visit his game preserve
in the Ozark Mountains of Arkansas, in company
with Col. W. J. Bryan. Many who do not know
Mr. Hogan intimately will imagine that there will
be heated arguments on the gold and silver question down there in the mountains, but there will
be nothing but good fun, and shooting, and eating, and there will not be a politic to be found all
day and all night. The writer believes that Hogan
and Bryan will go to their homes with an enthusiastic love for each other, and that they will be the
warmest friends. Few shooters of to-day know
that J. J. Hogan is one of the best shots in Wisconsin, with a shotgun, or a rifle either, for that
matter. For ten years or so he has not been shooting, and thinks he is getting to logy to tramp
around, but we will wager that he will tire out any

man on that trip in the Ozarks. He has a record of shooting ninety-five or more live pigeons out of a hundred, and when he used to go shooting game it needed a wagon along to carry what fell to his gun, and nothing gave him more pleasure than to go off on a tramp with a friend, a tenderfoot, and walk the friend forty miles about the bluffs of La Crosse, until the friend's tongue would hang out, and he cried quit. When the writer first struck La Crosse in 1871, Hogan sized him up for a chump, and asked him to go out for a day's partridge hunting. The invitation was eagerly accepted, and the two started off towards Viroqua, at daylight, and along towards noon struck towards the Mississippi river, near Bad Axe, and at night brought up six miles below La Crosse, in an exhausted condition, having walked near fifty miles, and never saw a partridge. After the writer got so he could walk, a couple of weeks afterward, the boys all told him that Jim Hogan tried to kill him, but "Jim" was pretty tired in his own right that night. That was a species of hazing they had in La Crosse in those days. If we could get word to Bryan, we should tell him that if Hogan proposed that they saunter through the woods for a walk, that he decline the invitation with thanks. Bryan might beat Hogan talking at a mark, but in walking or shooting he could discount the orator of the Platte. Hogan used to shoot a ten-gauge gun that he loaded so heavy that his arm was always black and blue, six drams of black powder being used, and wads clear up to the end of the shell. All the gang of shooters that used to go together knew better than to ever shoot Hogan's gun, unless they were tired of life. He used to offer to let any of the boys take his gun when they were going out, but nobody ever took it but once. One day a party of us were away up at the head of Pine Creek, opposite La Crosse, shooting teal ducks, and stopped on the banks for lunch, when a smart young farmer came down and wanted to know what right they had on his farm. Hogan was for taking him by the pants and chucking him in the creek, but Hatch said the best way would be to give him a drink of some vile whisky a man named Root used to take along for such cases, so he was given a drink. The drink went to his head and he wanted to shoot a crow that lit on a tree right over him, and Jim offered his gun to the farmer. The boys all turned pale as he put the gun to the top of his shoulder and aimed right straight up, and they began to scatter to get out of range. The farmer stood in a wet place on the bank, and when he pulled on that crow it sounded like a blast in a stone quarry. The man was driven into the ground about a foot, then he fell over in the mud, dropped the gun and put his left hand to his right shoulder, and groaned, and then the crow came down all over him, and the boys gathered around to congratulate him on being alive.

Hogan never moved a muscle, but put in a fresh cartridge, and asked him to take another shot at a blue jay, but he said he never liked to shoot more than once the same day.   The boys pulled his shoulder into place, and pulled him out of the mud, and he staved around a little while, finally asking

He fell over in the mud.

Mr. Hogan if he didn't load his gun a little heavy.   Hogan said he did, sometimes, when he was out shooting geese, but he had only snipe cartridges with him that day.   Before he went away, the farmer said the gun kicked him six times, once after he was down, in the mud, and wanted to know if it wasn't "one of these 'ere repeaters."   If Mr. Hogan has a good time down in Arkansas, and finds that he is as young as he used to be, and can shoot yet, and tire the boys out walking, he will very likely enter again into the sport of shooting, and never retire again, as long as he can see the sights on the old gun.

SCHLEY OUGHT TO HAVE SAID IT.

In the controversy over the battle of Santiago those who are interested in killing off the hero of that battle are publishing a report that at a critical time in the battle, when he gave an order to port the helm of the flagship, and was told by the navigating officer that he might run into the Texas, he said, "D—— the Texas. Let her take care of herself." The matter has become so serious that some of Schley's friends have tried to disprove that he said it, and Schley himself wants to forget it if he did say it, and wishes that he had not said it, or hopes that he didn't, and his enemies, finding they have got him rattled, are making the types jingle in the newspapers to ruin him. The writer believes he said it, and that he was justified in saying it. Suppose a chief of police was riding in a patrol wagon into a mob, to stop a riot, and he told the driver to turn a certain corner, and the driver was afraid of running over a policeman who was leisurely going to attend the riot, the chief might, in his excitement and anxiety to get there, and knowing the policeman never was run over before, might say "D—— O'Grady. Let him look out for himself." If the chief got there and broke up the row, and O'Grady didn't get run over, it would be a mighty mean trick for the board of police commissioners, who were miles away from the row, to impeach the successful chief for swearing about O'Grady in the excitement, taking the word of the driver of the patrol wagon, who was probably scared out of his boots for fear a brick would hit him in the ear. It would be fully as well for Schley to think the incident over, now at his leisure, and admit that he did say it, and tell the hounds that are on his trail that he would say it again under the same circumstances. Is Schley the only sailor that ever used a profane word in battle? If it had been Bob Evans who said it, these same papers that abuse Schley would be quoting his remark as beautiful to contemplate, and Bob would probably have said it if it was his turn to put in. Suppose Admiral Farragut had said something of the kind, they would have had it engraved on his monument. And now, suppose Admiral Dewey had said, "D—— the Baltimore. Let her look out for herself," under similar circumstances at Manila, wouldn't the papers have published the remark in big letters, and wouldn't every Fourth of July orator in the country have quoted the remark as the utterance of a world-

beater, and would not school children be taught
that it was not so bad for Dewey to say it? Since
Ethan Allen demanded the surrender of Ticon-
deroga, "in the name of the great Jehovah and
the Continental Congress," and General Jackson
made use of language not polite yet forcible, and
Farragut said words that almost burned the ropes
when he was lashed to the mast in Mobile Bay, it
comes pretty tough to see the Sampson wor-
shippers around the navy department, many of
whom would swear a blue streak at a street car
conductor who stepped on their patent leathers,
try to ruin the second naval hero of the Spanish
war because he used one little insignificant damn,
on Sunday, in the heat of a battle greater than
Manila.   If this persecution of Schley continues
much longer the people, who are onto the whole
thing, will take matters into their own hands and
place Schley where he can fix every mother's son
of his enemies, and send them out into the cold
world to saw wood, which they would have to do
better than they fight to hold a job long on a
respectable woodpile.

PUMPING A HANDCAR FOR FUN.

Two elderly men were standing on the lake bank above the railroad track recently, watching a gang of section men pump a handcar along the track at a good rate of speed, on their way home from the day's work, when one of the men said:

"I never cared to own a yacht, but I have often thought I would like to own a handcar, and have the right to run anywhere, on any railroad. I believe a man could enjoy the benefits of travel, and at the same time get plenty of exercise. Wouldn't you like to own a handcar?" and the speaker turned to his friend in a pleasant manner.

"Not on your life," said the friend. "You never pumped a handcar, did you?"

"No, I never did," answered the man who had opened the subject. "Did you?"

"I have helped pump a handcar forty miles on a hot Sunday, and I would not take a thousand handcars as a gift. It gives me a pain in the back to see one go by. About forty years ago, when I was quite a strapping boy, I lived at Whitewater, and one Sunday morning I dressed up in a white linen suit and went down by the depot, where some boys had borrowed a handcar, and were running it up and down the track. One of the boys suggested that we slip away and run the car to Janesville and just have a high old time, and I got on and we fairly flew westward. It was one of these old-fashioned handcars that run with a crank and belt. Before we got to Milton my coat-tail got in under the belt and wound around the shaft, and was chewed up and covered with oil and tar, but they pulled me out, and we pumped and pumped. I wanted to go back, but the boys insisted on going to Janesville. We all knew some girls there, and previous to my coat-tail being chewed up in the cogs I thought what a surprise I would give the girls by calling upon them. It was afternoon before we got to Janesville, and by that time my white trousers and shirt were a sight from tar, grease, perspiration and dirt. The boys seemed to be clean enough for society, and they went off to see the girls and left me on the depot platform to watch the handcar. It soon got noised around town that a man at the depot had been run over by a car, and while the whole population of Janesville was not five thousand at that time, I am almost sure that a million people came to the depot and looked me over. One leg of my trousers had been in the cogs also, and the trousers were torn so about half of one bare leg showed, and though I tried to keep the leg next to a hogshead of sugar on the platform, everybody saw it, and they commented on the accident, and asked questions till I thought I should die. I got hungry, and wanted to buy some luncheon, but found that I hadn't a cent in my pockets, or if I had any change when I started from home it had all fallen out of my pockets when I was drawn over the wheel and lost my coat-tail. I have been through some terrible scenes in my life, but I never suffered so from hunger and humiliation as

I thought I should die.

I did that hot Sunday. The boys did not come back till 10 o'clock at night, and they were half full and had had a good time. They loaned me money enough to get a sandwich and a boiled egg at a restaurant, and an egg never went further than that egg did. Then we had to pump the car home, twenty miles, there was no oil, and the

Janesville boys had put sand in the gearing. Oh, what a night! We got home at 3 o'clock in the morning, and found the citizens dragging the mill pond for our bodies. We were arrested for stealing the car, and our parents mauled us for running away, and taken all in all it was the worst day I ever spent in all my life. My own people made the punishment more severe by compelling me to put on those disfigured white linen clothes the next morning and have a tintype taken. It was the worst picture ever seen in the world, but I would give ten dollars for it now, if I could find it. No handcar for me, if you please," and the two old friends walked along the lake bank until they came to a saloon, and went in and took a drink, and the man who had expressed a desire for a handcar said he guessed he was cured, as he never did enjoy a backache, anyway.

SENTENCED TO SUNDAY SCHOOL.

One day last week a tough young colored boy was brought up before a Chicago judge for stealing apples. The judge talked to him kindly, and while he believed the boy was a regular little devil, he concluded not to send him to jail. The judge said: "I sentence you to go to Sunday

school every Sunday for two months." The colored boy turned pale, and sat there with his mouth
open, his underjaw dropping, and the perspiration
in great beads covering his forehead. He acted
much as one sentenced to be hanged might act,
but he said he would accept the sentence, and
carry out its terrible provisions, and he went out
of the court-room and had two fights before he
got home. The sentence was published in the
papers, and the truly good people of the churches
began to compete for the colored boy's custom at
their respective Sunday schools, sending him
cards, giving the hour at which the schools would
convene, and invitations to make himself at home.
He was not a clean boy, and his clothes were torn
and ill-smelling, and he hated to go, but with that
sentence ringing in his ears he felt that he had to
or go to jail, so he showed up at a church on
Sunday morning an hour before it was time, and
amused the other children by playing marbles,
standing on his head, turning cart-wheels, and
other things in his repertoire. One of the boys
guyed him about a hole in his pants, which showed
a black background of shining skin, when he
stood on his head, and he promptly slapped the
jaws of the white boy. He offered to wrestle,
catch-as-catch-can, with a nice boy dressed in
white marseilles, and rolled the boy over, three
points down, and when he got up there was a job
for the cleaner. He kicked off a white straw hat

for another boy, and it went in the sewer, and
when some girls took the part of the white boys,
and said it was only a little fool nigger, he got
down on all fours and barked like a dog and chased
them into the church. The school was called, and
he went in and sat in the superintendent's chair,
and when the school sang a hymn the colored boy
sang "There'll Be a Hot Time in the Old Town
To-night." The superintendent finally got him
into a class by himself, and the lesson was about
the Hebrew children, the fiery furnace, and Elijah
going up in a chariot of fire. The teacher asked
him if he knew anything about the Hebrew children, and he said he wished he had as many dollars
"as he knew about dem Hebrew children. I knows
every one o' dem chillun in de whole block, and I
can lick all of 'em." The teacher said he must not
talk that way or she would have him put out. He
said there were not guys enough in de joint to put
him out, when de judge sentenced him all right.
Asked if he knew anything about the fiery furnace,
he said it's one of these things you have to keep
shoveling in coal or the people upstairs will kick,
and when you get it going they kick because it is
too warm. "Dey kicks at a furnace whatever you
do," said the colored prisoner. Things were going
along quiet enough until the boy in white, who
had been having his clothes wiped in the toilet
room with a towel, came in, and shook his fist at
the colored boy, when he made a jump for the

boy, in the midst of the class, and was pulling his curly hair, and the teachers came to the rescue. He grabbed a lady teacher around the ankles in football style and threw her against the superintendent, and the janitor grabbed the colored boy by the shirt, the boy ran out the door leaving the shirt in the janitor's hands, and the children screamed, some one turned in a police alarm, and the boy escaped with his pants and one suspender, the school adjourned, and the white boy was sent to the laundry. The other churches that wanted the boy to attend their Sunday school are undecided whether they will close up for the summer or ask the judge to suspend the sentence and send the coon to a reform school. It is thought if the sentence stands he will break up all the Sunday schools in Chicago.

THE COLORADO BEAR HUNTERS.

The papers state that Governor Tanner of Illinois has been invited to participate in a grand lion hunt a few miles from Leadville, Colo., and that he has accepted, and is preparing his weapons for the event. It is more than probable that the smart fellows at Leadville are going to have some fun with his honor. There is not a lion within a day's ride of Leadville, but the Eastern tenderfoot does

not know it. Like the Englishmen who come over
here and begin to clean up their guns after they
pass Sandy Hook, to get ready for the shooting
of buffalo in Central park, the governor is getting
his guns ready to shoot lions near Leadville. They
will take him out in a hack, and station him on a
lion runway, and the governor will sit on a log,
and listen for the soft footprints of the king of
beasts, and at every little noise the cold chills will
run up his spine, and while waiting for the lion to
pass along on the path the governor will wish he
was back in Springfield, where there is no animal
more dangerous than a Chicago lobbyist, and
where the shooting is confined to "craps." The
Leadville boys who have a live governor on the
string will play him for all the fun there is in this
lion hunt. They have no doubt prepared a yellow
dog with black spots, to resemble the mountain
lion, and they will muzzle the dog so he cannot
bark and give the snap away, and send him down
the path in front of the governor after a stick, and
after the governor has had the lion fever and forgotten to shoot, he will see the lion return to
where the boys are, with the stick in his mouth.
Those Leadville sports have got a regular menagerie of tame animals that they use to give the
tenderfoot a chance to hunt big game, for nobody
ever kills anything. They have, to the certain
knowledge of the writer, a toothless old grizzly,
that is so tame he will eat huckleberries out of

their hands and go and lie down when they kick
him, that they take out in the woods when
they have distinguished guests to entertain
and let them shoot at Ephraim with smokeless
cartridges from which the bullets have been removed. There is a story to the effect that the
Leadville boys gave President Cleveland a chance
to shoot a grizzly, and after he had emptied the
Winchester at the bear, the animal came up to the
log on which the President was seated and stole
the lunch out of the pocket of his hunting coat,
and then growled, when Mr. Cleveland left his
gun and the tail of his canvas coat and went
down the mountain, breaking brush and frighten-
ing a tame goat that Mr. Lamont was billed to
shoot at, until it pulled up the picket pin and
dragged the rope clear to Leadville. This story
is denied, but many believe it to be true. Anyway, the grizzly is still doing business at the old
stand, and very likely if Governor Tanner survives
the lion hunting and does not kill the painted dog
and get onto the sell, they will give him a chance
to bag Ephraim. Usually the grizzly plays his
part better than he did with Mr. Cleveland. The
game is to let the tenderfoot shoot at the bear a
few times, and then the boys set a dog, a little
terrier, after the bear, and the animal is frightened
over the hills and far away. This usually occurs
on the last day of the hunt, and the boys tell the
distinguished guest that the bear has evidently

got a mortal wound, and they will follow him and
bring in the pelt, and after the bold hunter has got
as far east as Omaha or Chicago, they telegraph
him that they got the bear all right and are having
the pelt tanned for a rug and will send it to him

All about how the bear was killed.

later.   The tenderfoot tells everybody at home
how he killed a grizzly, and after a month has
passed the boys of Leadville express him a rug
made of the skin of a cheap cinnamon bear, that
smells like a cross between a tannery and the stock-

yards, but he does not know the difference, and he places it in his parlor and gives a reception, and tells his neighbors all about how the bear was killed, how he plunked him through the heart just as the bear was about to close his jaws on him, and all that rot. The boys out west have to have some fun, or they would die, and there is no better use that our public men can be put to than to let them engage in these dangerous bear and lion hunts. The only danger that is to be feared is indigestion from eating too much in the rare atmosphere, or loss of breath from running away from the bear when he becomes too familiar. Governor Tanner is now warned, and if he wants to let those Leadville boys have the laugh on him he can go ahead.

IN HIS STOCKING FEET.

Colorado is all broken up over the action of the governor of the state. The governor was attending a banquet, and during the meal he found that one of his shoes hurt his foot, so he removed it, and sat in his stocking until the guests arose from the table, when he put on his shoe and went out with the rest, and everybody is talking about it. The governor's experience was not a marker to one the editor of this paper had with a tight boot once. It was in 1870, when the writer was holding an editorial position on the New York Democrat. A press club gave a banquet at Delmonico's, then on Fourteenth street and Sixth avenue, at which all the distinguished editors of that city were present, Greeley, Beecher, Dana, Harper, Raymond,

and hundreds of others, and it was a rare experience for a fresh Western printer to see them, eat with them, hear them speak, and shake hands with them, and the writer went gladly, when invited. He had on a new pair of "boots," not shoes, tight enough when they were pulled on, but getting tighter every minute when

I went through the ceremony.

the feasting began. The first three courses he held his breath and wondered if he could live through eight more courses and four hours of speeches, with that right boot pinching like an old-fashioned instrument of torture. The foot was swelling and the boot was shrinking, and when the fifth course was reached it was found necessary to remove it part way, or

die, as he was becoming faint and dizzy. The
offending boot was gently placed behind the calf
of the left leg, and deftly pulled half way off, and
the relief was so great that perfect happiness pre-
vailed all around, the appetite returned and the
rest of the banquet was easy. Then came the
speaking, and for hours the eloquence was listened
to and the boot forgotten. When it came time to
rise from the table, the boot would not go on, pull
as the owner would. He pulled until he broke a
suspender, and nearly had apoplexy, and finally it
was necessary to take the boot in his hand and go
out in the parlor, to shake hands with the distinguished editors that he had gone from Wisconsin
to New York to become chummy with. The editor did not propose to miss any of the Greeleys
and Beechers that he had read about all his life, so
he marched out boldly, with his boat in his hand,
his white sock showing up terribly, and went
through the ceremonies of introduction to the
great men of the press of New York. As he thinks
of it now, he must have had more unadulterated
gall thirty years ago than he has got now, for he
remembers going up to Mr. Greeley with all of the
confidence imaginable, with the boot in his hand,
and he remembers how Horace looked over his
spectacles in astonishment, as though wondering
if the man with the boot in his hand was from a
dangerous ward in the lunatic asylum. Beecher
seemed to understand the situation, and had no

doubt had some such experience himself, as he laughed and said, "Better have swelled feet than head," and was so genial that the writer never forgot how lovely he was. Dana looked cross, when he saw the man with the boot in his hand, as though he was insulted, but the writer shook hands with him and limped away as though suffering from an old wound, and Dana looked after him as though ashamed at having misunderstood a wounded hero. Then came the hurrying to get out, and into a carriage, and the long hour on the cold sidewalk, waiting for number 85 to show up, with Brick Pomeroy making life a burden to the young editor by his funny comments on the tight boot, calling attention of passers-by to the condition of the man with the boot in his hand. It was a trying night, and was not over till almost daylight in the morning, when a cold walk was taken across the widest stone sidewalk in New York, and finally the bed was reached, and for hours the young editor from the West dreamed of going barefooted in a search for the north pole, and meeting Horace Greeley, polar bears, Beecher and a lot of walrusses, on an iceberg, singing "We Won't Go Home Till Morning." There is no one that can appreciate the condition of the governor of Colorado at a recent banquet quite as well as the editor of Peck's Sun, and he drinks to the governor's good health, and good sense, for taking off his boot rather than die in his tracks.

THE DUDE AND THE DUCKLESS
POWDER.

The discovery of smokeless powder has had a great effect on the army and navy, and the illustrations of the difference between black powder and the smokeless variety during the late war were not particularly creditable to the American side. Our people had plenty of chance to be supplied with smokeless powder, but on account of some jealousy between army and navy, or the fact that powder makers did not interest any of the senatorial steering bugs in the powder trade, we were short of the smokeless variety, and thereby lost many good men. Two or three years ago any duck hunter could have told the government that smokeless powder was the stuff, but no duck hunter was consulted by the secretary of war. When smokeless powder was first put on the market the sportsmen turned up their noses at it. It did not kick, and smoke up the surrounding country, and make a noise like the old black powder, and while it seemed to occasionally kill something, the old hunter would say that the bird would have died anyway, and that it was probably a cripple that some one else had shot before, with black powder. The champion shots got to using the smokeless at the trap, and doing good work, but the old

hunters said they were hired to use it. The duck
hunters prided themselves on big guns, that would
give notice when they were discharged, by making
a dent in a man's shoulder, and they gloried in
seeing a cloud of smoke, like burning a tar barrel,
go up from their blinds, and a man was known best
by the report of his old gun, which, away off
across the lake, would sound like blasting a stone
quarry, and the old duck hunters rather prided
themselves on having a headache at night, after
coming into camp with a lot of ducks, from the
concussion and kicking of the old gun. The Du-
pont people, who had discovered a good smokeless powder, which they had trouble hiring anybody to use in the field, were worried a little about
whether they could ever get the Wisconsin duck
hunters to use it, but the desire of a Mr. Rice,
who seemed to boss their business, to save life,
and get their headache cure on the market, caused
him to think a few thinks. He picked out a man
who had the lightest kind of a sixteen-gauge gun,
loaded some shells with smokeless powder and
chilled shot for him, and let him go to a clubhouse where there were a dozen old hunters with
the old guns. The man showed his little gun, about
big enough for a ten-year-old boy, and they
laughed at it, on the sly. He cut open a cartridge,
about as big as a six-grain quinine pill, and showed
the sawdust inside, and they laughed again. They
said the ducks would enjoy that kind of shooting,

and unless the man could get the ducks to swallow those "catridges" he would never get enough for a mess. One of the hunters threw a baked bean can up in the air and let the smokeless fellow fire at it. There was a slight noise, as though a cork had been pulled out of a bottle of citrate of mag-

Threw a baked bean can up in the air.

nesia, the can shot into the air as though struck with a club, and when it was examined there was shot all through it, making holes big enough for anybody. The smokeless man whistled, and handled the little gun as he would a rattan cane, and the old fellows winked at each other and finally put him in a blind where they knew the canvas-

backs would have fun with him. They wanted to
see him kill a full-grown duck with that sawdust.
He went out to the blind, and the old hunters got
together under a bank, in plain sight, to see the
fun, and watch the ducks come back after more.
The farmers around the clubhouse, on being told
of the fun there was going to be, looking at the
dude with the pop-gun, trying to kill ducks, quit
husking corn and came along, to enjoy the smokeless man's discomfiture, when he should try his
squirt-gun on able-bodied ducks. The ducks began to fly, and the dude would raise up occasionally, put up the little gun, there would be a sort
of "sput," a noise the old fellows could hardly
hear, and there would be no great cloud of smoke,
but a duck would double up and come down on
the water, and never kick. The little gun was kept
going all afternoon, and when the smokeless
young man came in with fifteen or twenty big
birds, many of them buck canvasbacks, the old
hunters gathered around and examined the birds,
firmly believing they had dropped dead from fright
or something, but when they found the sawdust
had forced shot clear through the toughest old
duck they were willing to at least take the smokeless powder into consideration, while the dude
put a drop of oil on his gun, and rubbed it around,
and then showed the old fellows how to make a
toddy that would carry the news all over them. An
old farmer went into a town near the lake the next

day, and after buying some stuff at a grocery, and counting out the eggs he had brought in to sell, said, "Saw the dumdest thing out to the lake yistidy. Feller there with no pants on below his knees, just sox. Had gun not biggern a pair of lead pencils, shot some kind of sawdust, et didn't make noise enough to wake a baby, and he knocked ducks silly. Just ruined ducks, and they never fluttered, and the dude just whistled, and shot, and the old hunters died right in their tracks. Damest shootin' I ever see. Didn't have to more'n pint at 'em, and they come right down. Duckless powder he called it."

That settled black powder, for within a month all those old black powder backstops, who had been kicked all their lives, began to use smokeless, and the noise of celebrations has ceased on the lake.

THE TENDERFOOT.

What would the jokers and funny fellows of this country do if it was not for the "tenderfoot." A tenderfoot is a man that is not onto your game. A New York man goes out into the mountains or on the plains, unused to the ways of the natives, and he becomes a tenderfoot, and everybody has license to play pranks on him, and if the mountain-

eer or the cowboy of the plains goes to New York,
he becomes the tenderfoot, and they don't do a
thing to him.   In all communities there are men
who are looking for the tenderfoot, and if a friend
is the tenderfoot it goes harder with him than if
he was a stranger.   It is on the same principle of
*he lodge that initiates the new man, or the college
that makes the freshman wish he had never been
born.   If a man who never has been fishing is induced to go out with his friends, they place him to
fish where a fish was never known to be, and if he
rows a boat they will fasten it to a root and he
pulls till his back aches and does not move an inch.
There is a gang of fellows here who have a shack
away up north on one of the lakes, and they never
have so much fun as when they can induce a friend
to go out with them for a week's outing.   They
jolly him all the way up there on the cars, and when
they arrive at the depot in the woods, and are met
by a team with a lumber wagon, then it is up to
the tenderfoot.   A few years ago a brewer went
north with these devils, a fat man with fun all
through him.   They got him into a springless seat
which laid across the wagon box, and started for
the shack five miles away, just at dark, and if there
was a stump that was not run over on the trip he
does not know it.   While he was dodging around
to keep the seat on top of the box, and part of
the time he was in the bottom of the wagon on the
dogs, the boys were sitting calmly smoking on the

back seats and talking about how much the road had been improved since their last visit, while the tenderfoot was frightened out of his wits, and yet not daring to show it. At a given signal the team ran away, as was their custom, and after half a mile of wild running, brought up at the camp, where the boys, who had nearly died from laughter, jumped out as though they had never had so en-

Part of the time on the dogs.

joyable a ride in their lives, and helped the brewer out, almost a dead man. These fellows had rather been killed themselves than to have missed the pleasure of initiating their tenderfoot friend. During the evening they told of the wild Indians in the vicinity, and how dangerous it was to be so near them, when they had firewater, and when the tenderfoot had got so nervous he could not sleep,

all retired, and along towards morning they all
sneaked out with guns, and just as the guest was
beginning to drop off to sleep there were wild Indian yells and firing, and after an engagement with
Indians of half an hour's duration a messenger
came back to the house after the tenderfoot to
come out and help bury the Indians and help carry
in the wounded hunters. No one will ever know
what that visitor suffered before he got out from
under the bed and went out in the dark night
looking for dead bodies of Indians, or how glad
and mad he was when he found it was all a sell
and that he was sold. They tell even now of the
tenderfoot shooting forty times at the head of a
deer that was fixed up so the head was just over a
fallen log, and how he ran away from a burned
stump that had been fixed to move when a rope
was pulled, and seemed to be a black bear. Oh,
the tenderfoot has his uses, and long may he and
his kind live to give joy to his friends who have
been there before.

THE THEATRICAL ORCHESTRA.

There is a movement on foot in the East to
remove the orchestra from in front of the curtain,
between the audience and the stage, and put the
players of instruments off on the side, away from

the view of the people, where the bass viol and
its torturer will not cut off the view of the heavy
villain, or the funny man.   While it has always
seemed wonderful that a bass viol could hide so
much of the stage, it is probable that the removal
of the orchestra will never become popular with
theater-goers, as there is much to amuse them in
looking at the orchestra, when the curtain is
down.   The snare drummer, who plays, incidentally, half a dozen other instruments, is clearly the
most interesting man in an orchestra, and all eyes
are on him, though he seems unconscious that he
is attracting more attention than the others.   His
chief instrument is the drum, but he is attached,
by wires and strings, to a tambourine, a triangle,
a string of sleigh bells, a bass drum, a xylophone,
and plenty of other instruments, and what he can't
play with his hands, and his mouth, he works with
his feet, and he keeps busy, flying from one instrument to another, always on time.   It is no wonder
that the snare drummer, who incidentally carries
the load of all these instruments, dies early, of
nervous prostration, but while he lives he is a
wonder, and yet nobody in the orchestra seems to
look up to him as they do to the man who plays
a solo on the cornet, the man who sucks in wind
from the ventilator that comes in through the
alley, and sends out sweet notes that you wouldn't
believe could be constructed of such foul air.   The
leader of the orchestra, who plays nothing but a

common fiddle, and rests his fiddle most of the time and beats the air with the bow, is perhaps the most important man in the orchestra, but he is powerless if the piccolo player gets full of beer and squeaks out a note that is not on the barb-wire fence in front of him, called music. It is a sad day for the leader when a company comes along with special music, and brings an orchestra leader,

Resemble some citizen of national reputation.

who comes into the midst of the musicians at the proper time, with a loud plaid vest, and usurps the place of the regular leader, who has to take a back seat, and see the new leader ogle the girls on the stage. It is strange how the most of the members of an orchestra will resemble some citizen of national reputation. In one orchestra there is a man playing a fife that looks so much like Grover Cleveland that one can imagine that the conundrum, "What shall we do with our ex-Presidents?" is in a fair way of being solved. There is a man rasping the stomach of a bass viol in an almost indecent manner, who looks so much like Billy Mason that Republicans in the audience almost feel like hissing him as he saws, while a player of the trombone in an orchestra looks so much like Bryan as he toots his silver instrument that the Democrats in the audience can hardly refrain from cheering him, as he gets in the brazen notes of a "Hot Time in the Old Town To-night." There is a snare drummer who plays a round of other instruments, and who changes constantly from one to the other, at the beck of the orchestra leader, who so much resembles McKinley that one is struck with amazement, until he turns his head and it is seen that his collar has been worn for weeks without rest. Looking at an orchestra is a good deal like looking into a fireplace where wood is burning, and you can see in the fire and ashes fanciful pictures and weird views. There is one thing about an orchestra that most people make mistakes about. When the orchestra comes up out of the basement, in single file, after the curtain has gone down, most people can imagine they detect an odor of beer about the place, and occasionally one picks his teeth, and the wayfaring man would swear the musician was dislodging a piece of Swiss cheese, or a firm and unyielding particle of summer sausage, but expert musical critics will assert positively that no member of a theater orchestra ever drinks between drinks, whatever they may do after the theater is over, and the house is dark. It is asserted that no man can play a musical instrument while under the influence of drink, and that there is an iron-clad contract with musicians that they shall not indulge in the beverage that cheers, and brings tears to the eyes, for joy. Next time you go to a theater, watch the orchestra, and see how each member resembles some distinguished man you have known, and the wait between the acts will seem much shorter.

WHEN THE CURZONS COME BACK TO CHICAGO.

Chicago may lose the stadium, whatever that is, that has been talked about so much in connection with her fall festival of foolishness, but there is something coming to Chicago, one of these days, that will cause her more notoriety than anything that has occurred so far in her history. One of her daughters has been honored more than any woman of history, and when she comes home, as she surely will, Illinois will be too small to hold Chicago. Miss Leiter, who married Curzon, who

is the viceroy of India, is becoming more of a
queen than anybody. The queen of Holland, the
queen of Spain, and all of them, have got to look
out for Chicago's Daisy. The last thing that has
happened to Mrs. Curzon is a herd of elephants.
One of those Mahdi's or something, who think
they rule over part of India, has presented the wife
of the viceroy with a herd of forty elephants, with
trappings covered with gold, silver, diamonds and
pearls, each elephant broke to all the gaits, to ride,
drive or fly, each one a royal brute far ahead of
any ever in captivity. The time will come when
Curzon will lose his job of viceroy, and he will go
back to England, which will be too tame for him,
and then he will naturally go to Chicago to visit
his wife's relatives, and he will be compelled to
bring the herd of elephants with him. Those who
have seen a Chicago crowd on the streets when a
common circus, with six common runts of elephants, who will not get along without a prod in
the pants with a spike, can appreciate the crowd
that would be massed in the same streets if forty
blue-blooded elephants should show up, draped in
bespangled garments, when diamonds are liable to
drop off any minute. Imagine the Curzons and
the Leiters, mounted on elephants, proceeding up
Michigan avenue toward the north side to make a
formal visit to the Potter Palmers, the old-Sheik
Leiter, sheiking across the Rush street bridge,
kicking his elephant in the ribs with his big, flat

feet, and watching over his left shoulder to see if his old partner, Marshall Field, has climbed up on the iron work of the bridge to see him go by, followed by Joe Leiter, on a "two-for" elephant, looking out on the lake to see if Phil. Armour's fleet of wheat transports has got unloaded yet and gone back to Duluth. Then will come the Curzons, the Prince and Princess of India, on elephants

When the Curzons come back to Chicago.

bigger than the whaleback, and the other thirty-seven elephants with friends of the family, and as they strike into the lake-shore drive Potter Palmer will be out in front of his house stopping runaway horses, and driving the cheap populace off the picket fence, and fixing a place to herd the elephants on the lawn while the folks are in the house

visiting and drinking champagne.   By the time
the visiting party is ready to depart it will be just
like Potter Palmer to give each elephant a large
bucket of champagne, and if he does there will be
a hot time in the old town that night, when the
Curzons and Leiters try to jab the herd of elephants back to the south side.   A tipsy man can
make trouble, but forty elephants with a champagne jag will cause Chicago to go wild.   Imagine
those good people trying to get the elephants by
the Auditorium Hotel, where the smell of champagne is coming out of every window and door,
and imagine Joe's elephant waving his trunk in the
air in a won't-go-home-till-morning way, and staggering by the Grand Pacific and the postoffice,
down towards the tenderloin.   Montgomery Ward
would get out an injunction to prevent the elephants from going on the grass on the lake front,
and the police would arrest the whole gang of
debauched elephants, and when they were sold at
auction to pay their fines for scaring automobiles
to run away, all the boys would buy an elephant
just to be in the swim.   There are great days in
store for Chicago, when the Curzons come home.

WHEN GRANT AND SHERIDAN CAME
TO MILWAUKEE.

The announcement that President McKinley will be entertained in Milwaukee next week, and that the old Light Horse squadron will escort him from depot to hotel, and about the town, and the remark made by some committeemen that it was doubtful if the squadron could keep up with the hack that would carry the distinguished guest, has brought a flood of recollections to the editor of this paper, who was an officer of the squadron when Grant and Sheridan were here in 1879, and who had charge of the platoon which surrounded the Grant carriage, and which rode at a gallop for five miles, through a solid mass of people, taking the carriage with its precious load from start to finish on a charge, the hottest day that ever was known, when Sheridan said, "Lieutenant, that ride reminds me of Winchester!" Wonder if that squadron can keep up with a hack now, after its twenty years of honorable service, its diplomas for rough riding, the badges and banners won against the best cavalry troops of this country, under the command of such thoroughbreds as Bob Hill, Will Collins, George Shoeffel, Charley Huntington, Will Grant, and others? It is the unanimous opinion of this writer that the squadron will keep up with the procession, and never turn a hair.

When the reunion of 1879 was arranged, and it was known that Grant and Sheridan were to be here, it occurred to a few old cavalrymen that we ought to have a cavalry company to do escort duty, and one night a meeting was held at the Newhall House, two weeks before the reunion, a company formed and officered, and drill began. Six times did the boys drill, and it was said they would do.   Uniforms were ordered, and received the night before Grant was to come.   The next morning the squadron appeared mounted, in uniform, and it was a thing of beauty.   Grant was received at the old Milwaukee depot on the south side, when Fred Underwood, a member of the squadron, run the train into the crowd, as conductor, at fifty miles an hour, changed his clothes for a uniform in the baggage car, and jumped a horse, and in three minutes the squadron had rescued the heroes of the war from the hundred thousand people and got them into a quiet place, away up on Juneau avenue, at the head of the line, which was to start at ten o'clock, go up Juneau to Chestnut, over to Grand avenue, and down through town. The writer, whose platoon was the third, and not supposed to contain the best riders, was placed in charge of Grant's carriage, containing Grant, Sheridan, Forsyth, and young Fred Grant, if memory serves, the other two platoons of the squadron taking the advance, and looking like an army, half a mile ahead.   The procession moved a block, and stopped, moved again, and stopped, and kept that up for an hour and a half, and hadn't got to the river yet, the crowds rushed in at every stop and shook the hands of the heroes until it seemed as though they would be smothered.   No one knew

When Grant and Sheridan come to town.

what was the cause of the frequent stops, but it afterwards proved that Captain Pabst had given orders to serve beer to all who passed the brewery, and five hundred brewery employes were engaged in lightening the white man's burden, stopping soldiers, **Grand** Army veterans and everybody in the procession to give them a Milwaukee welcome,

with foam on.   It was found that at the rate of
progress it would take a week for the procession
to pass a given point, if the beer held out.   Grant
and Sheridan began to get nervous, and at about
11 o'clock Grant called the writer to the carriage
and said:

"Lieutenant, I have got an engagement to dine
with the Loyal Legion at 1:30, and if I am going
over this line, I must start now," and he looked as
though he was going to go.

"If it is your wish, General, to go on," said the
Lieutenant, who was scared out of his boots at
taking the responsibility of moving without orders from the marshal of the day, "I will send an
orderly across town to head off the procession,
and stop it, and we will try to get through the
crowd, and get you to the dinner all right."

"Do it, quick," said Grant.

"That is the only way to make it," said Sheridan.

"Forward," said the lieutenant, and he gave a
couple of inches of spurs to the old roan horse, and
the charge of the Light Horse squadron was begun.   Sending two men ahead to shout to the
crowd to make way for General Grant, we charged
across the bridge at Chestnut street, and up the
hill, the rough pavement mixing Grant and Sheridan up a good deal, but the crowd on both sides
of the street yelled and it was a picnic.   Up the
hill by the big brewery we went, the smiling, white

aproned brewers, and the good old captain on his porch feeling hurt that anybody should get away without at least a schnit of beer, the carriage and the cavalry turned into Eighth street on a run to Grand avenue, and down that street, like a stampede, Grant and Sheridan trying to be polite by taking off their hats to the crowd, and bowing, but often bumping each other. The writer would occasionally look back to see if the distinguished guests were still in the hack, and to see if his platoon was still on horseback, and he can now recall some of his soldiers, who had never ridden off a walk before, jumping up in the saddles and coming down with a dull thud, right side up with care. He remembers J. F. C. Brandt, and F. Stilke, because they raised out of their saddles higher than the others, and looked as though they had not expected so warm a war when they enlisted, three weeks before, but who were the other members of that "four hundred" who made the charge, he does not know to-day.

Down Grand avenue to West Water, down West Water to Michigan, and over to Milwaukee street, went the crazy soldiers and the guests, and there was more noise than ever was heard before. Along Milwaukee street, lined up to the east curb, was a regiment of infantry, at shoulder arms, and as the guests came around the corner the infantry came to a "present," with a noise that scared the horses, and the writer remembers that the old roan horse

he was on gave one snort and landed at one jump
from the middle of the street to the sidewalk in
front of the Academy, but as soon as he found that
the infantry wasn't loaded he came back into the
road, and we were joined by the other two platoons of the squadron, and took General Grant
and party up Jefferson street to General Hamil-
ton's house, presented sabers, and he went in the
house, about as tired as he ever was in his life.
Then came the proudest moment the squadron
has ever known. General Sheridan came out on
the sidewalk, his little duck legs not long enough
for such a body, and addressing Captain Hill, who
had taken command of the troop, said:

"General Grant desires me to thank your squad
ron for its courtesies to-day, and to say that he has
never seen a handsomer or better drilled and
equipped troop of cavalry, and I join him in his
judgment, and I have seen more or less cavalry
myself," or words to that effect.

Did the squadron yell? Yes, it did yell, and as
we broke into fours and went down the street every
soldier hugged his neighbor and said, "How is
that for a cavalry company three weeks old?" and
then we broke ranks as the sun beat down at nearly
a hundred in the shade, and all went home and
took a bath.

Later, at the Loyal Legion dinner, the writer
met Grant and Sheridan again, and they couldn't
believe it when told that the squadron had never

drilled but six times before that day, and had never rode off a walk, and Sheridan said:

"Well, lieutenant, that was the prettiest ride I ever saw, now that it is over, and a wheel didn't come off, but you must have a lot of old cavalrymen in that company," and as he and Grant looked at the Loyal Legion badges on Captain Hill, Collins, Clinton, Van Norman, Graham, and the writer, Grant smoked his cigar and said:

"Course there's veterans amongst 'em."

DYNAMITING A DOG.

If there is any trouble that boys cannot find, and get into, nobody knows what it is. The trouble that boys have is greater during vacation time, because they have more time to find it. If anybody has a mess of kittens to drown they always find idle boys who will take the job on shares, and many a boy has had his heart touched for the first time by the piteous cries of a damp kitten that escaped from the bag and swam ashore. One of the most laughable tragedies in which boys have taken part recently, occurred in a suburb of Philadelphia, on Tuesday. A man had a dog he wanted killed, and he turned it over to a lot of boys to do the job. It was thought that poison would be too slow and uneventful a method, shooting was out of the question in city limits, drowning in the river involved too much uncertainty, because it might be a water dog, and starving the dog to death would be tedious, so one of the boys suggested that they get a stick of dynamite and blow the dog sky-high. It was considered a wise suggestion, and a stick of dynamite was procured from a quarry workman, and the dog was coaxed out to the deserted base-ball park, where the work of slaughter was to be accomplished. After long discussion the conspirators decided to tie the stick of dynamite to the dog's tail, touch a match to the fuse, and make a rush for the grand stand, where they could sit and see the fireworks, see the dog blown to pieces, and then watch the particles of dog go into the air, and rain down on the diamond, when the force of the explosive had been expended. The enthusiastic experimenters got the dynamite nicely tied on and after touching a match to the fuse they started for the grand stand on a run. Then something occurred that they had never thought of. Looking over their shoulders as they ran for the fence they saw that the dog had concluded there was some fun on hand and did not propose to be left alone in the field, so he had started after them, the fizzing fuse of the dynamite stick making a merry noise as the dog ran at their heels, barking and capering. The terror of the possible explosion in their midst frightened the boys, and they ran faster, and yelled

for the dog to "get out," but he wasn't one of those
"get out" dogs, and he ran faster, and kept well up
with them.   No crowd of melon-stealing boys,
chased by a farmer, ever ran faster than those boys
did, and no dog ever sprinted with better results.
The boys were scared out of their senses, and they

The explosion took place.

climbed up the fence in front of the grand stand
like cats, and just as they were about climbing over
the explosion took place, and pieces of dog, blood,
hair and feathers were painted all over the fence,
and silence reigned—silence fairly rained dog.
When the boys had recovered from the shock.

which blew some of them into the seats, they
looked down where they left the dog, but all that
could be seen was a hole in the ground, and a little
smoke. Nearly every boy was covered with blood,
and other things that go to make up an ordinary
dog, and they spent the afternoon scraping each
other off, and inventing excuses for their condition,
to repeat at their various homes. The noise of the
explosion, and the air charged with fragments of
dog, brought the neighbors to the scene, a patrol
wagon was sent for, and the police called a coroner
to hold an inquest on the fence, believing that a
boy had exploded, but when yellow dog hair and
toe nails were found sticking to the backstop of the
ball ground, the story of the boys was believed,
and they were simply arrested for cruelty to the
dog. Any person that has ever seen a flock of wild
boys out for sport, can appreciate the scene when
those Philadelphia boys were trying to get away
from the dynamite and the dog. Boys will be boys.

SELLING A HOUSE BY BUNCO METHODS.

There is an old house in the city of Ripon, this
state, that has historic interest to the people of this
country, it being the house in which the Republican
party was born. Mr. A. E. Bovay and some other
citizens met in the house, which was then a school-

house, and launched the party that has been such
an important organization so many years. Later
the schoolhouse was made into a dwelling house,
and was owned, thirty years ago, by the editor of
this paper. The present owner of the house desires
to sell it to some organization, which will keep it
as a sort of monument to the political party which
was born in it. In this connection it is perhaps
proper for the writer to make confession of a secret
which has been locked in his breast for thirty years,
and that is how he worked it to sell that house at
the drop of the hat, when he wanted to sell it, and
had got to sell it. The writer had received an offer
to go to New York and take an editorial position
on Brick Pomeroy's Democrat, and he had to go
within a week. He wanted to sell the house, and
several men looked at it, but no one made much of
an offer for it. It wasn't worth more than six hundred dollars, and he was offered about four hundred, just about enough to pay the mortgage on it.
He wanted enough money to buy a ticket to New
York. A gentleman living next door wanted it,
but he didn't want to pay much. He was a deacon
in the church, and as good a man as ever lived. The
house stood out in front of the deacon's house, cutting off the view, and he wanted it bad, but would
not produce very much. The editor thought that
if the deacon had an idea that anybody was thinking of buying the house for a saloon, that he would
take it too quick. It was a regular gold-brick game,

and the writer of this has hoped to be forgiven for it, but he went to a German friend who worked in a wagon factory, and deliberately hired him to come up to the house Sunday morning and look over the house as though he wanted to buy it. There are fellows in Ripon now, sitting around on

The German never said a word.

boxes, smoking pipes, who helped the writer entertain that German that Sunday morning, in looking over the house, and the yard, while the good deacon came out of his own house with his family and started for church. The German never said a word, but he smoked a long pipe, looked over the house,

paced off the number of feet in front, and got one
pace over beyond the line fence, onto the deacon's
lot, and just looked as though, if he bought that
house, the line fence would have to be moved. The
writer can remember now how the deacon and his
family looked back at least fifty times, on the way
to the church, to see what was going on. It is
doubtful if the good man heard much of the sermon that day, for thinking of that German and his
pipe, and wondering if he was going to be a neighbor. After the deacon had got safely inside the
church, a couple of blocks away, the German ceased
to examine the property, but all the boys sat down
on the steps and smoked until church was out. The
crowning infamy of the whole bunko game came
when church was out. One of the drivers for John
Haas' brewery came along, and the writer asked
him to hitch his horse and come into the yard. That
settled it. The deacon came back from church,
with several neighbors, and when he saw the German with the pipe, and John Haas' driver, pacing
off a space about fifteen feet square in front of the
house, visions of a beer garden and a music pavilion
within ten feet of his front door no doubt came to
him, for he sat down by his front door and heaved
a sigh. After the German and the driver had
talked a language the deacon didn't understand, for
a little while, with gestures in between the words,
and had said to each other "Sure," and "I bate
you," and "swei-und-swansy," and a few things like

that, they started away, the German saying, "Vell, Mishter Bake, I see you ober 9 o'clock tomorrow," and everybody went home. The deacon was visibly affected, but he was too good a man to talk business on Sunday, though along about dusk he came over to see if any of us were going to attend the evening service, and he incidentally remarked that he would like to see the writer right after breakfast Monday morning. The appointment was made, and in fifteen minutes he had offered the price that had been asked for the house, and he never breathed until the papers were made out, and the money paid over. Just as the transaction was completed the German came into the office, smoking his pipe, and said, "Mishter Bake, I vant to see you," and the good deacon shook the deed in his face and said, "There, I guess you won't have any beer garden on that corner." The German swore that he never had a thought of such a thing, that he only called on the writer to see if he couldn't borrow his duck dog, but the deacon always thought that he had the narrowest escape on record from having a beer saloon under his nose. It was the wickedest piece of deception that the writer ever engaged in, before going into politics, but he believes he has been forgiven, and certainly it shall never occur again. But that German wagonmaker was an actor! He could give points to Gus Williams and Fritz Emmett. He never said a word, but just smoked and acted.

ANOTHER TIME DAD WAS SCARED.

At the time Peck's Sun had about 80,000 circula-
tion and the "Bad Boy" had been published in
book form, with several other alleged funny books,
and many million copies had been sold, the "old
man," as the editor was called by the boys, got an
idea he would like to travel. He had never been
out of Wisconsin in all his life, except to go in the
army, and to make one trip to New York, and he
decided to go to California, so he packed up one
day, and with the partner of his joys and sorrows,
started for the coast, leaving the boys to take care
of The Sun. He was gone nearly two months, and
enjoyed the dust of California, got the worst cold
he ever had in his life, fought fleas and mosquitoes,
and ate oranges until he had cholera infantum for
six months afterward. When he got back he always insisted that he had the greatest time of his
life, and when asked if he found that people away
out there seemed to know that he was the author
of "Peck's Bad Boy," he blushed like a girl, and
said he struck one place where it came pretty near
being the death of him to be known as the aforesaid
author. It seems that on getting across the mountains, after a week crossing the plains, everybody

was too tired to live, and the "old man" left the
train at Colton, and went to a hotel, dead to the
world, and went to bed, about day-
light in the morning, prepared to
sleep a day, or a week if necessary,
to rest up. The better half was
also tired, and occupied an adja-
cent room. The editor was snoring away for keeps, when he heard
a few revolver shots out in the
street, and presently there was a
knock on his door that sounded as
though somebody was using an ax,
and he yelled "come in." The door
opened and a young man almost
seven feet high came in, with a revolver held by the muzzle, with
which he had been pounding on
the door. As he came in the editor raised up in bed, undressed

A young man sev-
en feet high.

and sleepy, and the man seemed to be getting taller
all the time and the revolver looked as long as a
crow-bar, and about as big. The editor felt that his
end had come, and when the tall man waved the
revolver and said, "Don't you move," he knew it.
The stranger looked at the man on the bed, and
asked, "Are you the Peck's Bad Boy man?" and
the editor did not dare deny it, and said that he
was, but was on the point of apologizing and saying that he would never do it again if spared this

time, and the man said, "I have been looking for
you every train for a week, because the Los An-
geles paper said you were coming, and I just found
your name on the register, and I told the landlord
I would just run up to your room and have it out
with you." The editor wondered what a man away
out in California could have against him, and why
he didn't go on shooting, and was on the point
of asking to be allowed a few minutes to make out
his will, and bid good-bye to his partner in the next
room, when the man dropped the revolver on the
table, and sat down on the side of the bed. He
was a rough, handsome fellow, with a flannel shirt
on, open at the collar, showing a strong neck, sunburned and bronzed. He had on leather boots that
came above his knees, long spurs, and a belt with
another revolver and half a bushel of cartridges.
The old editor tried to look as though he enjoyed
the visit, there was a rap on the door, the stranger
said "Come in," and a waiter brought in a tray with
a quart bottle of extra dry champagne. The editor
thought the man was at least going to fill him up
before filling him full of holes, anyway, so he could
die happy, at least. The man looked at the editor
and laughed, and said:

"Well, I'll be d—. It don't seem possible that I
am talking to the man who wrote Peck's Bad Boy.
Here, take a mug of this champagne," and he
handed over a beer glass chuck full and boiling
over.

The editor had not contracted the habit of drinking champagne before breakfast, but concluded he had rather drink it than be shot, so he said, "Well, here's looking at you," and took a couple of swallows on the emptiest stomach that ever was, got brave and said, "Who the deuce are you, and what are you going to do?" The man swallowed a whole pint of champagne, felt in his pocket and found a little package and gave it to the editor. It looked like a powder, but was as heavy as lead, and the editor opened it and found about ten dollars' worth of shot gold, and gold in flakes, and dust, and looked at the man in surprise, and the visitor continued:

"My name is ——. Keep the gold as a souvenir. I have got a mine up on the mountain north of Ontario, and it is a good one. I came from Illinois years ago. I have ten men at work for me, and we go down in the mine and work all day in the water, and come out at night, and get supper, and then there is two or three hours before bed time, that the men think about home, and want to get away, and do you know, the only way I can keep those miners from deserting and leaving me, is to sit up and read your books to them till they are sleepy, and then they go to bed, and are ready to go down in the shaft the next morning. I have read Peck's Bad Boy and your other books to them for two years, every night, until I can repeat the whole blamed business to them in the dark,

without missing a note," and the fellow reached
over with one of his big hands and slapped the
author on the bare leg, and laughed loud and long,
and then he continued, "I thought I owed you so
much for the pleasure you had given me, and the
facilities you had offered me for keeping my miners
from deserting, that I owed it to you to call on
you, and tender you the freedom of the state of
California. Why, I have got one Swede that does
not understand a word of English, and yet he is
tickled to death when I read the stuff and the other
boys laugh. Say, old man, you're a wonder," and
he filled up the beer glass again with champagne,
and the two took a parting drink, and the tall
man stooped as he went out the door, his revolvers
in his belt, his spurs jingling, and turning to the
editor he said, "If you will get off the train at Ontario and come up to my mine, I will treat you like
a president, and give you a shot at a grizzly bear,"
and he went out, and the editor got up and locked
the door, and wished all the day long that he could
get the champagne out of his system, but he was
awful glad he was alive.

GENERAL MANAGER AND STATION AGENT.

Not many years ago the editor of this paper was away out west shooting chickens, and being about ready to come back home, it happened that a special train load, composed of directors of the road, officials, etc., stopped at the station, and the editor, with his chickens, was invited to ride across three states, toward his home, with the distinguished people. It is needless to say that they ate up all his chickens, but he had the best two days of his life. The directors, millionaires from the East, who were inspecting the line, looked out of the windows occasionally, and made bets as to whether a particular field contained corn or flax, wheat or peanuts, but it did not make much difference to them what it was as long as it had to go to market over their road. They were fashionably dressed, and played poker for stakes that would have given heart disease to the editor if he had consented to sit in the game. The millionaires did not take the attention of the editor much, because millionaires all looked alike to him, but the general manager was a study, and the editor kept close to him. The train stopped at all stations, and the general manager jumped off first, and called the station agent Bill or John, or whatever his name might be, and

he knew them all, how many children they had if
married, and where their best girls lived if they
were unmarried. When he struck a station platform his smile lighted up the dingy depot and everything around it, and before he had got inside
the station and touched the telegraph key, to wire
a message to headquarters, his eye had taken in
the condition of the crops all about there, and he
could average the bushels to the acre that would be
threshed out from the number of shocks in a field,
and while the train stopped, in four minutes he
would give instructions to the agent that would
take him six months to carry out, and as the directors who had stepped out on the platform to stretch
their legs, climbed on board, the manager jumped
the last platform of the last car and watched everything to the next station, the condition of the track,
the fence, the telegraph line, and the crops all
about. His head didn't ache, though it was full
of different kinds of information, and when the
wine bottles were firing salutes he smiled and drank
water. All the day and into the night the editor
watched that manager, and wondered if the directors, who owned the road, appreciated that he was
greater than all of them, and of more value to them
than the locomotives and the cars. And yet that
manager's education was limited to about what he
had found out himself, and one of the colored por-
ters, who had graduated at Oberlin, before he became a he-chambermaid, no doubt had a better

education than the manager. The last night before
arriving home the editor and the general manager
sat up until after midnight on trunks in the baggage car, and he talked about the early life of a
station agent. The conductor and the baggage
man were his friends of the old days, and they sat
there, one on a barrel of ice water, and the other
in a cane-seat chair with the bottom gone, and listened to him. He said:

"Boys, I have had more comfort on this trip
watching the old station agents along the line than
associating with the directors, though all are good
in their places. I remember how I left school at 16,
and learned to telegraph, and was finally given a
country station in a town of 300 inhabitants, and
how I sat down to what I supposed would be an
easy life. At first all I had to do was to sell tickets, check up way freight, in and out, and telegraph, but gradually I worked into more business
than I could do to-day with a dozen clerks. I sold
salt and lime, sung in the choir, sold agricultural
implements and put them together for farmers,
and went out and drove them in the fields for a
trial. I boarded at the hotel, and helped wait on
table when there was a rush, painted the depot and
the water tank with paint sent from the shops. I
ran the caloric engine to pump the water into the
tank, and acted as undertaker when people died.
I became an insurance agent and wrote policies,
and a notary public, to execute papers. I helped

farmers to plow corn, or do their haying, and sometimes took a cradle and helped in the harvest field.
I was elected constable, and kicked tramps off the
platform and down the track, if they were drunk,
and fed them if they were sober and hungry. I
played shortstop in the ball nine, and was about the
only man that could make a sick horse drink medicine out of a bottle, and it got so every horse within six miles knew me. I wrote love letters for
young men to their girls, drove eight horses on a
threshing machine, bought wheat and green hides,
led the prayer meeting, managed the rag-tag-and-
bob-tail for the Fourth of July, fired off the rockets,
and helped amputate a man's leg that was injured
under the cars, bought eggs and butter, broke
steers to the yoke, drove a country trotting horse
at the county fair in 4:55, on a half-mile track, put
in tile drain on a tamarack swamp to prevent it
flooding the track, and sold coffee and doughnuts
to the freight train hands at night, was floor manager at dances, helped lynch a man for a brutal
murder, had an advanced class in Sunday school,
ran an engine forty miles to the end of the division
when the engineer was overcome with heat one
hot summer day, and got $40 a month, saved
money, and never looked cross a day in my life."

"Well, how did you get promoted?" asked the
editor.

"Oh, I don't know. They just found out I could
do most anything, and do it as well as anybody, my

reports were all ready the minute they were due, and they were always right, and after I had bossed the clearing of the track after a freight wreck, and taken the responsibility of burning some wrecked cars to get them out of the way for the fast mail, they began to move me around from place to place, and finally I got here, but some day I am going to resign and ask them to give me my old station, for I was never so happy as I was there," and the manager slid down off the trunk, took a drink of ice water in a tin cup, looked at a watch the boys had given him, as big as an alarm clock, covered with inscriptions, and said, as the train slowed up, "Here we are home. I must go up to the office and work two or three hours," and after midnight the editor took a car home, and the manager went to work, while the directors went sleepily to the hotel.

THE SHIPWRECKED BACHELOR.

There is no man in Wisconsin who is a more successful and happy all-around sportsman and business man than Mr. Willard Van Brunt of Horicon, the forty-five-year-old bachelor. He attends to business when the business season is on, and when the shooting season is on a man with business on his mind couldn't find Willard with a hound dog, for he would be just as apt to be on Lake Superior as the plains of Dakota, and he wouldn't leave his address when he went away. Willard made a vow early in life that he would not ever permit an unmarried woman to come within two feet of him, and he carries a foot rule in his pocket, and if one ever seems to be getting too close, he pulls out the foot rule and begins to measure off, and that settles it. The most genial man in the state, he is sound on everything except politics and matrimony, and while a thousand girls in Dodge county alone would hail his discarding of the two-foot rule plank in his platform, with joy, he just whistles and devotes himself to a married sister and a nephew that has been named after him. Willard comes the nearest to being the "Uncle Ike" that is written about, of anybody, in regard to bossing his nephew, and allowing himself to be bossed by the nephew. Not long ago he found that the nephew was getting to be a great tall boy, and wanted a sailboat, so Willard went off to a factory and bought one of the finest boats to be found, and shipped it to Fox Lake, where he and his nephew floated around all one summer. Willard did not know one dingus from another on a sailboat, but he had a vague idea that when the sail was pulled up the boat went better than it did when the sail was down, though it seemed to go where it pleased. He found that if he wanted to sail to any particular place it was best to point the boat the other way, and then if the

wind changed he might bring up where he wanted
to, either that day or the next. All last summer
he never made connections with a single meal, on
time, except breakfast. He would go off sailing,
and if the boat decided to come back at lunch time
Willard came with it, but the boat often landed
somewhere else, and Willard and the boy would
walk to camp, cheerful and hungry. For such emer-
gencies they got to taking along a piece of summer sausage, but after eating that for a week or
so they found that when they came ashore they
felt like kicking up their heels and whinnying, and
they concluded the sausage was made of horse
meat, and quit it. Last winter they had the sailboat hauled from Fox Lake to Horicon, where
they sat up with it nights, and painted it more than
fifty times, and read books on sailing, until this
season they became experts, and when the season
opened at Fox Lake, and the cottages were filled,
it gave Willard and the nephew pleasure to be able
to sail somewhere that they wanted to go, instead
of leaving it all to the boat. Their habit of sailing
the boat up edgewise, sitting on the gunwales and
hanging their feet over, caused the cottagers to believe that sooner or later there would be a ship-
wreck, and they all kept boats ready launched, with
oars in place, a teakettle of hot water on the stoves,
and dry blankets, whenever Willard started out, to
rescue him, the hot water to be made up with whis-

ky into a toothsome beverage, and the blankets to save life dear to them all.

The expected happened last Thursday, the day that the storm that wrecked Porto Rico reached out one of its tentacles into our summer resort region, a dark cloud that had a charge with soda water appearance, with a root beer color, hovered over Fox Lake, and in a moment a gust of wind took the Van Brunt yacht and turned it over, and the people on the bank turned their faces away and wrung their hands. The wind was blowing a mile an hour, the waves were over six inches high, the hail was coming down like eggs, and darkness shut out the tragedy. It was known that there were life preservers on board, and it was believed the two young boys would put them on and be saved, but as the life preservers were built to resemble a woman's corset, and laced up on the side, those who knew Willard were positive he would die, and become food for the garfish before he would put one on. It was an exciting half-hour, and tears were shed until it was necessary to dig trenches about the tents to carry the water away. Suddenly the light of the sun shone through the clouds, and the boat could be seen on its side, and a lady with a glass asked excitedly if anyone knew whether the boys had any canteloupes on the yacht, and it was decided that they did not. "Then," said she, "Willard is safe. I can see something that looks like the under side of a canteloupe, a white patch, and

I am sure it is the top of Willard's head, where the hair is not so very thick." It was true. Then boats were manned and womaned, and the wet fellows were brought to shore, and when they landed each cottager brought a teakettle of hot water, a bottle of whisky, and each made something hot for Wil-

"I can see something like a canteloupe."

lard. He says, now that the thing is all over, that he must have drank fourteen different mixtures. Any way, after his boat had been righted up, he looked out to where the accident took place, and asked his sister how many yachts there were in the fleet at anchor out there, and when she told him there was only one, he was satisfied he had drank enough hot stuff to keep him from taking cold, and he wrapped a blanket around his form, stuck a feather-duster handle down his back, gave a whoop and said he wanted to be sent back to his reservation. The kindness shown him when he got ashore, by the ladies, has had one good effect. Willard has abolished the two-foot rule, and his sister was the first to notice that girls, in their joy at his being saved, could get just as near to him as they wanted to, but it was argued that he was wet, and cold, and needed warming, but it is believed by those who know him best that when he gets good and dry they will have to keep their distance.

OLD KICKER ON DREYFUS, ETC.

"How do you figure out this Dreyfus business?" said the man with the checkered suit, and golf socks, as he came into the suburban train, about twenty miles out, and sat down with the Old Kicker, who had read all the testimony in the morning paper. "I believe they will convict that fellow again, and I don't know but he deserves it, for not killing some of those duffers."

"O, I don't know," said the Old Kicker, as he folded up his paper and kicked a telescope valise with a strong odor of fresh fish in it, which a young man with a sunburned nose had dropped on his foot. "I think that court will let him off, and when he gets outside they will hire an assassin to stab him with a dirk. If he is innocent it is no place for him in France for he will be the only innocent man in the army, and the army would go on a strike. Do you notice that the meanest whelp in the army, who is proven to be corrupt, a thief and a thug, gets the most vivas? That whole business gives me a pain," and the Old Kicker looked it.

"If that trouble was in our army, over here, you think it would be different, do you, that the guilty would be punished and the innocent would triumph," said the man with the golf socks.

"Well, by gum, I don't know," said the Old Kicker. "You know we get tangled up some ourselves, on army matters. I don't want to kick too much on France until we get this Carter business settled. I see Carter says he is not going to be any Dreyfus, and go to jail, while the other fellows who were in with him on a million dollar steal go around with their thumbs in the armholes of their vests. Do you know, if there is any senator who has been getting a rake-off on Carter's stealing from the government, I want to see him walk turkey, whether he lives in Ohio or Georgia."

"What do you think of the way we treated Alger?" asked the golf sock man.

"Say, that was pretty tough, wasn't it?" said the

Old Kicker, lighting a cigar. "Just as bad as Dreyfus, every mite. The whole outfit of beef boodlers was getting in its work to slide bad beef under the canvas of the commissary, and it would have taken an army of men to have watched them. If Alger had turned on them from the senator who plugged for contracts, to the brother of the administration who greased the ways so they would slide through, and had them all arrested, Alger would have been the greatest man around Washington, and the people would have had to be headed off or they would have put him in the white house, but he sort of weakened, and sawed the responsibility off onto Eagan, and said to himself 'O, I am not well enough to go around looking for trouble,' so the beef got in, the money went out, the packers went to Europe, and the soldiers went to heaven, and when the people got to rounding up the responsible parties, there was Alger in plain sight, and the other fellows were hiding behind something, so everybody took a pot shot at Alger. He was the buck, who stood out in plain sight, and got it in the neck. You never saw a drove of deer on the prairie, did you? There is a buck and two does and some fawns, and they scent danger, and all become nervous, and run this way and that, and get ready to stampede, with their big ears pointing toward the trouble. Then the old buck stamps his feet and snorts, and walks ahead of the drove toward the danger, and all the eyes are on him, and the drove admires him for his nerve, and thinks that with such a leader they are all safe. The buck knows they all admire him, and he goes a little too far, there is a puff of smoke away out there on the prairie, and a bullet strikes him and breaks his neck, and he falls in a heap, and bleats like a calf, while the herd that had admired his nerve a few minutes before, look at him bleeding and dying at their feet, and they stick up their white tails, say to themselves that he made an everlasting fool of himself, and they run away in a stampede, while Mr. Miles, who was hunting deer, comes up and skins Mr. Buck, takes the hams and leaves the rest for the wolves. That is about the size of it," and the Old Kicker got up to shake the dust and cinders off his clothes.

"Well, say," said the golf young man, "do you think Esterhazy would make a good teacher in a Sunday school?"

"There is a horsethief and a highway robber for your life," said the Old Kicker, as he flipped the ashes off his cigar into the eye of a passenger across the aisle. "The first time I saw a picture of Esterhazy, in the papers, I thought there is the heavy villain of the whole Dreyfus business. He looked like a composite picture of a sneakthief, a train robber, a poisoner, an assassin, a liar, a forger, a perjurer, a bunko steerer, a train wrecker, and an all-around villain, and now it is proven that he wrote the dossier, the pate de foi gras, and the

hors du overture. Say, that man ought to begin at
Devil's Island, where Dreyfus left off," and the Old
Kicker stamped out of the door as the train
stopped, as though he had been accused of having a secret dossier up his sleeve.